THE DUKE, THE WITCH, AND THE PARTY PLANNER

Love Regency Style

ROSEMOUNT MANOR
BOOK V

LOUISA CORNELL

Chapter One

⚜

Rosemount Manor, Scotland

TWELVE-YEAR-OLD KNOX LET THE EXPENSIVE SHEAF OF stationary slip from his fingers. The letter fluttered to the library carpet as he drew his feet up onto the thick window seat cushion where he sat. He folded his arms on his raised knees, then rested his cheek there and gazed out the tall, mullioned windows that overlooked the back gardens. Lightning flashed in the gloaming sky and illuminated the hedges, flower beds, and statuary, then the garden plunged back into the fading grey of evening. Thunder shook the house. No mean feat with a place as large as Rosemount Manor. His chest tightened. *My home.* Nae. Not any longer.

"What's this? To Lord Knox Alexander Wallace Innes, Marquess of—"

"Bloody hell!" Knox nearly jumped out of his skin.

His brother, Lachlan, always moved so quietly as to frighten everyone in the house. Which was why he was always the one to steal treats from Mrs. Gordon's kitchens whilst Knox played lookout.

"It's a letter," Knox muttered without turning away from the view out the rainswept windows. "Father gave it to me when he called me on the carpet after supper."

The power flickered off, then back on again. Somewhere down the corridor a television blared to life. His mother hated the monstrous big screen his father had installed in the drawing room. But at least it kept Father occupied most of the time, and away from the rest of the family.

Lachlan bounced onto the window, the letter in hand. "What'd ye do this time?"

"Nothing." Knox continued to stare at the rain.

The thunder rolled closer and closer with each flash of lightning. A blur of white in the gardens below disappeared around the entrance to the maze. His heart did a little flip, but he refused to acknowledge a thing. He was done with Elsbeth and done with all the trouble she'd caused him.

At twelve, Knox was supposed to look and sound like an adult. His father told him so at least a dozen times a day. He was too old to speak Gaelic. He was too old to spend time with his old pony. He was too old to steal biscuits from the kitchens. He was too old to have an imaginary friend.

"Ye saw her again, didn't ye?" Lachlan always sounded far older than a mere eight years.

"Who?" He finally looked at his brother.

Lachlan chewed on his bottom lip and swiped at his nose with the back of his hand.

"Ye shouldn't talk about her. It only makes Father angry, and makes Mother cry."

"Father makes Mother cry, nae me. Nae Elsbeth."

Lightning lit the sky and a boom of thunder followed immediately.

Lachlan's eyes widened. He pulled his legs up into the window seat and wrapped his arms tight around his knees. "Don't s-say her name."

"She won't come, silly. She never does when I want her. When other people are around."

"That's because she's *yer* friend. That's why no one else can see her." Lachlan became the solemn little soldier again. The one who stood there perfectly still whilst their father raged at them for the slightest misdeed, real or imagined.

"No one will be seeing her anymore. I'm going away." Knox pried the letter from his brother's grip and smoothed it out against his raised knees. "That's what this letter says. They're sending me away to school in England."

"Why?" Lachlan snatched the letter back and started to read, his lips moving as he did.

"Because they think I'm mad and school will cure me." Knox shrugged. "Maybe it will."

"But yer not mad, are ye? Ye see her, the Innes Witch. She talks to ye."

"It doesn't matter. I'm leaving Rosemount in the morning."

"But I don't want ye to go away, Knox. Where is Eton? Is it very far away?"

"Yes. Very far. And I don't know when Father will let me return. I want ye to promise me something." Knox blinked hard against the sting of repressed tears.

"No. I won't." Lachlan's bottom lip trembled. "I don't want ye to go."

"We don't have a choice. Maybe in a few years they'll send ye to Eton too."

"I don't want to go to Eton. I want to stay in Scotland. I want to stay home, and I want ye to stay home too." Lachlan's voice grew tighter and higher. He was ready to cry and Knox didn't want him to cry because if Lachlan cried so would he. Sons of the Duke of Turra dinnae cry. Ever.

"Well, yer not in charge and neither am I. We don't have a choice, and I want ye to promise me something right now.

Father won't let ye see me off. He's already said so. Promise me."

"I don't want to." Lachlan raised his chin and poked out his bottom lip.

"I'll let ye have my longbow." His brother continued to glare at him like one of the sheep in the high meadows, refusing to come down for the winter. "And all of the sweets in the trunk under my bed."

"All of them?" Lachlan's face brightened.

"Yes."

"What do ye want me to promise?"

"Promise me ye'll look after Gaisgeach." Knox's throat went dry. Even the thought of leaving the pony on which he'd learned to ride made him want to cry. "He likes Mrs. Gordon's oat cakes and lemon biscuits. Promise me ye'll visit him every day, and ye'll nae let Father sell him." Knox extended a hand.

Lachlan clasped his hand and shook it hard. "I promise. What about Nero?" Trust Lachlan to ask after Knox's hunter, the horse he was currently riding.

Knox still gripped his brother's hand. "Urquhart says Father has already arranged for him to be sent to Eton in a few weeks. Ye look after Geechy and the dogs. Agreed?"

Lachlan shook his hand again. "Agreed."

Knox released him and they both returned their attention to the storm. Knox spotted the figure in white at the edge of the maze. She moved in the direction of the terrace steps to the main house. He forced himself not to react. Lachlan was afraid of Elsbeth. Knox was afraid of her as well, but for completely different reasons. The French doors at the far end of the library rattled.

Lachlan gasped and grabbed Knox's hand. "She's here, isn't she?" he whispered, eyes wide and his face pale.

"Go to bed, Lachlan. I'll come up in a bit."

"Ye won't go without saying goodbye, right?"

"Right. Leave yer lamp on."

"On yer honor?"

Knox snorted at their old vow, the one they'd used when they played Knights of the Round Table in the fields beyond the stables. "On my honor. Go on now."

Lachlan scrambled off the window seat and, eyes on the French doors, padded quickly out of the library. Knox sighed and turned back to the show the Highland storm provided as it rolled across the estate. He wanted to cry. Badly.

Rosemount was all he'd ever known. And when his parents weren't in residence, he and Lachlan were happy. They had the run of the estate. Everyone from Mrs. Wallace, the housekeeper, to Abercrombie, the butler, to McGinty, the estate steward, had a hand in raising him and his brother. They'd been indulged but not spoiled. A series of tutors and governesses had come and gone. Their educations had been haphazard, but good. Why couldn't they go on like that forever?

Money. His father spent too much of the estate's earnings on his women and parties.

Revenge. His mother was determined to take her anger at Father out on all of them.

Elsbeth. Which meant this was all his own fault.

"You're too old for this nonsense. I'll not have people thinking my son is a mad boy who talks to ghosts," his father had railed earlier that day. *"I never should have allowed this to go on for so long. A few years in a good English boarding school will knock this notion of imaginary friends and Highland witches right out of your head."*

Father paced back and forth across his study rug, and as he did spittle gathered like foam at the corner of his mouth. His face went bright red.

Still Knox persisted. "I cannae help it if she appears to me.

I dinnae ask to see her. I dinnae want to go to England. I want to stay here."

His father's slap came so fast Knox didn't register the attack until he fell to the carpet. The hot sting across his cheek and the painful brush of the carpet across both knees, bared by his kilt blurred his vision.

"You will go to Eton, and you will not embarrass me with this talk of ghosts. You will stay in England until the English drive every bit of this Highland superstition from your head."

Knox raised his head and met his father's furious gaze. "And if they don't?"

"Then you won't be coming home until I'm dead and you're the duke."

Knox rose. "Done." He stuck out his hand, his head raised in defiance, and his knees knocking beneath his kilt.

Knox still couldn't believe he'd defied his father in such a way. The old bastard shook his hand and sent him out of the study like any other servant. That's what he was, a servant. He'd been born to two people who hated each other but had to carry on a name and a lineage he'd grown to hate. So, he'd go to England. He'd become English. He'd study architecture like he'd always dreamed and he'd never come back to the Highlands. Lachlan loved Scotland. He could be the duke. He could run the estate and carry on the family name. Knox was never coming back as long as he lived. Ghosts haunted places, not people. He'd leave his parents, Scotland, and the bloody Innes Witch behind and live the life *he* wanted. They'd see. He'd show them all. He would never—

"*Mo thighearna.*"

The French doors blew open and brought the icy wind and rain into the library.

"Go away." Knox continued to study the gardens. He tightened his arms around his knees.

"I am here to say farewell."

"Farewell. Now go away."

"Look at me, mo thighearna. Or are ye afraid?"

Knox unfolded himself from the window seat and turned slowly to face the spectral figure who glided toward him not quite touching the antique carpets. Her red hair shimmered in tight curls across her shoulders and down to her waist. Her skin appeared a golden brown in spite of her pallor. Elsbeth Dunhomme, the Innes Witch, had been his friend and companion for as long as he could remember. He'd never let the fact she'd been dead for hundreds of years stand in the way of their friendship. Until now.

"I'm leaving, Elsbeth, and I'm nae coming back." He stood as straight and tall as possible.

"Are ye now?" She smiled and shook her head.

"I am, and I want yer word on something."

"Oh?"

"Stay away from Lachlan. He's afraid of ye, and he'll nae understand why yer here. Yer word on it?"

"On my honor," she said, and her eerie laughter floated around the room.

"I mean it, dammit. Leave him alone." He had to be mad, arguing with a ghost.

"Yer the one leaving him alone with yer parents. And I meant what I said. I'll nae bother the lad."

"Good."

Knox clasped his hands behind his back and rocked on his heels a few times. For the first time since she'd shown up in his bedchamber to comfort him during a storm very like the one hammering Rosemount Manor now, Knox didn't know what to say.

"'Tis well, mo thighearna, I'll wait. I've waited this long." She came closer and the air around him grew bone-chilling cold.

"Wait for what? I mean it, Elsbeth. I'll nae return. I'll nae see ye again."

"As ye say. I can wait." With that she faded away into the darkness at the far end of the library. The French doors closed quietly behind her.

"For what?" he murmured as he gathered the stack of books he'd pulled from the library shelves to take with him.

"For ye, mo thighearna. For ye." Her voice came out of the darkness.

Knox shivered and hurried out of the library and up the stairs. He had to talk to Lachlan and then he had to pack to leave Rosemount Manor and Elsbeth forever.

Chapter Two

Rosemount Manor, Scotland
Mid-January, twenty years later

Knox Innes, Duke of Turra, fished around in the pocket of his heavy wool coat and pulled out yet another of the apples he'd filched from Mrs. Gordon's pantry. He offered it on his flattened palm to the old Shetland who'd been nudging his pocket for the last ten minutes. Urquhart, Rosemount's horse master, tutted at him and turned to give one of the lads some instructions about the horse in the next stall.

"Ye spoil that worthless old blighter, Yer Grace. He's gone ta fat, he has," Urquhart said without turning back to him.

"Leave be, Urquhart." Angus McGinty lumbered into the stables and kicked the snow off his boots before he came to stand next to Knox. "That old pony has earned a bit of spoiling. Teaching this hard-headed lout to ride."

"True enough," Urquhart muttered as he turned, touched his cap, and shuffled deeper into Rosemount's massive stable block.

"Is that any way to speak about a duke?" Knox asked.

"'Tis, when ye've changed the duke's nappies." McGinty's grin faded almost the moment it arrived on the bear of a man's wrinkled face. "She's here."

"Who?"

McGinty rolled his eyes. "Ye know who. The American woman. Miss…Witherspoon."

"Ms. Witherspoon."

McGinty loosed a particularly vile Gaelic curse. "Whoever she is, she's here with enough bags for an invading army, some *mòr* of a glass cage, and she wants to speak with *His Grace* before she starts preparing the house for whatever Sassenach nonsense that rich American director is paying for."

"Dear God." Knox ran a hand through his hair, gave the pony a last pat, then walked slowly out of the stable block. "Can't you deal with her, McGinty? You're my steward. I agreed to whore out my house and estate for this abomination. Do I really need to talk to these people?"

"Yer not whoring Rosemount out. You're repairing the harm yer father did the best way ye know how. There's hardly a laird in England or Scotland who has nae done something like this ta bring a bit of money in to keep his people in the black." McGinty clapped his bear paw of a hand onto Knox's shoulder and held him in place. "You've done well these last years since the Lord took yer father. Ye've saved our home and the jobs of most of the people in two counties."

Knox tried to look away.

"Ye've nothing to be ashamed of and ye know it. Even if no one else knows, I know what ye gave up ta come back here and save Rosemount." The old Scot gave his shoulder a last squeeze and they continued across the cobblestoned stable yard.

"The Lord wouldn't touch my father with a tabor. The devil took the old bastard and I hope he's roasting in hell. I didn't have much of a choice about coming back now, did I?" He shoved his hands into his coat pockets and hunched his shoulders as they walked into the bitter Highland wind that whipped up the path to the manor.

"Ye could have left it ta your brother."

McGinty didn't mean a word of what he'd just suggested. They both knew it too.

"No, I couldn't."

His brother had returned from the battlefields of the Middle East and gone to ground in the wilds of the estate like one of the foxes their father used to hunt. Knox's choice had been to stay in London and run his successful architecture firm or to return to Scotland and save an estate on the brink of complete financial destruction, thanks to his father.

"But I still don't want to talk to this…party planner, is it? I can think of a great many things to call this little money-making scheme, but a bloody party isn't one of them. You talk to her." They reached the corner of the manor and headed across the main drive to the front of the house.

"You'll have to talk to her eventually. Ye cannae avoid the woman for an entire year or more."

Knox stopped in his tracks. The wind had to be playing with his hearing. He clapped the heel of his hand against his ear a few times. McGinty looked at him as if he'd run mad.

"A year? A year!" His voice echoed across the circular drive, in front of the manor's monstrous front doors. "This is supposed to be a three-month Jane Austen house party, or some such utter nonsense. Who said anything about having Americans running loose in my home for a fucking year?"

"Actually, you did, Your Grace," a distinctly feminine voice, accompanied by the crunch of footsteps, announced her presence behind him. "When you signed the contracts I sent you after your conversation with Mr. Wentworth?"

Knox turned smartly on his heel to face the person who approached him from around the fountain in the middle of the drive. "Have you lost your bloody—"

His throat closed tight around his words. His blood drained to his feet so quickly he strained to hear the splash of water in the fountain. His heart thundered in his ears like the Edinburgh Tattoo. The world in his vision faded to a narrow strip of cobblestones between him and the apparition walking toward him. She appeared as if down a dark corridor of memory.

The woman was tall, though not as tall as him. She was slender with long elegant limbs. Her skin was a golden bronze color and her hair, caught up in a neon flowered cloth band that matched the floral pink, orange, and yellow pattern of her ankle-length frilly skirt, curled in a mass of ringlets of several shades of red and gold past her shoulders. She wore a bright pink entirely-too-thin-for-the-Highlands sweater. A large leather satchel that matched the material of her butterscotch boots hung over her shoulder. None of that mattered. Although somewhere in the far reaches of his scrambled brains the image of a 1960's flower child came to mind.

Knox closed his eyes tightly, counted to ten, and opened them again. He hadn't done that since he was a very young lad. Didn't help. Her face and hair remained the same. Each and every delicate line was a combination of Caribbean beauty and Highland strength. Her hair was a tumbled mass of taut curls in the golden red he'd thought unbelievably magical as a child. They were the face and hair, the woman, of his childhood memories. Now even he believed he had finally run mad. There was no other plausible explanation.

She stopped a few steps away and executed a very formal curtsy. McGinty elbowed him, though Knox hardly felt it. She extended a hand and glanced at his steward expectantly.

"Yer Grace," MacGinty's voice fairly boomed. "May I present *Ms.*—"

Knox reached out before the move even registered. "Els—"

"Eleanor Witherspoon," McGinty finished. He gave Knox a nudge and a stern look.

She took his hand. Knox started as if struck by lightning. Once her dainty fingers wrapped around his, he couldn't let go.

"I'm very pleased to finally meet you, Your Grace. I'm so looking forward to us working together." She smiled and his heart stuttered to a stop.

This had to be a dream or a nightmare or some wicked combination of both.

Knox dropped her hand, gave her a curt nod and, with no thought to the shame he was doing his Highland ancestors, spun, and walked one degree below a run into the house and straight up the stairs to his study. He was sure the shocked expression he'd glimpsed on her face in the instant before he'd turned followed hard on his heels. The memory kept him up half the night. He finally gave up just before first light and sat up on the side of the massive ducal bed. The wind howled like a scorned woman against the long windows next to his nightstand. He said the name he'd not even thought of since he'd left Rosemount as a child.

"Elsbeth?"

The wind only shrieked all the louder.

Eleanor glanced over her shoulder once more as she ascended the grand staircase behind Mrs. Wallace, the duke's housekeeper. The duke in question had disappeared like a date who'd been presented the check at a high-end restaurant after she'd told said date he wasn't getting any that night. Was it something she'd said? He hadn't given her the chance to say much. She gave her armpit a surreptitious sniff as she reached the first-floor landing and turned up the next staircase.

Her deodorant was still holding. Check.

She was decently dressed. Check.

She hadn't said anything rude or condescending or nosy. Check.

Then what the hell was the Duke of Turra's problem? He'd looked at her so strangely. Then he'd grasped her hand, held tightly for several seconds, then dropped it like a lit firecracker. Why had he done that?

Another staircase and a long corridor later, the poker-faced housekeeper finally stopped in front of a set of double doors. She pushed the doors open and strode into the room like a drill sergeant.

"Your rooms, Miss Witherspoon. I hope you will be comfortable." Mrs. Wallace paced to the huge fireplace and flicked a long piece of brocade with a tassel at the end. The bell pull if Eleanor remembered right. "If you need anything pull this and one of the maids or footmen will be up in a few minutes." She folded her hands at the waist of the stiff white apron she wore over an even more stiff black dress. "Is there anything you require?"

"Uhm," Eleanor stared as she turned in a slow circle and took in the gorgeous antique furniture in the room. "The bed? Where would the bed be?"

"This is your private sitting room." Mrs. Wallace pointed to another set of doors to the right. "Your bedchamber is in there. Robbie and Dougal have brought up your luggage and your…pet." Most people had to suck down a whole basket of lemons to muster up a pucker like the one the duke's housekeeper was wearing. Then again, Persephone, who went with Eleanor wherever she traveled, wasn't everyone's idea of a normal pet.

"Good. Thank you. I can't think of anything I need right now."

Mrs. Wallace inclined her head and turned to go.

"Mrs. Wallace?"

The older woman turned back. "Yes, Miss Witherspoon?"

"Has the duke told you what will be going on here for the next months and then the rest of the year? I mean, about the boot camp and the movie being filmed?"

"His Grace does not discuss his business with me outside of my running the house. Why do you ask?"

"He just seems kind of pissed I'm here to be perfectly honest. Make that very pissed."

A series of emotions flickered across the stoic woman's face. "I'm sure I wouldn't know." She nodded again and walked to the still open doors. "But you may be assured if Himself *is* pissed, as you say, you'll have no cause to doubt it." She stood with a hand on each of the two doors' handles and smiled. "No cause at all."

"Well, that's not scary as fuck," Eleanor muttered once the housekeeper was gone. She went to check out her bedroom next door. "Oh, hello." She stepped into the bedroom to find two young men in kilts, white shirts and black vests eying Persephone's specially designed travel crate as if they expected her to pop out and chase them down the stairs.

"Miss Witherspoon?" the dark-haired one asked.

"Of course she's Miss Witherspoon," the red-haired one said. "Who else would she be?" The two of them elbowed each other.

The travel-crate rattled and they took a step back. Eleanor tried not to laugh. Then she got a look at the room.

"Damn. Is there any room in this house that isn't fabulous?"

Everything from the four-poster bed-curtained bed to the antique carpets covering the floor to the wardrobe and highboy and other furnishings screamed "My family has been rich for generations." She couldn't believe she'd be spending the next year or so here.

The Innes clan has lived here for over five hundred years," the dark-haired one said. "Plenty of time to decorate. I'm Robbie, by the way."

"And I'm Dougal," the other one said as he blushed bright red.

"I'm Eleanor Witherspoon." She shook each of their hands in turn. "I see the guy from Edinburgh has Persephone's home all set up." She inspected the spacious floor to ceiling glass case very carefully. The temperature gauges indicated the perfect levels of heat and humidity. The various branches and platforms were in the exact right positions. Of course, she had sent the man carefully worded instructions on how to put the habitat together correctly.

"Oh, aye," Robbie said. "He left his card and asked that you call him. He wants to know who designed this…habitat." The footman pulled the card from his vest and handed it to Eleanor. She tucked the card into her bag and tossed the bag onto the huge bed.

"Come on, sweetie," she said as she opened the travel crate. "Let's get you settled." She pulled an undulating section of her albino python out and handed the thick coils to Dougal who didn't step back quickly enough. "Here, Robbie, take this." She turned around to find the poor guy frozen in place, save for the frantic shaking of his head. "She won't hurt you. I can't lift all of her myself. See, Dougal's doing it." She glanced at the other footman whose face had gone white as a sheet. "Oh, for God's sake, boys, don't tell me you've never seen a snake before." She gave them a wicked grin.

Robbie snickered. Dougal looked ready to faint. She pulled the rest of her pet from the crate and took control of the snake's head as she walked over to open the glass case. She fed Persephone onto the first climbing branch and the snake immediately crawled into the habitat in search of the platform in front of one of the heat lamps. Eleanor and Dougal supported her body until she fully slithered inside the habitat.

Dougal swayed on his feet. Eleanor guided him into a beautiful brocade upholstered chair. "Put your head between your knees. You'll be fine."

"She's orange," Robbie observed as he stepped close to the glass enclosure. "How much does she weigh?"

"She's an albino, a mutation, that's why she's orange. She weighed in at 120 pounds at the airport."

"Does Himself know about the snake?" Dougal asked when he finally raised his head and took on a better color.

"In theory? Yes."

The two footmen looked at each other and grinned.

"What?" Eleanor narrowed her eyes and tried to figure out what was so damned funny. "Is Persephone going to piss him off? Apparently, my presence here has already pissed him off, if the way he ran away after our introduction as if his kilt was on fire is any indication."

"Why? What did he say?" Robbie asked as he pulled Dougal to his feet and headed toward the door.

"He didn't say anything. He shook my hand, dropped it like I had leprosy, and ran." Eleanor tried not to sound insulted or hurt. She was actually shocked at how much his behavior stung.

"Trust me, miss," Dougal said. "If Himself were angry with you, you'd know it."

Robbie nodded so vigorously she half expected him to cross himself. They nodded to her and promptly left the room.

"What the hell have I gotten myself into?" Eleanor toed off her boots and started toward the fireplace to warm her feet. As she crossed the thick carpet, she spotted movement from one of the tall windows along the far wall of the bedroom. The duke. She recognized the walk, especially as he was walking away from the house just like he'd walked away from her. She went to the window and settled onto the cushioned window seat.

There was something familiar about his walk, something familiar about him, as if she'd met him before. She hadn't. She knew that. Still, his reaction to her was odd and she wished like hell she knew why. He wasn't a willing participant in her regency boot camp idea, nor in the idea of a period film taking up residence on his estate for at least a year. Tough shit. He was broke, and he needed the money. Himself's title was useless without money. Which was why he'd hired her, an event planner with no major event planning experience, to come up with a scheme to save Rosemount Manor.

She might be dependent on his grumpy grace's goodwill for her first big job as an independent event planner, but he needed her too. Eleanor watched as he strode out of the gardens below her window and into the fields beyond. Like something out of the period film that was about to be filmed at Rosemount Manor, he strode away head up, shoulders back. Which was why when he stopped and looked back at the house, she nearly fell out of the window seat. He was looking directly at the window where she sat. For a minute she wanted to duck down out of sight.

The hell with that.

She stood and braced her hands on either side of the window and stared back at him in the distance. He didn't look away.

She'd say it again. "What the hell have I gotten myself into?"

Chapter Three

The bustle of the kitchen faded into the background as Eleanor ran her fingers around the neck of her thick Scots wool sweater and refrained from sighing. Again. In two weeks, she had a veritable herd of actors, actresses, period film specialists, and God only knew what else arriving for the Regency experience she'd sold to Erik Wentworth, Hollywood's hottest young film director, as the perfect way for these people to prepare for his newest film project. For the last three weeks, she'd run herself ragged all over the Duke of Turra's ancestral home and estate planning events, planning every day, arranging for lessons, and classes, and wardrobe.

"Spend whatever you need," Erik had said.

And she had.

She'd signed off on bills for ridiculous amounts of money. More money than she'd ever seen in her life. She was terrified. She'd never planned an event on this scale in a place as magnificent as Rosemount Manor with as many moving parts as this *experience* required. She'd also never had to butt heads on a daily basis with such stubborn, narrow-minded, impossibly—

"Himself won't like it," Mrs. Wallace broke into her thoughts. "Ye'll have ta talk to Himself about something like that."

Mrs. Wallace, Rosemount's housekeeper, was going to need few adjustments to fit the role of the sort of woman who'd run a duke's home during the Regency. Jane Austen could have written this woman. She did write her, but in Jane's book she was Lady Catherine De Bourgh.

"I'd love to discuss a great many things with the duke if I could *find* him. I'm beginning to think the man is a ghost."

Whoa! The entire kitchen of servants went dead silent. A few of them crossed themselves.

"Ye want us all to wear the fancy togs, you want the electricity turned off in most of the house," the housekeeper said. "Ye want all the indoor plumbing locked up. Fireplaces as the only heat, and candles as the only light. And now ye want the staff to empty chamber pots and carry buckets of hot water up and down the stairs for these people to take a bath?"

Mrs. Wallace never raised her voice. She did, however, raise her nose to the point if it started raining in this big-assed kitchen the old woman would drown. Eleanor didn't begrudge her that attitude. She admired women who worked tough jobs and owned their position like a queen.

When she'd first arrived at Rosemount Manor, Eleanor had been amazed and thrilled at the number of people working in the house and on the estate. Like she'd stepped into a Jane Austen novel, there were servants and routines that hadn't changed in over two hundred years. She'd asked a million questions about who did what. Then she'd sat down in the humongous library and written out list after list, plan after plan, and ordered every sort of period clothing available to make certain not only the participants, but the staff lived the next three months or more as people did during the Regency, right down to the underwear or lack thereof.

Two things now stood in the way. First, Mrs. Wallace, the housekeeper, and Abercrombie, her cohort and the duke's butler, with whom Eleanor had had to fight for every little thing on her lists. Second, the damned Duke of Turra, who'd snubbed her the day they met and had refused to show himself ever since. The house and estate were huge, but damn. He'd disappeared like a fart in the wind.

She had no idea what she'd done to offend him. After mulling over the exactly seventeen words she'd said to him, Eleanor still had no idea. Which meant, the man was just your average, garden variety, aristocratic asshole. Assholes she could do. She'd dealt with them most of her life. Having a prominent surgeon father and a district attorney mother might make people think she'd led a charmed life. When the father was Black and the mother was White, even in California, sometimes the charm was hard as hell to come by.

So yeah, a snotty Scottish duke? No problem. If she could find him. Not that she needed him to settle the problem of asking people to work like nineteenth-century servants.

"Mr. Wentworth has authorized me to pay handsomely above your regular wages any member of staff who agrees to take on these extra duties and play the part of Regency servants." Eleanor hid a smile as the people assembled in Rosemount's *servants dining hall*—they still called it that? cool—began to talk loudly amongst themselves.

"And what constitutes *handsome* pay in America?" Robbie asked. The young red-headed man in a cable-knit sweater and kilt folded her arms folded across his chest.

"Check it out, Robbie." She handed him her clipboard onto which she'd put the pay schedule she'd compiled last night. Didn't say word, just handed him the clipboard.

His quick broad grin as he handed the clipboard to Dougal told her she'd come up with some good numbers.

Whilst the information made the circuit around the room, Robbie and the other young man sidled over to her.

"So, yer going to make these Americans live without electricity?" Robbie asked.

"Yes. And that means no computers, no cellphones, no electric lights. Nothing. They're going to live just like people in the time of Jane Austen."

"No mod cons and no indoor plumbing?" Dougal, asked.

"All the modern bathrooms will be locked. They'll have to use a chamber pot or the water closet on the second floor."

"The toilet with the wooden seat and the wind blowing up yer *arse* from the auld ruins?" Robbie started to laugh so loudly everyone in the room stopped and stared.

Dougal joined him but managed to talk between bouts of helpless laughter. "So the Yanks can either hope they hit the chamber pot and hope we show up ta empty it or they can get a rush of Highland air up the *arse*. That kind of money and watching the Americans suffer? I'm in, miss. I'm in!" Dougal fist bumped Robbie.

Mrs. Wallace rolled her eyes and glared at Eleanor with a loud huff.

"Aye," some of the others shouted.

"Ye can count on me, miss."

"Sounds like a right treat."

"I'll nae turn down the money."

"Oh"—Eleanor raised her voice over the noise to add— "some of the people attending are English."

The noise rose to a deafening level. She didn't know much about modern Scotland, but she knew there was still no love loss between the Scots and the English, especially in the Highlands.

She turned to Mrs. Wallace. "Do you still think we need to consult the duke?" Her smug smile faded when the housekeeper shrugged and adopted a suspiciously nonchalant expression.

"Ye may do as you please, miss. McGinty has said as much. Did this Mr. Wentworth consult with Himself about giving this lot extra money? Or did ye decide that all on yer own?"

Shit. The duke probably didn't give a rat's ass, but what if he did? She scanned the older woman's face in the hope of finding some sort of answer. The participants hadn't even arrived, and she might be pissing off the duke already. Or again. Or whatever!

Eleanor glanced at the antique watch she had pinned to her sweater that morning. "I'll tell you what, Mrs. Wallace, it is eleven o'clock. If you tell me exactly where *Himself* is this time of day, I'll go and ask his permission to pay your staff more money." Eleanor retrieved her clipboard from one of the younger women in the group and waited.

The woman smiled. Eleanor's blood ran cold and dropped into her shoes.

"Yer timing is perfect, Miss Witherspoon. I was about to send one of the maids up to his study with his tea tray. You can take it up."

Mrs. Wallace didn't give her a chance to answer. Not that Eleanor could at that point. Her brain sort of froze. The room cleared out save for the people who actually worked in the kitchen. Her sense of unease wasn't helped one bit by the sympathetic glances she got from the staff as they filed past her.

Before she managed to open her mouth to protest, Mrs. Wallace took Eleanor's clipboard and handed her a tray loaded with an ancient looking teapot, expensive pieces of very fine bone china, some delicious smelling scones, a pot of clotted cream, a pot of jam, some silverware and various other items. In other words, the damned tray weighed a ton.

How the hell did the little skinny girl they called Bridie, who now led Eleanor out of the kitchen by way of a worn narrow servants' staircase inside the walls of the manor, carry this thing?

"Are ye all right, Miss Witherspoon?" Bridie called down to her as they climbed two flights of stairs before reaching the door to the corridor that ran across the back of the first floor.

"I'm fine."

She was lying her ass off.

Once they went through the door, Eleanor leaned back against the wood for a moment to strengthen her grip on the tray. The last thing she needed was to dump the duke's tea all over what looked like three-hundred-year-old Persian rugs. When she caught her breath, she followed Bridie down the hallway. Eleanor glanced over her shoulder and found that the door was inset into the wall so that it was invisible. These soon-to-arrive movie people were going to *love* their Regency experience. If she could keep the duke and his minions from fucking it up.

Bridie stopped in front of an imposing double-paneled oak door. Sunlight streamed through the large window that spanned the entire end of the corridor. The sun's glow bathed the door's wood in a warmth that made the dark, highly polished surface shine with rich shades of brown, amber, and red. Eleanor stepped toward the window. She couldn't resist admiring the view of the expansive gardens behind the manor. This time of year, only the carefully sculpted evergreens offered a show of color. But she had taken a tour with Rosemount's head gardener, so knew the view from this window would be incredible come spring. The gentle rain that had been falling off and on all morning would make sure of that.

"Miss?" Bridie tapped her on the shoulder.

Eleanor started which rattled the china before she managed to steady her grip on the tray that grew heavier by the second.

"He'll be wanting his tea, miss. He's nae happy when its late."

"Is he ever happy, Bridie?" Eleanor wanted to kick herself for asking. Especially when the young maid's face turned bright red and she mumbled something about not knowing the mind of someone like *Himself*. Eleanor gave her a reassuring smile. "Don't worry about it. You run along. I've got this."

"Ye'r certain, miss?" Bridie's dubious expression did nothing for Eleanor's confidence, but she wasn't about to back down now.

"Absolutely."

Bridie gave her one more questioning look, bobbed a little curtsy, then hurried back up the corridor.

Eleanor positioned herself squarely in front of the door and knocked with her foot.

"Come."

Eleanor recognized that tone. The Duke of Turra's voice made a spot between her shoulder blades itch. She shrugged and used a few fingers of one hand to lift the door latch. She smiled at the use of a latch rather than a doorknob. So Regency. One of the reasons she'd wanted Rosemount for this project was the period details of the house, the grounds, the entire estate. She elbowed the door open, then used her butt to push the door back far enough to admit her and the tray that now weighed a ton.

"Put it on the tea table. I'll serve myself. Thank you." The arrogant…duke didn't deign to raise his head.

He sat behind a gorgeous mahogany land-yacht of a desk, eyes glued to a laptop screen while making notes on a stack of papers with an expensive Montblanc pen. At least he said thank you. Even if he didn't know who he was thanking. His two deerhounds, asleep before the fire, at least opened their eyes and raised their heads to acknowledge her before they returned to their nap.

She settled the tray on the tea table in front of the fireplace, released a silent breath at the sudden weightlessness in her arms, then contemplated how to announce her presence. The freshly brewed pot of tea, wrapped in the brightly colored knitted cozy, smelled heavenly. The selection of tarts and scones made her mouth water. So she did the only logical thing. Eleanor poured herself a cup of tea, added milk and sugar, and placed two tarts on one of the dessert plates Mrs. Wallace had included on the tray. She sat down in one of the comfortable chairs before the fire and took a long sip of her tea. He continued to ignore her or perhaps he truly didn't register her presence at all. She stirred her tea and dropped her spoon onto her little plate.

The duke slowly raised his head. The pen fell from his hand. He didn't say a word, but several expressions flashed across his face before he settled on a look somewhere between curiosity and disdain. Those first couple of expressions she filed away for further study. The curious disdain she could deal with, as she'd been doing all her life.

"Good morning, Your Grace. Tea?" She raised her cup and smiled before she took another sip.

He continued to stare at her. Which gave her the opportunity to study him more thoroughly than she'd had the chance to do the day they'd met. If you could call what happened in front of the house a meeting. More like a drive by snubbing. The duke was too damned good-looking for his own good. His face was strikingly handsome with high sharp cheekbones, deep blue eyes, a strong jaw, a stubborn chin with a small scar to one side, lips that were way too sensuous for such a cold sort, and black hair that begged to be mussed and maybe pulled just a little?

"Has there been some disaster in the kitchens, Ms. Witherspoon?"

"Not that I'm aware of, Your Grace. Why do you ask?"

"I assumed the entire staff must have called in sick if Mrs. Wallace has recruited you to deliver my tea."

"Oh no. I volunteered." Eleanor took a bite out of the tart on her plate.

His eyes widened for a brief second. His chest rose and fell beneath his black vee-necked cashmere sweater. It was a very nice chest too. The duke was tall and lean, but those pecs and abs couldn't be hidden by a mere sweater. She took another sip of tea to wash down the tart and to hide her self-satisfied smile. She was getting under his skin and took a perverse pride in doing so. He was, after all, human.

"You volunteered. And Mrs. Wallace allowed—"

"I needed to speak with you and, other than hiring a private detective to track you down, this seemed the most efficient way to find you."

"Find me? I wasn't aware I was lost." He stood.

The dogs lifted their heads and tracked his progress across the room to the tea table. The duke poured himself a cup of tea. Once he'd added one sugar and a splash of milk, he propped an elbow on the mantel and lifted his cup from the saucer he'd placed there.

"Yours is a selective lostness, Your Grace. You only disappear when I ask to speak with you. Magicians in Vegas could learn a thing or two from you. Are you afraid of me or am I simply too far beneath you for you to bother? Scone?" She offered him a plate onto which she'd placed a scone, some clotted cream, and strawberry jam.

He froze, cup halfway to his lips. "Afraid of you? Don't be

ridiculous." He returned his cup to the saucer with deliberate care.

She added two ginger biscuits and offered him the plate once more. This time he took the plate and placed it on the mantel next to his tea.

"I am a very busy man, Ms. Witherspoon. This Wentworth person hired you to arrange the use of my home. I suggest you get on with it. I see no reason for you to worry me with said arrangements. Now, if you will excuse me."

He picked up his tea and the plate as if to return to his desk. He paused only long enough to feed Tannus and Beira a ginger biscuit each. She loved the big hairy dogs and had asked Robbie their names first thing.

"No." Eleanor touched one of the silk napkins to the corners of her mouth. "I will not excuse you. Did you even read the contracts you signed for this event?"

He gawked at her as if no one had ever told him no. She struggled not to laugh. Poor guy.

He placed his tea things on the tea table and glared down at her. "I am not accustomed to reading every line of fine print in contracts with a party planner."

"An event that may well last over a year is hardly a party, Your Grace. But your disdain for my occupation is duly noted." Eleanor had had enough. "And sit down, please. You are not intimidating me, and I'm getting a kink in my neck from looking up at you."

"What?" He stared at her in such an odd way she almost felt sorry for him. Almost.

"Sit." She pointed at the leather armchair opposite hers. To her surprise he did as he was told.

"I hold neither you nor your occupation in disdain," he said, and actually managed to sound hurt. "A dukedom is a business. I am accustomed to running this estate as a business, not as some sort of renaissance festival for bored tourists."

Ah, there he was, the stick-up-his-ass-duke.

Eleanor topped off his teacup and handed it to him. "Drink. Tea solves all manner of problems, isn't that what you Brits say?"

"Scots."

"What?"

"We are Scots here. I suggest you remember that or your time here could be quite unpleasant. What sort of problems can I look forward to that I need to drink more tea to endure?" He took a long draught from his teacup before he returned it to the table and picked up the plate with the scone on it.

She almost wanted to laugh at the civility of his set down.

"Scots. Of course." She pulled the little notebook and pen out of her pocket. "Now that I have you cornered."

He stopped dotting cream onto his scone and blinked. Who knew a blink could say so much?

"Mr. Wentworth has offered to compensate your staff for the extra duties they will incur with bonus pay. Do you have any objection to this?" She crossed her legs and propped her notebook on her knee, pen poised to write.

"What sort of extra duties?" His voice dripped with suspicion.

"The sort of extra duties that will help to make the boot camp attendees experience authentically Regency. Things like—"

He raised a hand. "I don't think I want to know. If members of my staff don't object, I have no problem with any of them receiving extra money for extra work. So long as I don't have to participate in this, what did you call it, boot camp?"

"Actually...."

"Ms. Witherspoon"—he dropped the scone onto his plate —"I never agreed to participate in this ridiculous little charade nor do I intend to—"

"You did. When you signed the contracts, you agreed to dine with the guests and to participate in those activities in which I think being in the presence of a real live duke will be beneficial to their experience."

"Beneficial to their experience?" He was on his feet and halfway to his desk before he turned to stalk back toward her. "I am a duke, not a show pony to be trotted out on command."

"Any resemblance you bear to any part of a horse is strictly incidental, I'm sure."

"Ms. Witherspoon—"

"Please call me Elle if you're going to scream at me."

"I am not screaming," he shouted.

Eleanor gave him her sweetest and most insincere smile.

The duke huffed and crossed his arms. He had nice arms too. Very muscular. She glanced down at his kilt. Damn! Who knew a man's knees and calves could be so sexy? She gulped a large swig of her tea. He stood and all but tapped his foot. He didn't need to because his stony expression spoke volumes. He was *almost* at the end of his rope. Too bad. She hadn't hauled that tea tray up two flights of stairs to let him off the hook now. He could just tie a knot in his rope and hang on.

She opened her mouth to speak, then the large portrait on the wall behind his desk caught her eye. There were no portraits of the last duke and duchess anywhere in the house. She'd looked. The portraits in the long gallery went on forever and ended with this duke's grandparents. The portrait behind his desk was a large candid photograph in a gilt ornate frame that matched those in the gallery.

"That's you and your brother, isn't it?" She'd sort of

blurted the question before she thought about it. One of her many flaws.

Once more she'd caught him off guard.

He wrinkled his brow, followed her line of vision, and shook his head. "Could you please raise your hand when you decide to change the subject? Your conversational skills are somewhat disconcerting."

She inclined her head and kept her mouth shut.

"Yes, that is my brother, Lord Lachlan, and I a number of years ago, before he shipped out to the Middle East." He turned slightly and faced the portrait.

"He looks like a nice guy. Maybe he can take your place with the boot camp attendees. A duke's brother is almost as good as—"

"No." He reached her in two long strides and braced his hands on the arms of her chair. "You will *not* approach my brother under any circumstances. Is that understood?"

He brought his face so close to hers she could discern the shades of blue in his eyes. She refused to panic and she refused to look away. Not when the man had finally shown some raw emotion. Especially when her heart was racing and every inch of her body vibrated like a damned bell rung too hard.

Eleanor covered one of his hands with hers. His gaze dropped to where their hands met. An electric fissure simmered between them. She gasped softly. He took a deep breath. Very slowly their eyes met.

"My brother…does not socialize. He…has not yet recovered from…. The war was difficult for him. He cannot—"

Eleanor pressed two fingers to his lips. "I understand. I'm sorry. I shouldn't have suggested it."

She stared at her finger against his lips. Lips that were soft and warm. She'd imagined him cold to the touch, hard and emotionless. In this moment, he fairly shook with…not quite anger, but fear? Of her? She couldn't move. He didn't move—save the rapid rise and fall of his breathing.

Thunder rolled somewhere in the distance, but close enough to vibrate the windows. She yanked her gaze to his eyes to find them nearly as wide as saucers.

"Who are you?" he whispered against her fingers, his voice velvet and dark. "Why are you here?"

"I...." Staring into his eyes, she honestly didn't know.

Time stood still. Her heart slowed and nearly stopped. She took in a deep breath and blinked. Her fingers slipped away from his lips.

He leaned closer. "Who are you?"

She tasted the tea and strawberry jam on his breath. She couldn't move away. Thunder boomed like a cannon next to the house. The dogs leapt to their feet, growling, hair on their backs raised. The light rain turned to a deluge against the tall windows at the end of his study.

The duke snapped his head back. His face registered shock and confusion. He still loomed so close the subtle scent of his expensive cologne caught her by surprise. He smelled so damned good.

Her head spun, and she could only think to answer the strange question he'd asked before he kissed her. "I'm your horrible American event planner." As if the answer wasn't stupid enough, she added, "And I will likely make your life hell before Mr. Wentworth's film is done. But I will do my best to make certain your brother isn't disturbed by anything that goes on while I'm in charge." Ok, that last part might redeem her pride a little. Showed empathy, right?

The duke slowly straightened to his full height and took a step back, then another. "Thank you. I will review those contracts and do my best to provide your film people with, what did you call it, a Regency experience?"

"Yes. Thank you." Head still spinning, she picked up the

notebook she'd dropped at some point in their *conversation.* "Let's talk about what that might—"

"No." Before she knew it, he had returned to his desk in much the same pose as when she'd entered the room. "I don't have time to discuss this today." He once again looked at her as the duke, his face unreadable. "We'll discuss this tomorrow."

Eleanor got to her feet and somehow managed to walk to the door. The rain hammered against the windows and lighting hung in the sky outside like a lantern. It wasn't until she raised the latch and opened the door that a wave of anger swept through her.

She faced him. "Tomorrow, Your Grace?"

"Of course, Miss Witherspoon. Tomorrow afternoon."

"On your honor?"

"What did you say?"

"I have your word we will discuss this tomorrow."

"That isn't what you…. Yes, of course. Tomorrow. Good day, Miss Witherspoon." He picked up his pen and turned his complete attention to the stack of papers on his desk. "Is that all you wanted?"

The dogs returned to their place before the fire and settled immediately to sleep. Apparently, even they had dismissed her.

Eleanor turned and fumbled to open the door, then slammed it behind her before she set off down the carpeted hallway. She took three wrong turns before she found a blue tufted velvet bench in front of a broad floor to ceiling window overlooking the rolling hills of the estate. She dropped onto the bench and watched the storm. She was safe from the Highland weather. The storm going on in her head was another thing entirely.

"Is that all you wanted?"

Good fricking question.

Chapter Four

KNOX POLISHED OFF THE LAST OF HIS BREAKFAST AND returned his plate to the tray on the little table next to his desk. He poured himself another cup of tea from the Brown Betty teapot with its whimsical knitted Highland coo tea cozy and leaned back in his chair to enjoy the blessed silence. Whilst he'd managed to avoid Miss Witherspoon over the last week, he hadn't managed to avoid the noise her preparations caused all over the manor. He supposed he should be grateful for the noise, as the cacophony of laughing servants and her shouted orders of instructions allowed him to know where she was at all times.

He'd taken to having breakfast in his study in order to avoid the constant rehearsal sessions in the dining room, where Miss Witherspoon conducted classes in how to serve Regency-style breakfast, lunch, and dinner, and several other meals of which he'd never heard in his life. The servants sounded as if they were having a grand time. Knox, however, was not. His mood swung from fucking annoyed, to utterly mystified to…terrified that he might have finally run mad.

The first moment he saw her, he thought he was seeing a

ghost. Then she'd begun to find him in his study, in the stables, as he was getting into his car, in order to ask him a million questions about what she could or could not do in conducting this event that was bringing so much money into Rosemount's bank account he couldn't afford to turn the opportunity down. Every time he saw her, spoke to her, even thought of her, that sensation of having met her before got stronger. Which had resulted in a brief but uncomfortable encounter only a week ago in front of the manor house.

"Miss Witherspoon, for the love of God, you do not have to plague me with every tiny detail of this Regency Disney World. There is more to running a dukedom than allowing a mob of Americans to have free run of the place." He'd been about to climb into his Range Rover to drive to the estate's whisky distillery to tend to some issues there and perhaps drown himself in a vat of Rosemount's finest. "Ask Mrs. Wallace these questions and leave me out of it." Of course, once he saw her step back and the wounded look in her eyes, he'd felt a right bastard. What was he supposed to do? Tell her that her resemblance to someone who didn't exist made him want to run screaming?

"I have asked Mrs. Wallace," she shot back with that typical American *screw you* attitude that he was beginning to find arousing. "Every time I ask her a question, she says *'You'll have to be asking Himself about that'.*"

Knox had almost laughed out loud at Ms.—Miss, she had instructed him to address her by the Regency Miss—Witherspoon's spot on imitation of Rosemount's iron-handed housekeeper.

"I don't enjoy having to chase you down to ask permission for every little thing either. I'm an adult, not some Highland lassie begging permission from the master."

"I am well aware that you are an adult, Miss. Witherspoon." He put a bit more insinuation in that statement than intended. "What can I do to ensure you don't have to *chase me down*, as you so charmingly put it?"

"Handle Mrs. Wallace."

Knox snorted. "Not on your life. Do you have a pen and paper about you?"

She whipped out a legal pad and a pen from the leather satchel she always carried. He scribbled a note on a clean page and signed it with a flourish before he handed the pad and pen back to her. Miss Witherspoon read the note and smiled. When she looked up at him every ounce of blood in Knox's body froze. Other people only saw ghosts at night or in their dreams. His stood in the front drive of Rosemount Manor and smelled of gardenias.

"Are you okay, Your Grace?" She snapped her fingers in front of his face. "Hello?"

"Fine." He shook his head. "I'm fine. "That should handle any difficulties you have from now on. I have to go."

He fumbled for his keys and dropped them. She scooped them up and laid them into his open hand.

"Mrs. Wallace isn't going to like this." She indicated the note he'd written.

"No, but she'll do as I say. Good day, Miss Witherspoon." He practically fell into his car and started the engine.

"Does everyone here do as you say, Your Grace?" she demanded as he put the Range Rover in gear.

"Apparently not." He'd driven away but watched her in the rearview mirror until she was out of sight.

She was laughing.

To say he hadn't seen her since was a lie. The sound of her voice not only informed him of when to stay away, there were moments over the last week when he'd sought her out, not to speak with her, but to observe her. He had some wild idea that if he kept studying her and listening to her without her knowing, her ability to haunt him would lessen. No such luck.

He finished his tea, then dragged the stack of Rosemount's latest bills in front of him on his desk. At least now he had money in the estate's accounts to actually pay the many debts left over from the last years of his father's life.

"Yer Grace?" Mrs. Wallace marched into his study without knocking, which was unusual enough as it was. The expression on her face, however, signaled trouble of biblical proportions. She only ever turned this particular shade of red when someone was about to suffer an untimely death at her hands. "That woman has got to go. She is interfering with the maids' work and I willnae have that creature crawling about the best drawing room frightening those pur girls out of their wits!"

Knox raised his hands in surrender, as much as anything, and gave his head a good shake. "How is Miss Witherspoon interfering in their work, and what creature is crawling where?" He had no reason to ask who the *she* was, but he was having trouble with the creature's identity.

"That great bloody snake she keeps in her room, that's what creature! She has it crawling about on the Aubusson carpets like a pet dog. I willnae have it, I tell ye."

He'd never hear Mrs. Wallace curse in his life. Which was probably why he took a minute to sort through what she'd said. "There is a snake in the drawing room, my drawing room?"

The housekeeper rolled her eyes. "And who else's drawing room would it be, Yer Grace?"

"Show me."

He pushed out of his chair with a heartfelt sigh and followed her out of his study, down the stairs and down the corridor to Rosemount's main drawing room. Half the maids in the household were crowded around the double doors, along with Robbie and Dougal, who were likely wagering on who would blink first—Knox, Miss Witherspoon, or the snake. Did snakes blink?

He had a vague memory of signing off on her bringing her pet with her to Rosemount. He remembered reading something in the stacks of paperwork he'd signed about the pet needing a large glass enclosure, and that she'd have the creature's food shipped frozen from some exotic pet store in Edinburgh. Did that paperwork mention the pet was a snake? Probably, as he was so infuriated at the entire idea of hiring an event planner, he hadn't really read the contracts he'd signed. Then Miss Eleanor Witherspoon had shown up looking like…she did. Bloody fucking hell!

"Out of the way," he snapped. "Why are you all loitering about out here? Mrs. Wallace says you're supposed to be cleaning the drawing room."

"I'll not be going in there, Yer Grace. Not with that great bloo-ruddy snake in there." Bridie had worked at Rosemount since she'd finished school and had always seemed a sensible, no-nonsense sort of lass.

Knox glanced at Dougal and Robbie who backed away, shaking their heads.

"Oh, for the love of William Wallace." He grabbed the door latches of both doors, pushed them open, and started inside. He scanned the expansive stretch of antique carpets and exquisite furniture to find Miss Witherspoon sitting in one of the high-backed damask chairs before one of the large fireplaces in which a fairly large fire burned. "Miss Wither-spoon, I understand you have a—holy fucking shite!" He stopped dead in his tracks.

Stretched from a spot before the fireplace, across the carpet damned near to where he stood was the largest snake he'd ever seen. Not to mention, the damned thing was pastel orange. Who the hell travelled across an ocean with an orange snake?

"Can I help you, Your Grace?" Miss Witherspoon raised her head from the book and papers in her lap. She wore a tight pink jumper and a long pink and green plaid skirt. She had removed her shoes and the snake's huge head rested on one of her bare feet.

He ran through a series of things to say in his head. None of those things seemed to fit the occasion of finding one's party planner lounging in the formal drawing room with enough snake for several pairs of shoes and a few handbags to boot.

"Is there a reason this creature is currently lying about my drawing room and frightening my staff, instead of occupying whatever housing arrangements you made to keep it in your rooms?"

"Good morning to you, too, Your Grace. Persephone is just stretching her legs, so to speak. It isn't good for her to by cooped up in her enclosure all the time. It's too cold for me to take her outside, so this is the next best thing. Nobody ever comes in here. I know because this is where I come when I want some peace and quiet to go over the details of the boot camp before everyone gets here. She's perfectly harmless."

"Perfectly harmless? The maids are terrified. Mrs. Wallace is about to have a stroke. And if McGinty comes in here, the poor man will keel over dead. He has a mortal fear of snakes."

"If I was as big as Mr. McGinty, I wouldn't be afraid of Godzilla, let alone a little snake like Persephone."

"If this is yer idea of little, no wonder you're single." Knox had no idea what possessed him to say such a thing to a woman he barely knew, let alone one who worked for him.

He watched the wheels turn in her head and saw the moment what he'd said registered. She fell back in the chair laughing, a loud husky laugh that sent wicked sensations careening through his body. He had no choice but to grin, in spite of the heated flush that ran up the back of his neck. The snake raised its head and turned toward him, the entire orange body undulating slowly.

'What is it doing?" He took a step back.

"*She* is moving away from the fire because she's warm enough." Miss Witherspoon stood and dropped her books and papers into the chair. "She's been out long enough. Help me to get her back upstairs."

"Me?" He backed up a few more steps.

"Oh, for God's sake." She walked around him. "Let me get Robbie and Dougal so the poor duke doesn't have to deal with the big, bad snake."

"Wait just a minute." He caught up to her in two steps and clasped her hand. "Give a man a minute to think, will ye, woman?"

She glanced down at her hand, then back up at him. He'd never actually seen a woman who could shoot fire from her eyes. Eleanor Witherspoon came close. Knox dropped her hand.

"Sorry," he muttered, and ran his hand through his hair.

"My name is not 'woman'. You've obviously spent entirely too much time in the wilds of Scotland."

"I did apologize." He shrugged his shoulder that had begun to itch with irritation. "You cannot simply suggest a man pick up a great monster of a snake and not expect him to consider things for a moment or two."

"What sort of things?" She tilted her head to one side and pinned him with a hard stare.

"Death? Being bitten? Being eaten alive? How such a thing is actually done?"

She huffed loudly. "I rolled her down here by myself in one of Mrs. Wallace's laundry carts."

He looked around the drawing room. "Where is the cart now?"

"In the custody of Mrs. Wallace, who snatched it away and announced she'd allowed many things since my arrival, but she'd not be providing transportation for an American instrument of the devil in her best laundry carts." Miss Witherspoon folded her arms. He sensed Mrs. Wallace's set-down had hurt her feelings.

"She actually said 'instrument of the devil'?" He raised an eyebrow and fought a smile.

"Not just an instrument of the devil, an '*American* instrument of the devil'."

Knox winced, which made Miss Witherspoon laugh. "Very well. Transportation by duke it is." He took a deep breath, walked to where the snake now lay perfectly still on the carpet, and bent over and picked up a middle section in one hand. The snake immediately hissed and raised her head so that she was eye to eye with him. Her snake tongue flicked out at him several times. "Fuck. What did I do?" He stayed frozen in that position, bent over, snake in hand.

Highly amused and eerily familiar feminine laughter floated from behind him. He whipped his head around to make certain the sound was real or imagined, a voice from his childhood. "Female snakes don't like to be manhandled any more than women do, Your Grace. You startled her. Let's do this together."

"My apologies, Persephone," he said solemnly, and lowered her body back to the floor. "How do we go about this?"

"You carry and support one half of her body and I'll take the other half. I think we can manage to take the stairs that way." She positioned herself over the back half of the snake. He chewed his lip.

"Given a choice," he said as evenly as he could, "I'd prefer the half without the teeth."

"You're not afraid of a little snake bite, are you?" She stepped to the front of the snake and carefully lifted the animal so that the head and first section were draped over her shoulders. "She isn't venomous, you know."

"Neither are my dogs, but I still prefer they not bite me." Knox carefully stepped close to the back half of the snake. He tucked his hands underneath the cool, surprisingly silky body and hefted the creature up waist high. "Lead the way, Miss Witherspoon."

She rolled her eyes and strolled ahead of him as if walking about with a large reptile draped over her shoulders was an everyday occurrence. She was a singular woman, and had she not so resembled.... If things were different, he might be very interested in getting to know her.

Once they cleared the doors to the drawing room, he was treated to a large portion of his household staff standing open-mouthed as they watched him carry half a snake toward the stairs. Several of the maids squeaked in fear and scurried back against the walls. Robbie and Dougal, cowards that they were, offered him a respectful bow, whilst they backed away from the stairs.

"Don't you men and women have work to do? Mrs. Wallace?" Knox asked as he passed the housekeeper, who stood her ground, though she paled a bit.

"Aye, they do, Yer Grace. Ye heard Himself. Back to work the lot of ye."

Knox heard a flurry of footsteps behind him as he ascended the staircase.

"Robbie and Dougal, if I catch you wagering on this snake biting me, you'll be working for Urquhart mucking out stables for a week," he called over his shoulder. By the time they reached the top of the stairs Knox realized even half of

Miss Witherspoon's python was heavy as hell. "How much does this thing weigh?" he asked.

"She weighed in just under one hundred and twenty pounds when she had her vet check for the trip here. She's a little over thirteen feet long and still growing." The woman rattled off the numbers off like a proud mother reciting the size of a bloody toddler.

"Jesus," Knox muttered.

"How are you doing back there?" she asked, her voice laced with laughter.

"Perfectly fine, thank you."

"I forgot to ask you, Your Grace," she said as she opened the door to her room and they carried the snake through her sitting room. "Do you have a weak stomach?"

"Weak stomach? Not that I am aware of. Why do you ask?" Only after they came to the next door and took a few steps inside did he realize he was in her bedroom.

"Since you were so good as to give me the end of Persephone that bites, I thought I should warn you about the possibility of the other end taking a shot at you."

"The other end? What the hell happens at the other end?" He glanced at the tail of the snake hanging down from his right hand damned near to his ankle.

"What do you think?"

She stopped in front of the largest glass case he'd ever seen. The damned thing covered one whole wall of her bedroom and reached from the ceiling three quarters of the way to the floor where it sat on a sturdy wooden cabinet. She slid the glass door open and allowed the snake to crawl from her shoulder onto a thick tree branch inside the case.

What do you think? He stared at the length of reptile in his hand. She had to be joking. However, when he looked back up at her, the evil grin she wore told him she was in dead earnest.

"Snakes sometimes defecate as a defense mechanism," she explained. "And the smell is horrific. Stays with you for days."

"Please take her." He stepped closer to the sliding door and tried to hand the snake off to her.

She backed away. "You're doing great, Your Grace. Just slide her in there. You'll be fine."

Knox leaned into the glass case and did his best to stuff the rest of *Persephone* into her glass house. About the time he let go of the end of her body, her head swung down from the tree limb to look him in the eye again. Knox lurched back so quickly he backed into Miss Witherspoon who grabbed him to keep him from falling over. When he spun to steady her, he found himself in her arms.

"Are you okay?"

She blinked up at him, and he had the oddest sensation of falling. Her eyes were a rich dark brown with showers of gold flecks. The subtle scent of gardenias came to him, gardenias and not lavender and heather as he expected.

"I'm fine, thank you." He stepped back and straightened his jumper. "Is there a reason you travel with such an unusual pet?"

Eleanor shrugged. "She's quiet, hypoallergenic, eats once a month, and keeps me sane."

"Sane? Do you have problems with sanity, Miss Witherspoon?" He knew at once he shouldn't have asked that particular question.

"Don't we all at some time or another, Your Grace?" She stepped to the fireplace and stirred the low flames back to life before she settled into one of the overstuffed armchairs before the hearth. She indicated he should sit, but he shook his head and stood there, hands clasped behind his back. "We all go a little mad sometimes."

"Norman Bates, not a very good point of reference." He sounded like a prick but couldn't stop himself. One of his many defense mechanisms and in the presence of this particular woman he needed all of the defense he could get.

"Wow," she laughed. "You've seen Psycho. I never would have though it."

"Watched it on my father's satellite television one night with my brother. He had nightmares for weeks."

"But not you?" She was studying him again in that way he was beginning to find annoying.

"My nightmares are very different from my brother's."

"Still?"

"Still." He cleared his throat. "Thank you, Miss Witherspoon. This morning has been quite instructive." He turned to go.

"Eleanor."

He halted. "I beg your pardon?"

"My name is Eleanor. Any man brave enough to carry Persephone up a couple of flights of stairs can call me Eleanor."

Suddenly, her sitting there in her plaid skirt, barefoot before the huge fireplace carried him back to another time. Now he did smell lavender and heather, and he had to leave the room at once.

"Very well, Eleanor. Good day."

He left her bedroom, lengthened his strides, and fled out into the corridor and down the stairs before he stopped on the landing to catch his breath. If a snake could return someone's sanity, he'd have an entire herd of snakes delivered to Rosemount. Mrs. Wallace would kill him. If Eleanor Witherspoon' presence in his home didn't do the job first.

Chapter Five

Knox tossed another log on the fire across from his desk and used the poker to encourage the blaze to burn higher. He normally wasn't such a lowlander about the Highland chill that permeated the manor. However, landing arse over teakettle in his own fountain with nothing between that arse and the icy water but a kilt made a Scot's best friend a damned packed fireplace. He'd changed into dry clothes a few hours ago and his bones still ached. It was only March, so it wasn't surprising the water had been freezing, but damn.

"You're getting old and soft," he muttered as he returned to his desk and dropped back into his chair.

He dragged the old-fashioned ledger closer and tried to focus on the figures. No more than quarter of an hour had passed when he started at the sharp rap on his door. He knew that knock. Damn.

"Yes?"

The latch clicked and the door opened just enough for Eleanor Witherspoon to stick her head inside the room. She smiled. "Is it safe for me to disturb you for a minute, Your Grace?"

"That depends." He closed the ledger. "Do you intend to drown me in my fountain, then assault my ears with a screaming banshee of an American actress and two eight stone wrinkled bags of canine drool?"

"Not today." She stepped into the room, closed the door, and strolled to the chair opposite his desk, her satchel in hand.

She'd changed into a long tartan wool skirt and the sort of pretty white puffy blouse the lasses in the village wore on holidays or festival days. She'd tied her hair back with a tartan scarf, though her kinked curls never failed to escape any attempt she made to control them.

He admired her cheeky attitude and cocky American style. Not least of all because those things about her helped him to steel himself against the riot she set off in his mind.

"And will your Regency house party be bringing any more members of the animal kingdom to Rosemount before this little adventure is over?" He hated to sound like such a prick, but he dared not let his guard down around her. She'd already charmed most of his staff and half the village to do her bidding when it came to organizing this event that was to save Rosemount from bankruptcy.

"First of all, this is not a house party." Her eyes flashed and her cheeks flushed. He'd pissed her off. Again. "Second of all, what happened this morning was an accident, a simple accident. And third—"

"Tell that to my best kilt and my favorite Scots wool jumper. I thought Mrs. Wallace was going to have a seizure when I walked into the kitchens like some kelpie from a fairy tale. She knitted that jumper for me. I'll be in her black books for a month." He was piling it on a bit thick, but this event, whatever she called it, was still in its infancy, and he was already wishing it were over.

"You're not afraid of Mrs. Wallace, and you know it." She pulled her leatherbound notebook from her satchel. He never saw her without it. Of course, he saw her far more often than she saw him.

"Any person of sense is afraid of Mrs. Wallace. In fact, you seem to be the only person on the estate who isn't."

"Are you saying I have no sense, Your Grace?" She stopped flipping through her notebook and stared at him, pen in hand.

"I am certain in most areas of sense you have a fair amount. Your sense of self-preservation when it comes to Mrs. Wallace, however, may be lacking." He propped his elbows on his desk and steepled his fingers. "I will ask you again, will there be any more unmanageable animals arriving in the next few days?"

"Not that I'm aware of. Are you counting Miss Randolph as one of the wild animals?"

"I am counting her as a menace to the male sex and my eardrums. Keep her away from me and away from my male staff." Knox was no fool. The American actress had made a beeline for him the moment she saw him. He'd been fighting off women attracted to his title since he was fifteen.

"Oh, that's not sexist in the least." Eleanor pulled a stack of papers from her satchel and placed them on his desk.

"My sense of self-preservation is not limited to Mrs. Wallace. I recognize trouble of the female sort from a mile away. That woman is beautiful, sexy, and famous, and she knows it."

"She's not the only one who knows it. I caught your brother admiring her from afar." She blanched and bit her lower lip. "I didn't mean—"

"Remember our deal about my brother and gunfire?" A

cold chill swept through him followed quickly by a flash of temper. "That goes double for Miss Randolph. Someone like her is the last thing he needs."

"You really are an insufferable snob, you know that?" She flounced from her chair and paced back and forth in front of his desk.

Knox was mesmerized by the grace with which she moved, even mad as a wet hen. He needed to quit tweaking her because when she was put out with him, she was twice as dangerous to his peace of mind as she was under normal circumstances.

"Lachlan is a grown man and perfectly capable of taking care of himself no matter what you think. And the people coming here for this boot camp and staying to make this period film are all professionals. This is not some tropical resort they've come to looking for a hook up with the locals." She stepped up to his desk and shoved the stack of papers she'd placed on his desk closer to him. "Here are the schedules for the boot camp activities for this month. I have highlighted the ones that require your attendance."

"Lord Lachlan," Knox said. He began to study the schedules. "His name is Lord Lachlan."

"He has asked me to call him Lachlan and, unlike you, I happen to think he is adult enough to decide what he wants to be called."

She sat back down hard in the chair. The woman fairly hummed with energy. She was like that all the time from what he'd observed watching her when she wasn't looking. Then again, her energy now was anger directed at him and him alone.

"I see," he said.

"No, you don't, but I don't really care."

"I never agreed to attend all of these activities. I don't have the time to—"

"We are not having this discussion again." Eleanor blew a stray auburn curl from her face and rolled her eyes. "You agreed to attend the activities I feel would be enhanced by the presence of a real live duke. Unfortunately, you're the only duke on hand." She stood and dropped her notebook and pencil into her satchel. "Which means I expect you at the welcome dinner tonight in full duke regalia. Got it, Your Grace?"

His cock was so hard he was afraid it would start knocking at the underside of his desk. What was it about her that made him so angry and so turned on all at the same time?

"I hope you will allow me not to wear my robes and coronet to dinner. When I bow my head for grace the damned coronet falls into my soup."

Her lips twitched, but she refused to smile, which only made him want to grin like an idiot.

"Kilt and dinner jacket will suffice. I assume you have more than one."

"Kilt? I have twenty actually."

"Of course you do. Until tonight, Your Grace." She jumped to her feet, gave him an exaggerated curtsy, and made for the door.

"Knox."

She turned back as she opened the door. "Excuse me?"

"My name is Knox. I'm old enough to decide what I want to be called."

"When you start acting like Knox I'll call you Knox. Until then, Your Grace will have to do. Don't be late. And if you decide to pull one of your send a note and not show up tricks, I'll hunt you down and drag your ducal ass to the dining room whether you are dressed or not." She slammed the door so hard the antique vase on the table next to the door rocked in place.

He pushed his chair back from his desk and walked to the window that looked out over the fountain and front drive of the house. He'd seen Eleanor's face when the footmen hauled him out of the fountain. Her expression had been one of genuine concern at first. Once she saw he was unhurt, she went to help Miss Randolph, but he'd caught her smiling and trying not to laugh. Something about her face in that moment warmed him all over and scared the hell out of him. He glanced down to the front of his kilt, tented by the hard on he still had.

"You're not helping," he muttered, then stood, and opened the window for some cold air.

Chapter Six

ONLY TWO WEEKS IN, BUT ELEANOR WAS VERY HAPPY WITH THE way boot camp was going. As she and Samantha Higgins made their way across the bridge over the ha-ha to join the spectators watching Teddy Rousseau's shooting lesson, she took a moment to give herself a mental pat on the back. Director Erik Wentworth was already e-mailing her about extending boot camp into the actual filming of *A Matter of Honor*. The duke would be thrilled. Not! She scanned the area just beyond the shooting range Teddy had set up on the extensive front lawn. The duke stood with his arms crossed and feet braced like the lord of all he surveyed. Which technically was true, but that didn't give him the right to be such an ass about it.

He spoke to Samantha and when she replied, he actually threw back his head and laughed. Eleanor both loved and hated when he laughed. Loved because when he laughed, he looked so damned handsome and happy. Hated because she didn't want to be reminded of either of those qualities in the man who seemed determined to drive her nuts.

"Miss Witherspoon," the duke called to her. "Come to enjoy the show?"

The man should have been an actor. His expression could go from pleasant, sociable gentleman to hard-assed, stone-faced jerk on a dime. The fact he was always nice and accommodating to Samantha and always so damned serious with her had nothing to do with it. Well, two could play that game.

She deliberately turned away from him and spoke to Samantha. "Is Mr. Arneaux finally showing up that horse's rear of a sword instructor? How about it, Dr. Higgins? How is your boy doing? Oh my. He's impressive as hell in that kilt, isn't he?" She could almost feel His Grace's eyes burning into the spot between her shoulder blades.

Samantha said something about Arneaux wanting a kilt like the one worn by the first duke in the portrait in the manor's long gallery.

His Grace felt the need to remind them that he was a direct descendant of the guy in the portrait and that the first duke had fought at Bannockburn.

"So Dougal and Robbie said. But it was Mrs. Wallace who told us about the Innes Witch." Samantha's comment went over like a lead balloon.

His Grace stared at the poor professor like she was a bug who had dared to cross his lawn. So much for pleasant and accommodating.

"Indeed." That was his reply, one word that said it all. Himself, as the members of Rosemount's staff called him, was *not* amused.

Eleanor reminded herself, yet again, to find out more about the legend of the Innes Witch. Something about the story hit the duke like a hammer every time.

Teddy and Arneaux and a couple of the estate's ghillies had made their way up the hill. Eleanor and Samantha exchanged a glance. Danny Arneaux definitely looked hot in his Regency Scot's clothes with a gun in the crook of his arm. Of course, when she and Samantha made a harmless remark, Teddy had to come up with one of his typically snarky retorts. Teddy kept walking toward them. For some reason, Arneaux stopped and handed the duke his gun. In the blink of an eye, the action star had spun the swordmaster around and—

Crack!

Eleanor and Samantha screamed and jumped aside just in time for Teddy to fly past them, then slide back down the hill toward the duke. What the fuck? Arneaux had just cleaned Teddy's clock. The two ghillies slowed down, but the duke waved them on and, of course, they obeyed. Poor Samantha kept looking back and forth between Teddy and Danny, her face bright red.

"Nice one," His Grace commented. "Abercrombie, see to Mr. Rousseau."

The butler rushed to do his master's bidding. He wasn't too gentle about it either. He hauled Teddy up by one arm and pretty much dragged him toward the house. Samantha was furious. Danny tried to say something to her, but she was having none of it. Eleanor had no idea which disaster to address first.

The duke strolled up in all of his stuffy, superior glory. He was almost smug about one of the boot campers taking a swing at another.

Eleanor walked around him without a word and headed for the manor. "I guess I should go and check on Mr. Rousseau. After all, I am in charge of this little adventure."

"So I've heard," the duke remarked.

Eleanor turned back to where Samantha, Danny, and the duke stood. "Idiot man." She smiled. "I mean Mr. Rousseau, of course." She bobbed a curtsy.

"I'm coming with you," Samantha ran to catch up to her.

"Samantha, this wasn't your fault." Danny chased after his Regency coach, hand outstretched.

She slapped his hand away and lit into him on how unprofessional his behavior was. The entire time they argued, Eleanor locked eyes with the duke. She wanted him to laugh or say something stupid. To her amazement, he followed Samantha's confrontation of Danny with an expression of sympathy. In a moment, the professor ran toward Eleanor, swiping at her eyes. Danny started to chase her, but the duke stopped him.

"Don't even think about it," the duke said.

Danny stopped in his tracks, though it appeared to be the last thing he wanted to do.

"Sonofabitch is smarter than he looks." Eleanor looped her arm through Samantha's and led her toward the ha-ha bridge. "For a duke. Want to tell me what that was all about?"

"Nothing," Samantha said, her voice wobbly."

Eleanor glanced over her shoulder to see the duke in serious conversation with Danny. She'd give anything to know what he was saying. By God, she was going to find out. The last thing she needed was a snotty Scots duke interfering in her boot camp.

Settling Samantha's nerves, then talking Teddy out of having Danny arrested for assault took longer than Eleanor had planned. By the time she set out to question His Grace, she had missed lunch and had to bribe Robbie five pounds to tell her where the duke was. To her surprise, *Himself* was on the terrace enjoying a private luncheon tray, courtesy of Mrs. Gordon. He didn't even look at the sound of her Regency walking boots as she marched across the terrace.

"Have a seat, Miss Witherspoon," he said. He finished spreading butter on a slice of bread and placed it carefully onto the top of a stack of ham and cheese. "Would you care for a sandwich?" He did look up then. "And perhaps a cup of tea?"

Well, hell. She hated him when he was civil. She settled into the chair across the little wrought iron table from him. "Both, please. I missed lunch."

"So I heard. Here you go." He handed her the plate with the sandwich on it and poured her a cup of tea. Then he set to making another sandwich for himself.

"So you heard? From whom?" She bit into the fresh-baked bread stacked with the local ham, cheese, and butter, and slowly chewed so she could enjoy the delicious flavor.

The duke snorted. "From Robbie. He told me when I told him he could let you know where I could be found."

Eleanor swallowed her bite of food and washed it down with a sip of tea. "The rat. He made me pay him five pounds for the information."

"I shudder to think of the fate of England if Robbie Wallace ever decides to stand for Parliament. We had quite the morning, didn't we?" He smiled and took a bite of his sandwich.

"We? You aren't the one who had to talk Dr. Higgins of the ledge and prevent Rousseau from calling the police."

"Not to worry. The police won't step foot on Rosemount without calling me first. One of the few privileges of being a duke. Rousseau deserved what he got, and I, daresay, he knows it."

Eleanor sighed. "Of course, he did, but Samantha didn't deserve the embarrassment Danny Arneaux caused her by knocking Teddy on his ass."

"He knows that now." The duke pushed the cut crystal dish of Mrs. Gordon's pickles toward her. "I take it she's afraid his actions will indicate a relationship between her and our Cajun friend."

"Don't you see it that way?" She speared a pickle with her fork and devoured it. The duke watched her as if fascinated. You'd think he'd never seen a woman eat a pickle right off the fork.

"I try never to assume anything, especially about the affairs of others."

"Really? Then what were you and Danny Arneaux discussing so intently after Samanth and I left?"

He glanced up at her, his mouth full of sandwich and one eyebrow raised.

She shrugged. "I saw you two sitting out on the hill after Samantha and I went upstairs. Her windows overlook the front lawn."

"Do *you* think they are having an affair?" he asked once he'd washed down his food with some tea.

"None of my business."

"Precisely."

She huffed and glared at him. They ate in silence for a while.

"He realizes what he did was wrong," the duke finally said. "It wasn't his place to punch Mr. Rousseau."

"Whose was it?"

"Hers. He realizes she is perfectly capable of defending herself, and he should have let her do so." He returned to his meal once he'd refilled both of their teacups.

"Did he come to that conclusion on his own or did you help him?" Eleanor had no idea why she asked the question except she was having a real conversation with him, which was rare. Not to mention she wanted to know his view on women who were capable of being more than someone's wife or employee.

"I think we came to that conclusion together. Sometimes it is easier to decipher a mystery if you use someone else as a sounding board."

"Mystery? What mystery?"

"Women, Miss Witherspoon. You ladies are a deliberate mystery to men. Surely you knew that."

"Just making sure you knew." She smiled behind her teacup.

He actually snorted. "As if you would ever let us forget. I think he really cares for her, if that makes any difference. He hit Rousseau because he respects Dr. Higgins and thinks others should too."

"Yes, but by fighting her battles for her, he makes her think he doesn't respect her. Trust me, I'm an expert on men not respecting women." She gave him her most pointed stare.

"I respect you, Miss Witherspoon." His voice was that of the hard-nosed duke once more.

"But not enough to tell me why you blow hot and cold with me most of the time." She was in dangerous territory, but she was going to be dealing with him for at least a year, if not longer. She wanted desperately to know where she stood and nothing more. At least, that's what she told herself.

"Blow hot and cold?" He appeared genuinely puzzled.

"We are sitting here now having a simple conversation about some mutual friends. You aren't coming up with an excuse to run off somewhere. You manage to look me in the eye. You don't act as if I am your Great Aunt Gertrude, who might kiss you without your permission, or your Cousin Henry who might ask you for a loan."

"You have some interesting relatives, Miss Witherspoon. I have no idea what you're talking about."

"Bullshit," she said. "Don't tell me. I'll figure it out, eventually." She pushed her plate away and got to her feet. "I don't know if Danny and Samantha are having an affair, but they do have some sort of relationship, and they need to talk about it."

"Agreed, but that's up to them." He eyed her suspiciously as if he expected her to return to the previous subject.

Good. Let him worry about it.

"Actually, it is up to us. I have a plan, and you're going to help me."

"Excuse me?"

She loved his panicked expression a lot more than she should.

"Instead of running away after dinner this evening, you will join us in the drawing room for whist. Once the card games breaks up, you and I will put my plan in motion."

"Plan? What plan? Miss Witherspoon, come back here."

He was on his feet. She was halfway across the terrace. She waved at him and smiled.

"I'll see you at dinner, Your Grace. Don't be late."

A soft wind wafted down the terrace and surrounded her with the scent of lavender and heather. When she turned to go into the house through the French doors the duke was standing there with the most stunned look on his face. Poor guy.

THAT EVENING AFTER DINNER, ELEANOR SLIPPED BACK INTO the drawing room and signaled the duke. The card party was breaking up. Some people were already headed upstairs to bed. Others were milling around the sideboard for a last drink.

She sidled up to His Grace. "Here's the plan," she whispered.

"Did you not hear me when I said I had no interest in matchmaking? This is ridiculous. These are two adults." He rocked back and forth, his hands clasped behind his back.

"Two adults who need a little push. You agreed to help me."

"I did? When?"

"Stop whining. All you have to do is take Danny to the library. His dogs are waiting for you there. Tell him to give me a minute to talk Samantha into a walk in the gardens. Then he can come out into the gardens, I'll make an excuse to leave, and he can accidentally run into Samantha. After that, it's up to them."

"How nice of you not to hand them each a script with directions and dialogue."

"Give it a rest, Your Grace. Give me a minute to distract Samantha."

She pasted on a smile and strolled over to the fireplace where Samantha sat alone, sipping a cup of tea. When she sat down and looked back, the duke was glaring at her the way he glared at his dogs when they misbehaved. She looked pointedly at Danny and back at the duke. He rolled his eyes and called Arneaux over to him. After a short conversation, they left the room.

"How about a nice walk in the gardens before bed?" Eleanor suggested when Samantha finished her tea and stood.

"It's rather chilly out." Samantha glanced around the room as if in search of someone.

"We've got our shawls. We'll be fine." Eleanor pulled Samantha to her feet, looped arms with her, and walked across the drawing room to the French doors that led onto the terrace. In a few minutes, they were on one of the lamplit paths that meandered through the formal gardens. "Have you talked to Danny yet?"

"Talked to him about what?"

"I'll take that as a no. Do you intend to talk to him about what happened?"

Samantha sighed. "What's the point? He doesn't understand. Men never do when it comes to a woman's professional reputation."

"You could explain it to him." Eleanor shrugged. "Couldn't hurt."

"Like you could explain how confusing the duke's treatment of you is?" She looked at Eleanor sideways.

"That's different. I have no interest in the duke, and he has no interest in me." She said the words, but she wasn't sure she believed them.

"That's not what the Rosemount betting books are saying."

"Hell's bells," Eleanor muttered. She glanced back at the terrace. Danny stood there with his dogs. She maneuvered herself and Samantha around a turn. "Speaking of which, I just forgot Robbie wanted to ask me something about tomorrow's schedule. Sit here and I'll be right back. We're not finished with this discussion." She practically shoved Samantha onto the little stone bench and ran back up toward the house. Danny saw her, waved, and started down the steps with Marie and Laveau.

Eleanor caught the duke as he was about to go back inside. "Hang on." She grabbed his arm. "We may need to referee."

"I agreed to this madcap and unnecessary intervention. I have no intention of refereeing a lover's quarrel. That is not in the contracts you had me sign." He didn't appear to object to her hand on his arm so she wrapped her fingers around his bicep, as much as she could, just to keep her hand warm.

"Oh, come on, Your Grace, where is your sense of romance?" She asked the question in her lightest, most flippant tone.

"Romance is for novels. It seldom works in real life." He kept his head up as if he was studying the moonlit gardens.

"Don't you believe in love?" She forgot to fix her tone. He didn't appear to notice.

"For someone like Arneaux and Dr. Higgins? Perhaps. Not everyone is that fortunate. And some people aren't suited for love." He shrugged, but she didn't buy his attempt to be nonchalant.

"Have you ever been in love?"

She kept her hold on his arm but stepped a little in front of him to force him to actually meet her gaze. Slowly, he lowered his head to look into her eyes. A sudden shock went through her, and he felt that shock too. She'd bet her place here at Rosemount on that.

"Not really. No. I don't think I'm suited for love. You have to agree I'm not the most pleasant of men." He flashed his even white teeth in a self-deprecating smile, which faded way too quickly.

"No, you're not," she replied. He laughed. "But you have potential."

"Potential to be pleasant? Be still my heart."

"Potential to be loved." She would have made a joke or made some smart-assed remark, but the way he stared at her…. Eleanor meant every word.

"I shall take that under advisement, Eleanor."

Chapter Seven

ELEANOR ROLLED OVER IN BED AND GROPED AROUND ON THE bedside table to turn up the low burning oil lamp. After a few tries, she managed to fight her way out of the heavy bedclothes enough to sit up. The sound of voices and running feet moved up and down the corridor outside her room. Hells bells! What now? She scooted off the high bed and sifted around with her feet to find her wool mules. It was late March, and the room held a distinct chill. She glanced at the heart. The fire had burned down pretty low. She had a lady's pocket watch somewhere but a shout in the hallway made her decided not to look for it. It sounded like all hell was breaking loose outside her room. The last thing she needed was for the Duke of Pain in the Ass to hear this noise in the middle of the night.

After stubbing her toe twice and glancing over to check on Persephone, she shrugged into her wool dressing gown and yanked her bedroom door open. Every sconce in the hallway had been lit, which meant some of the footmen and/or maids were participating in what looked like a small riot, or some kind of twisted Scottish relay race.

"Bridie, is the house on fire?" she shouted after the maid who ran by at full tilt and turned the corner toward the main corridor.

The maid called back something incoherent about the American actress, a bat, and the Innes Witch. Eleanor groaned. She spotted Sylvan Goode and Bella Stepford talking with Anna Chase and hurried to join them.

"Would one of you like to tell me what—"

"Shewasstandingovermybedlaughing.   Shelookedjust-likeyou,Eleanor."

"Say what?" Eleanor grabbed Anna's wildly gesticulating hands. "Anna, what are you talking about?" From the corner of her eye, she glimpsed something small and black flit down the corridor, then back up to fly into one of the bedchambers. "Was that a bat?"

"The bat is the least of your worries, Miss Witherspoon," Sylvan Goode said.

She found listening to him difficult as he was dressed in a Regency nightshirt and nightcap.

"Miss Chase has had an encounter with the ghost of the Innes Witch."

Eleanor did a double take, but the old gentleman was serious. When she glanced at Anna Chase her fears were confirmed. If the duke heard about this, he'd go ballistic.

"Anna, honey, maybe you were having a bad dream. Let me see what is going on with the bat and we'll talk about what you saw back in your room."

Eleanor looked back up the corridor where Lily Randolph was having a major meltdown, Mrs. Wallace was shouting at the maids, and Dougal McPhee, the footman, was brandishing...some kind of net? Eleanor met Samantha Higgins gaze and they both rolled their eyes.

A cold, lavender-scented breeze swept down the corridor, accompanied by an eerie whistling. By the time the breeze reached the covey of maids and Mrs. Wallace, the maids were shrieking and running again with the housekeeper in hot pursuit. Suddenly, the maid, Emma, appeared behind them, running from the direction of Anna's room.

"The witch! The Innes Witch! I saw her. She's in the young lady's room."

"I'm going to kill somebody before this night is over," Eleanor muttered.

Anna grabbed the maid and tried to calm her. "I'm sure I was dreaming. I didn't mean to frighten you."

"What did you see, Anna?" Eleanor asked at the top of her lungs. Between everyone talking at once and Lily pitching a fit down the hall she could hardly hear herself, let alone hear anyone else.

"It's silly really," Anna shouted back. "I woke up to the smell of lavender, and my room was cold. I thought I saw a lady sitting in the chair in front of the fire reading my book. She was laughing. Then suddenly she was over my bed." Anna tugged her dressing gown more tightly around her and shuddered

"The Innes Witch," the maid screeched, looking about frantically as if just saying the name would conjure the poor maligned dead woman. "It was her ghost. I saw it."

Between the two incidents—the bat and the ghost—the noise level reached sports bar during playoffs level.

"I was only half awake," Anna shouted over the din. "I'm certain—"

"Quiet!"

The dark roar of a voice Eleanor would recognize in her sleep sent a shiver down her spine, a delicious shiver, but a shiver, nonetheless. The Duke of Turra came down the corridor from the direction of the landing, his long strides eating up the Turkey carpet runner. He wore a long, black, velvet robe that looked like something out of the Arabian Nights. Silence fell like a stone.

"There is no ghost at Rosemount Manor. Mrs. Wallace, will you take these girls in hand?" He waved toward the maids. "Where the devil is Abercrombie?"

Dougal emerged from Lily's room with the bat caught in his net, thank God. Lily started some sort of argument about Danny Arneaux and his dogs and where those dogs were sleeping. The duke ordered Dougal to release the bat outdoors so everyone could get some sleep.

What did where the dogs slept have to do with anything? Lily was obviously taking cheap shots at Samantha. Eleanor kept her eyes on the duke. She recognized his expression. Another five minutes of this midnight riot and the man would go off like a Fourth of July fireworks display. Oh, hell. Now the dogs were slobbering all over Lily, who fell flat on her ass. Worse, the duke went to help her up and got covered in slobber. Which Eleanor didn't mind too much. Served him right. She smiled.

"Marie and Laveau slept with you last night, didn't they, Miss Chase?" Dougal asked.

"They did, indeed," she replied. "I wish they'd slept with me tonight. Perhaps, I wouldn't have let my imagination run away with me and awakened the entire house."

"T'weren't your imagination, miss," the maid, Tildie, said. "I saw her too. Big as day, in the corridor outside your room. The Innes Witch—"

They needed to shut up about the Innes Witch before—

"There is no witch!"

And we have liftoff. The duke's shout echoed down the corridor and his expression grew stonier by the moment. Once he spotted Eleanor, all bets were off, and she was too tired and cranky to deal with him right now.

Danny's bloodhounds were baying their heads off.

"Quiet!" McGinty barked, one hand raised for emphasis.

Everyone, including the dogs shut up.

"Miss Witherspoon," the duke said, and stared down the hall at her, "will you please escort Miss Chase and Tildie back to Miss Chase's room and check for this spectral witch? It would be nice if we could all get some sleep sometime tonight." His Grace was well into high and mighty horse's ass mode.

Sylvan and Bella gave her a little wave but stayed put.

Eleanor glared right back at him. She bared her teeth in a fake smile, gave him a really bad curtsy, beckoned to the other ladies, and marched down the adjacent corridor toward Anna's room. Once inside the elegant bedchamber, Eleanor flounced into one of the chairs by the fire. Anna took the other chair, and Tildie settled onto the ottoman between them.

"Now," Eleanor said as she tried to shake off the storm of emotions the duke always provoked in her. "Tell me what you saw, Tildie."

"Everyone was running about and screaming. I came downstairs to see what was happening. Mr. Goode and Miss Stepford were talking to Miss Chase. And the Innes Witch came floating out of Miss Chase's room. She was kind of misty, but I know it was her. She put her finger to her lips and disappeared out the window at the end of the corridor. Then that cold wind rushed inside and down towards Himself." She crossed herself.

"What about you, Anna? What did you see?" Eleanor discovered a long time ago that if you wanted someone to tell the truth and not to second guess themselves you had to ask the question as if it was no different than any other question. She didn't know if she believed, but she knew these two women did.

"Sort of the same thing," Anna said. "A blurry figure, definitely a woman, definitely in medieval looking clothes. For a moment her face reminded me of you, but—"

"Miss Witherspoon, the duke said you must come at once." The footman, Dougal, stood braced in the doorway, slightly out of breath.

Eleanor rose slowly to her feet. "He said what?" Her whole body flushed hellfire hot. She was not a servant to be summoned like a dog.

Dougal took a step back. "Uhm. Well, that is. Mr. Arneaux is trapped in bed with your snake, and Himself said since the snake is yours, we best leave this to you and, please, miss. Mr. Arneaux is white as a sheet, and Himself is flummoxed, and 'tis quite a coil we're in and no mistaking it."

"Persephone is in bed with Danny?" It was official, Eleanor had landed in Looney Tunes land. "Hell's bells on steroids. Come on, Dougal." She hooked the footman's arm as she hurried out the door and down the corridor to Danny's room.

❧

KNOX WINCED WHEN DANNY SHIFTED IN BED.

"There aren't enough women in my room in one of the most humiliating moments of my life?" Dante muttered.

"Probably," Knox said. "But in this case, we don't have a choice. It's her snake."

"It's what?" Dante shifted up in the bed, but immediately stopped, eyes wide and breath suddenly short.

"That's what happens when you allow an American party planner to turn your home into Regency Disney World. The woman is a menace. Putting people in costumes. Disrupting my routine." Knox hated that he sounded like a disgruntled arse, but Eleanor Witherspoon had turned his life upside down in more ways than one. He'd tried to avoid dealing with her, but that hadn't worked. He was thinking about camping out in the castle ruins until sometime next year.

"Taking away cell phones," Lily declared.

Knox fought the urge to roll his eyes at the American actress. Speaking of being an arse, or at least a pain in the arse, he said, "And traveling with a thirteen-foot albino python. Unless, in addition to a supposed witch and a few bats, we have another *humongous orange snake* slithering about the house."

"This is ridiculous," Teddy Rousseau said. "There are five grown men in this room. We are more than a match for a python, no matter how large it is. Unless this is all a ploy for attention on Arneaux's part. We all know what drama whores actors are."

"Screw you, Teddy. Don't let the door hit you where the good Lord split you on the way out. I don't need your help."

McGinty let loose a deep belly laugh. Knox fought a smile. Arneaux had a knack for saying the very things to Rousseau that he longed to, especially when the swordmaster said rude things about Eleanor. Whilst it was fine when Knox said or thought them, when someone else did, his first reaction was to punch that person. Yet, another reason he'd be glad when she and this Regency boot camp were gone.

"Oh, I wouldn't miss this for the world," Teddy said.

"Mr. Rousseau is correct in one thing." Knox stepped closer to the edge of the bed. "There has to be a way to get you out of this without disturbing your scaly date. As much as Miss Witherspoon will hate it, I think we need to switch on the electric lights." He could just hear her now, declaring he was interfering with the guests' *Regency experience.*

"Certainly, Your Grace." Mrs. Wallace went to the wall switch and, in an instant, most of the other people in the room were squinting at the glare of the chandelier-like fixture overhead. They'd been living so authentically the last couple of weeks that electric light must have been quite a shock. Fortunately, Knox refused to live without electricity when not in the presence of Eleanor's campers.

"You ladies can leave if you like," Danny said. "It's after midnight, way past even your bedtime, Mrs. Wallace."

"You've got enough to worry about in your own bed, Mr. Arneaux. Keep your nose out of mine." Trust Mrs. Wallace to put him in his place.

"Yes, ma'am."

McGinty snorted, and Danny threw him a glare.

"At least you're wearing a nightshirt," Knox said.

"Keeps me from freezing to death when my traitor dogs decide they prefer Dr. Higgins's bed to mine."

"One can hardly blame them," Mr. Goode said.

"What the hell?" The actor flinched and nearly came off the bed.

"What's wrong with you now, lad?" McGinty asked.

"It licked me."

Knox couldn't resist. "Do we need to leave you two alone?"

"Screw you, Your Grace."

"As flattering as that invitation is, Mr. Arneaux, you are not my type, and you appear to already have a bed partner who is more than willing."

Danny shot him the bird. "I really hate you right now."

"What on earth is everyone doing in Danny's room in the middle of the night?" Eleanor stormed into the room, her glorious red hair and ivory skin glowing against the light blue of her wool robe.

"Apparently, we're about to watch *Danny* have sex with your pet," Lily said.

The room erupted into a chorus of coughing and muttering. Danny and Knox exchanged a look. This could get ugly, quickly.

"Excuse me?" Eleanor narrowed her eyes at the actress.

If looks could kill Knox would not be surprised to see Lily Randolph reduced to ash. He'd been the object of that glare a time or two himself. He actually found her rather sexy when she was angry with him. Until he remembered the reason she was angry was his behavior toward her, which he couldn't bring himself to explain.

"Your little pet has crawled into bed with Arneaux here and has been holding him hostage for hours," Knox said far more harshly than intended. "Were you aware this creature was on the loose, or do I need to appoint a footman to walk it along with Arneaux's beasts?"

She rolled her eyes. "Oh, for God's sake, someone unplugged her warming lamp. She came in here looking for heat. You should be flattered, Danny."

"Your snake gets an electric heater?" Lily asked.

"She's not in Regency boot camp, Miss Randolph."

"I'd be more flattered if I hadn't woken up with her wrapped around my leg."

"She's perfectly safe." Eleanor stepped to Danny's bedside and practically elbowed Knox out of the way. "Move over here and I'll—"

"Uh-uh." Dante grabbed her hand. "Do not try to move her."

"Why not?"

Miss Randolph said something rude and an argument ensued between her, Danny, and Dr. Higgins. The entire time Knox studied Eleanor. She always seemed to know when to interfere in these squabbles and when to let them work it out. An uncanny skill for anyone to have.

Dante signaled Knox with a crooked finger. He leaned in to hear what Danny had to say and choked back a laugh.

"Well," Eleanor said, tapping her foot. "What did he say?"

"Actually he…that is, there is a problem with…." Suddenly he sensed heat crawling up the back of his neck.

"Great job there, Your Grace. The damned snake's head is on my…groin." Arneaux's last word came out a hoarse whisper.

"What?" Dr. Higgins asked.

"Excuse me?" Teddy said.

"I beg your pardon?" Eleanor said.

"The snake has crawled up my shirt and is using my nuts for a pillow, okay? And, if it's all the same to you ladies and gentlemen, I'd rather she didn't get pissed off enough to bite me right now."

Knox winced, along with every other man in the room. Some things were universal.

Eleanor snatched the covers out of Arneaux's hands. "Persephone is not going to bite you. She's probably asleep." She threw back the bedclothes, then reached under the poor bugger's nightshirt.

"Whoa!" Danny tried to lever himself up the headboard on his fists. "Careful, Eleanor. That's not a snake you're grabbing."

"Sorry about that." She shot the other ladies in the room a quick glance. "Apparently those rumors are all true." She winked, which for some reason flew all over Knox. He'd had enough of this.

He pulled Eleanor away and stepped into her place.

"Oh, for pity's sake, woman. You'd think you'd never had your hand on a cock before." He reached under Danny's nightshirt and pulled a few feet of snake out, head first.

"Shit!" Danny tried to move away. "Her bottom half is still wrapped around my leg, and she's squeezing now. Thanks a lot."

"Oh, let me help." Eleanor pulled the bedclothes the rest of the way down and tried to bump Knox out of the way. She started to tug at the coils of snake wrapped around the besieged actor's knee and thigh. "Come here, Persephone. Come to Mama."

"Bloody hell!" Knox froze as the damned thing wrapped its coils around his hands. What the fucking hell next?

"Your Grace!" McGinty and Mrs. Wallace scurried to his side and tried to break him free.

Wide-eyed, Lily, Teddy, Bella, and Mr. Goode offered suggestions.

"Just relax."

"Try not to struggle."

"Try not to make it angry."

"It's not going to eat him, is it?"

"So not helpful," Knox muttered. He flexed his hands to no avail.

"Jesus, take the wheel." Arneaux closed his eyes and shook his head.

"Stop pulling," Eleanor ordered Knox. "You're upsetting her."

Knox motioned with his head for McGinty and Mrs. Wallace to back off.

"How can you tell?" McGinty asked as he and Mrs. Wallace obeyed his wordless command and stepped back.

The snake shifted her body from tail to head with one powerful undulation. Eleanor and Knox landed across Dante in a tangled sprawl of arms, legs, and pastel orange coils.

"You know," Dante said tightly. "My fantasies of a ménage à trois never involved a snake." He looked around the room. "Or an audience."

"Get. Me. Out. Of. This. Bed," Knox ordered. The scent of heather and gardenias surrounded him and his body was having a strong reaction to Eleanor's curves beneath him.

"Or a duke," Arneaux said. "McGinty, why don't you just go ahead and shoot me."

"Before or after I help His Grace?" McGinty wrapped a thick arm around Knox's middle and hauled him off the mattress, snake and all.

Samantha hurried to help Eleanor to her feet. The redheaded virago who featured in so many of Knox's erotic dreams lately laughed as she unwrapped the snake from around his hands. Samantha worked to free Dante's leg from Persephone's powerful reptilian grip.

"See," Eleanor said as she pulled the snake across her shoulders and allowed its head to rest in her outstretched hand. "She's perfectly harmless. All this fuss over—"

The snake lashed out and sank its fangs into Knox's upraised hand.

"You were saying?" He lifted an eyebrow at Eleanor and ground his teeth to avoid swearing at the pain.

Thud!

McGinty took one look at the snake attached to Knox and passed out cold.

The scent of lavender and a woman's spectral laughter floated through the room.

Elsbeth. Knox shook his head. Spending the rest of the year in the rooms at the top of the old castle tower was beginning to look like a great idea.

"Is this really necessary?" Knox asked minutes later, as he, Eleanor, and Dougal maneuvered the snake, still clamped onto his hand, through Eleanor's sitting room and into her bedroom where the beast's cage sat.

"It was a lot easier to move her like this instead of trying to pry her off you in a room full of people. Just in case you lose that stoic Scots attitude and actually scream in pain. Wouldn't want to embarrass His Grace, would we Dougal?"

The footman said not a word as he hefted his end of the snake into the cage. Dougal McPhee was no fool.

"Now hand me your flask of whisky." Eleanor held her free hand out to the footman.

"My flask, miss?" He tried that wide-eyed innocent Highland lad expression on her. Knox could have told him he was wasting his time.

"In your sporran. Hand it over." Dougal collapsed like a house of cards in a stiff wind. He fished into his sporran and dropped the silver flask into her palm. "Now go into my sitting room and bring the big box marked *First Aid* from the sideboard." The lad hurried to do as she asked.

"This really isn't necessary, Miss Witherspoon," Knox said, even as he winced in pain.

"What? Me getting Persephone to let you go, or me making sure you don't die of infection? Or did you plan to hang around in my bedroom until she decides she can't eat you?"

He did a double take and then he saw her grin. "Do your worst then, Miss Witherspoon."

"I keep telling you my name is Eleanor. Especially if you are the reason my poor snake is going to have a hangover tomorrow."

"What are you going on about...Eleanor?" He watched fascinated as she opened the flask one-handed and held it to the side of the snake's mouth. She tipped the flask so that one drop and then another dribbled over the creature's lips and past those razor-sharp teeth embedded in his hand.

"Take this." She put the flask in Knox's free hand and kept her eyes riveted on her pet's head. In a few minutes the snake's jaws relaxed. Eleanor gently pulled those jaws apart, and he slid his hand free. "There you go, sweetie." She tucked the rest of the beast into the cage and closed and locked the door. "Come on, Your Grace. Let's assess the damage. I'd like to crawl into bed before sunrise."

She took him by the arm and led him to a chair in front of her bedroom fireplace. If she saw the double entendre in what she'd said, she gave no indication. Of course, he was still learning to read her, whether he wanted to or not. He put the flask down beside him in the chair.

She grabbed a tea cloth from the table next to his chair, sat down on a leather ottoman in front of his chair, and began to wipe the blood off his hand. "Mrs. Wallace is going to kill us for leaving a blood trail all over her carpets."

"Oh, I expect her to add that to the litany of major sins committed against the manor since you arrived. I receive a daily sermon on the matter, though she does change the order of service from time to time to keep it interesting."

"No doubt." She glanced up at him and grinned. "Thanks, Dougal," she said as the footman returned and handed her a large box. "Go find your bed. You've had a long day."

Dougal looked to him for confirmation. Knox nodded. "Go on with ye. Leave the flask, just in case."

"Aye, Yer Grace." He bowed to Knox, nodded to Eleanor, and quietly went back through the sitting room.

Miss Witherspoon…Eleanor opened the box Dougal had delivered and began to sort through the contents. She placed several items on the table next to him.

"Is there a reason you have a first aid kit large enough to serve a regiment in your sitting room?"

"Have you *met* the people attending this Regency experience?" She folded the tea towel into a square and placed his hand onto the now thick fabric cushion. "Punching each other, cutting each other with swords, paper cuts with whist cards, scraped knees, getting thrown from horses. Shall I go on?"

Knox laughed in spite of himself and waved her off with

his free hand. "Forget I asked. Perhaps I should leave Dougal's flask with you."

"If I start drinking, I'll never stop." She tore open some alcohol wipes with her teeth, then used them to clean the last of the blood from his wounded hand.

"How did you know the whisky would persuade our scaly friend to release me?" He turned his head toward the large glass case where the snake had coiled up on a platform under a red glowing lamp.

"I realize you have not noticed, but I am a very detail-oriented person. Once I decided I wanted a Burmese python as a pet, I did my research, which included what to do if she bit me. She only needed a few drops, anymore might have killed her. There are entire online communities of large snake owners that are all too happy to share their knowledge." She was cutting lengths of gauze and bandaging material as she spoke.

"Why a snake, especially such a large specimen?"

"First, to piss off my parents. I was thirteen when I bought her with my own money."

"I completely understand wanting to cross one's parents. My entire life has been an exercise in disappointing mine."

"Does that bother you at all?" She glanced up to meet his gaze.

"Not anymore. How about you?"

"Absolutely not. My parents wanted me to be a surgeon like my father. Or a lawyer like my mother and brother. Persephone doesn't judge, and she travels well. I don't have to walk her. I've had her over fifteen years now. She suits the life I live now." Eleanor pulled out a brown bottle stoppered with a cork. "Brace yourself." She poured liquid from the bottle onto his hand.

"Fuck!" He shouted. His hand burned like the fires of hell. "What the bloody hell is that?"

"Witch hazel. Aren't you glad I didn't do this where your staff might hear?"

"Witch hazel?" He gripped the chair arm with his free hand. "Why witch hazel?" Knox tried his damnedest to keep the suspicion from his tone.

"Because it works. Why? Do you have something against witches?" She was smiling as if she'd made a joke. She had no idea.

"Are you a witch, Eleanor?" He couldn't take the question back, dammit.

"No, Knox, are you?"

Bloody hell, she was good.

"Not that I am aware of." Sweat trickled down his back as he attempted to keep his answer flippant, or as flippant as he could.

She blotted the excess witch hazel from his hand, then applied a white cream, which fortunately only stung a bit. Next, she set to bandaging his wound as efficiently as any nurse he'd ever seen.

"What did you do to piss off your parents. You don't strike me as the wild child type," she asked.

Her head was bowed over her work, which gave him the chance to study the tightly kinked red and gold curls that created the silky crown cascading over her shoulders and down her back.

"Everything. I did everything I could think of, even after they sent me away to school in England. Drinking, smoking, chasing unsuitable girls, was almost sent down from college more than once. Only thing that saved me was being the son of a duke."

"Why were you so angry?"

"Too many reasons to name." He didn't want to engage in this conversation. Not with her. Somehow over the last months, Knox had decided he didn't want her to think badly of him. "Even Mrs. Wallace would be impressed with this dressing." He held up his bandaged hand. "Though I suspect she'd die before she'd say so."

"There's a lot of that going around where I'm concerned." She began to place all of her supplies back into the first aid box.

"What do you mean?"

She snapped the box closed and finally looked him in the eye. "You, Your Grace."

"Knox. My name is Knox."

"Fine. You, Knox. You're sitting here with me now acting almost human. I could almost believe you respect me and don't have any problems with me."

"I do respect you. I don't have any problems with you. What gave the idea otherwise?" He knew. God help him, he knew, but he would never be able to explain that to her without coming off as a complete lunatic.

"In front of other people, you treat me with complete disdain. Hell, sometimes you treat me that way when we're alone. Then other times, you treat me like…a friend. What the hell is going on in your head where I am concerned? It has to be you. I know good and damned well I haven't done anything to you to make me have to check to see who I'm talking to half the time—His Grace, who talks to me like I scare him to death or Knox, who let my snake bite him and didn't bat an eye." She set the box on the floor. "You know what? It doesn't matter. I'm tired, and God knows what the fallout from tonight's activities is going to be." She stood and walked to the door that led to her sitting room.

"Take some ibuprofen for the pain, not aspirin. Aspirin might start the bleeding again. Thanks for not raising a fuss about Persephone biting you." Her face had gone a little pale, and she looked weary and more than sad.

He got up and grabbed Dougal's flask. "I suspect Perse-

phone was tired of being manhandled. Not lady likes that."
He stopped in front of her. "Whatever you sense in my treatment of you is not your fault. I can't explain it." He shrugged.

"Can't or won't?"

"A little of both? Eleanor. I know this isn't fair. There are things about you being here that I am doing my best to deal with…adjust to." He needed to stop talking. He wasn't helping. Her expression of confusion, skepticism, and hurt told him so. He had the sensation of sinking in a Highland bog and almost wished he was.

"Do you want to tell me what those things are? Maybe I can help." She put her hand on his forearm.

He lifted her hand and rubbed her fingers. An overwhelming sense of warmth and memory suffused him. "I wish I could, Eleanor. I truly do. Good night and thank you."

He opened the door to the sitting room and crossed to the hallway door without looking back. He hurried on shaky legs down the corridors to his own bedroom. Once inside, he closed the door, pressed his back against the thick oak wood, and slid down to the floor, cradling his wounded hand and wondering what the hell he was going to do about Eleanor Witherspoon.

Chapter Eight

Eleanor cursed as the toe of her slipper-clad foot caught on another small rut in the hallway of the original remains of the castle. She juggled the dishtowel covered plate she carried in one hand with the leather journal she carried in the other. She was sick and damned tired of asking Knox...the duke...Lord Stick-Up-His-Ass for permission for every little thing to do with her meticulously planned Regency experience. Especially after the *heart-to-heart* they'd had last month. He'd seemed almost human the night Persephone bit him. Now—

She blew out a frustrated breath. Now, she left schedules for him to review, sneaked into his study every morning and left notes on his desk with lists of each day's events. Which was how she'd found out that he slept on the big Chesterfield sofa in front of the fireplace at least two or three nights a week.

She never woke him up, but she did take time to study him while he slept. Asleep the man looked younger, but tired, always tired. Nine times out of ten, when she found him like that, she covered him with the thick wool blanket that hung over the back of the sofa and felt sorry for him for the next few hours. Then he'd skip out on lunch with the boot campers, or side with Mrs. Wallace on some nitpicky detail or other, and she'd remember why he was such a jerk. A tall, sexy jerk with a great ass who smelled like damn-I-love-his-cologne-let-me-sweat-it-off-him-with-some-first class-banging.

"Son-of-a-bitch." Eleanor stumbled again.

Regency slippers and dresses were no match for medieval ruins. Especially when she'd spent so much time tracking Knox down that the fading light of dusk was all she had to help her make her way to the old tower where he kept the office he ran off to when he wanted to hide. He had to be there. She'd looked everywhere else.

She'd hardly reached the huge wood and iron door into the bottom floor of the tower when she heard Tannus and Beira, whining and snuffling at the doorlatch. Eleanor raised the latch and bumped the iron-banned oakwood with her hip. The dogs danced in place as she used her butt to close the door. In spite of the high ceiling and the staircase that spiraled up to the other floors of the tower, the room was warm. The dogs followed her to the desk where she set the plate and her journal.

"Your Grace?" Eleanor glanced around the room as she gave each dog a good ear scratch. "Knox?"

"What?" The groggy sounding question emitted from the old horsehair couch to her left, followed by a loud thump and muttered Gaelic.

Eleanor leaned over the couch to find His Grace, the Duke of Innes, sprawled on a braided rug on the flagstone floor with the dogs sniffing his face. "Did I wake you?" she asked with her sweetest smile.

He shoved the dogs aside, then rolled onto his hands and knees and glared up at her as he struggled to his feet. The back of his kilt was hiked up, giving her a great view of his bare muscled butt. Unfortunately, he saw what she was looking at and snatched the plaid fabric down as he stood.

"Do you Americans have some sort of directive that forces you to try and see what a Scot wears under his kilt?" He braced one hand on his hip and ran his other hand through his hair a few times.

He snatched the plate from her.

Eleanor flexed her fingers and counted them to make certain the duke had not removed one of them when he grabbed the plate. "Hungry, Your Grace?"

He stopped, mouth full, mid-chew, and swallowed hard. "Apologies. Mrs. Gordon's tablet is a weakness of mine."

"I see that."

She came around the old couch and sat down. With her feet stretched toward the fire Eleanor studied Knox as he ate the next piece of tablet more slowly, eyes closed and savoring every bite. He finally settled onto a worn tapestry fabric covered ottoman across from the couch and the dogs dropped their butts onto the carpet at his feet and waited.

"I didn't mean to wake you," Eleanor said.

"I'm growing accustomed to it."

"Accustomed to what?"

"You bringing mayhem with you everywhere you go." He gave a half grin. "When you show up, I'm either dunked in a fountain, choke on my wine, am attacked by a snake, or fall off a settee." He offered her the plate. She took the smallest piece of tablet.

"None of those incidents was my fault. When is the last time you ate?" She noticed a teapot swathed in a knitted tea cozy and a half empty cup of tea on the fender next to the fireplace. Now that she looked closer, his face appeared a little pale and there were faint shadows under his eyes.

"I had breakfast in my study this morning." He offered her

the plate once more, but she waved him off. He covered the tablet with the cloth and set it on the small simple table behind him. "You come bearing tablet. What do you want?"

Knox's clear blue eyes turned blue-grey when he was suspicious or angry. She didn't know which at the moment, perhaps a little of both.

"About Lily learning to drive your phaeton." Eleanor had learned early on not to beat around the bush with this man. "Urquhart says you have refused. Why?"

"My antique phaeton. My decision. Anything else?" He sat with his hands clasped between his knees and gazed at her as if they were discussing the weather or what Mrs. Gordon had made for dinner.

"Fine." She stood and retrieved her journal from his desk. "There are several estates between here and Edinburgh where I can rent one and have it delivered. You, of course, will have to absorb the cost as I hadn't figured the rental into the price I gave Wentworth for the boot camp. Good evening, Your Grace." She started for the door followed closely by his dogs.

"Dammit, Eleanor, wait a minute." In three long strides he reached her side and grasped her arm. "Come back and sit down."

She glanced down at his hand which he quickly removed and raised in a gesture of surrender. Eleanor brushed past him, managing to step on his foot on the way, and flounced back onto the couch.

"I know you don't like Lily, Knox, but she is a professional. She's been riding horses and driving various vehicles since she was a child actress."

"The phaeton is not just any vehicle." He sat back on the ottoman. The dogs settled at his feet. "I've been driving it since I was eight, and even I have nearly come a cropper in it more than once."

"Come a cropper?" Eleanor raised an eyebrow. "How English schoolboy of you."

"Very funny. I cannot afford any extra expenses right now and that includes medical bills and an injury lawsuit for an American actress smashed to bits by a runaway antique carriage."

Eleanor rolled her eyes. "Lily has signed a release for all the boot camp activities. And Urquhart says there is no one better to teach her to drive the phaeton than Lachlan, so she'll be perfectly safe."

Her attempt to insert his brother into the equation casually went over like a lead balloon. Knox stared at her, his face like stone. He clasped his hands so tightly together between his knees she saw every vein and tendon. He didn't say a word, but she refused to break the silence. Even the dogs raised their heads and regarded their master as if he might suddenly erupt.

"I realize," he finally said, his voice rusty and harsh. He cleared his throat. "I realize it has been some time since we talked about my rules concerning my brother and this little party of yours."

"This is not a little party. This is a major event leading to the filming of a major motion picture, which will result in a major dump of cash into your bank account." Eleanor fought the simmering heat that suffused her body. She didn't want to lose her temper with the man who was essentially her employer. Not matter how big a dick he was being. "And I have it on the best authority, Lachlan's, that you are not his father, nor are you assigned the task of making rules for him."

"You are telling me he agreed to this ridiculous plan? To teach that woman how to drive my phaeton?" Now he was losing his temper, and she was glad.

"I'm saying he offered to do anything within reason to

help me make this Regency experience and boot camp a success. Urquhart said Lachlan is the best carriage driver on the estate, except for you. I assumed you wouldn't volunteer, so your brother is Rosemount's designated driver." Neither she nor Urquhart had actually told Lachlan who his student would be, but Eleanor wasn't about to tell Knox.

"I have no intention of participating in this farce any more than absolutely necessary." He sounded like the snooty aristocrat now. Which would be sexy if he wasn't so damned arrogant.

"That's a relief. You'd probably murder poor Lily and dump her body in the loch, tied to a chair." His face went white. What had she said?

"Knox?"

He stood abruptly, grabbed the poker from the stand beside the hearth, and stirred the fire. "If someone dumped Miss Randolph in the loch tied to a chair, she'd probably float." He replaced the poker in the rack and leaned against the mantel, arms folded across his broad chest. "Tell me. Eleanor, do you lie awake at night and come up with ways to see how far I will go to save Rosemount? Of do you just want to humiliate me for being less than receptive to this entire operation?"

She snorted. "I don't lie awake at night and think about you at all. I sleep soundly because I am constantly fighting to make certain everything runs as smoothly as possible. And as far as what you will do to save Rosemount, so far, I have had to fight you every step of the way."

He strolled over to the couch and gazed down at her intently.

She swallowed hard but refused to look away. "And I doubt the woman has been born who could humiliate you... Your Grace." This close his eyes suddenly appeared blue as the Highland skies over the loch. She licked her lips. Her journal dropped to the floor.

"Then you sleep far better than I do, Eleanor," he said softly. "I lie awake at night and think of ways to resist you, but I must confess I don't come up with much. I used to think the woman who could humiliate me had never been born." He bent and leaned close, his lips a breath away from hers. "Until recently."

"This is not a good idea, Knox." Eleanor had trouble catching her breath.

"What isn't a good idea?" His breath tasted of tablet and tea.

"This."

She fisted her hands in the skirts of her Regency walking dress. If she touched him, she'd be lost. Dammit, this wasn't what she'd traipsed across that medieval courtyard in the dark for at all.

"This isn't what I came out here for."

He sighed and slowly straightened. "You started it." Something in his expression made her want to apologize, but she didn't quite understand why.

"I know." She twisted and slid her way off the couch, then brushed her skirts back into place. He scooped up her journal and handed it to her. "You'll tell Urquhart you'll allow Lily to have lessons in your phaeton?" She had to resort to business or she'd lose her resolve.

He gave her his usual cynical smile. "I usually don't sell myself for something as cheap as a plate of tablet, but I'm tired and live in hope this will be a disaster and you'll stop persuading me to make decisions I know I'm going to regret."

A sad sort of disappointment washed over her. His cynicism stung.

"I'm an American, Knox. There are no limits to what I'll do to get the job done."

She pushed past him, stopped to give each of the dogs a pat and walked quickly to the door, which she opened with one try. Not hard when she was as pissed off as she was, at him and at herself.

"I didn't mean that, Eleanor." He stood in the doorway as she took a few steps across the broken cobblestones. The moon was out in a clear sky. She'd have no trouble finding her way back to the manor. "You know I didn't mean that."

She turned and looked back at him, standing in the doorway to the tower like a medieval lord with his dogs at his side. "Didn't you?"

"No, I didn't. I'm tired, hungry, and whatever this is between us is driving me mad." He smiled and even managed to appear a little embarrassed.

"Well, that is some compensation. Don't forget to send word to Urquhart. Nobody on Rosemount dares defy you, Your Grace."

"Nobody, Miss Witherspoon?" He crossed his arms and gazed at her dubiously.

"Almost nobody." She bobbed a curtsy and waited until she was nearly at the entrance of the courtyard before she looked back.

He was standing in the doorway laughing.

Chapter Nine

Knox stood in front of the ornate mullioned windows at the far end of Rosemount Manor's largest and least frequently used drawing room and watched what was becoming a familiar scene play out. Had someone told him in January he'd be hosting three weddings and four wedding receptions before the end of June, in the middle of something called a Regency boot camp—which was now to be a year-long production of a period film—he would have….

He sighed. Who was he fooling. He'd be doing the exact thing he was doing now. His father's financial excesses made this entire farce necessary. Knox released a breath and tried to concentrate on the string quartet that played in the corner, left of the hearth.

"Drink, Yer Grace?" Robbie Wallace, footman and the estate's resident bookmaker, sidled up to him almost out of thin air.

The lad's grandmother had taught him well. Mrs. Wallace had been Rosemount's housekeeper since before Knox was born. She'd forgotten more about serving in a duke's household than most people would ever know. And she knew the value of a servant's ability to do his or her job as silently and seamlessly as possible. A skill Knox often wished he might acquire. Being a ghost had its appeal.

"No thanks, Robbie. I've had my fill of champagne for the day."

Knox did his best not to turn his head toward the distinct melodic laughter of the author of his now farcical existence. He failed. Eleanor Witherspoon, dressed in a deep blue Regency gown that made her look like a model in a Thomas Lawrence portrait, stood with the latest happy couple

"Mr. Arneaux suspected as much. He sent ye this." Robbie handed Knox a heavy crystal glass filled with what smelled like whisky from Rosemount's own distillery.

"I think that Yank must have been a Scot in a former life." Knox took a sip of the whisky and reveled in the burn as it slid down his throat.

"Ye'll get no argument from me, Yer Grace." Robbie grinned and sauntered off to offer his tray of champagne glasses to the nearest group of guests, milling around the drawing room.

Knox worked to not look in Eleanor's direction and, instead, thought back to the last real conversation he'd had with her. Two months ago, the night her pet python crawled into bed with Danny Arneaux, then bit Knox. He flexed the hand Persephone had bitten. Eleanor had tended to the wound and he'd healed right as rain. He still remembered the warmth of her fingers as she'd bandaged his hand. That memory had kept him awake more nights than he cared to admit.

He gave Eleanor a last lingering look, then scanned the drawing room in hopes the reception might be winding down. Unfortunately, the wedding cake hadn't yet been cut, and the spread Mrs. Wallace and Mrs. Gordon had laid out meant the guests weren't going to leave anytime soon. The string quartet started a new piece, Beethoven, if he wasn't mistaken, and he never was.

Danny Arneaux caught Knox's eye, raised his own whisky glass, and nodded. Knox saluted him in kind. The American whispered something to Dr. Samantha Higgins, now Arneaux, his bride of a few months, and strolled across the drawing room to join Knox.

"Why is it you're dressed in twentieth-century clothes and you look more uncomfortable than I am in this Regency get-up?" Arneaux ran his finger under his neck cloth and shuddered.

"Because Scots formal kit is uncomfortable no matter the era. And this is the fourth time in as many months I've had to wear it." Knox glanced down at the lace-edged fall of his neck cloth.

Arneaux winced. "You look like you were born in this outfit. I look like I'm being strangled. And the happy couple look like an advertisement for a Scots wedding venue."

"Bite your tongue. Four weddings and a period film are all the Regency experience I am prepared to tolerate at this point. I do not want Rosemount Manor advertised as a wedding venue any more than it already is, if you don't mind. That way lies madness."

"Madder than allowing the Battle of Waterloo to be fought in your mountain glen and sheep pastures over and over again while a squadron of cameras film it?" Arneaux knocked back the last of the whisky in his glass.

"When is this happening?" Knox put on his ducal all-is-well face as a trio of wedding guests walked by and gave him deferential nods.

"End of next week after Bas and Teddy return from their little honeymoon."

"Bloody hell," Knox muttered.

Arneaux snorted and pulled a large silver flask out of the

antique sporran at the front of his kilt. He topped off Knox's glass and poured himself two more fingers of whisky. He took a sip and paused. Knox followed his gaze across the drawing room.

"Incoming," Arneaux said behind his glass.

Eleanor crossed the room, half lithe elegance and half drill sergeant. Knox would never admit it, but her approach made him smile, followed closely by making him want to back her into a corner and kiss her until neither of them could breathe.

"Is she coming for me or for you?" he mused.

"My money's on you, Your Grace."

"You spend entirely too much time with Robbie, *Mr. Arneaux*. How much did you lose to the lad on today's wedding?"

Arneaux took Knox's glass and his own, then set them behind a monstrous flower arrangement on the marquetry table behind them. "Fifty quid, thanks to you. How did you talk Teddy's mother into showing up? He still can't believe it."

"She had an affair with my father." Knox looked to where Teddy Rousseau stood talking to his mother, Millicent, Countess of Chawton, and his new husband's mother, Mrs. Salazar. "Twenty years ago."

"Blackmail?" Arneaux looked impressed.

"A suggestion that her son would appreciate her presence no matter her reason for attending."

"Bullshit. You blackmailed her because you knew Bas's entire family was coming and you didn't want Teddy to be ashamed."

"Which is exactly the reason he only blackmailed the mother. Teddy's father is a homophobic nightmare. God help us if he showed up. You're looking very Scots duke handsome, Your Grace." Eleanor bobbed Knox a curtsy and reached around him to grab one of the empty whisky glasses Arneaux had hidden. "Give me some of what you're hiding in your sporran, Mr. Arneaux." She held the glass out for the actor to fill.

"I'm a married man, Miss Witherspoon. What makes you think I'm hiding anything in my sporran?" Arneaux pulled out the flask and filled the glass.

"You and the duke are over here looking entirely too relaxed."

"Why wouldn't we be?" Knox asked.

"Our little regency boot camp has had great success in the marriage mart. Wonder who will be next?" She directed her question to Arneaux and deliberately didn't look at Knox. Or at least he assumed she did so deliberately.

"You're up, Your Grace," the annoying Yank said. "I've already caught my limit."

"I shall be certain to tell your wife you compared her to a fish. However, as I have no intention of participating in Miss Witherspoon's little matchmaking sideline, I would suggest McGinty as a safer bet. Mr. Salazar's grandmother seems quite taken with him."

Knox, Eleanor, and Arneaux glanced as one to the spot in front of the large ornate fireplace where McGinty, in full Highland kit, stood deep in conversation with the senior Mrs. Salazar. They were joined by the book critic, Hadrian Cross, and his new wife, Anna Chase, author of the book on which the film project that started it all was based.

"I don't have a matchmaking sideline for you to partici-pate in, Your Grace. I pity the matchmaker who tries to find a woman to take you on." She handed her now empty glass to Knox as if he were a footman. "Whatever romantic power is at work here has nothing to do with me. I will, however, take credit for how perfectly this wedding went today. Bas and Teddy look so happy."

She sighed deeply, and Knox marveled at the light in her eyes and the glow of her expression.

"It was a beautiful wedding," Arneaux agreed. "But the best part of this entire thing is that being with Bas has turned Teddy Rousseau into someone I don't want to punch in the face at least once a day."

Eleanor laughed. "I have to agree with you. Teddy is much more pleasant to be around these days. It's amazing what the love of a good man can do."

"One wonders how much of the change in Mr. Rousseau is due to his new husband and how much of it is due to his finally admitting he is gay and not giving a damn what his father thinks."

Eleanor and Arneaux stared at Knox as if he'd sprouted a second head.

"Damn, Knox," Arneaux said.

"Did I say something wrong?" He and the American actor had become friends of a sort. He didn't want to offend him, or anyone for that matter.

"I think Danny is simply stunned by your insight. Smacks of the voice of experience just a little." Eleanor looked at Knox in such a way his heart gave a little stutter, torn between a desire for her to see him and the fear that she might do just that. See a part of him he preferred to keep to himself.

"I know what it's like to never be able to meet a father's expectations. I simply wonder how much of Mr. Rousseau's being a complete arse was a result of trying to be someone he hated for someone who would never be satisfied." He concentrated very hard on not allowing himself to blush under Arneaux and Eleanor's intense scrutiny. Especially Eleanor's. "When were you going to tell me about turning my estate into the Battle of Waterloo, Miss Witherspoon?"

Eleanor made a little noise in her throat. She tightened

her jaw, which turned her lips into a thin line of pique and determination. Her widened eyes gave the only indication his question had caught her off guard. Arneaux elbowed him in the side.

"On that note," Arneaux said. "I'm going to join my wife in congratulating the grooms on tying the knot. Play nice, Knox. Kick his ass, Eleanor." He clasped his hands behind his back and strolled toward the other side of the room. But not before Eleanor called after him.

"I'll deal with you later, snitch."

Arneaux wiggled the fingers of his clasped hands at her. *Cheeky bugger!* Trust the American to leave him alone with a very angry woman who already held a low opinion of him.

"Snitch?" Knox smiled a little in spite of himself. "Did you not intend to tell me about the reenactment of a major historical battle on the grounds of my estate?"

She rolled her eyes and folded her arms across her chest. "You have had a complete schedule of all boot camp activities from me and a complete schedule of every single scene Erik is filming here from him on your desk since the first of March. I have had a copy of the script pages and the daily scenes to be filmed delivered to your study by McGinty every morning. Do you ignore everything on your desk or only the items with my name on them?"

The gold flecks in the depths of her deep brown eyes lit up when she was angry or frustrated. He suspected she was both at this point.

"I trust you and Wentworth to take charge of all of this movie activity. There is no reason for me to be involved. I would never ignore you, Miss Witherspoon. You are rather unignorable."

"Flattery. Be still my heart." She studied his face for a moment. She rested her hand on his forearm. "You're worried about your brother." He managed a brief nod. "I don't care how much Wentworth is paying me, I would never do anything to hurt Lachlan. You must know that."

"Of course." The words came out in a hoarse whisper. He concentrated on the spot where her hand rested. Even through his formal jacket and shirt the heat of her touch slowed every sense to the narrow space between them. "He is doing so well since he and Lily married. I don't want him to return to the way he was."

She squeezed his arm. The comfort of the act astonished him.

"Lachlan is taking Lily, Hadrian and Anna, Sylvan, and a few other cast and crew members who won't be filming on a fishing trip at the lodge."

"Lily is going fishing?" Knox had a hard time envisioning his Hollywood star sister-in-law on a Highland fishing expedition.

"They'll be lucky if they get Lily out of the lodge let alone into a boat." Eleanor hadn't moved her hand from his arm. Knox could kick himself for the tiny sense of belonging such a gesture gave him.

"I agree. I'm surprised Robbie hasn't started a betting pool on that very subject."

"He has. He's laying even odds Lily ends up walking back to the manor out of sheer boredom."

"Good God."

Eleanor laughed softly.

"Perhaps you should tell my brother to keep the door to the lodge locked at all times," Knox suggested.

"You can tell him yourself." Eleanor gave his forearm a pat, then grasped his elbow. "But for now, it's time for you to deliver a toast so they can cut the cake."

She dragged him halfway across the room before he was able to put up a fight.

"Where in the Regency etiquette book *and* in the

contracts I signed does it say I am obligated to give a toast. Will you stop pulling me as if I am a hooked salmon?"

"Will you stop acting like such a cold fish? And everyone knows if one has a duke handy, said duke must make a toast at a wedding reception. Especially one he is hosting."

She stopped in front of the table which held the ridiculously large wedding cake and proceeded to arrange him like a piece of furniture, adjusting his clothing and slapping his hands apart when he clasped them in front of him. She patted his frothy neckcloth and straightened his sporran which set his cock to twitching and his blood to racing.

"There you go. Be ducal. Speak." She signaled the string quartet that had been playing in the background and smiled at Knox.

The room grew silent and entirely too attentive to suit Knox.

"A duke is not wedding entertainment, Miss Witherspoon," he muttered, and accepted the flute of champagne Robbie handed him.

"Of course not," she replied as she took her own glass of champagne. "Entertaining is the very last word I would apply to you. Say something. It doesn't have to be terribly romantic. We all know how you feel about romance. A simple thank you for coming will do. Now speak."

He held her gaze for a moment or two. Her expectant expression reminded him of one of the many tutors he and Lachlan had gone through during their haphazard childhood. Expectant was perhaps the wrong word. Resigned better described her faint smile and unamused eyes. He turned his attention to the rest of the room. Arneaux, the arse, grinned and gave him a thumbs up.

Well shite, as McGinty would say.

"Miss Witherspoon has gently reminded me," Knox began, "that as host it is incumbent on me to say...something." A ripple of laughter went round the room. "To the family and friends, some of whom have traveled a long way to attend this wedding, welcome and thank you. To those of you who keep showing up at my breakfast table thanks to Miss Witherspoon's efforts, I am certain the staff appreciates your continued presence, but could you please stop marrying each other? These weddings and receptions are a great deal of work."

"Not to mention the money we all keep losing on Robbie's wedding betting pools," Hadrian Cross called from his place next to Anna Chase, recently Anna Chase Cross.

More laughter.

"Bas and Teddy—" Knox's throat tightened as he turned to Rosemount's newest married couple. Never had two people been so completely opposite of each other. But the way these two men, dressed in full formal Highland kit, looked at each other stunned and amazed him. "I'm not much of a romantic, or so I've been told. So, I offer a toast to you with a few words from Thomas a Kempis that seem especially appropriate."

He took a quick breath to loosen his throat. "Love feels no burden, thinks nothing of trouble, attempts what is above its strength, pleads no excuse of impossibility; for it thinks all things lawful for itself, and all things possible." He raised his glass. "To Bas and Teddy, who have shown us the truth of those words."

"To Bas and Teddy," echoed throughout the drawing room.

Knox turned to touch his glass to Eleanor's. As he sipped from his crystal flute, she stared at him open-mouthed.

He leaned in close enough to prevent anyone else from hearing. "It is customary to actually drink the champagne after a toast."

With that, he downed his own drink, gave her a slight

bow, and strolled across the room to where Arneaux stood with McGinty, both of them grinning like loons. He stepped between them and observed as the reception stirred back to life. Samantha had joined Eleanor, and a few of the other women appeared to be organizing the cutting of the cake. Good. That meant the party would soon be winding down.

"That was nicely done, Your Grace," Arneaux said.

"Which?" McGinty asked. "The toast, or shocking the devil out of Miss Witherspoon?"

"Both," Arneaux replied.

"Nonsense." Knox continued to study the room.

He made certain his expression was that of the ducal host. But he couldn't keep his eyes off Eleanor. Except when she glanced over her shoulder at him with that confused and even a bit irritated look on her face. Then he turned his attention to his brother, Lachlan, and Lachlan's wife, Lily. Their happiness made him nervous, which kicked in a bothersome load of guilt.

"Stop frowning at yer brother," McGinty said. "If his wife sees you, she'll smack you, duke or no duke."

"I'm not frowning."

"You are," Arneaux said. "And you do *not* want Lily to smack you. Especially not wearing that rock of an engagement ring Lachlan gave her. Go back to staring at Eleanor."

"I am not— Gentlemen, congratulations." Knox was saved when Bas and Teddy sauntered up to join him and the two thorns in his side.

"Thank you, Your Grace," Teddy said solemnly. "For… everything." He glanced to where his mother stood chatting with Teddy's new husband's sister. The Countess of Chawton actually appeared to be enjoying herself.

"That toast." Bas's voice was rough and hoarse. He cleared his throat and shook his head. "Thank you."

Teddy squeezed his arm.

"Of course," Knox replied. "I meant it."

They all had a sudden attack of foot shuffling and polite coughing.

"So, tell me." Arneaux's expression grew less serious.

Knox knew him well enough to know he was about to stir the pot, which was exactly what they all needed. No one in this group of men did public emotions well, least of all himself.

"Tell me, *Lord Staines*, do we *my lord* you and your husband or just you?"

Teddy Rousseau, sword master and weapons expert for the film, was also a peer of the realm. His father was the Earl of Chawton. Teddy was his heir and held the title of Viscount Staines, a fact they'd all only recently learned, much to Teddy's chagrin.

"Screw you, Arneaux." Teddy said with an insincere smile.

"For God's sake don't start that with my mother and grandmother," Bas said. "They're already impressed that their new *semea* is a viscount."

"I told you not to tell them." Teddy's behavior had improved monumentally since he'd fallen in love with the Basque stuntman, but he could still be a grump. Funnily enough, Knox understood.

"As if that lot would have kept it a secret from your female relatives." McGinty nodded toward the gathering of ladies next to the table that held the wedding cake.

"True that." Arneaux signaled Robbie, who stood next to the stand globe tantalus.

The young footman wasted no time and raided the decorative liquor cabinet for five glasses and a decanter of whisky. He hurried over to Knox and the other men, distributed the glasses, filled them, and was back at his post quick as a flash.

"Whatever you're paying that kid, it isn't enough," Bas observed, and took a sip of his whisky.

"He'd be paid more if he weren't such a cheeky bugger," McGinty said.

"Mrs. Wallace keeps him honest enough." Knox checked the progress of the cake cutting preparations. He wanted the reception over so he might retire to his office and decipher his last encounter with Eleanor without the entire cast and crew of a period film watching his every move.

"To answer your inane question, Arneaux," Teddy said. "There is no precedent for addressing the husband of a viscount, so far as I know." He and Bas shared a brief smile, the sort of smile Knox suspected only people in love understood.

Knox sipped his whisky. "I would suggest you set your own precedent, Lord Staines. You and Mr. Salazar have more than earned that right. Ah! I believe Miss Witherspoon is summoning you two to cut the cake. Shall we?"

Once again, Knox found himself the subject of curious and even amazed stares from his companions. He didn't blame them. The time he'd spent surrounded by these people, the people Eleanor had recruited into her *boot camp*, as they called their stay at Rosemount, had forced him to consider things he hadn't contemplated in a very long time. Or perhaps his newfound insights and questions were a direct result of the presence of Eleanor Witherspoon, an enigma on a multitude of levels.

The five of them joined the crowd around the beautifully decorated table that held the towering and exquisite wedding cake. On closer inspection, Knox recognized the cake as a white and florid replica of the tower ruins on the estate where Rousseau had proposed to Salazar. Laughter and applause ensued when Eleanor handed Teddy a Regency era sword with which he and the other bridegroom cut the cake.

Not long afterwards, the happy couple were hoisted onto the shoulders of Mr. Salazar's stunt crew members and carried unceremoniously to the front steps of Rosemount, where a carriage festooned with ribbons, balloons, and a tail of old boots and horse shoes awaited them. They didn't have far to go as they had chosen to honeymoon at the hunting lodge across the estate. The filming schedule was about to begin in earnest, and they were only allowed a few days away from the set.

Another hour passed before the guests began to leave the drawing room, some to go home and others to return to the rooms they occupied in the manor. Knox was about to leave himself when he noticed the Regency boot camp group stood together in a tight little gathering in front of the fireplace. He noticed them because at random intervals one or two of them would glance in his direction.

"What are they up to, McGinty?" he asked his steward, who had handed Salazar's family over to the care of several footmen and maids and come to stand beside him.

"I have no idea, Yer Grace, but they're up to something, that's for certain. And Lord Lachlan and Lady Lachlan are in the thick of it. Look there, she handed Miss Witherspoon a key."

"Perhaps they mean to lock me in the attic for the rest of this boot camp and film making chaos."

"Would that be so terrible? Mrs. Wallace would feed ye and there's plenty of furniture up there to choose from."

"Don't tempt me, McGinty. A little privacy would be—"

Eleanor turned to stare at Knox and the look in her eyes stopped him cold. He and McGinty had both been joking about the now close-knit group being up to something. If Eleanor's gaze meant anything, they were past the phase of *up to something*. Someone had told Rosemount's American events coordinator something that had her looking at him as if he were a Victorian villain and she was a female Sherlock Holmes.

"Should I have Mrs. Wallace air out one of the rooms in the attic?" McGinty asked.

In the words of his Cajun friend, Knox was in deep shite, and he had no idea what the hell he'd done. However, he suspected he was soon to find out.

Chapter Ten

Teddy and Bas's wedding day had gone perfectly. Now all Eleanor wanted was a cup of tea and a good night's sleep. She dropped onto her bed and bent down to untie the ribbons of her Regency slippers. In moments, she kicked them off and wiggled her toes against the thick Aubusson carpet beneath her feet. Her embroidered reticule made a distinct clunk when she dropped it onto the bedside table. That key. The mysterious key she refused to deal with today, if ever.

She unpinned the antique watch from the collar of her pretty blue watered silk dress. Nearly eleven o' clock. After a late supper with the remaining wedding guests and the Regency *boot campers*, as they'd taken to calling themselves, she'd checked to make certain all the wedding detritus had been cleared away and beat it up the stairs before she risked running into the duke. The duke and the key, two things she fully intended to ignore for as long as possible.

Especially after the little tête-à-tête she'd been subjected to at the end of the reception. Lily and Lachlan, Danny and Samantha, and Hadrian and Anna had all talked at once, which meant Eleanor only caught about half of what they'd tried to tell her. Something about the duke keeping a secret that she needed to know. Then Lily had handed her the antique key and told her they'd make everything clear to her later, whenever later might be.

Knox Innes, Duke of Turra, irritated and surprised her most days, but he'd really outdone himself today. First, he acted like he was being led to his own execution when she asked him to give a simple toast. And then? Well then, he delivered one of the loveliest and most romantic wedding toasts she'd ever heard. *Asshole!*

"He does it to piss me off." She slid off the bed and padded to the wardrobe in search of a nightgown. "Just like he calls me his party planner to piss me off. Jerk." She paused at the quick rap on her door. Her tea had arrived just in time to save her from a complete rant on the many vices of the Duke of Turra. "Come in."

"Good. You're still up." Lily Randolph, no Lady Lachlan as she was now called, stormed into the room with her usual full head of steam.

She brushed past Eleanor, followed by Samantha and Anna.

Lily rummaged through the wardrobe. "Here. Get dressed. Where are your ugly-assed boots?"

"Got 'em," Anna said from the other side of the bed. "Stockings?"

"I'll get them." Samantha went to the top drawer of the highboy and dragged out a pair of Eleanor's thick gray Regency stockings.

"Come on." Lily shoved one of the plainer period dresses in Eleanor's wardrobe into her hands. "Get dressed. We need to get moving."

"Moving? Where are we going? I *am* dressed, by the way."

"Girls' night out." Anna dropped the boots at Eleanor's

feet and began to help Lily undo the buttons at the back of Eleanor's dress. "Or girls' night in…or under and up."

"What the hell—I can dress myself you know." Eleanor turned and backed away from them.

She shed the gown she'd worn to the wedding along with all of the accompanying undergarments. Then tossed them one at the time onto the bed and wiggled her way into the dress Lily had handed her. Once she'd sat on the bed and pulled on her stockings and boots, she stood and turned so Samantha could lace up the back of the dress.

"Now. Would one of you ladies tell me what the bloody hell is going on?"

"She cusses," Lily observed. "Not very well, but she did cuss. Is that ladylike, Miss Witherspoon?"

"Kiss my *arse*, Lady Lachlan."

Eleanor didn't like the jittery sensation that suddenly struck her. She trusted these women, it wasn't that. She couldn't quite put her finger on the cause of the almost electric current that danced through her.

"Later," Lily said. "Where's the key?"

Eleanor nodded toward the bedside table. Lily went to retrieve the key from the reticule while Anna and Samantha each grabbed one of Eleanor's arms and steered her to the bedchamber door. Anna opened the door wide enough to poke out her head and look up and down the hallway.

"The coast is clear." She snorted. "I've always wanted to say that."

"Oh hell." Lily pushed the key into Eleanor's hand. "Let's go before the guys decide to call it a night and come looking for us." She pushed past the rest of them and marched out of the room.

Eleanor stumbled as Samantha dragged her along in Lily's wake with Anna bringing up the rear of their little expedition.

They didn't go far. Lily ducked into Teddy's room and waved the rest of them inside. Samantha closed the door behind them. Eleanor decided she'd fallen asleep and the last few minutes had to be a bizarre dream. Nothing else explained her creeping across Teddy's room into the dressing room that connected his and Bas's rooms.

"Is there a reason you don't want your husbands here with us?" she asked. Dream or not, she really wanted to know what the hell was happening.

"Yes," the three women said in unison.

Lily and Anna each picked up one of the two oil lamps that had been left burning low on a table in the dressing room.

"Robbie?" Eleanor asked.

"Robbie, bless him," Anna replied. "Where's the door, Samantha?"

"Here." Samantha stood at the rear of the closet where a medieval-looking door made of heavy dark wood and iron bands was set into the wall. The Regency coach and consultant for the film looked at Eleanor expectantly. "We told you about a secret," she said, suddenly very solemn. "Unlock this door if you want to find out what the duke has been keeping from us."

Eleanor turned the key over and over in her palm. In spite of the ridiculous way they'd set the stage, she discovered she truly wanted to know what possible secret the duke might have that was so terrible he would keep it from everyone, that he would keep it from her. She unlocked the door. It took she and Samantha both to tug the door open wide enough for them to slip inside one by one.

They were out of their minds, all three of them. Eleanor stood on a small stone landing and stared down the beginning of a steep, narrow, twisting flight of stone stairs. Once Lily moved around her, the light from the lamp the actress carried illuminated the path all the way down to another landing.

"You expect me to go down those tiny worn-out steps by lamplight?" she asked. Her voice held an eerie, hollow tone against the hard rock walls on either side of the staircase.

"Well, if *someone* wasn't so insistent on us living the real Regency experience, Robbie might have left us flashlights instead of lamps, but the poor boy is scared to death of you, so here we are. I'll go first, and Anna can bring up the rear with her lamp. We'll be fine. Come on." In typical Lily fashion she started down the stairs, and with Samantha and Anna behind her, Eleanor had no choice but to follow.

Torn between the fear of breaking her neck and the thrill of discovering this, heretofore, hidden part of Rosemount Manor, she tried to take in the twists and turns as they traveled under the gardens, according to Samantha, and underground all the way to another treacherous staircase that led up into the tower of the old castle ruins.

"You do realize His Grace could be in his duke's version of a man cave." Eleanor studied the rounded walls of the tower as the four of them wound their way higher and higher.

"His hideaway office is on the ground floor, which we have already passed," Samantha replied.

"Yes, and he ran away to his study in the manor right after the reception ended," Anna added. "I think you frightened him."

Eleanor snorted. "Nothing short of a visit from God Almighty would frighten the duke, and I'm not sure even that would scare him."

"You might be surprised," Lily muttered, which caused her two accomplices to break out in simultaneous throat clearing and coughing.

Eleanor had endured about as much of this mystery and

intrigue as she cared to at this point. She opened her mouth to say so when they arrived on a landing near what had to be the top of the tower. Despite it being June, an icy, damp breeze whistled down from above them.

"Look, ladies," she began.

"No, you look, Eleanor." Anna gave her a little push forward as Lily put her shoulder into the ancient wooden door at the top of the stairs and shoved.

Eleanor nearly fell on top of Lily when the door opened. She righted herself and everyone else followed them inside. The dim light from the two lamps cast meager light in the room, which was exactly what Eleanor expected of a solar in the ruins of a hundred of years old castle. Except for the clean, thick glass of the large window on the wall to the right overlooking the loch. She took two steps toward the window. A bit of moonlight spilled in through the glass and the bars on the window were far enough apart not to block view of the lake.

"This room must have been the lady's favorite," she murmured.

The light brightened behind her and Eleanor turned. She glimpsed the lone chair sitting to her right, facing, not the window, but the far wall where Lily and Anna had placed their lamps on a long table against the wall and turned them up. To her surprise, a large vase with an arrangement of fresh flowers sat in the middle of that table.

Above the table— She frowned and stepped closer. A heavy, ornate gold frame bordered a large portrait. The artist had so perfectly captured the texture of the fabric and the gold ribbons of the dress the woman in the painting wore, Eleanor could almost feel the green velvet beneath her fingers. In an instant, her mind took in the small leatherbound book she held, the red, gold, and black Persian carpet beneath her golden-slippered feet. The slashed sleeves of the gown that trailed to the floor, one draped over the crossed paws of the giant deerhound lying next to her. And the golden-red hair hanging in thick spiral curls to her waist.

In the next instant, Eleanor stared at the woman's face. The features, the golden-brown skin, every single line and aspect save for the eyes, were hers. She might as well be looking in a mirror. And those eyes, those brilliant blue eyes, they met her gaze as if to dare her to deny the uncanny resemblance.

Eleanor shivered as if someone had walked over her grave. "Is this some kind of joke?"

"No," Samantha said. She and the other two women came to stand close behind Eleanor. Samantha put her arm around her shoulders. "This is a portrait of Elsbeth Dunhome, the Innes Witch."

Eleanor jerked her eyes onto Samantha. "You can't be serious?" But Samantha's solemn expression was all the answer she needed. Eleanor returned her attention to the painting. "How did you know this was here?"

"Bas and Teddy found it," Anna said. "They wanted to tell you when they found it, but then they broke up and so much was going on, and…."

"They chickened out," Eleanor murmured.

"Pretty much," Lily said.

"All your husbands have seen it?"

"Yes." Samantha squeezed Eleanor's shoulders. "Are you okay?"

"The duke knows about this? He's seen it?"

"Look around, Eleanor. This tower is hundreds of years old, but this room is spotless. Those flowers are fresh. The only chair faces this portrait. He has an office at the bottom of the tower, and he won't agree to filming in or on top of this tower. What do you think?"

Eleanor couldn't tear her eyes from the woman. "If the room is spotless, Mrs. Wallace—"

"Has never been in this room," Lily cut in. "None of the servants have been. No one is allowed in the tower at all, except *Himself.*" Lily stepped in front of Eleanor. "I've already asked Lachlan all these questions. Why are you making excuses for—"

"I'm not making excuses," Eleanor murmured, her attention still on her doppelganger.

He'd practically run away from her the moment they met. He came up with excuses not to meet with her for weeks after she first arrived. Once she began dressing in Regency costume, he wavered between leaving any room she entered and staring at her when he thought she wasn't looking. At times, his eyes burned with an intensity that set her body to humming with erotic awareness. Then there were times when she couldn't interpret his expression at all. Fear? Disdain? A deep sorrow?

She'd made allowances for his odd behavior. Now this. She'd held her tongue and ignored being snubbed and dismissed by him. He didn't like having to rent out his ancestral home, and she respected him in some ways for that. And if he had of treated her well—or at least decently—she would have understood him not telling her about her resemblance to the Innis Witch, the ghost he believed had haunted him as a child. Hell, it was downright weird. But he hadn't treated her well. Between his obvious desire for her and his disdain….

"Superstitious asshole," 'she muttered, and headed for the door back out the way they came. "Damn you, Knox Innes. Damn you to hell."

"Oh shit," Samantha said.

"Catch her," Anna ordered.

"This should be good," Lily said.

"Lily, stop her!" Samantha cried.

Eleanor reached the stairs and cursed. She'd forgotten how dark they were. She yanked up her long skirts and started down, her free hand braced on the cold stone wall.

"Eleanor," Samantha called down into the dark. "You'll break your neck."

Eleanor halted a half dozen steps down. Samantha was right. And if she broke her neck, she couldn't confront the duke. And break *his* neck. The sound of footsteps echoed down the stairs and the bob of lamplight grew nearer.

"Okay, Zena Regency Warrior Princess." Lily grabbed Eleanor's arm once they reached her. "As much as he deserves it, I don't think it is legal to kill a duke in Scotland."

"Don't be ridiculous." Eleanor pulled her arm free. "I'm not going to kill him."

"Well, damn," Lily muttered.

"What Lily is *trying* to say," Samantha said as she took the lead and shone her lamp ahead of them as they began to descend the stairs, "is that you need to think about it before you confront him. I'm certain he has his reasons for keeping something like this from you."

"He has his reasons for keeping it from the rest of us," Anna said. "Keeping something like this from Eleanor is…." They all stopped to look at Anna. "Well, he should have told you, especially if the existence of such a painting makes him uncomfortable to be around you. Let's go. The guys will be looking for us." She waved them forward.

"He isn't uncomfortable to be around me. Oof!" Eleanor ran into Anna who ran into Samantha at the bottom of the stairs.

"Ex*cuse* you?" Lily jiggled her lamp as she side-stepped to avoid slamming into Eleanor's back. "He isn't *uncomfortable*?" They pinned Eleanor with are-you-kidding-me glares as they hurried forward and began the twists and turns that boggled Eleanor's mind. "All you two do is fight, followed by days of not speaking to each other, followed by him fleeing any room you walk into, followed by you—"

"So we have issues," she shot back.

"Issues?" Anna said.

Samantha led them around another bend, then straight on.

Moments later, they reached the staircase back into Teddy and Bas's dressing room.

"What you two have is sexual tension so hot it should come with its own porno film soundtrack and more denial between you than a river in Egypt," Anna said.

Lily and Samantha howled with laughter.

"You three have had way too much champagne."

Eleanor thanked whatever powers that were in charge of her current madhouse universe that her three deluded friends couldn't see her face. Her entire body, let alone her face, burned with embarrassment. They clambered up the stairs in silence, crept into the dressing room, and closed the heavy door behind them. Eleanor quickly locked the door and dropped the key into her bodice.

She hurried from the dressing room to the door and out into the hallway, then practically ran down the antique carpets to her own bedchamber. She didn't move fast enough because Lily, Samantha, and Anna pushed into the room behind her.

"So, what are you going to do?" Samantha asked.

"About what?" Eleanor dropped into one of the pretty brocade chairs in front of the fireplace and leaned toward the low fire burning there. "Get warm, ladies. The walk was chilly."

"What are you going to do about your resemblance to a seven-hundred-year-old ghost." Lily flopped down into the chair opposite her. "A ghost who cursed the duke's family. A ghost who was said duke's imaginary friend when he was a child and got him sent away because his family thought he was nuts. A ghost who—"

"Thank you for the clarification, Lily." Samantha gave the actress the sort of scowl mothers gave children right before they send them to their room.

"What is the curse exactly?" Eleanor knew a little about the duke's relationship with the ghost. However, she'd never really heard the specifics of the curse.

The three of them exchanged a glance, then Anna said, "Apparently, when the first duke's mother had Elsbeth strapped to a chair and thrown into the lock to determine if she was a witch, Elsbeth cursed the—"

Samantha cleared her throat.

"Right before she drowned," Lily added. "Anna's husband has been researching the legend. Lachlan gave him—"

Samantha gave Lily a kick.

"I think we need to let Eleanor go to bed." Samantha stood. "She's had a busy weekend and she needs time to digest this new information." Samantha motioned them to the door. "We can talk about the rest of this later."

Before Eleanor could say another word, they hustled out of the room with excuses about waiting husbands and a need for a good night's sleep.

Suddenly alone in her way too quiet room with a head full of questions, Eleanor wrestled her way out of her dress and toed off her boots, which she kicked under the bed.

"Elsbeth's not the only witch in this house," she muttered. "Why drag me into that tower and show me that portrait, then leave me hanging like this?"

She draped her dress and stockings across the back of a chair, found a heavy cotton Regency nightgown in the wardrobe and drew it on over her head. Not until she climbed into bed, did she realize she had the damned nightgown on backwards. She rolled out of bed, adjusted the nightgown, and went to the window that overlooked the formal gardens at the back of Rosemount Manor. The moonlight made the neat hedges, graveled paths, and beautiful flower beds appear almost ethereal, like something out of a fairy tale.

Or a memory.

Knox Innes wasn't the only one in denial when it came to Rosemount Manor. Eleanor settled onto the window seat and leaned against the cool glass. From the moment she'd set eyes on the Highland mansion and the medieval ruins, she'd had the eeriest sensation. Most of the time she didn't give her reaction any thought. She was too damned busy keeping the Regency experience on track and searching for more ways to make the estate a desired destination. She didn't have time to explore ridiculous superstitions or that weird flip in her stomach when déjà vu threatened to overwhelm her.

The Innes Witch was a great selling point for the estate. Ghost stories, old legends, family history, and superstitions drew in tourists, historians, and all sorts of paying customers. The stories had nothing to do with her. The duke himself said it was all nonsense and that the staff were victims of having been born and raised in the area where they'd been spoon-fed the stories at their grandparents' knees.

His Grace could deny everything about the Innes Witch from now until hell froze over. But there was no denying that painting and the fact he'd kept it hidden, probably even from his own brother.

"He wouldn't have kept it a secret unless it bothered him." She jumped to her feet and ticked each item off on her fingers as she paced. "His reaction to me the day we met proves something. What? The way he shuts down any discussion of a harmless ghost story that could attract more money to the estate he is trying to save means somewhere deep down he is afraid the story is neither harmless nor just a story."

Afraid? Him?

She stopped in front of the window seat. Her legs went shaky and weak. Eleanor flopped onto the window seat again. He was afraid. The tough, stoic, arrogant bastard might be who he had become, but the little boy with the imaginary friend and the parents who thought he was mentally ill was still in there. The staff and the locals weren't the only ones who had heard the legends from the cradle. For a moment, her heart ached for that little boy and maybe, a little, for the man he'd become.

A ghost who cursed the duke's family.

Eleanor didn't believe in curses. She wasn't sure she even believed in ghosts. What she did believe was that the Duke of Turra wasn't sure what he believed.

She needed to find out everything she could about Elsbeth Dunhome, the Innes Witch. And she'd start by cornering Hadrian Cross, Anna Chase's husband. She'd start tomorrow and….

"Oh, damn," she muttered.

The film director she'd persuaded to allow her to run his Regency boot camp was arriving in Scotland tomorrow. Erik Wentworth was pouring all sorts of money into the Duke of Turra's bank account, in order to use the Rosemount estate and Rosemount Manor as a film location. She didn't have time to keep him happy and to solve the mystery that was Knox Innes.

She stared out the window past the gardens to where the ruins and the tower waited in the dark.

She'd make time.

Chapter Eleven

THREE DAYS. ELEANOR HAD ENJOYED THREE DAYS OF COMPLETE triumph where Erik Wentworth was concerned before all hell broke loose. Now she stood in Rosemount's ballroom and watched all her hard work evaporate in what was shaping up to be the fight of the century between a completely confused Hollywood director and one very pissed off Scots housekeeper.

Erik had been wowed by Rosemount Manor and the gorgeous scenery of the duke's estate, both of which he'd only seen in photos and videos before his arrival. His first night, Eleanor had arranged a Regency dinner and an evening of cards and other Regency entertainments. Wentworth had been so enthusiastic about her "boot camp" he'd insisted they carry on for the rest of the film shoot. Since the duke hadn't bothered to show his face since the wedding reception, he wasn't there to scowl and grumble about the actors and others continuing to live and dress like they were at some "overblown costume party."

The duke's absence hadn't been all bad. Rude where Wentworth was concerned, but not completely useless.

Eleanor had had time to think about how she wanted to approach Knox about the painting and about the other aspects of the Innes Witch legend. Not that she'd decided anything, but at least she wasn't fantasizing about tying him to a chair and tossing him into the loch.

With Erik's arrival, she hadn't had a moment to spare, so hadn't been able to corner Hadrian Cross. The house and estate had to be perfect for him, in spite of the fact that he'd chosen to stay in his monstrous travel traveler parked next to the inn, where the crew was staying. He'd had the behemoth flown over in a cargo plane. It had become quite the tourist attraction in the village. The cast and the film consultants who made up her Regency experience had been on their best behavior, for the most part. Lord Lachlan had even attended the Regency dinner with Lily. He and Erik had gotten along like old friends.

She should have known it was all too good to be true. If Mrs. Wallace's face got any redder, Eleanor was afraid the old woman would explode.

McGinty sidled into the ballroom and moved as stealthily as a man his size could to join Eleanor in front of the wall of French windows that led out to the gardens. At least she could make a quick escape if fists started flying. Robbie and Dougal left several members of the film crew and sauntered across the ballroom floor to take up position on Eleanor's other side.

"I think Mrs. Wallace can take him," Robbie said softly. He nodded to where the housekeeper stood pointing to a long, deep scratch in the polished ballroom floor. When she aimed that pointed finger at the young director's chest, he actually took a step back.

"Aye, that's a safe bet and no mistaking it," Dougal replied.

"You two are not helping," Eleanor said, between gritted teeth.

"Were we meant to, miss? Oww!" Robbie rubbed the back of his head where McGinty had smacked him.

"Are you going to…." McGinty nodded toward the two combatants.

"Are you?" Eleanor cast him a sideways glance.

"Someone should," McGinty replied. "Poor lad looks ready to faint. What set this off?"

"Yon director dared to put a scratch in Mrs. Wallace's three-hundred-year-old floor with the wheels of his camera," Robbie said. "And she wants to banish *all* cameras from the house this instant and forevermore."

McGinty muttered something in Gaelic. Eleanor hoped it was something rude, crude, and socially unacceptable. She sighed and strode across the ballroom. McGinty lumbered along behind her.

"What seems to be the trouble?" What a completely idiotic thing for her to have said.

"He—"

"She—" Erik ran his hand through his hair and gave a little bow to indicate Mrs. Wallace should speak first. Smart man.

Mrs. Wallace folded her arms. "I wasnae told ye'd be dragging cameras and motorbikes into the house. This floor is ruined. I'll nae have it, Miss Witherspoon. Ye'll have to make yer movie somewhere else." She glared at Erik the entire time she spoke to Eleanor.

"Are you fucking kidding me?" He threw up his hands.

"Watch yerself." McGinty stepped in front of Erik who stopped dead in his tracks.

"Sorry," he muttered. He turned back to face Mrs. Wallace. "I apologize for my language."

She rolled her eyes and Eleanor nearly cracked up. "Apology accepted. Yer not the first man to curse at me. Won't be the last. But ye will be the last to do damage to this house. Take yer crew and that monstrosity and get out." She pointed at the dolly-mounted camera as if it were a dog with muddy paws.

"Mrs. Wallace, you don't exactly have the authority to throw Mr. Wentworth and his crew out of the house." Eleanor caught sight of McGinty out of the corner of her eye. He was shaking his head in vehement warning. Her stomach sank. *Oh, hell's bells.*

"Yer right, Miss Witherspoon," the housekeeper said, and headed for the ballroom's double doors. "But I know who does."

Robbie and Dougal exchanged a look and a grin and scurried after her.

"Shite," McGinty muttered, and hurried after them.

Eleanor wanted to kick something or someone. She should have stayed in bed. She should have stayed with the party company. She should have stayed in med-school.

"What?" Wentworth said, when she grabbed his arm and dragged him out of the room.

"You're about to meet the duke," Eleanor told him. "Brace yourself."

"I thought this was all a done deal," he said as she dragged him down the stairs toward the foyer.

"It was, until your camera crew took a bite out of a floor that is polished by hand three times a week and has been since it was laid down in that ballroom in 1720. Crap!" At the top of the stairs Eleanor came into a scene out of one of her worst nightmares.

In the foyer, just outside the drawing room doors, Knox Innes, Duke of Turra, stood listening to Mrs. Wallace but staring at Eleanor with that ever-present expression of superiority and consternation. At the bottom of the stairs, Anna Chase and her husband, the elusive Hadrian Cross, glanced back and forth between Eleanor and the duke as if in anticipation of a twisted tennis match. Just inside the open front doors of Rosemount Manor, Danny and Samantha and Lord Lachlan and Lily waited as if afraid to enter what was fast becoming a Scots version of the Gunfight at the OK Corral.

"I'll nae have it, Yer Grace," Mrs. Wallace said, and pointed at the director as he and Eleanor descended the stairs. "That man has destroyed the ballroom floor. I've nae spent the last fifty odd years preserving this house to have the likes of him and his film people desecrate—"

"Desecrate? This place is supposed to be hundreds of years old. I thought the floors would be made of stone like any decent castle." Erik reached the bottom of the stairs and crossed his arms as he glared at Mrs. Wallace, who glared right back.

Eleanor leaned close and whispered to Eric, "Please don't antagonize her." With a quick prayer, she started across the marble floor. "Your Grace, I don't believe you've met Erik Wentworth, the director of *A Matter of Honor.*" She motioned Erik over. "Mr. Wentworth, this is His Grace, the Duke of Turra."

The two men eyed each other like a couple of Highland stags. Eleanor almost expected one or both of them to paw the floor or snort. Finally, they stepped toward each other and shook hands. Briefly. The duke turned his attention to Mrs. Wallace for a moment. He didn't say a word, simply nodded. The housekeeper bobbed a brief curtsy and at her usual going-to-war pace left the foyer by way of the corridor that led to the back of the house.

"I didn't mean to piss off—I mean—tick off your house-keeper," Erik said. "I'll pay for whatever damage is done to the house and grounds while we film, but—"

"I wasn't aware there would *be* damage to my home and estate, Miss Witherspoon." He pretty much ignored the director, of course. *Arrogant ass.*

"It was in the contracts you signed but didn't read," Eleanor replied sweetly. "Your Grace. The film is insured, I assure you."

"I see. And how precisely does insurance intend to replace hundreds of years of my family's history?"

The man looked like an advertisement for Scotland GQ in his kilt and sweater, until she saw the look in his eye. That was the look of his Scots ancestors—ready to defend his castle with bloodshed and mayhem. Could this situation get any worse?

"Look, why don't I pack up my cameras and my crew and my actors and find another location for this shoot?" Erik said. "I mean, this place is perfect, but maybe Rosemount Manor is too delicate for this sort of thing."

Apparently, the situation *could* get worse. Eleanor's heart sank. Especially when the duke's expression of triumph caught her eye. All her hard work, her big chance, and the stubborn, lying, son of a—

"Couldn't you film the ballroom scenes with Steadicams, and save the dolly cameras for outside shots?" Danny suggested as he stepped farther into the foyer.

"It isn't that simple, Arneaux. You know that." Wentworth ran both hands through his overlong hair. He was frustrated as hell.

Eleanor wanted to say, *"Welcome to my world."*

"He could always film some of the indoor shots in the old west wing," Hadrian suddenly said. "The floors are stone in that part of the house."

Eleanor couldn't decide who was more stunned—her, the duke, the two open-mouthed footmen, McGinty or Wentworth. She'd always wondered what *so silent you could hear a pin drop* sounded like. The moments after Hadrian's suggestion definitely fit the bill. This was the first Eleanor had heard of anyone being allowed in the old unused wing of the house. She'd never seen that part of Rosemount Manor. The strange thing was the other members of her Regency experience didn't appear surprised at all.

"And how would you know about the floors of the old west wing?" the duke demanded.

Erik glanced at Eleanor and winced. He raised his eyebrows in inquiry. She shook her head, blindsided by the whole turn of events. Hadrian coughed, but other than that wasn't cowed so far as she could tell. Good for him.

"I've been spending a good part of every day the last few weeks in the library and archives stored in that wing, researching my book actually."

"Who gave you permission to invade a closed wing of this house and plunder my family history, Mr. Cross?" The duke glanced at McGinty who raised his hands as if to say, *"Don't look at me."*

"I did." Lachlan strolled closer to his brother.

Lily hung back with Danny and Samantha, grinning.

"You did say this is my home, too, did you not, Your Grace?" Lachlan raised his brows.

Eleanor gnashed her teeth. Erik Wentworth's introduction to the duke had turned into a Scots version of a Greek tragedy or maybe a Shakespearean farce. Everyone appeared to be enjoying the current scene except her and Knox Innes. She had to come up with a way to diffuse the situation before her entire Regency experience and film location business went up in smoke.

"The west wing hasn't been used in decades," the duke said.

The muscle in his jaw flexed so tight, Eleanor was surprised he could speak. His expression might be hard as stone, but when he looked at his brother, the Duke of Turra's eyes spoke volumes. Her heart tightened. In the middle of what might end up a disaster the bastard still had the ability to make her feel for him.

"I'm not certain it's in fit condition for you to visit, Mr. Cross, let alone have a film crew in there."

"Don't let Mrs. Wallace hear you say that, Knox," Danny said. His easy Cajun way and his oddly close friendship with the duke took some of the tension out of the moment. "There's not an inch of this place she doesn't inspect for dirt and decay. I'm pretty sure she doesn't sleep just so she can walk the halls and run a white glove over the windows and bannisters."

"I can vouch for that," Hadrian said. Anna wrapped her hands around his bicep and squeezed. He glanced down at his wife and smiled. Eleanor marveled at the depth of love conveyed in that single gesture. He returned his attention to Knox. "I haven't explored the entire wing, but what I've seen is spotless."

"Are the floors really made of stone?" Erik perked up a bit, and Eleanor prayed this was the solution that would keep him and his money at Rosemount Manor.

"The west wing was built on the medieval manor. It was remodeled and added on to over the centuries, but the stone floors remain," McGinty said.

The duke gave him one of those ducal glares and the burly steward clamped his lips shut. Erik turned his head so only Eleanor could see his face and grimaced comically. She shook her head and tried not to laugh.

"The wing was closed for a reason," the duke said.

The hair at the back of Eleanor's neck stood up. He was staring at her. She didn't have to check. His attitude toward her had grated on her nerves from the moment they met. The events of the past few days had pushed that grating to the bone. Her face flushed with heat. Her hands rolled into fists. Her jaw tightened to the point of pain.

She cleared her throat to speak, but Lachlan beat her to the punch.

"The wing was closed because it was costing a fortune to heat, and Mama thought the rooms were too old-fashioned. You've kept it closed because you deemed it impractical to use it when we didn't need the space." Lachlan, the reclusive lord of few words, nodded toward the Hollywood director. "It just became practical. Give over, Knox."

For a moment Eleanor wasn't sure what might happen. *Give over, Knox.* This was the first time she'd heard Lachlan speak to the duke, as one brother would speak to another. Marriage to Lily had done wonders for him. Was there hope the change in the young Scot might do the same for the staid, tightly wired duke? Probably not because the duke in question continued to gaze at her as if he wished he could shoot fire from his icy blue eyes and incinerate her on the spot.

"Very well," the duke finally said. "I am certain Miss Witherspoon can arrange with Mrs. Wallace for you to have access to the west wing, Mr. Wentworth." The duke turned to his brother. "Lachlan, since you have seen fit to allow Mr. Cross access to our family archives and you wish for Mr. Wentworth to have access to every inch of our ancestral home, perhaps you can assist Miss Witherspoon."

"Not a problem. Thanks, Knox." He actually slapped the duke on the back and he and everyone else in the foyer gathered around Erik to discuss exploring the west wing to decide which rooms might suit which scenes.

Eleanor stood on the periphery of the group and pulled her little notepad and pencil out of the pocket of her pretty green muslin Regency day gown. Changes like this were a pain in the ass, but disaster had been diverted and that was all that mattered. There would still be filming in the main house, and she had to find a way to keep Mrs. Wallace happy about—

"Miss Witherspoon."

Eleanor jumped. The duke stood so close that his kilt brushed against her skirts. "Yes, Your Grace?" Her voice broke.

Her hands shook the tiniest bit so she thrust them—notepad, pencil, and all—behind her back. The Hollywood group, Lord Lachlan, and even Robbie and Dougal, the traitors, headed up the main staircase *en masse*.

"When you have finished arranging everything with the director I would like to speak to you." He glanced up at the retreating group of people. "I'll be in my study." He gave her one of those lord-of-the-manor bows, the least inclination of his head possible, and started up the stairs. Eleanor let go of the breath she'd been holding and waited until he got to the landing.

"Good," she said loud enough for him to hear. He stopped mid-step but did not look back. "I want to speak to you too. *Your Grace*." She imbued those last two words with as much disdain as she could manage. He continued up the stairs, his back ramrod straight, and she went in search of Mrs. Wallace.

❧

ELEANOR SPENT THE REST OF THE MORNING TREKKING ALL over Rosemount Manor, upstairs and down, closed wing, and open wings—every damned where. She'd followed Wentworth and his merry band of actors like some secretary in a nineteen-fifties movie, taking notes and smiling and nodding agreeably. If her "meeting" with the duke hadn't lurked in the back of her mind, she might have enjoyed the work. She was fascinated by the discussions about where to shoot certain scenes and what kinds of cameras to use in order to avoid the wrath of Mrs. Wallace. Lachlan hung back with her, but Erik sought his advice frequently, and Lily's normally taciturn and even anti-social husband actually helped the young director by giving him the perspective of someone who knew every inch of the manor, the ruins, and the estate.

Mrs. Wallace put on a lovely Regency-style luncheon, and the conversation around the table alternated between laughter inducing stories about filming movies and enchanting tales from the family archives that Hadrian had been studying. She shouldn't have lingered. She should have excused herself and gone up to the duke's study.

She didn't.

She found every excuse to avoid the confrontation she'd sworn to have with him a few nights ago. Finally, after she'd convinced herself, and more important, had convinced Erik Wentworth that all was well, she'd started down the hallway toward the duke's study. At the last minute, she ducked into a small sitting room and collapsed onto a silk brocade settee to gather her thoughts. She flipped through the handwritten schedule of scenes and locations for the next month to which Erik and Mrs. Wallace had agreed. The two of them had come to a tentative truce. *Thank God.*

Now if Eleanor could just— No. She didn't want a truce with the duke. She wanted answers. He'd treated her with disdain, with exasperation, with suspicion, and yes, at times, with the kind of interest a man had in a woman he desires. And now, thanks to Lily and the other ladies, she had a possible reason for his attitude toward her. A reason that made no sense. If he didn't believe in ghosts, what the hell difference did it make if she was a dead ringer for that ghost, the woman who had been executed and gone for seven hundred years?

Dead ringer. Not a good choice of words.

"Time to get this over with," she muttered, and pushed off

the settee. She checked her appearance in the gold filigree framed mirror on the wall next to the double doors out of the sitting room. "Give it your best shot, Your Grace." She crossed the Persian carpeted hallway and knocked on his study door so loudly she winced.

"Come." He didn't invite, he commanded as if she were some lowly servant called in to explain why there was a spot of dust on his desk.

She flung the door open and marched into his study.

"Close the door, please, Miss Witherspoon."

He sat behind his mahogany land yacht of a desk in his high-backed leather chair designed to look like nothing less than a throne. Head bowed over some papers, he continued to scribble notes on the pages while she closed the door, then faced him and waited. She counted to twenty in her head, then sat down in one of the two smaller armchairs in front of the monstrous slab of heavily carved wood.

Very slowly, he raised his head and put down his pen. He gazed at her in what he probably thought was an intimidating silence for several minutes.

She was too pissed and too tired to be intimidated. "What can I do for you, Your Grace?" Eleanor detected the petulance in her tone, but she didn't give a damn. A prickly energy began to build from the soles of her feet, up her legs and into the rest of her body.

"What can you do for me?" he repeated. "You can stop allowing people who have no respect for my family's history access to parts of the house I expressly told you were off limits. You are in charge of this film misadventure, and I expect you to take charge. I realize this is a rather large and long party, but as party planning is your profession—"

"I am *not* a party planner.' She slammed a fist onto the arm of her chair. "I am the event coordinator for Rosemount Manor, which includes arranging events for every aspect of the corporation that is associated with this estate. And what I am coordinating is *not* a misadventure. It is a Regency experience and training camp, and the location for the filming of one of the biggest and most expensive period films of the last five years. Shall I give you a rundown of how much money this misadventure has dropped into your bank account and will continue to drop into your bank account until the filming is completed?"

"I am well aware of the financial arrangements, Miss Witherspoon. No one is more aware when it comes to Rosemount's finances."

"You could have fooled me. You didn't read the contracts. You never read the daily schedule of events. How am I supposed to know if you've read the financial records?"

"I always read the financial records, but I also read the expenses associated with this period film."

"So do I." Eleanor tried to slow her breathing and to lower her voice. She wasn't entirely successful. "What Erik Wentworth is paying you is more than compensating for the expenses. I know because I check those expenses every day." She jumped out of her seat. "And as for that little scene this morning, the only thing that is keeping that money coming in is your brother's quick thinking and my ability to deal with a pissed off film directing genius and a stubborn, fussy Scots housekeeper."

She rounded the desk and he rose quickly to his full height as if he thought she might attack him. Which Eleanor was seriously considering.

"If you have a problem with Lord Lachlan allowing Hadrian to explore the west wing and suggesting that wing be opened for some of the filming, I suggest you speak to him about that. You are capable of speaking to your brother, aren't you, Your Grace? I realize you are out of practice."

"Don't be ridiculous. Lachlan is generous to a fault and

people take advantage of him. He doesn't realize there is information in the archives about our family that is no one's business but ours. And as for allowing that rude American director to—"

"Rude? Rude! You're the one who was rude to Mr. Wentworth, not the other way around. Although, I shouldn't be surprised. You were just as rude when we first met and your treatment of me has improved little since then."

"I don't remember being rude when we met, Miss Witherspoon. I was busy and—"

"Bullshit."

A few tiny beads of sweat had popped out above his upper lip.

Do not look at his lips, Eleanor. Every time she did, she wondered what it would be like to kiss him.

"I beg your pardon." His eyes widened.

"It is a little late for that. You have blown hot and cold with me, and frankly it has been more cold than hot. And now I know why."

"Oh?" He relaxed a little and propped a hip on his desk. "Enlighten me."

"I've seen the portrait."

He stilled as if he'd been turned to stone. There wasn't a sinew of relaxation in him now. His nostrils flared slightly. His blue eyes changed from a bright sapphire to a stormy slate color.

"What portrait?"

"You know good and well what portrait." Did he think she was stupid as well as incompetent? "The portrait hanging in the room at the top of the tower above your hidey hole."

"I don't have a, what did you call it, *hidey hole*. And—"

"Elsbeth Dunhome's portrait. The Innes Witch. The ghost of Rosemount Manor." With every description she stepped closer. "The woman who could be my twin. *Her* portrait."

With the last two words she poked him in the chest. His harsh gasp and the unnamed fire in his eyes thrilled her. She'd shocked him. Good.

"You had no right," he muttered. "No right at all."

"I had no right? You had no right, no right at all to keep my resemblance to her a secret. No, wait. You had no right to make me pay for every bit of hate and superstition you have where she is concerned. I've spent the last several months being judged, ignored, belittled, and stressed out all because I look like some ghost from your childhood and I'm not going to put up with it. You will—"

He trapped her hand between his. "There is no such thing as ghosts." His voice fairly boomed and shook the windows.

"Who are you trying to convince, *Knox*? Me or you?"

He stared down into her face. His broad chest rose and fell beneath the tight confines of his dark blue cable knit sweater. He opened his mouth as if to speak only to close his lips so tightly together they nearly disappeared into one thin line of barely leashed anger.

"That room is spotless, but Mrs. Wallace nor any other member of your staff have stepped foot in there," she went on. "That painting is over seven hundred years old, but it looks as if it was painted yesterday. There are fresh flowers. I know your history with the Innes Witch. A man doesn't honor the memory of a childhood friend if he doesn't believe she exists. I-I can understand why you didn't tell me. It's—" She waved her hand. "You shouldn't have penalized me for resembling the woman."

"Who do you think you are?" His hands, wrapped around hers, trembled.

"I am the woman who is trying to help you save your ancestral home. And I'm doing so without an ounce of help from you. I am no ghost, Your Grace. I am flesh and bone, and brains and determination. You cannot wish me away by denying my existence."

He let go of her hand. "Denying your existence?" The duke pulled her into his arms so quickly Eleanor forgot to breathe. "I can no more deny you than I can the air I breathe, you ridiculous creature."

He kissed her so hard she saw stars.

Chapter Twelve

SHE TASTED LIKE PEACHES. HER LIPS, SOFT AND FULL, possessed such heat, possessed him to the point he couldn't think. Eleanor brushed her hands up his chest, across his shoulders and suddenly she tangled her hands in his hair. She cupped the back of his head and leaned up and into him so closely he had neither the power nor the will to pull away. He pressed his hands to her back and pulled her closer. The curve of her breasts against his body sent spears of arousal to his cock. If she continued to make those little noises in her throat while her thighs rubbed against the front of his kilt, he—

Crack!

Knox stumbled back into the corner of his desk. His ears rang. Eleanor backed up a step, the fingers of one hand over her lips and her other hand stretching and closing at her side. Her eyes wide and her breath coming in short gasps, she stared at him with a horrified expression. One side of his face burned as if he'd sat too close to the fire and had fallen asleep. The sound of the slap had reached him first. Now the sting set in and assured him he was *not* asleep. Not asleep, but definitely not caught up with what had just happened. In his mind he was still kissing her, tasting the sweetness of her lips, feeling the erotic curves of her body, and warming himself with a kind of heat he'd never known.

Bloody hell!

He'd kissed Eleanor…Miss Witherspoon. He'd kissed her soundly and was well on his way to kissing her senseless before she slapped him. Hard. He studied her face but had no idea what she was feeling.

Say something, you idiot.

"Miss Witherspoon, I apologize. I-I should never have—"

"Miss Witherspoon? Miss Witherspoon?" She stepped toward him her delicate hands clutched into not so delicate fists. Her slap packed power. He didn't want to experience her punch. "You just kissed me."

"I'm well aware of that, and I want to apologize. I…."

Not his best choice of words if her reaction was any indication. She made some sort of incoherent noise, threw her hands in the air, and stalked toward the doors. Only to turn back, march right back and grab his face between her hands. She kissed him and backed him into the bookcases behind his desk chair. Which prevented him from falling down. He'd lost control of his knees about the time her lips met his.

She plundered his mouth like a woman starved. Her tongue swept the roof of his mouth, and he shivered. He gripped the bookshelves with both hands to keep himself from grabbing her and laying her across his desk. As quickly as she started kissing him, she was done. She snatched her mouth away from his, swiped a hand across her lips, and took two steps back.

"Why did you kiss me and then apologize?" she shouted.

"I don't know why I kissed you, and I apologized because you're an employee and, unlike my father, I don't screw the people who work for me," he shot back.

"You don't know? You don't know?" she shot back. "And I guess you don't know why you didn't bother to tell me about the painting and how much I look like the Innes Witch either?"

"One has nothing to do with the other." He had to get away from her. This conversation was a disaster and could only get worse.

"Bullshit, Your Grace. Complete and utter bullshit." She turned and stomped to the doors which she flung open so hard they banged against the wall. Once she stepped out into the corridor, she turned back to him. "Some advice, Your Grace. If you regret kissing a woman enough to apologize, then you shouldn't have kissed her in the first place. Never assume because a woman works for you, she wants to screw you. Don't stick your aristocratic turned-up nose into my money-making event for the rest of the time it runs. And deal with whatever is going on with you and the local ghost because I am *not* going to pay for another woman's sins, especially one that has been dead for seven hundred years!" She leaned in to take a door handle in each hand and slammed the doors closed so hard they rattled.

Knox fumbled for the back of his desk chair. Took him a few tries to find the back and to slide his hand onto the heavily padded arms so he could drop into the seat right before his legs gave way. Impossibly, the room echoed. How silence echoed he didn't understand, but Eleanor Witherspoon had taken every bit of sound and air with her. He stared at the neat stacks of paperwork on his desk. Surely, if he focused his attention on something, his brain might stop ricocheting against his skull.

"What the hell just happened?" he muttered.

He inhaled deeply. *Mistake.* She'd taken the sound and the air, but she'd left behind the hint of her gardenia scented perfume. He closed his eyes and relived the moments he'd held her in his arms. She was with him every step of the way. Until she wasn't. He leaned all the way back in his chair.

I've seen the portrait.

He should have gotten rid of that painting a long time ago. The moment his father died, and Knox had become the Duke of Turra, he should have called McGinty and…and what? Told the old Scot that the boy who had claimed to have befriended the family ghost had discovered the portrait, locked it away in the tower, and left the key under the floorboards in his bedroom? Not bloody likely. The truth was, no matter how hard he worked to put those memories and the ghost of the Innes Witch behind him something always held him back. Somehow, he'd sensed the story wasn't over, would never be over, and so he'd kept the portrait and waited for answers that never came.

"Oh, stuff it, Knox."

"Am I interrupting something?"

Knox sat up so quickly his chair nearly pitched him across his desk. Papers and files scattered onto the floor. He glared at Danny Arneaux, who stood in the open doorway. How had the man opened the door without him hearing?

"What the hell, Arneaux? How long have you been standing there?"

"Long enough to hear you tell yourself to stuff it." The Cajun actor crossed to his desk and gathered up some of the documents, then dropped them onto the desk before he settled into the chair Eleanor had vacated. "I can leave and come back if you want to continue this executive session with yourself."

"What is it you say? Kiss my arse. Why are you here?"

Knox got busy sorting the papers into the proper stacks. Which made it easier to have a conversation with Arneaux without actually looking at him. Didn't fool the damned Yank. He simply gathered up the rest of the papers from the floor and started organizing them on the other side of Knox's desk.

"I ran into Eleanor outside the ballroom."

"Please don't tell me they're filming in the ballroom again." Knox didn't think he had the strength to sort through his feelings about that kiss *and* deal with Mrs. Wallace in high gear.

Arneaux laughed. "No filming. Dance lessons. Don't change the subject. What'd you do to our Miss Witherspoon?"

"What makes you think—"

"Do you *really* want to know what she was calling you under her breath when she nearly plowed into me? I'd have to say at least five Hail Mary's for repeating the words."

"We had an argument."

"Tell me something I don't know." Danny handed him a folder marked *Regency Boot Camp and Period Film*. "Does this have anything to do with the portrait in the tower?"

Knox put the folder directly in front of himself. He fiddled with the tab that identified the contents. His friendship with the actor had grown since they first met. But he wasn't the sort to trust others easily. He hadn't been since the first time he told someone about seeing and speaking with Elsbeth.

"Is there anyone currently squatting in my house in the name of period film that has *not* broken into a locked tower and viewed a portrait that was never meant to be on public display?"

Danny Arneaux blew out a noisy breath. When he looked back up at Knox he had that half grin on his face, the one that said *well, actually....*

"This is why opening the estate for this sort of thing was the very last thing I wanted to do to make money. Having my home invaded is one thing. Having my privacy invaded is intolerable."

He flattened his hand on the folder and tapped his index finger in agitation. His life had started a slow spin from the moment McGinty called with the news of Father's death. He'd agreed to the event use of the estate in a moment of weakness and desperation, two states with which he'd had little to no experience once he'd been banished to England as a child. But Knox had taken one look at Eleanor Witherspoon the day they met, and from that moment forward his life had become a demented carnival ride with no brakes in sight.

"Trust me, I know all about doing things you don't want to do for money. At least yours doesn't involve your naked ass on a movie screen." Danny leaned back in his chair and rested his folded hands on his chest. "You should have told her, you know. Keeping it a secret means she has to come up with your motive. You do *not* want a woman coming up with a motive for something you've done. She will always pick the worst one."

"Worst one for what? I'm the one who should be questioning motives. Who broke into that room? Who took her to see the portrait? And why?" Knox saw the flicker of guilt in his eyes and pinned him with his coldest stare. "And don't try telling me you don't know. Start talking, Yank."

"Yank? Kiss my ass, Duke." He gave an exaggerated sigh. "I'll hit the highlights, but if you tell anyone I told you, I'll deny it. Although, no one will give a damn at this point. Your secret is out and the whole boot camp is in on it."

"I'm listening." Knox ignored the knot in his stomach, He despised being exposed. He'd worked hard to avoid being vulnerable, even with his brother. Especially with his brother.

"The matchmakers in the group arranged for Bas and

Teddy to have the key to the dressing room between their rooms so they could get their freak…get together. They found a door in the dressing room. The key fit so they—"

"The tunnel to the tower. I'd forgotten all about that." Knox shook his head. He'd worked so hard to forget all about Rosemount Manor, inheriting the title, and especially Elsbeth, that he'd forgotten things like the tunnels and secret passages he and Lachlan had explored as children. "So, they took Eleanor to see the portrait?"

"Not exactly. They took all of us to see the portrait. They left the key with Eleanor at their wedding reception and the wives sort of kidnapped her and dragged her through the tunnels and into the tower."

"The wives?"

"Samantha, Anna, and Lily."

"Lily. Of course. My sister-in-law never misses an opportunity to make my life difficult. Why did they feel the need to show her a portrait they knew would upset her?"

"You'll have to ask them. But warn me before you do. I don't want to be anywhere near that conversation, and I doubt if Hadrian and Lachlan will either. Besides, that isn't the question you need to be asking."

"Oh?" He didn't really want to know what he should be asking, he suspected he knew. Did he want to know the answer to that question? Probably not.

"You need to figure out why you didn't tell Eleanor from the start that she looks like the Innes Witch, especially after the way you treat her."

"And how do I treat her?"

"Depends on the day, according to my wife. Some days you are, how did Samantha put it, you're quite civil to her." He sat up and grinned. "Other days, you treat her like a bastard at the family reunion."

"I have never—"

"Now me"— Arneaux cut in as he pushed to his feet— "I think Eleanor scares the hell out of you. That's why you don't know how to treat her, and why you fucked this up so badly." He ran his finger under his Regency neck cloth and made a face. "I hate these damned things. I don't know what is going on in your head, Knox. Curses and ghosts and all of that, whether you believe or not has to screw with your head."

"You don't believe in that nonsense, do you?" He tried to make the question sound like a joke. Neither of them laughed.

"I'm from New Orleans. Of course, I believe. But what I believe doesn't matter. You're the one who has the hots for a woman who looks like the family legend. You've lived with this from childhood, and I get that you did what you had to do to survive. You can deny it all you want, *ami*, but this stuff speaks to you, and all the crap your parents told you, and all of the things everyone else tells you won't change that. I spent half my life trying to be what people told me I was because I believed what they said about how my life would turn out. Don't fall for that shit. Don't be afraid to buck the odds and go after what you want."

"I'm not afraid of anything, my Cajun friend. Least of all Eleanor Witherspoon." Knox took the marked file and shoved it into his bottom desk drawer.

"Keep telling yourself that, Your Grace." Arneaux walked to the study doors. "But if I were you, I'd stay out of her way for a while. You might find yourself tied to a chair and thrown in the loch." He walked out of the study laughing. As he didn't bother to close the doors, Knox heard him laughing all the way down the corridor.

Avoiding Eleanor sounded like a great idea. He opened the drawer and pulled the file back out. Too bad he wasn't the sort to ignore a problem. He opened the file and began to go through the various documents and reports until he found the schedules she'd left on his desk a few days ago.

Knox managed to stay busy the rest of the day, in spite of the memory of that kiss invading his thoughts at least once an hour...once every half hour.

That kiss.

He pushed out of his chair and placed several files and papers in his desk drawer. One particular file, however, he picked up, then strode from his study. He descended the stairs to the first floor, where the doors to the dining room stood open as the servants cleaned up the remnants of yet another Regency dinner arranged by Miss Witherspoon. Eleanor. He'd asked Mrs. Wallace to arrange for his dinner to be brought to him in his study. After he'd read through all the schedules of lessons, activities, events, and filming to take place in the next several weeks and months, he'd decided his ability to remain civil to this Wentworth fellow had withered away to...less than nothing.

When Robbie had fetched the dinner tray, he'd informed Knox that the director had returned to his luxury caravan in the village. The others, the "boot campers" who had been sharing his home all these weeks, were presently in the drawing room playing cards and likely gossiping about him and the portrait they had no business ever seeing. Be that as it may, he intended to speak with Miss...Eleanor, dammit, about some of the things she and Wentworth intended to put Rosemount through in the name of this period drama nonsense.

He had no intention of causing a scene. He was perfectly capable of drawing her aside and having a civil conversation with her without either of them raising their voices. Or jumping each other like a couple of horny teenagers. He hoped. Once the drawing room doors came into view he slowed. He tapped the file folder against his chin.

Lightning filled the arched window that spanned the end of the wide corridor. The glare nearly blinded him. He was still blinking when he finally stepped into the drawing room. A noisy and somewhat unorganized conversation taking place around the fireplace drew his attention. That is until they all saw him standing just inside the doors and they shut up like a bunch of guilty children.

"Am I interrupting something?" He started across the room toward the chairs and settees in front of the hearth.

A clap of thunder shook the house. Knox stopped in his tracks. An icy shiver slithered down his spine. At Eleanor's insistence, the room was lit solely by candles, lamplight, and the fire in the hearth. No sooner had the thunder's last echoes died than lighting lit the room by way of the stained-glass windows that overlooked the front drive.

"With a prelude like that I'd say you're interrupting something," Lachlan said softly.

"The storm has been brewing all afternoon," Knox replied, and continued the last few steps to where they sat. "I doubt it has anything to do with me. The little confab I walked in on, however...." He raised an eyebrow and waited for someone to say something. Anything.

The wind howled outside the floor-to-ceiling windows. Driving rain beat a steady tattoo against the glass. The thunder continued to roll louder and louder down the glen. He could not remember a storm such as this since....

"What were you talking about?" he suddenly demanded.

"Whoa," Arneaux said. "Pump your brakes, Your Grace. We were discussing what Hadrian here has discovered about your family history digging around in the library in the other end of the house."

"I see. I assume you will allow me to read what you write *before* you publish it, Mr. Cross?"

Knox was of two minds on the subject of his family's history. Half the time he didn't give a damn what the world learned about the lairds of Rosemount. The rest of the time he lived in dread of what might come out should anyone investigate the family history too closely.

"Of course, I will, Your Grace," he said. "On two conditions. Your opinion will not change what I write and you start calling me Hadrian, for fuck's sake. Mr. Cross makes me sound like somebody's English teacher."

"Fair enough." Knox bit back a smile. "*Hadrian.*"

"They want to dig up the first duke." Lachlan announced as casually as if digging up a man buried seven hundred years ago was as common as watching a football match on—

Crack! Thunder roared.

Everyone in the room flinched. The house shook for a full minute whilst the room appeared in stark relief by the blaze of the nearly simultaneous lightening. They all laughed nervously except Lachlan and Knox.

"I beg your pardon?" He never took his eyes off his younger brother, seated on the arm of the chair occupied by his new wife.

"Sounds like someone doesn't like—" Anna Chase went silent when Knox raised his hand.

Knox kept his gaze fixed on his brother. "What did you say, Lachlan?"

Lily started to stand but was stopped by his brother's subtle headshake as he kept his eyes locked on Knox.

"You heard me, Your Grace. The consensus is that the first duke needs to join your friend, Elsbeth, on the island in the loch."

"My friend?"

Knox looked at the faces of the other people in the room.

He did so deliberately and tried to avoid Eleanor at all costs. Their expressions were a mixture of amusement, shock, and anticipation. They expected him to go off the deep end no doubt. He wanted to. Badly. Between the simmering sensation of heat up his veins and the exponentially increasing force of the storm, he was ready to roar at them like a lunatic.

"Your Grace? Knox?"

He started at the pressure of a small hand on his forearm. With the slightest turn of his head, he looked into the dark brown eyes of Eleanor Witherspoon.

With her free hand she tapped the file he held now clutched tightly in his hand. "Was there something you wanted?"

His focus dropped immediately to her full rose-colored lips.

They want to dig up the first duke.

"I want to know what the hell is going on when *guests* in my house are contemplating digging up my long dead, *very* long dead relatives."

"We'll be back," Eleanor told the others. She smiled her enigmatic *I'll-smooth-this-over* smile, gently cupped his elbow, and steered him around toward the doors out of the drawing room. "You didn't come into this room in search of a fight with your brother, Your Grace. You came in search of a fight with me. Shall we?"

Shock. The shock of Lachlan's announcement combined with Eleanor's competence as she dragged him down the corridor and into the small ladies' parlor, the green parlor, accounted for his lack of resistance. She didn't release his arm until she closed the door behind them and propelled him into a chair in front of the rounded window seat that looked out over the fountain at the center of the front drive. She dropped into the chair opposite him.

"I wasn't trying to pick a fight. And I won't be dragged about my own home by a managing female, no matter how much I'm paying her to keep my estate from going down the tubes." Knox flung the file folder onto the window seat.

Eleanor merely smiled at him in that cool, calm, annoying as hell way she had.

"Of course, you were. You still are. Looking for someone to fight with you, that is. A man of mystery you are not, Your Grace." She crossed her legs at the ankle and folded her hands in her lap. "And, as I did drag you here like some bullying child, what you are paying me does not enter into it, unless I will be paid a bonus for keeping you from acting like a complete wanker in front of a room full of people. Not to mention—"

"I think you've mentioned quite enough." Knox needed her to stop talking because when she spoke her eyes lit up and her mouth made every bone in his body hurt. Every. Bone. "I'm not finished with the subject of digging up my dead ancestors as an exercise for your Regency boot camp."

"*Quelle surprise.*" She actually rolled her eyes.

"But I will table that discussion momentarily to go over this shooting schedule you and that cocky director have devised."

"Which shooting schedule?"

He wasn't fooled by her demure Regency lady act, not one damned bit.

He kept his eyes trained on her face and scrabbled around in the file folder with one hand until he drew out a stack of papers held together with a colorful enamel butterfly binder clip.

"This one. The one that involves setting up shop in a wing of my house that has been closed for years, turning a large portion of the glen into a battlefield, and using enough pyrotechnics to send every sheep, coo, and horse on the estate running for Edinburgh after my shepherds and stockmen have spent the past several months moving them from the lower pastures into the Highlands for the summer."

"Oh." She took the papers, glanced at them, and handed them back. "That schedule."

"Yes." A clap of thunder shook the house again and drew his attention away from her. Lightning flashed, held. The front of the house from the fountain across the front lawns to the ha-ha stood as if in the noonday sun. The hair at the back of his neck stood on end.

"The storm is getting closer." She stood and moved close to him, her arm brushing his. She flinched as an explosive blast of thunder rattled the windows.

"The storm is here, Miss...Eleanor. I haven't seen a summer storm like this in years." He wondered which was worse, the pounding of the rain outside or the pounding of his heart. No woman had a right to smell as enticing as she did.

"Wentworth knows to make certain Lachlan is nowhere near the explosives. I've explained everything to him, and Lily has threatened to kick his ass if he so much as irritates your brother. I'm not sure what to do about the livestock, but there are animal handlers on the crew and a humane monitor who will make certain no animals are harmed in the film." She gave his arm a light punch. "And the medieval part of the house is almost as indestructible as you. I'm certain—"

"Lachlan doesn't remember about the west wing." He continued to stare out the window. He wanted to draw the storm around him like a shield, but she stood next to him, a buttress of stone in the middle of a river. Where she was an aura of calm seemed to live and breathe. "I don't want Lachlan going in there. I don't want him to see or hear or even know about the visions of war your director friend will unleash on this place."

"Knox."

"I left him here." He turned his head to meet her gaze. "I ran away to England and left Lachlan to deal with…everything. My parents at war. My father's rages. I could have come home after Eton. I could have come home after Cambridge. I could have come home before he decided the only way for him to escape was to join the army and march into a different kind of hell." He never meant to say any of this, especially not to her. Eleanor's eyes lured him in, trapped him, and opened the gates to his soul.

"He was a grown man when he went to war, not the little boy you are imagining you…." She paused as if searching for the right word. He knew the right word.

"Abandoned? It wasn't the first time I did so. Our father was quite creative in his punishments. He pitted us against each other. He locked us up in the old wing of the house at night, and we were forced to find our way out in the dark. Alone. If we helped one another, we were both taken deeper into the west wing, into the dungeons. The one who found his way out first, alone, was tucked up in bed with a hot meal, and a *good lad* from the old bastard. I learned my lesson well. So well, I walked away and let Lachlan go somewhere that nearly destroyed him." His throat burned and threatened to close. "I won't do that again, Eleanor. Not for you. Not for Wentworth. Not even to save Rosemount. Never again."

None of that matters now." She placed her delicate hand on the forearms he'd crossed over his chest. "He has Lily now. She'll help you keep him safe. We all will."

"It matters to me." He tried not to stare at the place where her warmth and strength flowed into his body. "And Lily Randolph won't help me do anything except perhaps fall into a well."

She laughed, an erotic throaty laugh that sent sparks shooting throughout his body as if he'd swallowed a star shooting across the Highland night sky. "If you weren't such a horse's ass to her, she might be less inclined to push you into a well. And her name is Lily Innes now."

"Her name is Lady Lachlan."

"Her name is Lily. She is your sister now. Didn't you want a sister growing up?" She moved her palm up and down his forearm.

"God no." Her expression brought him up short. "No, not because…I would never have wanted a sister to have to live the childhood Lachlan and I did." He shook his head.

"I thought perhaps Elsbeth was—"

"Elsbeth was a figment of my imagination. Nothing more." The storm rattled the windows. The wind howled very much like an indignant woman.

"Which came first? Your imagination or the portrait? Did you see the Innes Witch before you discovered her lurking around on canvas in the tower?"

"Before. Long before."

"And she looked…." She stared at him so intently even in the light of the fire and the lightning-streaked sky outside the windows he was drawn to the amber flecks in her fathomless brown eyes.

"Exactly as she is in the portrait," he said quietly.

"Exactly like me?" She stopped rubbing his arm and rested her hand on his flesh bared by the pushed-up sleeves of his sweater.

"Exactly," he breathed.

"So, you conjured her out of your imagination?"

"Yes." He glanced at her full, rose-colored lips and shivered.

"You're sure of that, Your Grace?"

She stepped into him, her body brushing against his like an inferno. The air around them grew icy cold. Rain pounded against the bow window in torrents.

"Knox. And I'm not sure of anything at the moment, *Eleanor.*" He eased his arms around her. He splayed his hands against her back and pulled her flush against his chest. "Except this." He touched his lips to hers and his entire body sighed. "Yes?"

"God, yes."

She kissed him so hard he stumbled back a step. Not that anything would stop him from answering her kiss with one of his own. She opened to him at once, and their tongues slid together in a sensual rhythm that drew him deeper and deeper into the inferno that was her. She sighed and hummed into his mouth, hungry and seeking. He clutched the back of her gown and turned his head to catch a breath before diving in once more.

He lost the power to think or worry or do anything, save discover the wonder of her lips, her tongue, her scent, and her passion. Eleanor's passion seared him. He never wanted to stop. He kissed her and received her kiss in return as if they shared a feast only they could share. She was a banquet of curves, heat, and intoxicating scents he drew in like oxygen. Like breathing, let this glorious moment never end. Let—

The room shook. The blast of a horn echoed in waves. They gasped in tandem and glanced around still wrapped in each other's arms. The sound blared through the air again, from a distance, but still so loud and eerie Knox sensed it in his chest.

"What the hell was that?" Eleanor asked, her voice a hoarse whisper.

She jumped at the next clarion call. Knox clasped her hand and faced the large window. The night was black save for the lightning and raging assault of sideways rain against the manor.

"That," he said, as he led her toward the hallway doors, "is impossible." The bugled notes rang out closer now. When he and Eleanor reached the middle of the corridor headed toward the drawing room where they'd left the others, Knox bent to press a tender but emphatic kiss to her mouth. "To be continued." He grasped her hand and strode toward the drawing room.

Knox shrugged against the icy sensation beginning to creep into his veins. His fear of what kissing Eleanor might mean raced through his mind. Followed closely by the dread he had run mad. The horn blasting over and over again hadn't been heard since the time the Romans invaded. Eleanor's Regency boot camp was about to get a lesson in Celtic history they hadn't bargained for, and Knox had no idea what the hell he was going to tell them. What he was going to tell her.

Chapter Thirteen

THE MOMENT THE DUKE OPENED THE DOOR AND PULLED Eleanor into the corridor, a mad scramble of barking dogs and running footmen added to the rumble and roar of the storm and the weird horn. She held tight to his hand as he maneuvered her around two adult deerhounds, two bloodhounds, Lachlan's little scrap of a dog, and a deerhound puppy. The footmen weaved in and out of the canine circus trying to round up the dogs. Eleanor concentrated on staying on her feet.

She slipped, stumbled, and nearly fell as Knox pulled her into the drawing room. She had no control over her body, whether due to the eerie horn still sounding as if from every side of the manor or due to the mind-blowing kiss she had shared with Knox, she had no idea. Personally, she wanted to blame being tugged along like a child's toy by a big ox of a duke for the fact her arms and legs had practically turned to jelly. Worse, that damned horn had set up an odd vibration in her chest that scared the hell out of her.

Knox stopped suddenly. Eleanor plowed into his back and clutched his arm with her free hand. The dogs spilled into the room ahead of them baying, yapping, and barking at full volume.

"Quiet!" Knox roared.

The dogs dropped to the floor, instantly quiet. She didn't look back but she wouldn't have been surprised to see the footmen sitting next to the dogs on the expensive antique carpets. In the ensuing silence, the haunting horn blared even more stridently above the storm.

"What the fuck is that?" Danny Arneaux demanded.

Eleanor took in his expression, then did a quick study of the other faces in the room. Apparently, she wasn't the only one scared witless by the cacophony that raged against the walls and windows of Rosemount Manor. Lachlan's hard expression and protective stance in front of Lily told her one thing—the Innes boys knew more about the mysterious horn call than anyone else in present company.

"If I didn't know better, I'd say someone was sounding a Celtic battle horn called a carnyx." Hadrian Cross stood at the huge windows at the near end of the drawing room, the ones that looked out over the front of the house. "But there hasn't been a working one of those in existence in nearly two thousand years, except the one at the Museum of Scotland." He turned toward Knox and gave the duke an inquisitive grin. "Unless you have one hidden in that wing of the house you're so eager to keep closed."

"Don't be ridiculous," Knox replied. He paused as the horn sounded once more. "If I had one, I'd have sold the damned thing long ago and perhaps avoided having my home turned into a Regency amusement park."

This elicited a combination of laughter and eyerolls from everyone except Lachlan. He continued to stare at his brother, some unspoken communication flying between them.

"Oh, I don't know." Hadrian glanced from Lachlan to the

duke. "I suspect you two have heard this horn before, or am I just imagining things?"

"Yes."

"No." Lachlan countermanded his brother. "We have heard it before, but it was a long time ago. We were just children. Our parents told us we were dreaming, didn't they McGinty?"

Only then did Eleanor notice the older Scot standing in the shadows at the other end of the room, gazing out the French doors onto the terrace.

"There's a piper on the tower," he said without turning around. "Listen." They all hurried to the French doors, all but Knox and Lachlan, who took their time, still not speaking a word to each other.

"How the hell can you hear a piper over— Holy shit." Arneaux glanced at Eleanor before he took Samantha's hand and followed the others out onto the terrace.

They crowded beneath the shelter of the overhang that jutted out several feet and gave them some shelter from the rain. Except, McGinty, who stepped to the railing. Fortunately, the driving rain lashed at the front of the house and lost much of its force by the time it reached the back terrace and gardens.

Thunder still shook the house. Lightning kept flashing as bright as day, then plunged the night back into pitch blackness. The horn continued to sound, but there was something different about the volume and direction. Eleanor started when Knox moved from behind her to stand between Danny and Hadrian. At almost the same moment, Lily pushed in next to her. Knox and Lachlan stepped up beside McGinty. The three of them stared at the tower. Tannus and Beira trotted around in front of Eleanor and backed into her legs as if to keep her from following the men.

Wind whipped the three men's kilts and lightning lit the

ruins up in one long flash. Then bagpipes filled the air as clearly as if the piper stood at the foot of the terrace steps below them. The obnoxious blare of that damned horn blasted once more, but faintly and far away, then stopped. The pipes played on over the storm. She could just make out a lone figure on top of the tower in the distance.

"*Highland Laddie*," Lily said. "He's playing *Highland Laddie*."

Lachlan and Knox turned as one to stare at her. Lachlan grinned.

"What?" Anna Chase asked, her hands wrapped around Hadrian's bicep.

"A Scot's battle air," Hadrian said. "A call to war."

"Lady Lachlan called it right," McGinty said, as he continued to stare up at the tower.

"Well done, my lady," Robbie said.

"I married a Scot, didn't I?" Lily grumbled. "Who is he, and why is he up there playing in a thunderstorm?"

Eleanor kept her focus on Knox. He had returned his attention to the tower, but she had caught sight of his pale face. Lachlan's expression was only a little better. Something had them spooked. Badly.

"Can one of you tell me do you—"

"Know the piper?" Knox cut her off and placed his hand on McGinty's shoulder.

"Aye. So does Lord Lachlan."

"Is it?" Lachlan asked.

"Aye. Sure as I'm standing here."

"Why is he—" Eleanor began.

"Show's over," Knox said abruptly. He squeezed McGinty's shoulder, turned, and gave Lachlan a meaningful look. "Everyone back inside, please."

"What the fuck do you mean?" Danny asked. "What was all that about?"

"Good, damned question," Hadrian muttered as they all

shuffled into the drawing room and continued toward the fire.

Eleanor glanced back to see Knox, Lachlan, and McGinty in conversation. Rain glistened on Knox's wind-blown hair. He looked as formidable as that horn had sounded.

McGinty inclined his head to the duke and went out the rear doors of the drawing room. Dougal followed him, while Robbie remained in the drawing room. Lachlan gave his brother one last distinctly unbrotherly glare, then joined Lily on the loveseat in front of the fireplace. Lily and Lachlan's little black and white dog crawled into Lily's lap. Hadrian and Danny tossed a few logs onto the blaze. Everyone was damp, cold, a little scared—and more than a little curious. Her most of all.

Knox stood at the French doors his head tilted at such an angle he had to be studying the piper, who continued to play over the now quieter storm. Danny's two bloodhounds ambled over and collapsed before the hearth. Hadrian's deer-hound puppy, Elsbeth, climbed across Anna's lap as Hadrian settled onto the sofa across from Lily and Lachlan. Tannus and Beira stood sentry on each side of Knox. Eleanor sat in one of the arm chairs next to Lily and Lachlan. No one said a word. All eyes were on the duke.

The storm still lashed at the windows and shook the house. The bagpipes, however, subsided, then went abruptly silent. Knox turned from the French doors and started across the room, the dogs on either side of him. He had nearly reached where they sat before the fireplace when he stopped and stared at the stained-glass windows on the opposite end of the drawing room overlooking the front drive. Eleanor glanced at the others and started to rise. Lachlan waved her back into her chair.

"The window is cracked," Knox said quietly.

He rested his hand on Tannus's head. Everyone jumped

up and rushed to inspect the color floor-to-ceiling trio of windows. A long crack extended the entire length of the middle window decorated with the Innes family crest and the Duke of Turra's motto and symbols.

"The horn," Lachlan said softly. "Like before…."

"Nonsense." Knox shot his brother a censoring glare.

"So you two *have* heard the carnyx before tonight." Hadrian grinned knowingly at the rest of them.

Eleanor elbowed him in the solar plexus.

"No," the Innes brothers said in unison.

"Could you repeat that please?" Danny asked. "My bull-shit monitor was going off so loudly I couldn't hear you."

Everyone laughed, except for Knox, Lachlan, and Eleanor. She didn't know why, but something about the way the two men were acting made her think some very private door into their past was being pried open. In her experience that sort of opening often didn't end well. For anyone.

Anna went to the window and traced her finger along the crack. "Mrs. Wallace is going to be so upset." She turned to Robbie who had hurried over with the rest of them. "I don't think it's leaking, but if it does, it'll ruin the carpets. Can you find some plastic to cover the window seat and the carpets, just in case?"

Eleanor shot her a grateful smile. Anna was often the one to diffuse tense situations in their little band. She was so unassuming no one dared argue with her.

"Yes, Mrs. Cross. Ghost horn or not, there will be blood if the rain reaches those carpets." He gave her a quick bow and rushed out of the room.

"Ghost horn?" Danny said.

"Well, boys," Hadrian said, ignoring his wife's furious expression. "To quote our Cajun friend here, which one of you is going to cut bait and tell us what's going on?"

Knox opened his mouth to speak, but Lachlan beat him to

it. "We heard the horn during a storm like this when I was four years old. Knox was eight. We were told we imagined it all, but something else happened that night."

"And?" Lily nudged her husband.

"Lachlan." Knox conveyed a warning and a command in that single word.

"And that is not my story to tell." He shook his head and took Lily's hand. "Knox is right. The show is over. You all have a big day tomorrow. I'm for bed."

"Now wait a minute. Oww. What?" Hadrian rubbed his arm where Anna had pinched him.

"Might I suggest, Lady Lachlan," Knox said, all ducal efficiency suddenly, "that you and my brother stay here in the manor tonight? The storm may have damaged the way back to your cottage and—"

"Don't tell me how to take care of my husband, *Your Grace*." Lily picked up their dog, Leonidas, and dragged Lachlan toward the doors.

Lachlan grinned and waved as they left the drawing room.

"I wouldn't dream of it, *sister*," Knox called after them. "Good night, everyone."

Something like, "Fuck you, Your Grace." floated back down the corridor.

"My sister-in-law has such a way with words," Knox murmured. He actually sounded amused, though his voice still held some tension. At least to Eleanor's ears.

They all shuffled their feet and muttered.

Eleanor clapped her hands once and petted Danny's bloodhounds as they trailed after Samantha. "Lord Lachlan's right. We have a lot to do tomorrow, and I think we have had enough excitement for one night."

They kept grumbling but picked up various candelabras and meandered out of the drawing room down the corridor to the stairs that led to the second-floor bedrooms.

Robbie and Dougal came running in with a large piece of plastic stretched between them. "Want us to take the dogs, Your Grace?" Dougal asked as he and Robbie worked to cover the windowsill, window seat and antique carpets.

"No. They'll bunk in with me tonight. Everything all right at the lodge, Dougal?"

"Oh, aye, Yer Grace. Power went out for a bit, but the generator kicked in by the time McGinty and I drove up."

"Drove up?" Eleanor asked. "Generator?"

"They *are* on their honeymoon. Did you really expect them to spend the little time they have building fires, lighting candles, and—"

Eleanor cut him off with a wave of her hand. "I concede, Your Grace."

"Very kind of you, Colonel Witherspoon." He clicked his heels and bowed. "And I assumed you wouldn't mind if McGinty drove a Land Rover to the lodge to check on Bas and Teddy. He declared himself too damned old to go on horseback, and Urquhart would skin both of us if he took a cart and horse."

"Of course, I don't mind," Eleanor said. "Although I wouldn't mind watching Urquhart skin someone after the fright we've had tonight. This was *not* on my Regency experience schedule."

"They heard the horn. And the bagpipes. The viscount and that big Basque fellow will want an explanation, just so you know, Your Grace." Dougal never looked so serious. Something had him spooked.

"They're not the only ones." Eleanor looped her arm through Knox's. "Come on, dogs. Good night, Dougal. Good night, Robbie." She picked up the last of the branch of candles with her free hand.

"Good night, miss." They nodded and offered her a conspiratorial smile.

"Come with me, Your Grace. I'll walk you to your room, and you can tell me what the hell just happened."

To her amazement, he didn't resist when she led him from the room, followed closely by his deerhounds. They were halfway down the corridor almost to the stairs and he still hadn't said a word. When she glanced up, he was studying her as if he'd never seen her before and a chill snaked through her.

"Come here."

She guided him into the music room just before they reached the stairs. Once she set her candelabra on the side table inside the door Eleanor grabbed him by his lapels and hauled him to her for a fiery kiss. Knox kicked the door shut and collapsed against the heavy oak slab with a groan. He framed her waist in his hands and held her close as she ravished his mouth with her lips and tongue. No man should have lips like his, full and soft and searing all at once.

Thunder shook the house and a flash of lightning hung in the sky long enough to illuminate the shadows in the room. In the split second that Eleanor opened her eyes a figure moved along one wall and disappeared. She gasped and pulled away from Knox. He reached for her, but she held up a hand to stop him. The lightning faded and the candelabra bathed them both in a small circle of golden light. She jumped when something brushed against her skirts. Beira and Tannus stared up at her. They leaned against her on either side, and she gave each of them a pat on the head.

Knox snorted. "You have them wrapped around your little finger, just like the rest of us."

"Tell me what this is all about, Knox. You and Lachlan are keeping secrets, and I'm not putting up with it a minute longer." She poked a finger in his chest.

He shook his head hard and blinked a few times. "What?" He spoke slowly, like a man coming out of a daze. Poor thing.

"I used small words, Your Grace. Which one didn't you understand?"

"Is this some sort of mad American female tactic?" He ran his hands over his face. "You bloody kiss me senseless and then ask me about the weather?"

Oh, now he was the duke again. What a pain in the ass.

"The weather?" She snatched up the candelabra, opened the door and stepped out into the corridor. The dogs followed her.

"Eleanor, wait." Knox clasped her elbow and turned her to face him. The dogs dropped their butts onto the carpet on each side of her. "What do you want to know?" he asked.

"What do I want to—" She took a deep breath and counted to ten. Otherwise, she'd bash him in the head with the candelabra. "That horn? The bagpiper? Any of this ring a bell? Because it damned sure appeared to ring a bell with you and your brother when it was happening. You two spoke more with looks and head twitching in the last hour than I've seen you actually speak to each other the entire time I've been here."

"Oh really? And what did we say with these looks and, what did you call it, head twitching?" Knox folded his arms across his chest.

"'Oh shit' and 'don't say anything.' That was the gist of the conversation. You two have heard and seen all of this before, and I want to know when and why, to start."

"I should think a woman like you would have figured it all out by now. The entire thing was a prank, probably put in motion to celebrate the arrival of your Mr. Wentworth. You are the exception, but most Americans tend to bring out the pranksters in the Highlands. Some of the servants decided to put on a show of ghosties and beasties for your director friend. He's been asking about ghosts and other nonsense since he got here."

She raised the candelabra to get a good look at his face and to give him a good look at hers. "You just don't like him."

"Do you?"

"What?" An interesting idea niggled.

"Like him?"

Knox Innes was jealous of Erik Wentworth. Eleanor bit back a smile. Until she realized he still hadn't answered her question about tonight's events.

"Oh, for fuck's sake. Do you really think anyone who works for you would pull this sort of prank?"

"Excuse me? Have you *met* Robbie and Dougal?"

Eleanor had to laugh. "Point taken." She patted her leg. The dogs lurched upright to follow her and Knox to the stairs. "It wasn't a prank all those years ago when you and Lachlan were children." She didn't look at him, but she did loop her free arm through his as they ascended the stairs.

"No, it was not."

"What happened that night?"

"The same as tonight. The horn sounded. The piper played. There was a violent storm. That was the first time Elsbeth actually spoke to me. I was about seven years old. Lachlan must have been three."

They reached the second floor and continued forward.

"She protected you from the storm." Eleanor didn't understand how she knew, but she knew.

"Yes. She did. Then five years later, she cost me everything. Or at least my silly obsession with her did. There is no ghost, Eleanor." They stopped in front of her room. "Just an all too human man forced to take on a title he never wanted, doing a job for which there is no training." He held her gaze as he lifted the latch and opened the door to her little sitting room.

"I see," she said.

"I hate it when you say that." He heaved an exaggerated sigh.

"Why?"

"Because you do. See, that is. Far more than I want you to see, dammit."

"Poor you." Eleanor stepped past him inside the room, halted, then patted him on the chest. "You'll get used to it."

"That's what I'm afraid of."

He bent and kissed her, a slow gentle kiss that curled her toes in her Regency slippers. When he raised his head, his eyes shifted over her shoulder to the giant glass case lit by a huge electric heat lamp where her python, Persephone, no doubt peered back at him. He shuddered.

He kissed Eleanor again, then looked up and down the hall. "To be continued?"

She pushed up on her toes and nipped his chin. "Maybe." She slid her hand beneath his kilt and wrapped her fingers around his rock-hard cock. "Just as soon as you tell me what this all has to do with the Innes Witch, and what you're so afraid of." She kept her hand on him, shoved him into the corridor, and slammed the door in his face.

Chapter Fourteen

ROSEMOUNT'S BUTLER, ABERCROMBIE, STOOD JUST INSIDE THE study door, his lips pursed and his face such a mask of disdain, Knox choked back a laugh. He dared not look at McGinty sprawled in the armchair in front of the desk, or he would—how did Arneaux put it—*lose his shit?* Even now, the old Scot coughed and cleared his throat repeatedly in obvious attempt to fight laugher.

"Are you certain Mr. Wentworth needs to see me?" Knox finally managed. He picked up some documents in order to avoid the vision of Abercrombie's put-upon expression. "Perhaps he means to see Miss Witherspoon."

"I suggested that, Your Grace." Abercrombie sniffed which sent McGinty into another fit worthy of an asthmatic on his last legs. "Apparently Miss Witherspoon informed him his request comes under the command of the duke. Yourself."

"Command?" Knox shook his head.

Of course, Eleanor said that. One more way to put him in his place, or at least in the place she intended to make certain he occupied, whether he liked it or not. Then again, when she'd wrapped her hand around his cock last night then shoved him out the door, Eleanor Witherspoon had only added to his confusion about his place in her life. And hers in his.

"Shall I tell him you're busy, Your Grace?" Abercrombie glanced at McGinty, then at Knox's paper-strewn desk.

Knox sighed. "Do you think it would matter, Abercrombie? He is American, after all."

"As you say, Your Grace." The butler inclined his head and stepped outside the study door. "His Grace will see you, Mr. Wentworth."

The American director, sporting sweatpants, a tie-dyed t-shirt, and bright green trainers, strode past un utterly unimpressed Abercrombie and approached Knox, his hand outstretched. Knox half rose, gave the man's hand a brief shake, and indicated the leather chair next to the one McGinty occupied. With his buzz-cut hair and golden tan, Erik Wentworth looked more like a surfer trying to recapture his glory days than he did the most acclaimed director in Hollywood. A title Eleanor had used again and again to persuade Knox to allow this entire Regency circus to land on his doorstep.

"I cannot think of anything to do with the Regency *experience* nor the film that Miss Witherspoon is not more than capable of handling for you, Mr. Wentworth." Knox indicated the various papers on his desk. "After last night's storm, McGinty and I have more than enough on our plates. Wind damage to the distillery. Trees down in several pastures. Damage to several tenants' homes." He paused and waited for the director to respond.

"Don't you people have FEMA or something like that?"

"When it comes to this estate and a number of the surrounding villages, Rosemount *is* FEMA."

"Why?"

Knox took a short breath. McGinty beat him to the

punch. "Because His Grace owns most of the bloody county, including the villages." The old Scot rolled his eyes and added a derisive snort for good measure.

"That is neither here nor there." Knox had had enough. "What can I do for you? Make it quick. I'm sure you have a floor to damage or a field to blow up this morning."

"Fine." Wentworth leaned forward and planted his hands on Knox's desk. "A couple of my cameramen stayed here last night. They went outside and caught some really interesting footage of the storm, a weird-assed horn blaring from God knows where, a dude playing bagpipes on that fucked up tower, and a crack running down that impressive stained-glass window."

"What makes you think one thing has anything to do with the other?" Knox asked.

"Nice try, buddy. The footage is time-stamped. I want to use that footage in the film, but Eleanor says I need your permission."

Buddy? McGinty mouthed.

"I see." Knox, irrationally enough, wanted to punch the man in the face for the way he said Eleanor's name. "Don't you need a release from the piper to use him in your film?"

"Well, sure, but who the hell can tell who it is?" He pulled a small iPad from his pocket and placed it on the desk. A still image of the piper on the tower filled the screen. "That's the best shot we have of him. How many people around here play the bagpipes?"

"At least a dozen," McGinty said. "And those are the ones who play for weddings, parties, funerals, and such. This one" —he tapped the screen— "doesn't play in public."

"Doesn't play in public?" Wentworth shifted toward him. "What the hell do you call that?" He nodded at the image on the iPad. "Wait. You know who he is? Have you talked to him?"

"Not in several months." McGinty said, and caught Knox's gaze.

Knox shook his head ever so slightly.

"Then how do you know?" The reddening of his tan and the tone of his voice indicated Wentworth was well on his way to being pissed off.

Good. Knox was all too ready to join him.

"I know every piper in the county by the sound of his piping," McGinty said.

"Bullshit."

"If he says he knows, he knows." Knox scooped up the iPad and tossed it into Wentworth's lap.

"Speaking of weddings." Wentworth had apparently caught on to the fact he had gotten both Knox and McGinty's backs up. "I saw the video your people shot of the last wedding here. Its big news in the States—American stuntman marries British viscount. I don't suppose you'd let me use that to promote—"

"That was a wedding between two men who took a long journey to be able to marry. It isn't a bit of entertainment. Is there anything else, Mr. Wentworth?"

Knox had grown tired of playing the unflappable Scots duke. Knox Innes, architect and businessman, stood a better chance of dealing with someone who saw Scotland as nothing less than an amusement park with funny accents and bagpipes.

"I guess not." Wentworth blew out a noisy breath and pushed out of the armchair. "Since no one seems to want to tell me the name of the piper." He tried to give McGinty and intimidating glance. "You're the boss here. You could give me permission to use the footage my men shot last night in the film."

"You'll have to get a release from the piper. Contrary to what you Americans believe, a duke is not a king. Rosemount is not my fiefdom, and I don't rule over everyone on the estate."

"Could have fooled the shit out of me," Wentworth mumbled as he trudged out of the study.

When Abercrombie followed him into the hall and slammed the door behind them, Knox and McGinty exchanged grins.

McGinty slumped back into his chair. "He'll go to Miss Witherspoon."

"Aye, and if he does, I'll feed his arse to Mrs. Wallace," Knox replied.

"That should do it."

"Who is the piper, McGinty? And what the hell was he doing on the tower in the middle of a damned thunderstorm?"

"Robert Gordon's brother, Callum." McGinty shifted in his chair. "The one who went to war with yer brother and came back just as broken."

"Jesus." Knox ran a hand through his hair. "They live in one of the restored crofter's cottages, right?"

"Aye, up the high meadows. Robert works in the distillery. His brother manages a herd of coos and those cross-bred sheep. Produces some damned fine wool."

"When he isn't piping his head off on a ruined tower in a lightning storm." Knox studied McGinty's face. "Why was he up there? What was last night all about? And please don't give me some mince about the Innes Witch."

"Mince? So you havenae forgotten all your Gaelic."

"McGinty."

"I dinnae ken why young Callum was up there. And I dinnae think 'twas the witch last night. But ye may want to ask her about it." McGinty hefted himself out of the chair.

"Her?"

"Elsbeth Dunhomme."

"I am not going to ask an imaginary witch about something that has a perfectly reasonable explanation. Ask Robert Gordon about his brother."

"Aye, Yer Grace. Ye might want to ask that Mr. Cross what he's stirred up digging about in the west wing because something woke up last night." He rose and lumbered to the door. "And it dinnae wake up happy. By the by, what were ye doing last night when the horn sounded?"

"What was I doing?" Knox kept his expression neutral as a flush of heat crept up his neck. "What does that have to do with anything?" He blinked against the sudden flash of an image of him and Eleanor in an incendiary kiss. An interrupted kiss, dammit. "I wasn't doing anything."

"As ye say, Yer Grace. As ye say. I'll be telling ye this for nothing. What happened last night isnae over. Whatever ye were doing when that horn sounded, ye might not want to do it again." The old bastard laughed all the way down the corridor.

Do it again? Knox shoved out of his chair and paced from his desk to the fireplace and back. Hell, he'd dreamed of nothing else since she'd slammed that damned door in his face. He'd dreamed of nothing but a long and completely uninterrupted kiss followed by....

"You don't have time for this," he muttered.

What did he have time for? He dropped onto one of the ottomans in front of the hearth. From there, he had a perfect view of the large, framed photograph of him and Lachlan taken only a few years ago. He'd lived a lifetime in those few years. But so had Lachlan. He scrubbed his hands over his face.

What had Hadrian Cross discovered in the family archives? Lachlan had no idea what was in those cases upon cases of old records and diaries and other things. He gave little credence to superstition, but sometimes superstition had a way of becoming reality. Badly.

"Right." He stood and began to pace again. "I have a bunch of actors and movie-types playing dress-up twenty-four hours a day, who have suddenly expressed an interest in digging up the first Duke of Innes, my ancestor. I have some fool blasting an ancient horn, and another fool playing bagpipes in the middle of the worst storm we've had in years. I have a director who wants to catch every minute on film and turn my home into an episode of some ghost hunting show, and a housekeeper and butler who want him and his entire crew packed up and sent back to America on the first plane available."

Knox halted and sat in the massive chair behind his desk. "And I am ridiculously attracted to the woman who started this entire fiasco in the first place, a woman who works for me and is therefore off limits." He crossed his arms on his desk and lowered his head to rest on them. "What the actual fuck?" he groaned.

Someone knocked the study door.

"Go away! Please!"

The door opened and he didn't have to lift his head to know the intruder was Eleanor. She entered the room in a rustle of silk skirts and the scent of gardenias. She'd imprinted the sound of her step and her barely-there perfume onto his brain almost from the moment they met.

"We have a problem," she announced, and slapped her hand down on his desk quite close to his head.

"Take a number, Miss Witherspoon." He didn't raise his head.

She leaned over and whispered in his ear, "I've got your number, Knox Innes. And is it really necessary to address the woman who had her hand around your cock last night so formally?"

"It is, if she didn't do anything with said cock. Oww!" She'd smacked him on the back of the head. He sat up and rubbed the spot. "Fine. What problem would you like to add to my current ever-expanding list of problems for the day?"

She pinned him with those beautiful brown eyes and he forced himself to push the erotic ideas she provoked to some back corner of his brain. "Can you please tell me how you have managed to piss off Erik every single day since his arrival, including days the two of you haven't even seen each other?"

Erik?

Knox leaned back in his chair. "I have already seen him this morning."

"Yes, and you pissed him off. Why won't you allow him to at least speak to the piper about using the footage of last night? He said McGinty won't even give him the man's name? What harm can—"

"He went to war with Lachlan and came back just as bad. Should I subject him to your director's ghost hunting shite in addition to everything else he has suffered. He doesn't have a Lily Randolph to fight for him."

Eleanor settled into the chair Wentworth had vacated to go and carry tales to her. *Snitch.* "I'm sorry. Erik didn't tell me."

"He didn't know."

She threw up her hands. "You could have told him."

"Not my story to tell." At least not to Erik Wentworth. "Is there anything else?"

"Yes, but let me help you solve one of your problems."

"What?"

"Where's this list of yours? There has to be one thing I can help you settle. Try me."

She wore a pretty peach-colored Regency era gown with puffy short sleeves, a simple round neckline, and a ribbon in a darker shade of peach tied just beneath her full breasts. The color was perfect for her, flattering to her gorgeous bronze skin and curly light auburn hair that was piled up on top of her head in some elaborate hairstyle. He gave himself a mental shake. Her offer suddenly reached his brain.

"As a matter of fact…." He rose and opened a drawer on his desk then fished around and pulled out a very old iron ring of ancient keys. "There is one problem you can help me with." He came around the desk and glanced at her shoes—plain, brown ankle boots, but fairly sensible. "Come with me." He grabbed her hand and pulled her out of the chair and out the study door.

"Wait. Knox, where are we going?" She stumbled a few times, then fell into step with him.

Fortunately, they didn't run into anyone between his study and the front door. He waited until they had crossed the front lawn and walked up a narrow cobblestone lane out of sight of the manor before he told her way they were going.

"Before all hell broke loose last night," he said as he opened the gate near the top of the hill and directed her up a smaller stone-covered path toward the large ominous building at the hill's crest, "you and your Regency playmates were discussing digging up the first Duke of Turra."

"Well, when you put it like that." Eleanor stopped at the bottom of the wide steps that led into the Innes family mausoleum. In spite of last night's storm, the sun shone brightly and caught the various veins of color in the marble façade topped with the crest of the Dukes of Turra carved from one piece of black marble. "Why are we here?" She seldom allowed him to see her uncertain about anything, but she damned well didn't appear the serene lady she acted most of the time. Good.

"I'm going to introduce you to the first Duke of Turra. You can tell himself that you'd like to move him from the place he's rested for hundreds of years to entertain a bunch of American actors and writers." He held the keyring out to her.

"You're being a fucking asshole, Your Grace, and you know it. That is *not* what I am doing. There are very good reasons those so-called actors and writers were discussing the *possibility* of moving this man. You just weren't interested in listening."

He shook the keyring again. "Fine. I'll listen while you tell him all about it. Shall we?"

"Asshole," she muttered, and snatched the keys.

She took the steps, unlocked and opened the towering wrought-iron gates and heavy wooden medieval doors, then stormed inside before he reached the covered colonnade entrance.

Once inside, he remembered why he hadn't visited the mausoleum since he was a lad of twelve. Even now at thirty-two, he fought the instinct to turn and leave as fast as his legs could carry him. The chill that swept from the soles of his feet to the top of his head had nothing to do with the fact he'd chosen to wear a kilt today instead of trousers. Then he caught sight of Eleanor and shivered with a different chill.

She stood before the two massive tombs at the center of the room, two marble *tumbas* topped with marble effigies, one man and one woman lying as if asleep, and so life-like down to the last details of their seven-hundred-year-old clothing. He'd seen the sculpted monuments, studied them in his childhood. Now, he studied Eleanor bathed in the gorgeous sunlight streaming through the stained-glass windows at the far end of the mausoleum. He couldn't decide which she resembled most, an angel or some fae creature from Scotland's folklore. She reached out as if to touch the feet of the two effigies, then her hand back sharply.

Knox came to his senses and remembered the purpose of

this little pilgrimage. "Miss Eleanor Witherspoon allow me to introduce you to His Grace, Connor Angus Innes, Duke of Turra and Alice Tabitha Wallace Innes, his mother."

She turned, her brow furrowed, which made her nose scrunch up in the cutest way. "His mother? He is buried next to his mother?"

"Entombed beneath the floor, and yes, she had herself placed next to him, in charge him even after death." He walked around to the head of the two *tumbas*.

"Where's his wife? His second wife, the one you're descended from?" Eleanor glanced around and took in the entire mausoleum. Her eyes widened as she spotted the dozens of plaques set into the walls on each side from floor to ceiling. Each bore the name of the ancestor whose remains lay behind their respective plaque.

Knox pointed at the plaque in the middle of the wall closest to the duke. "She's in there. Died in childbirth. Her son was the second duke. His is the plaque just beneath her, but his wife lies next to him."

Eleanor crossed to the wall and touched the name of the first duchess. "She was only twenty years old. How sad." She traced the dates carved into the duke's monument with her forefinger. "He only lived ten years after she died. Who raised their son?"

"The *auld bitch* as McGinty calls her." Knox nodded toward the effigy of Alice Innes.

Eleanor gave a little laugh, then clapped a hand over her mouth.

"Go ahead and laugh. McGinty's right. She murdered Connor's only love, forced him to marry the daughter of the chief of the Gordon clan, and before her body was cold, tried to marry him off to some other clan chieftain's daughter. Connor filled the pockets of his coat with stones and walked into the loch."

Eleanor gasped. Her eyes filled with tears that clung to her long lashes, poised to fall. "He killed himself?"

"Yes. And left that little boy to be raised by a monster." Knox tried to keep the bitterness from his voice.

"He must have loved Elspeth very much. He must have—"

"Very romantic," Knox cut in, and, this time, couldn't keep the bitterness from his voice. "He loved her more than he loved his son. He left that boy to shoulder a legacy no man could possibly be prepared to take on. Nor any man that followed."

Eleanor wiped her eyes "You're angry at him." She walked around the mausoleum, touching a plaque here and a heavy brass candlestick and marble urn there. "Aren't you?"

"Angry? I never knew the man. He's been dead for a few years, you know."

"I wasn't talking about the duke." She came to stand next to him. "I was talking about Lachlan."

"Lachlan?" Where had that idea come from? He would never if he lived to be one hundred understand the workings of the feminine brain. "Don't be ridiculous."

She cocked her head and smiled that enigmatic patronizing smile of hers.

"Actually, I am angry with him at the present. He's allowed Hadrian to run tame through our family archives. He's the reason your director is playing Regency role play all over a wing of the house that is supposed to be closed, not to mention pissing off my staff. And, apparently, he's the head of the lets-dig-up-an-ancestor-for-sport brigade. So yes, I am angry with my brother."

He'd run out of breath and out of things to say, and still all she did was smile.

Then she put a hand on his arm and squeezed. "It's all right, you know. To be angry with him."

Knox clenched his fists and shrugged against a sudden

flood of indefinable emotion. He hadn't planned on her reaction to the mausoleum and the terrible stories of his ancestors.

"I brought you here to convince you to forget this idiotic notion of reuniting the duke with his lost love. Digging up the dead is not on your or Wentworth's schedule and it wasn't on the list of activities you gave me when you proposed this misadventure. Are you convinced? I'd rather not spend the entire day here surrounded by my dead relatives."

"Whatever you want, Your Grace." She ran her hand over the chest of the effigy of the duke. She reached to touch other effigy, but once more drew her hand back against her chest.

"Stop Your Gracing me. Its bloody annoying when we're alone." He took the keys from her and strode toward the gates. She followed, then waited next to him as he locked the doors and then the gates.

"I have to say the mausoleum is beautiful and very well kept," she said as they went down the steps and started down the path toward the lane. "Not a speck of dust anywhere. Who would worry about dust in a tomb?"

"Mrs. Wallace," they said at the same time.

Eleanor laughed and took his arm. "I wonder who she assigns to this job?"

"Probably the footman who has put her knickers in a twist the most that week."

"Knickers in a twist?" Eleanor hooted with laughter. "Knox Innes, you should be ashamed of yourself."

"I often am, Eleanor Witherspoon."

"Why?" She stopped and gazed up at him, her eyes deep brown pools of sincerity and concern so potent his chest hurt. "What have you done to be ashamed of?"

"We don't have that kind of time, and there are some things a gentleman never confesses." He hoped that last bit might make her at least smile and get her off the subject.

She shook her head. "Fine. Don't tell me. What is that? I don't remember seeing that before?" Eleanor pointed over his shoulder.

He turned and looked at where she pointed to the pineapple shaped folly on top of the next hill. "I don't know how you missed it. The folly has been here for several hundred years." Knox had avoided the folly nearly as much as he avoided the mausoleum, but for different reasons. "McGinty didn't show you when he gave you the grand tour?"

"It was freezing when I arrived, if you remember. He didn't bring me to the mausoleum either. Can we go inside the folly?"

"If you like."

They took the second path that split off for the lane and managed the steep climb to the folly, laughing and teasing each other with mountain goat references. The last stretch, Knox pulled her up to the folly steps. She laughed so hard she couldn't speak. Head thrown back, her face aglow, her beautiful smile took his breath away.

She released his hand and ran up the stairs to the folly's covered portico, which wrapped all the way around the structure. At intervals, there were floor to ceiling openings that had once been left open to the elements. At some point recently, one of the dukes had covered the openings with door-like shutters to protect the sculptures and furnishings within. Eleanor stood at the top of the stairs and waved toward the manor.

"Look at this view." Her eyes sparkled. "This is incredible. No wonder McGinty wanted to keep it a secret." She ran around the building and came back to Knox who grinned in spite of himself. "Can we go inside? Please tell me there are no more tombs or dead dukes and their mothers in there."

Knox fished in his sporran for the keys and unlocked the double doors into the folly. While Eleanor oohed and aahed over the Greek sculptures, Knox went to each set of shutters and flung them open to let the sunlight bathe the folly's interior with light and heat. As he opened the shutters at the far side of the circular room, he caught sight of the meadows stretching out endlessly to the mountains. The river that fed into the loch crossed his view like a silver ribbon across fields so green they hurt his eyes.

"Eleanor," he said softly.

She glided next to him and took his hand so swiftly and sweetly he closed his eyes against the emotional overload. The view. Her touch. His life to this point.

"Oh." She rested her head against his arm. "So beautiful. And you own all of this, Knox."

"Do I? More like Rosemount owns me."

Eleanor turned him to face her. She cupped his cheek in her hand. "Is it so terrible to be owned by a place? To be joined irrevocably to something you cannot even name?"

Knox grasped his hands on her waist and pulled her closer. "I've always believed so." He lowered his head and touched his lips to hers, first in a brush of a kiss and then more firmly as he savored the taste of her, tea and honey and Eleanor, always Eleanor. "Until now, I have hated the idea of belonging to anything…or anyone."

"I don't want to own you," she whispered as he trailed his lips down the side of her neck and nipped at the spot where her throat and collarbone met. She shivered, then drew her free hand up his thigh and gathered his kilt to slip her hand beneath the heavy tartan. "Just parts of you."

She wrapped her fingers around his cock and gave a slow stroke against which he had no choice but to hiss through his teeth and rest his forehead on her shoulder. She stroked again, and he groaned.

"You've owned that part of me since the day we met, damn you."

He sifted his hand through her tight curls, scattering hairpins on the stone floor, and cupped the back of her head as he raised his head and trapped her full mouth in a demanding kiss. She sucked his tongue into her mouth. He fumbled with the sleeves of her dress and tugged each one down her arms. When he reached around for the buttons down her back, he popped the first two off. They pinged across the floor and Eleanor reached beneath his kilt and pinched his arse.

Knox flinched and drew back from their kiss just enough to speak. "No?" He refused to do anything she didn't want him to do.

"Don't ruin the dress. Bella Stepford will kill us both." She seized his bottom lip in her teeth, tugged, then released him. She twisted her arms around and attacked the buttons.

"Can't have that." He slid to his knees. "Tell me, Eleanor, how authentically are you dressed today?"

He gathered the hem of her dress and raised the gathered fabric higher and higher as he kissed his way up her stockinged leg to the point where her garter was tied. No underwear. She was hot and wet and the scent drove him mad. He used the fingers of his free hand to part the tight curls between her legs and found her sex with his tongue.

"What are you—oh! Knox. Oh, damn!"

She arched into his seeking mouth and set up a rhythm with her hips that he followed, flicking, licking, and sucking as she gasped and moaned incoherently. He gripped her hip when she tried to escape his relentless savoring of her pussy. Her body shook and then locked. She cried out his name and still he refused to let up until her legs shook and she nearly collapsed. He rose slowly, licked his lips, and marveled at the electric sexual excitement that rammed through him. He kissed her and when he stopped, she dropped her head to his shoulder, panting softly.

"Beautiful," he murmured.

He cupped the breasts she'd freed from her dress and some sort of Regency undergarment. The undergarment, pulled down, did a great job of presenting her luscious body. He swirled his tongue around one rose-tinted brown nipple before he caught the tip gently in his teeth. Eleanor ran one hand through his hair as a moan sigh vibrated in her chest. He suckled her breast deep into his mouth. His cock throbbed with desire. She fumbled rather expertly at his traditional kilt, then grabbed his belt and yanked it free of its loops. Belt and kilt dropped to the floor and left him bare-assed and rock hard.

She framed his face in her hands and drew him forcefully away from her breast. "I want you. *Now.*"

Knox seared his lips to hers and maneuvered her over against the wall between two of the unshuttered openings. "Are you sure?" He rolled up her skirts more tightly and shoved them into one of her hands. He bent and swept up his kilt, then shoved it behind her head to cushion her against the hard wall. "I don't have anything with me to—"

"Implant." She threw her arms around his neck, then jumped up and locked her legs around him. "I'm safe if you are. Stop talking, Knox and fuck me."

"Aye, Miss Witherspoon."

He wound one arm around her so her arse rested on his forearm. He took his cock in his other hand and rubbed the head against her wet labia before he gave one swift thrust. "That I will. Bloody hell!"

She was tight and hot. He clasped her arse with both hands and angled her up so his cock brushed her clit with each stroke. She clasped his shoulder with one hand so fiercely her nails dug through his sweater and t-shirt. With her other hand she grabbed the back of his head. She tugged his hair to the point of pain until he raised his head for her to take his mouth in an open tongue-tangling kiss.

Knox shuddered against the fiery sensations that flashed through his body. Never in his life had he ever experience sex like this—wild, fierce, unthinking and passionately free. He didn't think. He only savored the feel of her lips on his, the crush of her breasts against his chest, the frantic pumping of her hips as her pussy clutched his cock and refused to let go. She ended their kiss with a sharp cry and threw back her head. Knox thrilled at the sounds she made, pleasure and joy in wordless sounds as she matched him stroke for stroke and tightened her legs around him.

"I can't," he gasped as he thrust faster and faster with no desire except to join with her. "I can't…slow down. I can't."

"Don't. Don't you dare. More, Knox, damn you. More!"

She clutched his back and lowered her head to bite his ear. Her hot breath drove him harder. Her body began to quake around him. For a moment he worried he'd hurt her as he pressed her into the wall with every stroke. With every groan and gasp she pushed his worries aside.

"God, yes!" she screamed. "Knox, yes!"

Her walls tightened around him in near pain. One thrust and then another and he shook from the soles of his feet to the top of his head.

"Fuck," he groaned as he tried to catch his breath with each slow thrust until he had milked more pleasure from his cock than he thought possible.

He rested his forehead on her shoulder. She stroked his hair, her own breath finally slowing. He marveled at the intimacy her touch evoked, more intimate in some ways than what they had just enjoyed.

"And I thought the storm last night was amazing," she said with a laugh. "You can put me down now, Knox. I think."

"No," he murmured, and kissed her cheek. "Don't want to."

He backed up, Eleanor still wrapped around him. She managed to lean down and snag his plaid. He reached one of the old fainting couches in the middle of the folly.

"Turn sideways. Let me spread this over that couch, unless you want your balls to rest on scratchy old brocade."

"No, thank you."

He tilted her toward the couch and she managed to lay one end of the plaid over the couch. He lowered them down onto the cushion and rolled so that they lay chest to chest, her draped on top of him. She reached across and pulled the plaid over them.

For this moment in time, Knox allowed a sense of peace and rightness to settled around him. He drew in her scent, gardenias, an earthy musk with a hint of fresh-baked bread and sex. She rested her cheek over his heart and the unique texture of her fiery hair caressed his chin. He relaxed completely with a long, deep sigh. The sun shone through the open shutters. The room was cool, but not cold and they were surrounded by the gorgeous light, sounds and warmth of a Highland June morning.

"Knox?"

"Hmm?" He closed his eyes and tightened his arms around her.

"You didn't really answer my question." She reached beneath his cable knit sweater and traced a fingernail around his nipple. "Although your diversionary tactic was... incredible."

"What question?"

"Do you resent Rosemount and your title because they own you or because of what they cost you?"

Damn! He should have known that moment of peace was too good to be true.

Chapter Fifteen

Knox stilled beneath her to the point she swore he wasn't breathing. Eleanor went from lying on a warm sculpted body to a hard piece of human marble in the space of one breath. She had a hit nerve. Hard. She had a gift for that—digging to close to the heart of someone's issues.

"Sorry," she said when he didn't answer. "Too many years studying psychology."

"You have a masters. I was surprised to discover you didn't major in hospitality. Or perhaps military command."

She pinched his nipple with her nails.

He flinched. "Oww."

"Military command, my ass," she said.

"A very nice arse it is too." He slid his hand under the plaid and cupped her butt cheek.

"My parents would have been horrified if I'd majored in hospitality. It was bad enough I majored in psychology."

"What did they want you to study?"

"Medicine. I was supposed to be a surgeon like my father. Got into Harvard Med School." She tried for an air of casual interest in a part of her life she still found painful.

Somehow, confessing to Knox, the pain didn't hurt as much.

"And?" He began to relax again and stroked her hair, offering comfort, but not condescension, or at least that's how she took it.

"I discovered I was too squeamish to cut into a human body."

"Good to know."

She had to laugh, and she did until she realized he'd distracted her again. Two could play at that game. "Did your parents want you to study architecture? Your degrees are in architectural design, aren't they?"

"My parents didn't give a damn what I studied so long as I studied it in England. How did you—"

"Same way you did," she interrupted. "I checked you out before I agreed to work for you. I assume you checked me out as well."

"I read your resumé, but I don't remember sending you a copy of mine."

"There's this thing called Google. And your name was all over the London papers. Especially after you sold your architectural firm to pay the death duties on Rosemount. Is that why you hate this place so much, Knox? Because of what the title and the estate have cost you?"

He stopped stroking her hair, though he still had a handful of her curls wrapped around his fingers. "I don't hate Rosemount. I simply never wanted to be the duke. I never wanted the responsibilities and the duties, but I had no choice in the matter. I try not to waste time resenting what I cannot change."

"How's that working for you?" She shifted her position so she could rest her chin on her folded hands and see his face.

"How is what working for me?" He frowned and looked genuinely confused, poor thing.

"Trying not to be resentful? Because from where I'm standing, you're having a tough time with that, with not resenting something…or someone."

His expression changed so quickly she swallowed a little gasp.

"Someone? What are you talking about, Eleanor? I don't resent you." He sat up and pulled her across his lap. "I might have when you first arrived, but I know you are trying to help. You're good at what you do. My male ego is a bit bruised that you are doing more to save Rosemount than I am, but I'll get over that."

"Eventually," they said together.

Eleanor laughed.

"I have no right to be resentful," he continued. "I gave up a company and a life I enjoyed. Lachlan gave up a great deal more because of Rosemount, because of our father, and being a part of our fucked-up family. If I had stayed, he would never have gone to war to escape. He should have been born first. He loves Rosemount. He would make a far better duke than I, if he…if things had been different."

"If he hadn't come home broken," Eleanor whispered. "If he had never gone or had not come back with PTSD you would still be in London living your life and he would be here with all of the responsibilities of being the duke. It's only human to resent your brother for that."

"I don't resent Lachlan, dammit." He picked her up and set her on the far end of the couch. With a quick jerk he pulled his plaid after him and strode to one of the openings in the folly. "I resent the title. Thank you for allowing me to say so. Being the Duke of Turra has cost me everything, and I think I have the right to be a wee bit resentful."

God, he was beautiful. Eleanor sighed and turned her attention to straightening her dress. "You do have that right. And you even have the right to feel a little guilty about leaving your brother here alone." She tucked herself back into her Regency stays, then looked up to find he had turned and was staring at her. "But you need to decide which one you resent more, the title for what it cost you, or Lachlan for what his not being able to cope cost you."

"We need to get back." He scooped up his kilt from the couch and tried to wrap it around himself, but his hands shook. His voice shook.

She knew she had no business talking to him like that. Perhaps she was wrong. She didn't want what had been a lovely morning to turn into a big mistake. Eleanor got up and walked to him.

"We both have work to do. And I—a—"

"Stop." She batted his hands away and wrapped his kilt around him like she'd been doing so all her life. She pulled him over to where the belt had fallen to the floor, then grabbed it and wrapped the leather around his waist, low on his hips. "Knox, I know you love your brother. He knows you love him, but he also knows you blame him for not being able to take on Rosemount. Talk to him." She grasped his hands. "McGinty says you two were as close as any two brothers he's ever known. You need Lachlan, even more than he needs you."

"I do need to talk to him," Knox snapped. "I need to find out why he feels the need to dig up the first duke and whatever else Hadrian Cross has dug up nosing through our family history."

"What are you so afraid of Hadrian finding?"

Knox pulled his hands free and checked his kilt. "You did a good job."

"Mrs. Wallace's sister showed me when she fitted Danny for his kilts." She adjusted his sporran. "I thought it might come in handy." She pulled the key out of his sporran and walked away to start closing the shutters they'd opened.

When she got to the last one, she paused and gazed out at the fields. "I could stare at this for hours."

She sighed and leaned against the open shutter. He walked up behind her and wrapped his arms around her.

"How can you not be as one with the land that has been yours since before you were born?" she asked.

"How can you be so much one with this land, and you were not born here?"

She laughed. "I honestly don't know."

"Join the club." He kissed the top of her head and took the keys from her. "As much as I would love to spend the rest of the day up here with you, we both have jobs to do."

"Perhaps another time?" She closed and locked the last shutter and joined him at the door.

"I'd like that."

She'd more than like that, she craved it. She craved more time with him, time in his arms, and even conversation with him about things he couldn't bring himself to say to anyone else. Even when her insight into those things pissed him off.

He locked the folly doors and gates behind them and they started down the path that led to the lane back to the manor. He clasped her hand and held tightly until they came in sight of the house.

"I don't want people to know," he said softly. he kissed the back of her hand and slowly let her go. "Whatever this is between us…I don't want them to know."

Her heart stuttered. Eleanor had made love to him with no expectations, only an inexplicable desire. Yet….

"Don't want everyone to know you're banging the help, Your Grace?" She smiled to the point her cheeks hurt.

"Don't joke." His eyes turned that flat blue grey color they turned when he was deadly serious. "I don't want anyone to treat you with anything less than the respect you deserve, especially those Hollywood types. People are cruel, Eleanor.

My family history proves that." They started down the lane once more. "I'd hate to have to throw your American director or some of his crew into the dungeons under the west wing."

She snorted. "You'd love that, and you know it. Are there dungeons under the west wing?"

"Absolutely. Lachlan and I used to play there when we were children. There are all sorts of tunnels down there. We loved to pop up from one of them and scare the hell out of the sheep or the gardeners."

They crossed the lawn, and the spray from the fountain drifted across her face as they drew closer to the front door of the manor.

"Did you ever see Elsbeth down there?"

He slowed one step the only indication he'd heard her. "No. Have you ever seen a ghost here, Eleanor? Really? Have you ever actually seen the Innes Witch?"

"Up close and in person? No."

"Ah. Then until you do, I suggest you stop listening to old legends, no matter how romantic they seem. Elsbeth Dunhomme is dead. She met a nasty end at the hands of the woman buried next to the man you and your friends want to dig up. But do come and see me should she introduce herself."

She wanted to slap the condescending grin off his handsome face. "Who are you trying to convince, Your Grace? You or me?" She pushed up on tiptoe up to kiss his cheek and whisper in his ear, "By the way, you have a magnificent ass, Knox Innes, and your cock's not bad either."

She pulled back, then clasped her hands behind her back and strolled up the steps and into the house. When she reached the top of the foyer stairs, she turned to find him standing inside the doors, looking as if he'd been hit over the head.

Once she reached her room and sat down on her bed, she knew how he felt. Her legs shook. Her body hummed like a tuning fork. She'd had some damned good sex in her life. A Regency miss she was not, but damn! Eleanor refused to think about what more there was to whatever was going on between her and Knox. That way lay a whole world of heartache. But he'd talked to her, answered her questions even when he didn't want to, and that had both shocked and touched her. She'd asked because she wanted to help, but who did she want to help more, Knox, Lachlan or herself?

A knock sounded at the door. "Are you there, Miss Witherspoon?"

"Yes, Bridie, come in."

Eleanor jumped up from the bed and checked her appearance in the framed mirror next to her dressing table. She didn't look like a woman who had just shagged a duke. She smiled. But she damned sure had and shagged him well.

"Mr. Cross sent you this note." Bridie crossed the room, a folded piece of paper, sealed with wax, no less, in hand. Hadrian had not really signed up for the Regency experience, but he was a good sport. "And Dougal says you best come to the west wing quick. Mrs. Wallace is at it with that Wentworth man again. Odds are ten to one she's going to take him down this time."

"Shit." Eleanor took the note and crammed it into her dress pocket. Knox had been right. They had jobs to do. She snatched a shawl from the foot of her bed. The west wing was cold in spite of it being June. "What has Erik done this time?"

FOR THE REST OF THE DAY AND MOST OF THE NEXT, ELEANOR settled the dispute between Erik and Mrs. Wallace, listened to every opinion and theory imaginable about the mysterious horn and bagpiper, made certain everyone was still adhering to Regency boot camp rules, while wondering when she and Knox might find the time to jump each other's bones again like sex-starved teenagers. To her delight, and even a little bit of shock, Knox had kissed her in his study and in various empty drawing rooms, and they'd stolen several memorable minutes in a linen closet. And like guilty teenagers, they'd been interrupted by threats of discovery, real and imagined, to the point where she began to wonder if there was some higher, or maybe lower, power at work. Or perhaps Knox regretted starting an affair with her that had no chance of going anywhere.

"Stop it," she muttered as she joined the boot camp holdovers in the drawing room the following evening for cards, tea, and gossip—not necessarily in that order.

"Stop what?" Hadrian asked as he followed her to the sitting area in front of the larger fireplace closest to the French doors leading onto the terrace.

"Nothing." She dropped into one of the overstuffed silk upholstered armchairs where Anna, Samantha, Lily, and Lachlan sat. She nodded assent when Anna offered to pour her a cup of tea from the service on the coffee table in front of the couch.

Eleanor picked up the saucer and cup, took a small sip, then and set the tea on the side table to her left. "How is your research going?"

"Funny you should ask." Hadrian cast a furtive look at the other end of the drawing room where Knox and Danny sat on either side of a marquetry card table deep in discussion.

"What are you up to?" Eleanor caught the look Hadrian exchanged with the others. "What are you *all* up to?"

"Nothing," Samantha replied. "But we need to hurry. I don't know how long Dante can keep the duke distracted."

"Distracted? Wait a minute. The last time you put your

heads together I ended up finding a portrait of a ghost who looks like me. What have you—"

"Did he explain why he didn't tell you about your resemblance to Elsbeth?" Lachlan asked.

"Not really." Eleanor shifted in her seat and hoped the heat that crept up her neck to her face didn't show. "I told him how I felt about it, but then Wentworth arrived and well…we had other things to talk about."

She took in their dubious expressions. That lame excuse didn't fool anyone. Still, she'd rather them ponder that than tell them that she and Knox had discovered their physical attraction. Which made her an idiot. But she'd worry about her idiocy later.

"Doesn't matter," Lily said. "Tell her what you've found, Hadrian, before Arneaux bores Knox to tears, and they both come over here."

"Play nice," Samantha chided. "My husband is many things, but never boring."

"Yes, but he's not going to bed with my brother-in-law."

The group erupted into laughter. Trust Lily Randolph, now Lady Lachlan, to have the last word.

"What have you found, Hadrian?" Eleanor asked. "We're already in trouble with His Grace for suggesting we dig up the first duke. He took me to the mausoleum yesterday. Digging up your ancestor won't be easy, Lachlan. Did you know he's buried next to his own mother and not next to his wife—the second one, not the one his mother murdered."

"I love how she says that as if having your mother murder your wife happens every day." Anna shook her head.

"What do you know about your ancestors, Eleanor?" Hadrian asked.

"Not much. My dad's family is from Jamaica. My mom's family is from Boston. Why?"

"Because, before she married the first duke, Elsbeth

Dunhomme was handfasted to a sailor from a little village not far from here. His name was Malcolm Witherspoon."

The room wavered back and forth for a minute. Eleanor blinked to bring her eyes back into focus.

"She gave birth to his son and then his daughter, before he died at sea, before she saved the duke after Bannockburn," Hadrian continued. "He was wounded and dying, and she was the local healer, very skilled from all accounts."

"Are you sure?" Eleanor asked, despite already knowing the answer. Hadrian Cross was nothing if not thorough.

"I now understand why the duke didn't want me poking around the records in the west wing library. The first duke's papers and diaries are there. It's obvious some sections have been removed, but the records of Elsbeth Dunhomme's family are there, even the ones that tell what happened to them after the duke's mother accused Elsbeth of witchcraft."

Eleanor picked up her tea, then realized her mistake when her hand shook. Carefully, she took a sip, then slowly replaced the cup on the saucer. "What happened to her family?"

"The old bitch had most of them rounded up and killed. There is supposedly an empty, burned-out village at the far edges of the estate," Hadrian replied. "The duke's mother wanted to erase Elsbeth's existence,"

"My family is nothing if not efficient in their cruelty," Lachlan muttered.

Lily clasped his hand.

"Tell them the rest," Anna urged her husband.

"According to the notes I found, the duke managed to get Elsbeth's son and daughter and a few cousins onto a ship and out of Scotland. He ordered the local priest to tell his mother they were among the dead after the village was razed to the ground. He sent them to Elsbeth's mother's family. In Jamaica."

"Damn," Lily said. "That explains a lot."

"I'd say so," Lachlan agreed. "Eleanor, on behalf of my family I'd—"

"Stop." Eleanor wanted to jump from her chair, but the duke chose that moment to glance at her and the rest of the group gathered around Hadrian Cross. "This doesn't mean anything. A bunch of dusty records buried in some library nobody uses have nothing to do with me."

"They weren't buried," Samantha said. "Were they, Hadrian? There's a reason the duke got his knickers in a twist when he found out Lachlan allowed you free reign in the family archives, isn't there?"

Hadrian shifted in his chair. "I doubt the duke wears knickers, especially under his kilt." Anna punched his arm. He smiled gently at her, then went on. "The records of what happened to Elsbeth's family were spread out on a table in the library. As if someone had been looking at them. I didn't have to dig to find them. Someone has been digging through a lot of those records. And some volumes of the first duke's journals are missing completely. Deliberately removed from the way the empty spots on the shelves look. Recently."

"What are you saying?" Eleanor knew. Of course she did, but she wanted someone other than herself to say the words out loud.

"My brother has been hiding more than Elsbeth's portrait from you, Eleanor," Lachlan said in a low voice.

Danny and the duke were rising from their chairs.

"You need to ask him what and why."

"I'd love to be around for *that* conversation," Lily said, and pasted a pleasant smile on her face.

Anna pressed something cold and metal into Eleanor's hand. Another key. *Shit!*

"I left everything out in the west wing library," Hadrian said in a low voice. "Go in the morning and don't forget to lock up after yourself." He raised his head and exchanged a nod with Danny. "Whether Lily is there to see that conversation or not, you need some ammo if you're going to take on the duke about his ancestors."

"What are we discussing so intently?" Knox asked as he and Danny joined them.

"Whist," Eleanor said as she slid the key into reticule on her wrist. "Are you two in or out. I am feeling extremely lucky tonight."

The others made quick work of leaving the seating area and moving to where the tables were arranged for Regency card games. Knox offered her his arm. She only hesitated a moment before she rested her hand on his wrist. The way he studied her told her he didn't believe her whist ruse. At the moment she didn't give a damn. This wasn't the way she'd planned for Knox Innes to keep her up all night.

❧

ONE ADVANTAGE TO DRESSING IN REGENCY CLOTHING WAS THE warmth provided by a full-length dress and wool stockings. Eleanor had a whole new appreciation for the style. She'd slipped into the west wing of Rosemount Manor just after dawn in hopes of avoiding detection by servants, movie people, or the occasional nosy duke who had the habit of showing up when she least expected him. Never in her bedroom, but a girl could dream. Once she slipped into the empty ancient wing of the house, she regretted the hour because the damned medieval hallways and high stone ceilings were cold as a winter's night even if they were well into the month of June.

"Now I know why all those ladies took shawls everywhere they went." She raised the candle lantern she'd brought from her bedroom and glanced up and down the wide hallway. "I should have paid closer attention when I was down here with Erik."

A flicker of white farther down the corridor to her left caught her eye. She headed in that direction. After what seemed like miles, she finally found the heavy wood and iron doors to the library and archives. She took a few minutes to heave one of the doors open and the long, loud creak of the hinges reminded her of something out of horror movie.

Lantern raised high, Eleanor crossed the stone floor to a series of heavy tables that ran down the middle of the room. The three in the middle had been organized, Hadrian's work, no doubt. The others were covered in dust, cobwebs, and haphazard stacks of books, papers, and scrolls. In the middle of one of the neater tables, where Hadrian said he'd placed his research on Elsbeth's family, was a huge blank space.

"Mother fu—" She placed her free hand on the heavily scarred wood table and in that same instant a bone-chilling wind blew through the room.

Eleanor turned in a circle. Where the hell had that come from? There were no windows, something about preserving the items stored there. The only doors were behind her. The wind had come from the far end of the room to her left. She lifted her lantern higher and started in that direction. Something tugged at the skirt of her dress. Suddenly, an even colder wind blew from behind her. The contents of the neatly arranged tables erupted in a cyclone of swirling parchment and falling books.

"This is so not funny."

Her lantern winked out. The hair on the back of her neck stood on end. The door hinges squealed behind her.

"What the—"

Eleanor dropped her lantern, hiked up her skirts, and lunged for the closing doors. The whistling wind became an eerie howl. She reached the doors, grabbed one door edge, and yanked. For an instant, she could have sworn someone else pulled while she yanked. Then the door gave way, and she stumbled backward, still gripping the door. Eleanor caught herself and staggered forward.

"Come," a voice whispered.

An unseen hand shoved between her shoulder blades, propelling her out into the corridor. The door slammed shut with a boom that bounced off the walls and hit her ears like a bomb. Eleanor swung to face the door, heart pounding, ears ringing. She'd fought to get those old hinges to open the door at a snail's pace. How the hell had those big doors slammed shut? She slowly backed away in the darkness. Next time, she'd make Hadrian and Anna come with her. Maybe she'd wait until Bas and Teddy got back from their honeymoon and bring them too.

"Bullshit," she muttered, and turned.

She didn't need muscle to read some old records in a scary wing of an ancient manor house. She just needed a better lantern, and a fucking map. Without her lantern, the hallway was as dark as her ex-boyfriend's heart. Eleanor felt her way along the wall until she reached a T. Thankfully, miniscule moonlight trickled in through small windows in both directions. But which way to go?

She turned left, but after walking what she estimated was ten minutes, realized that nothing looked familiar at all. There were no doors, just miles of stone walls with an occasional narrow slit of a window with iron bars between her and the thick glass. She backtracked and turned a corner. A black shadow appeared in front of the narrow window way down the hall. The temperature dropped along with her stomach.

"Eleanor." The quiet, distinctly feminine voice came from a staircase just behind her.

The shadow started toward her. Eleanor backed up to the

staircase leading down into darkness. By the time the dark figure got halfway down the hall, Eleanor carefully backed down one step, then two more.

"Eleanor, come."

"I'm going to kill them," Eleanor growled. "Every single one of them. Starting with Hadrian Cross." The hazy figure passed a window and the feeble moonlight streamed through the apparition. "Fuck it."

Eleanor turned and hurried down the slick stone stairs. She braced a hand on each side of the walls as the stairs they wound downward, round and round until she spilled out into a narrow stone corridor, with a—Damn fuckers. A torch flickered in an iron sconce halfway down the hallway.

"You shits," she muttered. "You rotten shits."

She wasn't losing her mind. Her Regency boot campers had played a nasty trick on her. They would soon discover payback was a bitch. She'd have them taking cold baths and using the chilled metal chamber pots before this was over.

Eleanor hated herself but couldn't halt her legs from half running to the sconce. She'd make them pay for that too. She lifted the torch from the sconce and turned to look back toward the stairs. A shiver ran through her. Nothing there. Nothing. When she looked forward again, she glimpsed a white shadow disappear around the corner at the end of the corridor.

"Hello?"

Eleanor half ran to catch up. She resisted the urge to glance over her shoulder. No way she'd give the pranksters the satisfaction of knowing they'd managed to frighten her. The damp and earthy smell and the now complete lack of light except for her torch told her she was somewhere beneath the manor. She had no idea if she was heading toward the old ruins or some other part of the estate or—she shivered—the dungeons Knox had told her where he and

Lachlan used to play. Every time the corridor turned, she glimpsed the lady in white. Did she really just think that? Worse, she was following this person with no idea where she was leading her.

All this time, even with nearly everyone in their little group having supposedly seen the Innes Witch, Eleanor didn't want to believe. Despite the portrait that looked so much like her, she refused to entertain the idea that there was a connection between her and the local legend. She'd come into the west wing to see the proof Hadrian had supposedly found, proof that was now gone. Someone was determined she take her quest for the truth no further. Was it Knox?

A loud rumble in the distance caused her to jump. "I have got to find a way out of here or they won't be digging me up to take me to some island. I'll be a pile of bones in a nice dress." She looked back but couldn't bring herself to face whatever had chased her down the narrow, slick stone stairs into what was basically an underground tunnel probably to the dungeons.

"Fine, I'll just—" Eleanor halted.

A mirror. Someone had hung a mirror at the end of the narrow corridor. She wasn't close enough to be reflected in the mirror, yet she stared at a shimmering reflection of herself. But the person in the mirror wasn't her. Not exactly. The eyes were greener, the hair more red. The dress white. Not to mention, this woman's expression was serene instead of scared shitless. Her own breathing marked the time, loud and harsh. Her entire body went cold. The woman was not close enough for her to touch, but she was close enough that Eleanor couldn't deny….

"Elsbeth?"

Another rumble rolled overhead. The woman in white blinked slowly, smiled, then drifted around the corner to the right. Eleanor turned, eased forward, and followed. The thunder-like noise grew in intensity as the corridor sloped upward. Eleanor walked faster, but the woman stayed well ahead of her.

After what seemed like forever, another heavy, medieval-looking door came into view up ahead. Eleanor stopped. The rumble had grown thunderous and sounded as if the source lay just beyond that door.

A shrill wail roared behind her, approaching fast. Eleanor's heart jumped into overdrive. She couldn't make herself look back. The ancient door scraped open several inches and light poured into the hallway. Eleanor dropped her torch and ran for the door.

A dark ghostly figure, nothing like the shimmering Elsbeth, rushed past her. The wail became a shriek. Eleanor reached the door, turned sideways and shimmied through faster than she thought possible. The last thing she saw as she looked back was the ghost of the Innes Witch disappear into a thick black darkness.

Eleanor faced forward and broke into a run. Stone walls ran along each side of her, and a cloudy sky hung over the thick hedges that topped the walls. She reached a steep flag-stone incline, slowed, then stopped and turned to look back. Set deep into the hillside stood the door from which she'd exited. The door that was now firmly shut. She took several backward steps and found that the outside wall of the wing she'd been exploring was barely visible from this distance.

Where had she come out?

How long had she been down there?

She picked up her skirts and raced up the rise. The sudden roar of voices filled the air. And the—was that the pounding of horses' hooves? A loud boom sounded just as she crested the hill. What the— Eleanor had come out in the middle of the Battle of Waterloo. The meadow below her was the one she and Erik had chosen to stage the battle scenes. Which meant she'd covered a couple of miles in those tunnels. She covered her ears against the noise of cannon fire, men shouting, horses galloping and God only knows what else.

Wait. She spotted Hadrian talking to Erik and someone in a kilt and white shirt. She hurried down the grassy slope ready to give Anna Chase's husband a piece of her mind. Oh hell, the guy in the kilt was giving Erik hell. And she'd recognize that plaid covered ass anywhere.

Suddenly, a dark wave of sound drowned out all the other noise. The sky went dark as the earth several feet in front of her erupted, then showered down on top of her. Several voices shouted, one in particular cut through the din.

"Eleanor!"

She had the sensation of earth and air picking her up and slamming her into the hillside. Then everything went black.

Chapter Sixteen

ELEANOR DISCOVERED ONE OF THE FEW ADVANTAGES TO working for the Duke of Turra was that when he skidded his Range Rover to a stop in front of the entrance of the local emergency room like a NASCAR driver making a pit stop, doctors, nurses, and a veritable army of medical personnel spilled out with a gurney. They had her stripped, strapped into a hospital gown, and on her way to x-ray before she could say a word. Now, an hour later, she sat in a wheelchair in a room she had no intention of occupying while arguing with a young Scot's doctor who kept deferring to a very dirty and pissed off duke.

Eleanor glanced at Lily for help, but she only shrugged and clasped Lachlan's hand.

Eleanor returned her attention to the doctor. "I'm going to ask you for the last time, Dr. McIntosh. Do I have any physical injuries that make it absolutely necessary that I stay here overnight?"

"Well, I...." He fiddled with the stethoscope around his neck and glanced at Knox.

"If you look at him one more time, I will beat you do

death that clipboard you're holding. The duke is not my husband, nor my father, nor my brother. He's my employer, nothing more."

Knox coughed.

She glared at him. "I have no concussion, no broken bones, no stitches, and barely any bruises. I want to go home and sleep in my own bed. Now!" She pushed out of the wheelchair. "Lily, find my fucking clothes."

Knox gave his sister-in-law a dark look, which she promptly ignored and retrieved the plastic bag at the foot of the bed, where the duke and the doctor had been trying to get Eleanor to lie down.

"Your clothes are filthy, girl," Lily said. "Lachlan, go get the plaid and the mac out of the Range Rover."

Lily didn't have to ask her husband twice. He left the room at a jog.

"Miss Witherspoon," Knox said, "I really think you should stay the night. You had half a meadow dumped on you and you were unconscious for—"

"Three minutes at most and it was nowhere near half a meadow. I had some dirt spray me in the face and a stray rock hit me in the head. That's it. I was awake by the time you and Erik dug me out, and the reason I know I was awake is because I could hear you two swearing at each other like a couple of drunk sailors. I want to go back to Rosemount. Now."

Lachlan strode back into the room, grinned at his brother, and handed the plaid and the raincoat to Eleanor. She took them, rose, and went behind the screen in the corner, where she did her best to wrap the plaid around herself like a sarong. She refused to listen to the discussion going on between Knox and the doctor and concentrated on slipping into the mackintosh, which she fastened up to her neck.

"Where are my shoes?" she asked as she emerged from behind the screen.

Lily began to dig through the plastic bag again.

Knox stepped closer. "Are you determined to ignore the doctor's recommendation and—"

"I want. To go. Home." Eleanor stood toe to toe with him and emphasized each phrase with a poke to his chest.

"Fine," he all but grunted from between gritted teeth. He scooped her up into his arms and headed for the door. "Lady Lachlan, bring her belongings and get the orders and medicines from the doctor."

"Don't order my wife—"

"Shut up, Lachlan, and get to the car."

Eleanor peered over Knox's shoulder to see Lachlan make a rude gesture at his brother's back before he turned to address the doctor.

"Put me down, Your Grace," Eleanor ordered. "I can walk."

"Not barefoot you can't. You're lucky you're not dead."

Eleanor wasn't about to bury her head in his chest to hide from the stares of the other patients and hospital staff as the Duke of Turra carried her down the hallway, so she nodded like a princess and smiled as if she were riding on a float in the Macy's Day parade.

They reached the Range Rover still parked just outside the ER doors and he settled her into the passenger seat. Apparently when a man was a duke he could park wherever the hell he pleased and not worry about getting towed. He climbed into the driver's seat and slammed his door so hard the vehicle rocked. Eleanor stared at him in disbelief. Knox reached across her to fasten her seatbelt.

Once he had the belt in place he raised his head to stare into her eyes. "You frightened me, Eleanor."

"I'm sorry," she murmured.

"Don't do it again." He settled back into his seat and started the car just as Lachlan and Lily climbed into the back seat and closed the door behind them.

By the time they were halfway back to Rosemount, Eleanor was ready to scream. No one had said a word. It was sometime after noon. The others had to be as hungry as she was, but no one mentioned food. She shifted in the seat and did her best not to give away the fact that her body had started to ache from the beating she had taken. She'd told Knox it was nothing, but she had to admit being slammed into the ground at a high speed was a little more than "nothing."

"Are you okay?" Lily asked as she leaned forward between the front seats.

"I'm fine really. Just a little sore." She mustered up a smile and pulled the mackintosh closer around her. "It's kind of funny, but—"

"There is nothing funny about it." Knox was practically growling. Not to mention speeding along the narrow roads toward Rosemount. "You could have been killed. What the hell were you doing there? What was Wentworth thinking allowing you to be there when—"

"Allowing?" Eleanor turned in her seat to face him. Her body flushed with heat. "Allowing? Erik Wentworth isn't my father either, *Your Grace*. In case you have forgotten, I run this lucrative little boot camp and film project. I will go wherever I need to go to make certain everything is running smoothly." She crossed her arms over her chest. When she glanced into the back seat, Lily and Lachlan sat on the edge of their seats with matching smirks on their faces. Damn them.

"I see." Knox lifted his phone from the center console, hit one button, and in a few seconds, he was quietly firing out what had to be orders in Gaelic.

Eleanor turned to Lachlan who waved his hands and leaned back in his seat as if to say *Don't drag me into this.* Lily elbowed him, but he refused to budge. The duke ended the conversation and dropped the phone back into the console. For the rest of the trip Eleanor wondered precisely what *I see* meant. Nothing good, she'd bet her month's salary on that. She really needed to stop spending so much time around Robbie and Dougal.

The moment they pulled in front of Rosemount Manor, the imposing front doors burst open and a crowd of servants and boot campers spilled out to surround the Range Rover. Lachlan and Lily got out on the side closest to the house. Knox exited the car and pulled Eleanor's door open before she even got her seatbelt off. He had her in his arms and had elbowed his way past the crowd into the foyer before she managed to protest.

"For God's sake, Knox, I can walk. Put me down." She wished she could take the words back because once he set her feet on the marble floor of the foyer, he made a beeline for Erik Wentworth who was coming down the stairs with half a dozen of his crew close behind

"What the bloody hell were you doing setting off an explosion with non-film people about? She could have been killed."

"I had no idea she was there. She came out of nowhere." Erik peered around Knox at Eleanor. Poor guy wasn't afraid of Knox. He just looked worried and genuinely concerned. "Shouldn't you be at the hospital? Are you sure you're okay?" He started toward her, but Knox grabbed his arm.

"We're not finished yet." The duke's voice sent chills down Eleanor's spine. The man was spoiling for a fight.

"I'm not discussing this with you," Erik snapped. "It was an accident. Accidents happen. She's not hurt. No one is hurt. Tomorrow I'll make sure the set is cleared before we—"

"There will be no more explosions or stunts done on my property until Mr. Salazar and Viscount Staines return from their wedding trip. You are fortunate I am allowing this project to continue at all."

"Allowing?" Erik's face had turned a nasty shade of red. In fact, they both looked like a couple of bulls facing off in the middle of a pasture, with Knox being the bigger bull in more ways than one. Wentworth blinked and glanced at Danny who had edged his way closer to Knox, probably to keep him from killing the director. "Mr. Salazar? Viscount Who?" Erik said.

"Bas and Teddy." Danny put his hand on the duke's arm, but when Knox glared at him, he raised that same hand in surrender and backed away.

"Look, Your Highness." Erik ran a hand through his hair. "I have a schedule to keep. If I can't keep that schedule, I will shut this fucker down and—"

"I don't give a flying fuck about your schedule." The duke glanced around. "Why is the entire household standing around in the foyer? Lily, take Miss Witherspoon upstairs and put her to bed."

"Now wait just a damned minute, Lord Asshole," Lily said.

All hell broke loose.

"I have a film to make, your lordship," Erik said. "I don't give a fuck what you say."

"Not until I say so," Knox replied. "I have allowed enough people to be hurt in my life. No more. You two." He pointed at Robbie and Dougal. "If I hear of a single bet about this, you'll lose your jobs."

The two young footmen began to splutter and stammer out replies.

"Look, Knox," Danny said.

"Everyone, calm down." This came from Samantha.

Sylvan Goode, the dance master, and Bella Stepford, the costume mistress, came to the top of the stairs from somewhere down the first-floor hallway. Several of the movie crew started in the front doors but stopped in their tracks.

Eleanor saw Robbie take the plastic bag from Lily and try to edge around the shouting crowd of people. Mrs. Wallace came to Eleanor's side and tried to steer her toward the stairs. Anna waved her over in that direction, all the while keeping an eye on Hadrian who was trying to get between Knox and Erik. Every time Eleanor opened her mouth or tried to get to Knox someone, several someones, interfered. Her head began to throb. The cacophony of pissed off voices echoed off the high ceiling of the foyer.

"*Gu leòr!*" The commanding voice boomed so loudly Eleanor thought she'd gone deaf for a minute.

The veritable pin dropping would have sounded like a gunshot in the silence that dropped over Rosemount's entrance hall. Knox. Knox stood there, arms crossed and barked out Gaelic orders in that same bombastic voice. Servants scrambled like something out of a cartoon. Sylvan and Bella began to back down the hallway. The movie crew fell over each other getting out of the house.

Mrs. Wallace tugged at Eleanor's arm. "Come along, lass. Please."

She dragged Eleanor up the steps but kept her eyes on the duke. Erik stood there like a deer in the headlights. Knox gave them all one last steely glare, a glare that softened when he caught her eye. He focused on her face for a moment, swallowed hard, then turned and slammed out of the house. Eleanor tried to go down the stairs after him, but the sturdy Scots housekeeper was more than a match for her at this point. The Regency boot campers followed Eleanor to her room in complete silence. Once Mrs. Wallace had her settled in bed and the servants left, Eleanor and her friends exhaled on one long noisy breath.

"Okay." Hadrian dropped into the chair next to Eleanor's bed. "What. The fuck. Was that?"

"That," Lachlan said, and kissed Lily's cheek, "was the Duke of Turra." He went to the door and opened it.

"He's always been the duke." Danny sat on the foot of Eleanor's bed and pulled Samantha into his lap.

"No." Lachlan looked over his shoulder at them. "He hasn't."

"What do you mean?" Eleanor asked, almost afraid of the answer.

"I'll let you know." He left the room and closed the door behind him.

For a few minutes they all sat there, contemplating what Lachlan had said. Eleanor glanced around and realized these people, Danny and Samantha, Hadrian and Anna, Lily and Lachlan, and even Teddy and Bas when they were there, had become something of a family. They cared about her. And as hard as he made it to do so, they cared about Knox.

She cared about Knox, far more than she ever dreamed possible. Something profound had happened to him today. Oh, she'd had one helluva day, no doubt about that. But for Knox...something had changed. A deep emotional level had shifted in him, and she didn't know if that was a good thing or a bad thing. She needed to think. She needed to talk to him.

"Eleanor?" Hadrian's voice startled her. Everyone was staring at her. Again. "I'm going to ask the question everyone is thinking," he finally said. "This morning you were in the west wing, in the archives, right?"

"Yes, but—"

"And you ended up coming out of an underground tunnel

and nearly got your ass blown up, right?" he cut in, and Anna shoved his shoulder.

"How did you know I—" Eleanor wished he'd sit closer. She'd do more than shove his shoulder.

"I saw where you came out right before the shit hit the fan. So…." he shifted forward in his chair. Everyone else leaned in as well. Eleanor was reminded of that stupid television commercial. "What happened to you in the west wing and how did you end up getting buried under a dirt pile?" he asked.

She clutched the old counterpane in her hands and sat up straighter against the pillows Mrs. Wallace had piled behind her back. Might as well dive right in. "I think I saw the ghost. And I think she tried to kill me."

🙘🙚

Knox looked up and realized he was completely alone in the stables. He'd allowed the *shush shush shush* of the curry brush over the old pony's coat to fill his mind to the point he'd shut out everything else. He didn't remember the walk from the manor. Nor did he remember grabbing the curry brush and some horse treats from the tack room before he let himself into Gaisgeach's stall. He paused in brushing the animal and held out his free hand which no longer shook with…whatever.

"More?" he murmured as he pushed Geechy's head away from his sporan. "Urquhart will have both of our hides if you colic from too many treats."

He continued to brush the pony and fought to rid his mind of the images of Eleanor flying backwards, collapsing under a barrage of dirt, lying in the hospital bed. He had no right to take her injuries personally, but he did. He'd catalogued every scratch, every bruise, every wince and vowed with each to pound Erik Wentworth into the ground. In fact, had he not left the house, he likely would have wrung the bastard's neck, film deal or no film deal.

But he'd looked at Eleanor. Big mistake. As much as he despised every aspect of her project to refill Rosemount's bank accounts, that was how much she loved every bit of the boot camp, the film production, and the entire idea of creating something successful and profitable her first time out as party planner…fine, as event coordinator, for the estate. She wanted desperately to make a success of the project that had nearly killed her. Because for some reason she wanted to stay, to stay and work at Rosemount, to make her home here.

"Why?" he muttered as he walked around to Geechy's other side and begn brushing even more vigorously. "She feels this place in her bones. I was born here, and I don't want to live here."

"Then don't."

Knox paused. The pony stamped his feet and snorted. "Don't be ridiculous," he said without turning around. No need to as he'd recognize Lachlan's voice anytime, anywhere. "Go back to the manor. Or better yet, take your wife and go back to your cottage."

"You can order the rest of them around, *Your Grace*, but don't try that shit on me." Lachlan walked into the stall and leaned back against the wall on the other side of Gaisgeach, one foot raised to prop against the heavy oak panel. He crossed his arms. "And stop ordering my wife around or I'll turn her loose on you and they'll never find your body."

Knox bit back a laugh. "Don't threaten me with a good time."

"The pony'll be bald if you keep at it like that."

"He's not complaining," Knox replied, but he stopped and placed the curry brush on a shelf behind him.

"He wouldn't, would he. No one complains about the Duke of Turra."

"Fuck you."

"You're not my type. What was that all about?" Lachlan fixed him with that unwavering, demanding gaze of his, the one he'd been using on Knox since they were children. The one that meant he wouldn't stop until he got what he wanted.

"What was what all about?"

"You can't shut down the film operations, Knox. We need the money, and Eleanor has worked too hard for you to—"

"She bloody well could have been killed. No job is worth that, and I won't have her added to my list of mistakes. I've already failed to keep…." He reached into his sporan and offered Geecy another treat. "I have enough to deal with at this point. When Mr. Salazar returns they can go back to shooting the film." He glanced up at his brother. "Perhaps you should take McGinty and some of the lads to the upper meadows for a few days. Check on the condition and supplies in the bothies."

Knox grabbed the water bucket from the hook in the stall and walked past his brother to the spigot just outside the stall door. He washed out the bucket and refilled it. The icy cold of the water over his hands settled the prickles of heat dancing along his nerves. He hadn't had this long a conversation with his brother in a very long time. The scents of the stables, hay, oats, horses, even horse dung, they all proved a brief distraction to Knox. A distraction he sorely needed. He didn't want to fight with Lachlan and break this fragile truce between them. However, he didn't want to discuss Eleanor or being the duke or the damned film people either.

"Perhaps you should return to London," Lachlan said.

Knox had to try twice to hang the water bucket on the hook in the pony's stall. He stole a short breath before he retrieved the curry brush and began brushing Gaisgeach on the other side, which put the short, fat equine between them.

"And leave Erik Wentworth and Eleanor to manage all of this? Talk about a recipe for disaster. Mrs. Wallace would kill one or both of them within a week. I can't leave that *and* the running of the estate on McGinty." He snorted. "Besides, I don't have the time for a holiday." He concentrated on the rhythm of the brushstrokes across the horse's broad back.

"I'm not talking about a holiday. Just leave. Go back to London and let me take over."

Knox paused for a beat, then went back to brushing. "Don't be ridiculous."

"Why not? What's ridiculous about it?"

"First of all, your wife would have yet another reason to kill me in my sleep. And she knows where I sleep."

"She doesn't need another reason. She has a list. Trust me, if she decides to kill you, she'll want you wide awake."

Knox grinned in spite of himself. "And yet, you married her."

"Yes, I did."

"My point exactly. You're married now. Her life is in California or on a movie set. Not here."

"Can you see me in California?"

"Yes. You should...put all of this behind you." Knox rubbed his sternum with his free hand. He said the words, but the idea of perhaps never seeing his brother again....

"This?"

"Our childhood. The wars. All of it."

"You're the one who hates it here, not me."

"I don't hate it. I can't leave. I have responsibilities."

"But I'm not one of them, Knox. Not anymore. I won't be the reason for your guilt."

"You have never been—"

"Bullshit, to quote my wife. You're threatening to shut

down the film may be about Eleanor now, but you've wanted to since the day you found out about the battle scenes."

Knox turned and slammed the curry brush onto the shelf. "I'm trying to protect you," he shouted far louder than intended. "Jesus, Lachlan, you were catatonic when you got home from Afghanistan."

Geechy bumped him with his nose. Knox scrathed the pony's ears and forehead absently and took a deep breath.

"I'm better now. I can handle it, and what I can't handle, Lily can. And I'm seeing a therapist, one who specializes in PTSD."

Knox nodded. Thank God for that small favor. "You shouldn't have to 'handle it', not here. You served your time here after they sent me away. Rosemount has enough bad memories as it is without creating new ones."

"Those bad memories are yours too. Father's cruelty. Mother's indifference. The punishments in the West Wing. The fights between them. Your memories are just as bad as mine. And none of what I went through was your fault. None of it. You did the best you could."

"I have to stay here. You don't."

"I want to stay here. You don't."

"My life has been full of things I didn't have to do but have done anyway. Staying here is the least of them."

Lachlan tilted his head and stared at Knox for a full minute. Knox saw the moment what he'd said became a huge mistake, a mistake that gave his younger brother a look into a place in Knox's head he didn't want anyone to go.

"Things, like keeping everyone out of the west wing? Making sure Hadrian Cross doesn't dig up all of the family's dirty secrets? Denying the existence of the Innes Witch when we both know she is as real to you as Eleanor Witherspoon?"

Knox scoffed. "You of all people shouldn't want anyone to get lost in the west wing."

"I got over it. Haven't you?"

"Of course I have. Do you want someone digging into our family's ancient secrets? Digging up the bloody first duke, for Christ's sake?"

Lachlan shrugged. "Those secrets have nothing to do with us. And as for the duke? I think it is about time he was allowed to be with Elsbeth."

"The first duke is dead. So is Elsbeth." Knox ran his hands through his hair and began to pace back and forth across the stall.

"Maybe. But you're not dead. Its about time you started living your own life and stopped living under the shadow of our fucking father."

"I am living my own life. I'm the Duke of Turra. That *is* my life."

"Is it?"

Knox really wanted to wipe that smug expression off his brother's face. And he would if he wasn't so glad to see Lachlan fighting back.

"Does this little intervention have a purpose or did you just come out here to harass me for ordering your wife about? Or did McGinty send you out here to chastise me for frightening the servants just now? I swear I—"

"You didn't frighten the servants, Your Grace. You impressed them. You might want to try it more often." Lachlan pushed off the wall and walked out of the stall.

Knox strode to the door and shouted after his brother. "What the hell is that supposed to mean?"

Lachlan turned, but didn't come back up the wide stable corridor between the various stalls and loose boxes. "You've just been going through the motions, Knox. There is more to this duke business that keeping the bills paid. The people here need a real duke, especially now. In case you haven't noticed, some seriously spooky shit is going on at Rosemount. We need you to commit, to *be* the Duke of Turra, and listen to the people who live and work here. Something is going on, and they expect you to handle it. Up until today, I don't think they thought you had it in you. I've always known better, and now so do they. Wake the fuck up, about Rosemount, about what the people here need, and about who you are." He threw up his hands and walked to the stable door.

"Lachlan."

His brother stopped, but didn't turn around.

"I am sorry. For not coming back. And I am *trying*."

Lachlan looked over his shoulder at him. "You're a good brother, Knox. Too good sometimes. Try being a good duke." He grinned. "And while you're at it, wake up about Eleanor Witherspoon before its too late."

Chapter Seventeen

KNOX MANAGED TO AVOID NEARLY EVERYONE FOR THE REST OF the day. Which was fortunate for the American director because he still wanted to punch the bastard for putting Eleanor in danger.

Eleanor.

He was still trying to wrap his head around his brother's last cryptic order at the end of their conversation in the stables. Oh, he knew what Lachlan meant by the remark. He just wasn't too certain about how *he* felt about it. Having flashes of his and Eleanor's passionate encounter in the folly didn't help. He'd gone to bed with his fair share of women in London. Why wouldn't he? He ran a successful architecture firm. Even in the twenty-first century women seemed to be attracted to someone with an aristocratic title. And money.

Why? He had no fucking clue. Certainly hadn't done a thing for his father. The man had died separated from his wife, estranged from his sons, and surrounded by mistresses who left the minute the money ran out. Knox had no interest in any of that. No wife. No children. And definitely no mistresses.

One thing he'd write down in Robbie's betting book as a sure thing. Eleanor Witherspoon would never agree to be any man's mistress. Ever. Lover on her terms? Yes. Mistress on his terms? Hell, no.

He raised his head at the sharp rap at his study door. Without waiting for his response Mrs. Gordon, Rosemount's cook, opened the door and peered around the heavy oak slab.

Knox took one last swig of his now cold cup of tea and added it to the tray of dishes on his desk. "You didn't have to come for this yourself, Mrs. Gordon. I could have called one of the footmen."

She bustled across the floor and set to restacking the various plates, cups, and saucers on the tray. He wasn't fooled for a minute. She was checking to make sure he had eaten what she considered enough of the feast she'd sent up after he'd slipped into the kitchens and asked her to send his supper up to his study. He hadn't been specific because when he walked into the kitchens the busy hive of activity had suddenly become as quiet as a tomb. He sensed their staring eyes on him all the way up the back staircase he'd climbed to reach his safe haven without encountering Regency boot-campers, movie personnel, servants, or anyone else for that matter.

"Most of the lads are down the pub with those film folk, shooting darts. I've been carrying trays up and down these stairs since before any of you were born." She lifted the tray and gazed at him for a moment. Her grim expression softened. "Did you have enough to eat, lad?" Suddenly he was ten years old and sneaking down to the kitchens after his father sent him to bed without supper.

He stood, came around his desk, and bent down to kiss her cheek. "I did, Mrs. G. Thank you."

She sniffed and her eyes looked suspiciously bright.

"There's a good lad. Its late. You'd best get some rest if you intend to take on that American lout in the morning."

Knox laughed. "Robbie and Dougal?"

"Oh, aye. I've a fiver on you knocking the man on his arse by tea time." She curtsied. "Good night, Your Grace."

"Good night, Mrs. G."

She fairly beamed at his use of his childhood name for her as she waddled out the door and down the corridor.

Knox glanced around the room and rubbed his eyes. He hadn't bothered to check the time, but he suspected it was at least eleven o'clock, if not later. He'd heard Eleanor's loyal subjects come up the stairs from the first floor as the grandfather clock in the corridor chimed the half hour. They seldom quit their card games and other Regency activities before ten. Perhaps Mrs. Gordon was right. A good night's rest might do him good. He turned out the lights and headed toward the third-floor.

When he turned down the corridor that led to his bedchamber, Tannus and Beira, who had been lying outside the closed doors at the end of the corridor, leapt to their feet and stretched. He had nearly reached them when he turned back and followed the line of closed doors until he saw the door into Eleanor's room. Light shone from under the door which surprised him. She and the other boot camp participants didn't have electricity in their rooms. They used oil lamps, candles and firelights. Well, except for the elaborate heat lamps and uv lights that shone on the glass enclosure where Eleanor's huge pet python was housed. The damned thing even had a name—Persephone, of all things.

He stood there for a moment, debating what to do. He hadn't checked on her since they'd returned from the hospital. And he hadn't asked Mrs. Gordon or anyone else how sje was doing, though it had been torture not to do so. He took a deep breath, signaled the dogs to lie back down and walked quietly back down the corridor to her door. He glanced around to make certain there was no light under any of the other doors. The Regency boot campers were worse gossips than the village women at the church fete. He knocked lightly on Eleanor's door.

"Come in."

At least her voice sounded strong. He lifted the latch, slid in the door and closed it behind him. For a moment he simply stood there with his back against the door. The room was lit by a low fire in the hearth and oil lamps on the bedside tables on either side of the huge four poster bed. He blinked a few times to accustom his vision to the lighting. Which might have been a mistake. A big mistake.

Eleanor sat propped up in bed with the covers pulled up to her waist and her glorious fiery hair spilling down over her shoulders like a spiralled waterfall across the pristine white of her old-fashioned nightgown. She looked like the heroine of some romance novel. A hot heroine. She put down the book she was reading and smiled. His heart did a little flip in his chest. What a silly thought.

"I came by to see how you're doing." he said, his voice husky and dry. He cleared his throat. "Shouldn't you be asleep?"

"Shouldn't you?" She waggled her eyebrows.

He snorted and strolled over to sit in the chair at her bedside. "I've been sleeping most of the afternoon. I'm wide awake now. Are you okay?"

"Me? I didn't have a lorry load of good Highland soil dumped on me at high speed. Why wouldn't I be okay?"

"That little scene downstairs when we got back from the hospital? Ring a bell?" She was cute when she was smug.

"Hmm." He tapped his chin. "I have a vague memory of dressing down the man who nearly got you killed. What of it?"

"Dressing down? You cussed him out, then screamed at everyone else in Gaelic. Robbie and Dougal were still shaking when they brought my supper up this evening."

"Of course they were shaking." He gestured to the floor to ceiling glass case across the room, the only spot lit by electric lights. "They had to deliver your supper and worry about becoming supper for your giant orange pet." As if on cue, the snake lifted her head and stared right at Knox.

"Please." She rolled her eyes. "You frightened the servants. And everyone else within hearing distance."

"According to Lachlan, I impressed them."

"You talked to Lachlan?" She sat up, far too interested for his liking.

"More like he talked to me. That wife of his is a bad influence on him."

"Lily is a bad influence on everyone."

"You'll get no argument from me on that. What has she influenced you to do?"

"Oh, nothing much." Eleanor picked at the heavy comforter. "Perhaps climbing to the top of the tower and discovering a seven hundred year old portrait of a woman who could be my twin?" She gave him a sweet, utterly insincere smile.

"Why am I not surprised that my sister-in-law instigated that little foray into my family history? How about today's episode. Is she the one who sent you into the dungeons of the west wing?"

"Dungeons?"

"The place where you came out can only be reached by the stairs down into the dungeons. Though how you found those stairs and unlocked the door is a question for another day. Did Lily send you wandering about the west wing or did it have something to do with the film?"

"Actually Hadrian sent me down there. He found some

information about Elsbeth Dunhomme's family that he thought I needed to see."

"That *he* thought you needed to see?" Knox fought not to show the anger and fear boiling up in him.

"Yes, but apparently someone thought I didn't need to see it. When I let myself into the archives most of the articles he'd left out for me were gone. You wouldn't know anything about that, would you, Your Grace?" She pursed her lips. The gold flecks in her brown eyes sparked.

"If you were in the archives, how did you end up downstairs?"

She narrowed her eyes. "You're not going to answer my question are you?"

"No, I did not have anything to do with that. Are you going to answer my question?" This entire conversation would be easier if he wasn't hard as a rock and trying desperately not to crawl into bed with her. Who knew a plain white nightgown could be so bloody sexy?

She rubbed her arms and shuddered. The glow of her golden brown skin faded and her eyes grew large and bright.

"Eleanor?" Knox stood, toed off his shoes and crawled on top of the covers next to her. He put his arm around her shoulders and pulled her close. "What is it? What happened?"

She put her palm over his heart. He soaked in the up and down motion of her breathing against him. She remained silent so long he didn't believe she'd speak at all.

"You won't believe me," she finally said.

She shook her head and fiery golden red curls brushed against his chin. He nearly laughed at the irony of him not believing her.

He used his free hand to tilt her head up so he could look into her eyes. "I promise, whatever you tell me, I will believe you experienced it. Will that do?"

She pretended to bite his finger, and he drew his hand back in mock horror. They grinned at each other.

"You're a cagey one, Your Grace."

"Comes with the territory. Now tell me. Start at the beginning. Why did you go slinking off into the west wing at the crack of dawn and what happened that caused you to flee into the middle of the Battle of Waterloo?"

"It was not the crack of dawn. I was there to look over what Hadrian found out about the possible connection between my family and yours, but someone else got there first and removed some of the records. Oh, and I saw the Innes Witch." She looked up at him expectantly.

"You *did* have a full morning. And you're certain the person you saw was Elsbeth Dunhomme?" He removed all skepticism from his voice so as not to provoke her back into silence or, worse, have her dump him onto the floor.

"The shimmery, spirit I saw? Yes. She's rather easy to recognize, as I look just like her. Remember?"

He cleared his throat, but didn't say anything.

"But there was…something else there in the archives. And then in the tunnel at the bottom of the stairs."

She shivered and he wrapped his other arm around her. She didn't fight him at all, and he detected a tremor in her delicate form. This was no joke. Eleanor Witherspoon, the indomitable boot camp general, was spooked. He cringed. Not a good choice of word.

"What do you mean "something else"? What was it?"

"I don't know, but it didn't want me poking around the archives. It chased me out and came after me. No matter where I ran, it was behind me. Would have caught me, too, if not for the Witch."

"Her name is…was Elsbeth. And what do you mean 'it chased you'? What was it?"

"I don't know. When I tried to look at it, all I saw was this sort of blackness opening up in front of me. It was cold and gave me the creeps. It didn't have eyes, but it was watching me. *Elsbeth* dragged me out of the library, but it followed me. Then when I ran down the tunnel, it almost caught me, but Elsbeth pushed me out the door."

"Into an explosion." Knox's head began to spin with all of the information she was throwing at him. Information he didn't want to hear.

"Given the choice between the explosion and whatever was down in that tunnel, I'll take the explosion."

He did a careful study of her face. She truly believed what she was saying. What the hell did that mean? Eleanor was no silly girl in search of proof of some ghost story she read online. She was infinitely sensible. Except for her obsession with all things Jane Austeny and the damned snake.

"What do you think this black cloudy thing was?"

"I don't know, but I've only felt that sensation one time before." She slipped her arm behind his back and wiggled her way even closer into his arms. "The night of the storm. When that horn blew and the piper was out on the tower. Something was out there." Her voice shook. She took a deep breath. "Something was out there and that piper drove whatever it was away."

"So, your phantom is not fond of bagpipes. Good to know."

She drew back and shoved at him. He grabbed the headboard to keep from landing on his arse on the rug-covered hard wooden floor.

"I told you, you wouldn't believe me. Fuck you, Knox. Just get out." The only thing hotter than Eleanor in an old fashioned nightgown was Eleanor in an old-fashioned nightgown and mad as hell.

He wrapped his arms around her and settled them back against the mound of pillows piled up against the headboard.

"I wasn't making fun, Eleanor. Whatever is going on here has you truly frightened. I get that. I really do. But having grown up here, I can tell you that, between the ancientness of the west wing and all of the local legends being stirred up by this film production, it's little wonder everyone's imaginations are working overtime. Not to mention you are constantly on the go, don't eat enough, and get hardly any sleep."

"And how do you know all that?" She looked up at him, eyes narrowed.

"Because I've been watching you since the moment I met you. I can't help myself and its a bloody pain in the arse, if you must know. There. Satisfied?"

"Hmmm. Maybe. Please tell me this doesn't have to do with some weird childhood fascination with the Innes Witch. And before you go into your denial spiel, just don't."

"Denial spiel?"

"Yes. Your 'I am the Duke of Turra and I declare there is no such thing as the ghost of the Innes Witch and therefore she does not exist' spiel."

"We will have that discussion at another time. But no." He gazed down into her rich brown eyes and ran his thumb across her full bottom lip. "My fascination with you has nothing to do with my childhood, the Innes Witch, or anything else except you Eleanor Witherspoon." He gave a brief but determined kiss. "All you, all the time."

"I rather like the idea of being a pain in your arse."

"I'm sure you do. But listen. Please?"

"O…kay." She drew the word out in two long syllables of dubious intent.

"I don't know what happened to you this morning. I'm going to have McGinty and some of the men go into the west wing and check it out. Promise me you won't go back down there, at least not alone."

"You're not going to lock the whole thing down and keep everyone out, even Hadrian and the film crew?"

"It wouldn't do any good if I did. Your Regency boot campers are the most nefarious gang of snoops, lock pickers, and misadventurists I have ever met. And so long as the film crew is working in the west wing that means they aren't blowing up my meadows or detonating my housekeeper's temper. If I don't let them film down there, Erik Wentworth may end up in Mrs. Gordon's stew pot."

"Oh, and you would hate that."

"Of course I would. Do you have any idea the paperwork involved in explaining a dead American to a Scottish judge?"

She laughed.

"Promise me?"

She sighed. "I promise. *If* you promise to at least *consider* admitting what you know about Elsbeth and at least *consider* the possibility that there is something unexplainable going on here. Deal?"

"Deal." And because he couldn't resist, he brushed his lips across hers and then sank them both into a deep open-mouthed kiss that he wanted to go on forever. When they turned toward each other and she winced he reluctantly drew back. "You need to rest and I need to get out of here before we end up doing something against doctor's orders."

"Spoilsport."

He slid off the bed and began to look for his shoes. A sudden loud thump sounded from across the room.

"Persephone? What's the matter, sweetie?" Eleanor cooed.

Sweetie?

She tried to get out of bed.

Knox waved her back. "I'll check on her."

He strode to the huge glass cage with no idea exactly what he was supposed to be looking for. However, something was definitely off. The snake's head and a couple of feet of her length were raised up and she appeared to be looking at something in the area of the fireplace. She struck at the glass and Knox jumped. He glanced back at Eleanor.

"That's really weird. She never does that."

Almost as if the creature had heard her, the orange reptile sank back into a coiled position.

"Whatever it was she seems to be over it," he said.

"Probably a mouse or something."

"Don't say that where Mrs. Wallace can hear you." Knox walked back across the room and picked up his shoes. He made his way to the foot of the bed. "We have a lot to discuss, I think." Not that he really wanted to discuss anything with her. Eleanor Witherspoon was too damned intelligent and, even worse, too damned sensitive to what was going on his head, the one place he didn't want her to be.

"You have no idea." She gave him that frightening, not quite smile of hers.

"In the morning." He'd need at least that long to figure out how to deal with her curiosity. "Good night, Eleanor." He turned and headed for the door.

"Knox?"

When he looked back at her she suddenly looked very small and frail in that big bed. The glow of the bedside lamps lit up the fiery highlights of the tight spirals of her hair. She was as beautiful as ever, but her eyes held something he couldn't remember ever seeing in her expression. Fear.

"Can you stay? Can you stay with me tonight?" She opened and closed her hands around the edge of the thick quilted covers.

For a moment he had visions of himself sneaking out of her room at dawn. And being busted by one or more of the Regency boot campers. Then he looked at her face once more.

Damn!

He dropped his shoes. "Scooch over. And keep your hands to yourself. You're injured, and I won't be accused of molesting an injured woman."

She moved over to the middle of the bed and threw back the covers for him. He slid into the bed and rearranged the pillows so he could lie down. Eleanor snuggled close and rested her head on his shoulder.

"Better?" he asked even as every nerve in his body fired at once.

"Much. But I cannot promise not to molest you."

"Control yourself, woman. Threatening the life of a Hollywood director takes it out of man. Rest. Now."

"Yes, Your Grace. As you wish, Your Grace." She put her arm across his waist.

Knox snorted. "If only you were so obedient about everything. Ouch!"

"More Neaderthal talk like that and I'll pinch lower than your side next time."

"Sleep, please. You're keeping the poor snake awake." Knox looked at the snake and hoped like hell the thing couldn't get out of its cage.

Knox jerked awake. It took an instant to realize he was in Eleanor's room and not his own. Knox didn't know how long he'd slept. Eleanor's soft snores let him know he hadn't disturbed her. What had woken him? He looked at the snake. The bloody thing was undulating back and forth across the glass. Perhaps the snake had struck the glass again. It froze, as if something had caught its eye. Wait. Eleanor said snakes couldn't see well. They sensed heat. And the room had suddenly grown very, very cold.

He actually checked to make certain he was still under the covers. Check. And Eleanor's body was warm against his. He sat up slightly, still holding Eleanor close, and glanced around the room. The fire still glowed in the hearth, although it was pretty low. The oil lamps had been turned down, but they illuminated the bedside tables and an area around each one. However, in addition to the sudden cold, which seemed to come from the area across the room in the corner to the right of the fireplace, the room had grown unnaturally dark.

Knox blinked a few times and shook his head. Then he spotted the snake again. The damned thing seemed fixed on a spot across the room. In that same corner by the fireplace. The corner where a dark cloudy shape began to cover the walls and the door.

"This is ridiculous," he muttered. "Ghost stories and legends." He started to slide back down in the bed.

The darkness stretched toward the ceiling. The snake thumped against the glass. He looked down at Eleanor, still asleep in his arms.

"Fine," he said to the snake. "We'll both keep watch. You can't close your eyes anyway. But if you get out, don't crawl into bed with me. I'll turn you into a pair of boots."

He stayed awake staring at that corner until just before dawn. Which wasn't hard for him to do, as every hair on the back of his neck had decided to stand on end the entire time.

⚜

Eleanor decided the person who said injuries hurt worse the day after than the day of was an asshole. An accurate asshole, but an asshole nonetheless. It three tries to get out of bed. She'd managed to slip into her simplest Regency day gown, the one that buttoned up the front, but she didn't even attempt the undergarments and stockings. With luck she wouldn't find herself in a situation today where someone might discover she'd gone commando. Unless the discoverer happened to be the lord of the manor.

Down, girl. Don't let this situation get out of hand.

She'd woken up late, or at least later than she usually did. By the time she sat up on the side of the bed and checked the clock on the mantel it was past nine. Which was precisely when she realized that Knox wasn't in bed with her and must have left the room a while ago. His side of the bed was cold and his shoes were gone. She'd never known a man who made a room lonely simply by his absence. Mrs. Wallace had given her the largest room on the corridor, other than the duke's room, of course. Eleanor loved this room and had never been anything but comfortable and happy in it, until this morning. The sensation was unsettling to say the least.

The door swung open, and Lily marched into Eleanor's room without knocking, unless you counted the bang of the door against the antique paneling.

"Good, you're up. Bring it in, boys."

Eleanor straightened a little where she sat propped up on the bed as Robbie and Dougal entered, pushing a cart loaded with food and a huge tray with a tea pot and an array of porcelain teacups

"How are you feeling? Over here on the table in front of the fireplace." Lily waved them in that direction, and the two footmen made quick work of arranging everything in front of the fireplace.

"She's up." Danny sauntered in and sat on the oversized ottoman near the hearth.

"Did she have a choice?" Samantha crossed the antique carpeted floor and settled into the chair next to Danny's ottoman.

Eleanor threw up her hands as Lachlan, Anna, and Hadrian made themselves at home and began to fill the little plates they got from the rolling cart. Hadrian, Eleanor noticed, had brought a satchel with him and set it beside the seat he'd chosen. Lily gently pulled her to her feet and attempted to half support, half drag her to sit on the settee in front of the fireplace.

"I can walk, Lily. I'm perfectly fine." She limped over and sat down. "Was having breakfast in my room on the schedule for today?" She took the cup of tea Anna handed her.

"Actually, what was on the schedule for this morning was shooting more battle scenes." Danny snatched some bacon from Hadrian's plate. "But after the little scene in the foyer a little while ago, I don't see that happening anytime soon."

Eleanor started to get up only to have Lily shove her back into the chair and hand her a plate of food. "Eat," the arrogant actress ordered. "You're going to need your strength."

"What scene and why do I need strength?"

"The scene where my dear brother-in-law repeated his order to Erik that no filming of battle scenes or any other stunt or explosion scenes will be done until Teddy and Bas are back." Lily sat on the arm of Lachlan's chair and spoke between bites of a piece of toast slathered with Mrs. Gordon's blackberry jam. "He was scary as hell, actually."

"Knox? I mean, the duke?" If she wasn't already aching all over Eleanor would kick herself a that slip.

"Oh, yes," Samantha said as she filched the bacon from Danny's plate and gave it back to Hadrian. "According to Robbie, the yank stomped out of the manor, climbed into his jeep and is currently licking his wounds down the pub."

"He and Dougal cleaned up on that bet," Hadrian pulled pen and leatherbound journal from his satchel. "I lost ten pounds."

"You bet on that?" Eleanor took the toast corner Lily handed her, tore a piece off with her teeth, and washed it down with a swig of tea. Her delusions of controlling Regency boot camp with an iron hand had been blown to hell by a grumpy duke and a couple of enterprising footmen bookies.

Anna shrugged. "They also bet on how many days Mr. Wentworth will sit and sulk in that monstrosity of a trailer of his before he comes back to Rosemount. I put five pounds on five days."

"Anna!" Eleanor cried.

The authoress grinned, speared a large piece of sausage, and shoved it into her mouth.

Eleanor sighed and put her plate and cup onto the table. "Does anyone know where the duke is right now? I need to straighten this out before it becomes a full-blown disaster."

"That ship has sailed, lass," Lachlan said quietly. "Give the director some time and he'll come round. This is business and money for him. With Knox, its personal. Him coming round will take longer."

"Besides," Hadrian said, "we have questions for you, and some interesting information as well, courtesy of Bridie."

"Bridie? The maid?" Eleanor asked.

Samantha nodded. "The very same. She told me something very interesting this morning when she brought some of my dresses up from the laundry."

For a moment all conversation and eating stopped. Eleanor studied their faces. A whisper of cold air brushed across the back of her neck. So real, she reached back to wave it away.

"Does this have to do with what you found out about my possible connection to the Innes Witch?" She kept her words even and as unemotional as she was able.

"That and more," Hadrian said. "There is some strange shit going on at Rosemount Manor. I happen to think there's a logical explanation for it all. However, my fellow boot campers think differently. Whichever it is, I think we can figure it out if we put our heads and our past experiences together." He looked at Lachlan expectantly.

"The duke grew up here too." Eleanor noticed the tightening of Lily's features. The actress tried to appear tough as nails, but her love for the duke's brother had softened her. She obviously wasn't crazy about Lachlan spilling his guts in this little endeavor. "Shouldn't we include him in these discussions?"

"Not if we want to get anywhere," Danny said. "As far as His Grace is concerned, his life started the day he arrived at that hoity toity Brit boarding school."

"The school is called Eton." Samantha sounded so much like a snooty Oxford professor Eleanor nearly laughed.

"He's right." Lachlan glanced at this wife. She nodded and took his hand. "But Knox has every reason to want to erase his childhood. We both do."

Chapter Eighteen

ELEANOR HAD OFTEN WONDERED WHAT THE EXPERIENCE OF pieces of a puzzle falling into place might feel like. Actually, she'd always considered the entire idea a bit cheesy, a device writers and film makers used to explain something that never happened in real life. Until now. Listening to Lachlan tell them about his childhood, Knox's childhood, in that soft, nearly emotionless brogue, she imagined Knox as the older brother who bore the brunt of their father's rage and it was all she could do not to burst into tears. She glanced at Lily, Anna, and Samantha and gave thanks she wasn't alone, as their eyes also shone suspiciously bright.

Hadrian looked up from the pad he was scribbling on. "You mean to tell me he took you two into the west wing with no flashlights, no nothing in the middle of the night and locked you in?"

Eleanor wanted to hug Anna's husband for interrupting Lachlan's recitation. The more he spoke, the more horrific the story loomed in her mind. Two little boys locked in the dark in that frightening place. Knox had mentioned his father locked them up. Still...who did something like that?

"Our father locked us in there quite frequently," Lachlan said as if it were the most natural thing in the world. "Trust me, sometimes being down there in the dark was better than being in the main house listening to our parents try to destroy each other."

Samantha shook her head. "Why on earth would your father—"

"Because he was an asshole," Lily cut in.

"It was a game." Lachlan squeezed his wife's hand. "He thought it would make us stronger. He would leave me at one end of the west wing and Knox at the other. We were supposed to find our way out in the dark, alone. We weren't supposed to help each other. If we did, he'd lock the one who helped the other one into a room in the dungeons until morning."

"Let me guess," Danny said. "Knox spent a lot of time in the dungeons. Which explains a lot."

Lachlan smiled sadly. "He always said he wasn't afraid because the Innes Witch would keep him safe. He'd made a deal with her never to appear to me. I'd never seen her, but I was terrified of her. Knox would come and find me, lead me to an open window or a coal shute, and Father would find me fast asleep in bed long before dawn. Which infuriated him. Not as much as Knox talking about the Witch did, but enough."

"So, at some point, your brother did believe in the Innes Witch," Eleanor said.

"I cannot remember a time he didn't believe, until they sent him away to school. After that, he did his damnedest to make certain no one believed."

"That will happen when someone decides a child having an imaginary friend makes him certifiably insane." Hadrian shook his head in disgust.

"Certifiably insane?" Eleanor spoke the words, but had no

idea why. None of this made sense in any other world. But here, in Rosemount Manor? She didn't know what was real and what was the tragedy of having rotten parents.

"There are letters in the archives," Hadrian explained. "Lachlan, your father tried to have your brother locked up. He couldn't find any reputable shrink that would sign off on it, so he sent him away."

"Damn," Danny muttered. "No wonder Knox doesn't want to even think about her being real. Can you blame him?"

"I think there's more to it than that," Anna said. "If he believes in part of the legend, then he has to believe in all of it. The Innes Witch cursed all future dukes to unhappy marriages. If he believes she exists and she was his friend, how does he feel about that?"

"What?" Eleanor searched her memory. "I don't remember that part of the story."

"Oh yes," Samantha said. "Apparently your long lost ancestor *was* a witch and cursed all of the Dukes of Innes. At least that's what Bridie told me."

"Well that explains a lot," Eleanor murmured.

"Not necessarily." Hadrian spoke so softly she wasn't sure she heard him correctly.

"I don't think Knox gave much credence to that part of the legend even when he did believe in the Witch," Lachlan said. "He always said our parents' marriage didn't need a curse to make it an unholy mess because the curse didn't make our father a womanizing mean drunk who pissed the family fortune away on whores, drugs, and booze. The old bastard did that all by himself."

"I don't think we need to worry about His Worship being involved in our plans," Lily said. "No matter what he believes or doesn't believe. Lets talk about what Bridie said, and what Eleanor experienced in the dungeons."

She was glad for the change of subject, but the idea that Knox might blame her ancestor for some supposed curse, no matter how ridiculous and silly the idea sounded, settled into the back of her mind like it intended to pay rent.

"What did Bridie say, Samantha?" she asked.

Anna began to go from person to person, topping off everyone's cups of tea. Eleanor took pride in the fact they'd all settled into the Regency way of life and seemed to have become addicted to drinking tea at every opportunity.

"Our mysterious piper is her cousin," Anna began. "He is who McGinty said he is. He went into the military with you, Lachlan."

"He did. Came home with me too."

Everyone looked at Knox's brother as if they expected him to elaborate. Eleanor didn't. He had a way of uttering the few words he did say in a way that she'd begun to understand. His voice faded when he'd said all he intended to say, especially when it came to his time in the Middle East.

"Bridie asked him how he ended up on the tower piping in the middle of a storm."

This time their gazes moved to Samantha in expectation.

"What did he say?" Eleanor asked.

"He hasn't the foggiest notion. He was asleep on the settee in his cottage. Something woke him up. A sound. Then someone or something came over him and the next thing he knew he was on top of the tower."

"Tell them the rest," Danny said.

"He said whilst he was up there, some sort of dark, damp cloud came up behind him. It, whatever it was, tried to crowd him off the tower. He nearly fell, but a hand reached out and pushed him back and the cloud disappeared. He doesn't remember much about climbing down the tower or about getting home. But when he did, there was a fire burning in the hearth and a kettle boiling."

Samantha turned her attention to Eleanor, which made her want to shift in her chair. She broke off a piece of bacon and shoved it into her mouth instead. A trick she'd learned from the male boot campers when they didn't want to answer a question, spoken or unspoken.

"What's so odd about that?" Lily asked.

"He lives alone," Hadrian answered. "I took the liberty of speaking to him a few days after the storm."

"And?" Lily buttered a tiny piece of toast and began to nibble on it.

"I'm a skeptic, folks. You know that. I don't know if I believe all of this black cloud stuff, but I know he does. He's not lying. I'm a New Yorker. I know my liars."

They sat in silence, sipping tea and polishing off the contents of breakfast. Eleanor didn't care anymore. If they thought she'd lost her mind, so be it.

"When I told you what happened in the west wing, I didn't tell you everything." Not surprisingly, she had their full attention. "I told you there was something in the archives with me, and the Innes Witch helped me get out of there. But I know exactly what the piper described. That's what was down in the tunnels with me. It was cold and dark and damp, and I could see through it. Something inside that darkness scared the hell out of me. Whatever it was chased me out onto Erik's battlefield." She took a deep breath. "And if it hadn't been for the Innes Witch, I think whatever it would have killed me."

Anna placed a hand on Eleanor's wrist. "What do you think it was?"

"I don't know. But this isn't the first time I've sensed that something or someone is watching me. Someone who wants me gone or…." She swallowed and shook her head.

"Dead." Lily said.

"Lily," Anna said in unison with Samantha's "Good Lord," and Danny's snort.

"What?" Lily threw up her hands and glared at them. "You're all thinking the same thing. Something has been going on since we first set foot in our little Regency boot camp. It was funny at first. Sort of a touristy, kitchy sort of thing."

"Yeah, well its not funny anymore." Danny stood up and crossed his arms. "So what are we going to do about it before one of us really gets hurt, including Knox?"

"What do you suggest?" Hadrian closed his journal and shoved it into the satchel at his feet.

"Well, Grandmere always said spirits don't walk for no reason. And they don't always have control of what comes with 'em. Lay the spirit to rest, and what came with her has no choice but to leave." Danny shrugged and glanced at Lachlan.

"So we go with Bas and Teddy's plan?" Eleanor couldn't believe she was saying this out loud.

"Move the first duke to the tomb on the island?" Anna shook her head. "His Grace isn't going to like that one bit."

"Would you if someone suggested we dig up one of your ancestors?" Hadrian asked.

"One of her ancestors isn't wreaking havoc in the middle of a film production." Trust Lily to put things in perspective. "This has been going on since we got here." She held up one finger. "These occurences, whether any of us believe them to be supernatural or not, are getting worse." She gave Hadrian a pointed look as she held up a second finger. "And *if* we believe all of the pieces of this legend we've been told, I think Elsbeth has suffered enough. Even if she was a witch, she deserves to finally sleep with her man."

"If anyone would know what a witch is feeling, its Lily." Danny grinned and blew her a kiss as she shot him the bird.

"Knox is the only one with a key to the mausoleum, so far as I know," Lachlan said. "And I don't know where he keeps it."

"He keeps it in a drawer in his desk in his study." Eleanor bit back a curse.

Too late. They all stared at her as if to say *How do you know that?*

"We need to give him one more chance to be involved in this little expedition before we go all *Mission Impossible* and figure out a way to do it without him finding out," Danny said.

Eleanor could have kissed Danny for diverting the attention away from her.

Hadrian grinned. "Good idea, Arneaux. Why don't you talk to him? You're his new best friend."

"Fuck that, Mr. Historian. These titled dudes take betrayal seriously. My Cajun ass ain't built for dungeon living. How about asking McGinty or Mrs. Wallace?"

"Lets leave his employees out of it." Eleanor used one of the silk napkins to dry her sweaty palms. Strange because the rest of her body was cold as ice. "Its not fair, no matter how much they believe in the legends."

"I agree." Lily pinned Eleanor with one of those scary expressions of hers. Danny's witch comment wasn't too far off sometimes. "So why don't you approach him, Eleanor? Tell him this is part of the whole Regency experience. He likes you, and you've got practice talking him into all kinds of things...for the sake of the film." Her voice was laced with insinuation and had everyone else in the room looking anywhere but at Eleanor. Damn them.

"He thinks my ancestor cursed the dukes in his family to bad marriages in perpetuity. I'm the last person who needs to talk to him about digging up his great great whatever grandfather." Eleanor had no intention of telling the other reason she wasn't going to go anywhere near Knox with this crazy plan.

Thunk!

"Jesus!" Danny jumped and glared across the room at Persephone's habitat. "What the hell?"

The snake's head stood nearly at the top of her enclosure and her gaze was fixed on a spot over Danny's shoulder, a spot on the other side of the fireplace.

"Looks like your girlfriend wants you." Lily snickered, then her expression changed. Everyone's did. The room had grown cold, cold even for a drafty stately home in Scotland in June.

"Very funny." Danny rubbed his arms bared by the rolled up sleeves of his Regency linen shirt. "What is she staring at, Eleanor?"

"You, Snake Boy," Lily teased.

"Tough," Danny declared. "When I have to piss in a china soup tureen by candlelight, and she gets electric heat and lights and water circulated by an electrc pump, thumping on the glass is not the way to my heart or any other part of my anatomy."

Everyone cracked up. Eleanor's shoulders relaxed for the first time since they'd invaded her room.

"I'll do it," Hadrian said.

Silence fell like a ton of bricks. All heads turned toward him.

"Do what?" Lily asked.

"I'll talk to the duke." He grabbed his satchel and slung the strap over his shoulder before he kissed Anna. "I have something I need to check into first in the archives. I'll talk to him tomorrow after I confirm...what I need to confirm."

"Want one of us to come with you?"

"You can't, Mr. Arneaux. The rest of you all have lessons and film schedules to keep." Eleanor rose and gingerly made her way to the beside table where she grabbed her boot camp journal. "Come along, children. We have things to do before we plan our grave robbing expedition."

She hoped they were buying her *I'm in charge* bravado. She damned sure wasn't. Everyone grumbled and grabbed last food items from the breakfast tray, but they filed out the door with Hadrian bringing up the rear.

Eleanor grasped his arm and stopped him. "Are you sure about talking to His Grace, Hadrian?"

"Nope. But there is something I need to give him a chance to take on before I have to do it myself."

KNOX HAD ATTENDED ENOUGH BREAKFAST MEETINGS IN THE corporate world to know when everyone in the room was studying him for some expected or unexpected reaction. He had no idea why he'd decided to join the Regency boot campers at their historically correct morning meal. Well he had some idea. The presence of a certain person, a person he'd not seen at all yesterday and had managed to force himself not to visit last night.

Eleanor looked none the worse for her near death experience on Wentworth's Waterloo recreation battlefield. In fact, in her pretty light green Regency gown with her glorious golden red hair done up in some elaborate antique style, she took his breath away. Even if she was one of the people stealing glances at him as if he might do something ridiculous at any moment.

"What's on the schedule for today?' he finally asked when he'd had enough of their perusal. "Are we blowing up my horse pastures or giving my housekeeper a seizure?"

"Do you have a preference?" Eleanor asked sweetly.

"You've been spending too much time with my sister-in-law," he muttered. He glanced down the table. "Where is the lovely Lady Lachlan this morning?"

"She and Lord Lachlan went home last night," Miss Chase, no Mrs. Cross now, said. "I think they wanted some peace and quiet and a chance to wind down before Wentworth's shooting schedule picks back up." The authoress was decked out in Regency dress, but she had a very modern looking bound script next to her plate and was marking in it with a red pen.

"She wanted the chance to take a real shower instead of a horse trough bath," Danny said once he'd swallowed half the sausage on his plate. "And to sneak online and see what the gossip rags are saying about the movie without Eleanor catching her."

"What she does in her own home is none of my business," Eleanor replied in her prim Regency general voice that drove Knox crazy for some strange reason. "But once you cross the line into the back gardens or the stables you are in my territory and boot camp rules apply."

"Aye aye, Captain." The cajun actor gave a smart salute, then grunted when his wife and Regency coach elbowed him in the gut.

"Finish your breakfast," Eleanor ordered as she stood and gathered her journal and other papers. "You have dance lessons in less than half an hour, correct Sylvan?"

"Indeed," the short round dance instructor said though he didn't move from his place at the table. "If you will get them all to the ballroom, I'll be along in a bit to put them through their paces."

"When will Teddy and Bas be back?" Arneaux grabbed a piece of toast and a piece of bacon as his wife dragged him away from the table. "I need reinforcements."

"In a few days, from what I understand." Hadrian Cross stood but made no move to follow the others out of the dining room. "They sent word to McGinty to send the Land Rover for them the day after tomorrow."

"Does Miss Witherspoon know they're using non-Regency transportation?" Knox asked as he and the former book critic made their way into the corridor.

"I suspect not, but I make it a policy *not* to inform on men who blow things up or use lethal weapons for a living."

"Good policy. Is there something you want, Mr. Cross?" Knox stopped outside the door of his study."I have a lot to do today."

"Hadrian. Please.This won't take long, but it isn't something I want to discuss out here in the hall."

"I see." Knox walked into his study and strolled to his desk waiting for *Hadrian* to follow him. He indicated one of the chairs in front of his desk. "I don't supposed you have come here to tell me you no longer wish access to the archives in the west wing, do you?"

"Why would I?" He dropped his satchel at his feet and settled into the chair.

"After what happened to Miss Witherspoon I simply thought—"

"You thought I'd be scared off by the ghost?"

"I think we both know there was no ghost involved. I spent hours in that part of the house as a child. The walls produce odd shadows and odd noises. In the right light anyone might be frightened, even the commander of your Regency boot camp."

The American laughed. "She is definitely the commander. I didn't come here intending to join Wentworth's little training regime. I was conscripted."

"Marriage will do that to a man."

"I have no intention of abandoning my research in the archives, Your Grace. Unless you intend to lock the doors and forbid me entrance."

"I don't really have a choice. My brother gave you permission."

"So your brother has the same power to make decisions at Rosemount as you do?"

"Almost." Knox respected Hadrian Cross's tenacity and his sharp wit. He didn't like being at the other end of that wit and tenacity, but he had to admire the man. But he damned sure didn't want him digging too deeply into the family history, for lots of reasons. "He's given you access. I won't deny you. Though what you hope to find about a ridiculous legend is beyond me."

"I've already found a good bit of information that tells me this legend is rooted in fact. And if certain items would stop disappearing from the archives, I think I might find some insight into why these odd occurences keep happening."

"Odd occurences?"

Hadrian rolled his eyes. "Come on, Your Grace. We're grown men here, not some kids swapping ghost stories. *Something* is going on here. You can deny it all you want, but there is something up here at Rosemount. Do I think it has to do with the supernatural? Maybe. I'm a real sceptic when it comes to these things, but what do I know? I will tell you that some of the things I set out for Eleanor to look over about her possible ancestors were gone when she went into the archives, and she had the hell scared out of her. But that isn't the only time and those aren't the only things that have gone missing. And I don't think some ghost or banshee moved those things. I think someone alive and well did." He fixed Knox with a steady gaze of expectation.

"Me? You think I went down there and moved something?"

"*Removed* something. The first duke's diaries. I found them hidden in a locked chest inside a small locked room off the main archives."

"Locked? Someone gave you a key?" Hadrian's mention of the duke's diaries was like a punch in the gut. But where the hell did he get a key? Knox clenched his fist under his desk.

"Misspent youth." Hadrian shrugged. "If you don't want a reporter to go after something, don't lock it up. Especially if his best friend in high school did time for breaking and entering before he went to the police academy. How I found them doesn't matter."

"It doesn't matter to you." Knox flexed his fist as a thousand thoughts raced through his head, most of them about Eleanor and what she might discover thanks to the American reporter's interference.

"What does matter is that I didn't leave them for Eleanor to find, but I did put them up on a shelf, hiding them in plain sight, and she noticed the now empty spot where they were. I went down yesterday, and low and behold, all but one of them is back on the shelf, but not in the order or position I put them. You should have paid closer attention when you removed them. My question is, why remove them and then return them, Your Grace?"

"The last time I saw any of those diaries was when I locked them back in that chest in that little room. Which was before you ever arrived here. I have neither seen nor touched them since." He leapt from his chair and began to pace. He had to do something or he'd punch the man in the face. This was why Knox never wanted to open Rosemount Manor up to tourists, let alone the kind of people who were involved in making a damned film. "And for fuck's sake call me Knox."

"Okay, Knox. So you're saying a ghost moved them? Why?"

"A ghost? Please. Don't tell me you believe in ghosts."

"You don't?"

Knox glared at him.

Hadrian raised a hand in surrender. "Fine. We'll talk

about that later. Someone moved the diaries and someone is hanging on to the last one, the one the first duke wrote before he died."

"Offed himself," Knox corrected.

"Whatever. The point is, something is up here. Human interference or supernatural interference, it doesn't matter. I have two questions."

"Only two?" Knox finally walked back to his desk and propped a hip on the corner farthest from Hadrian. He relaxed his shoulders. This conversation was heading in a direction he had no desire to explore.

"First question. Who do *you* think is doing all of this? If you don't believe in ghosts, who is responsible?"

"I don't know. But I'm certain there is a reasonable explanation for all of this. Second question?"

"Have you read the last diary, and when are you going to tell Eleanor the truth?"

Knox dragged in an icy breath. "That's three questions."

"I'll take that as a yes to the first question. I suspected as much."

"Of course you did," Knox muttered. "What do you intend to do with that information? Information which, by the way, is nothing more than the ravings of a man at the end of his tether who killed himself soon after writing that entry."

"I intend to set the record straight. And I intend to set that record straight starting with Eleanor. She deserves to know. You may not want to admit it, but she is descended from Elsbeth Dunhomme. I set a geneaologist friend of mine on the trail, and I have the proof. Lily's not the only one who sneaks to Lachlan's cottage to use the computer. You know the truth about Elsbeth, the duke, all of it. Either you tell her"—Hadrian stood and picked up his satchel—"or I will." He walked to the door.

"This is ridiculous." Knox's stomach sank as if someone

had poured a bucket of cement down his throat. "You're an intelligent man. You can't believe in this witches and ghosts and curses nonsense."

"Doesn't matter what I believe.This is about what you believe, Knox. And I think it's about time you figure that out. Tell her. You have three days."

Knox stared at the closed study door and listened as Hadrian's footsteps faded down the corridor. He finally stood and walked to the floor to ceiling window that looked out over the front drive and fountain. The morning had been clear until now. Storm clouds had formed across the front lawn. They hovered over the grounds and stretched back to the folly on the hill, where he and Eleanor had made love for the first time. The faint sound of period music floated out from the ballroom. The dancing lessons had begun.

"Fuck."

He strode to his desk, found the key to the bottom drawer and opened it. Inside, he found the ancient leather-bound diary and the chatelaine ring of keys. Suddenly, there wasn't enough air in the room. Or maybe there just wasn't enough air in his lungs. He walked to the fireplace where Dougal had lit a small blaze in the hearth because the study was always so damned cold in the mornings. Before he even tried, Knox knew he would never burn the fucking diary. He wanted to, God he wanted to rid himself of the first duke's lunacy.

"Fuck. Fuck. Fuck."

He shoved the keys into his sporran and tucked the diary behind some books on the bookcase next to the door. Before he knew it, he was down the stairs and out the front doors. If he passed anyone on the way they likely dodged out of the way. He didn't see a soul. The more he ran over the morning's conversation in his head, the hotter his skin grew while whatever was running in his veins turned to loch water, cold and dark. Once he crossed the lawn and traveled behind the wall of hedges around the base of the hill where the family mausoleum stood, he broke into a run.

Knox reached the massive stone monument to his ancestors and slid down with his back against the medieval iron gates. From here, he had an unobstructed view of the manor house, the stables, the mews, the loch, the castle ruins, and more. He propped one arm on a raised knee and considered…everything. As far as he could see, the land, the buildings, all of it belonged to him. Before Eleanor, Knox hadn't really considered things that way. For him, Rosemount was a job, an obligation, a test.

Every morning, he climbed out of bed and debated heading to his study or heading to the airport. Or at least he had, until a cold January morning when a woman he'd convinced himself he'd invented floated across the front drive and knocked him metaphorically on his arse. If her arrival hadn't coincided with a sudden eruption in ghost sightings, assorted accidents, and bloody romances that led to marriage, he might have dated her, explored the connection between them, and perhaps fallen in love. Not that he intended to do anything about if he did. Fall in love, that is. Which he hadn't. Yet.

He couldn't. Knox had two carefully cultivated lists of reasons why his attraction to Eleanor had nowhere to go. Practical reasons that had to do with her being an employee. Impractical reasons that had to do with curses, real or imagined, and superstitions and….

Shite!

He didn't believe in this nonsense, dammit. He'd erased all the legends from his consciousness while he was away at school, at university, and then buried in creating his architectural firm. Surrounding himself with hard twenty-first century reality, Knox had grounded his life in facts. Then McGinty had dragged him back to Scotland with one phone call. And one look at the shell Lachlan had become had cracked open the door to those old superstitions just enough for the events of the last six months or so to....

Have him talking to Elsbeth as if he'd never left Rosemount. Have him reading his ancestor's diaries and discovering what he thought he knew about the family curse he didn't know at all. All the while, he'd sensed the insidious tendril of doubt creep into the back of his mind. Knox scrubbed his hands over his face and pushed himself to his feet. What the hell was he doing and why was he doing it?

Eleanor. That was why.

He took two steps toward the stairs that led down to the mausoleum. The clink of the keys to the mausoleum stopped him. Without thinking, Knox pulled the old metal ring from his sporan and unlocked the iron gates and then the iron-banded door. The interior was dark and cool and edged in shadows. He pushed the doors wide open to let in the light.

"Well, you mama's boy lunatic," he said as he stood at the feet of the first duke's tomb. "Are you happy now? You started this. I'm descended from a long line of suicides and madmen. All of whom were visited by the ghost of your murdered first wife. All, but you, of course. Is that why you did what you did? You figured the only way she would to come back to you was if you made certain none of us were sane or happy?"

Outside the mausoleum, thunder rumbled in the distance. The light began to fade as the clouds he'd seen earlier moved closer. The rain was on its way. Typical June weather in Scotland. As sure and certain as old legends coming home to roost. Legends he'd fought all his life to ignore and then erase. He clasped one hand on the corner of the duke's tomb and the other on that of the man's bitch of a mother. Suddenly he knew exactly how Eleanor had felt when she saw that wall of dirt and stone come toward her on Wentworth's battle set.

The price of returning to Rosemount, the way he felt about Lachlan, the darkness he'd discovered about his ancestors, the sheer weight of running the estate and knowing he could never leave—all of that and more pressed down on his shoulders until he actually bent over the stone monuments and touched his forehead to the icy marble. He couldn't find air to breathe or light to see the way out of the shit storm his life had become.

But he knew where he could find light and air. All he had to do was tell her the truth about everything. And pray she'd understand and not blame him for madness and cruelty of his ancestors. Of course she wouldn't. She was Eleanor. His Eleanor. Such a simple solution to the mess he'd made of his life. All he had to do was drag her into the mess with him.

Suddenly, the thunder shook the mausoleum. The light disappeared as the sound of heavy rain approached the hill. A soft voice spoke from the far end of the tomb. Slowly, Knox raised his head. She only appeared for an instant. When the lightning flashed behind the stained glass window, she was gone.

"I don't believe this shit?" he shouted. He clutched the marble tombs until his hands shook and turned white. "Do you hear me? I don't believe."

A chill wind blew in from the open doors and whistled around the closed in room.

"What did you do? What the fuck did you do? Damn you!"

Chapter Nineteen

ELEANOR TRIED FOR THE TENTH TIME TO FOCUS HER attention on the various schedules, notes, and lists she'd arranged on the little marquetry table next to the drawing room window seat. She found she coultn't concentrate at the little escritoire closer to the area where a couple of card tables were set up and occupied by her Regency boot campers. She had to smile at the term. Such a silly, modern idea for what was supposed to be a total immersion on all things nineteenth century England.

After a beautiful and very delicious formal dinner, they'd all decided cards and conversation were the order of the day. Which meant whist and talk of the recent "spooky" events and how they might go about solving the mystery and therefore the disturbances. As Bella and Sylvan joined them, the rest of Eleanor's charges kept certain things out of the discussion. Like the idea of digging up the first duke. Actually they kept the current duke out of the conversation as well.

Eleanor hadn't seen or heard from Knox all day. Actually, no one had. Not even Lachlan or McGinty. She didn't question the servants as she didn't want to stir up gossip. Or at least any more gossip that Robbie and Dougal's betting books created. She'd only had a moment alone with Hadrian to ask how his conversation with the duke had gone. Anna Cross's taciturn husband's response of "As expected." was no help at all. Hadrian's expression, however, gave him away. He was hiding something.

Eleanor blinked against the brilliant flash of lightning that illuminated the front drive below her window seat. The wind tossed heavy raindrops against the glass like a group of rowdy teenagers throwing rocks. The storm had broken after lunch and had only grown more wild after dark. She shivered and drew her shawl around her more tightly.

"Eleanor, Sylvan is cheating." Danny reminded her of her brother complaining because she was sitting too close to him in the car.

"I would never," Sylvan replied indignantly.

"You would never if you thought you would get caught," Lily said. "Otherwise all bets are off."

"You're just mad because he and Bella are whooping your ass. Ouch!" Hadrian gave Anna a dirty look.

"Watch your language, Mr. Cross. You are in Miss Witherspoon's Regency experience now."

"Very well, Mrs. Cross. Apologies, Miss Witherspoon. Mr. Arneaux, you are just mad because Sylvan and Bella are whooping your *arse*. Another game. Whose turn is it to deal?"

Eleanor rolled her eyes. "You are hopeless, Hadrian Cross. Absolutely hopeless."

"Mine." Lily gathered the cards into a pile. "And Samanatha's at your table, Danny, so you cannot accuse poor Mr. Goode of cheating this time."

"Never stopped him before," Lachlan said.

"Quite right, my lord," the dance instructor said with a decisive nod and a wink for Samantha.

Eleanor laughed even as the storm began to pound furiously against the window. The lightning lit up the front drive again and thunder shook the house.

"Wonder if we'll hear our mysterious piper tonight." Bella Stepford, dressed as a Regency era dowager, peered over her historically correct spectacles and studied her cards.

"What if he does?" Sylvan fanned out his own cards, then glanced at Danny. "You grew up in New Orleans, yes?" Danny nodded. "Did you ever have any experience with the supernatural, with voodoo, that sort of thing?"

"My mother was Creole and my father was a Cajun straight out of the swamps. Of course I did. Why do you ask?"

"It seems to me we have some restless spirits here at Rosemount Manor. And if Miss Witherspoon's experience in the west wing is any indication, one of them is very angry."

"You could say that," Hadrian muttered.

Anna gave him a *shut up* glare.

"What does your experience with voodoo tell you needs to be done?" The dance instructor was looking at this cards when he asked the question. After a few moments of ensuing silence he glanced up. "In theory. If one believed in that sort of thing."

Eleanor stood. She swept her papers into a neat stack and stuck them in her leather-bound journal. This conversation needed to end. Immediately.

"I'll admit I was too interested in chasing girls, playing football, and drinking beer," Danny replied.

"That explains a lot." Lily and Lachlan grinned at him.

"Fuck both of you," Danny said.

"Dante!" Samantha punched his arm. "Language."

"Sorry, Eleanor." He turned back to Lachlan and Lily. "Fornicate both of you."

The group erupted into laughter and Eleanor joined

them. She glanced out the window at the next flash of lightning. A figure moved across the front lawns coming toward the front of the manor. Who the hell was out in this mess?

"I will tell you this." Danny's voice became so serious Eleanor turned back to the group. "I once asked the local mambo about ghosts and curses. She said ghosts always come back to settle unfinished business, and it usually ain't good business. And sometimes, when they come back they bring things with them, things they had no intention of bringing. And the only way to lay the ghost and those other things to rest is to settle that business."

"I see." Sylvan shuffled and reshuffled the cards.

"What did she say about curses?" Hadrian asked. "Did she ever curse anyone? How do curses work?"

Eleanor kept her eyes on the storm and the front of the house. But Hadrian's question piqued her interest. He wasn't asking a hypothetical. He was up to something. She didn't look at him as she had decided he was far to good at reading people.

"Curses are simple, according to her. Doesn't matter whether you believe in them or not. What matters is what the curse and the power of the person laying the curse can *make* you believe."

"Interesting. Whose play is it?"

Just like that, Hadrian turned the conversation away from the supernatural, almost as if...Eleanor turned her head to meet his gaze. He nodded. The sky lit up behind her just as a loud clap of thunder boomed. Everyone else looked up for a moment, then went back to their cards. Eleanor got ready to sit back down when she saw someone striding in the pouring rain from the front lawn onto the drive in front of the fountain.

Knox!

"Excuse me." She pasted a stiff smile on her face and

walked as slowly as she could manage to the drawing room doors. "Keep playing. I need to check with Mrs. Wallace about something."

With measured steps, she made it to the landing and started down the stairs. She turned her head back and forth in search of any stray servant or some straggler from the film crew lurking in the shadows. When she reached the foyer, Dougal came running down the stairs behind her.

"Shhh." Eleanor raised her finger to her lips. "You saw him?" she asked softly.

"Yes, miss. I was upstairs putting out the candles in the dining room chandalier." He paused to catch his breath. "Saw him coming across the lawn."

"Run up to his room and get blankets and towels. Turn on the electric heat. Then try and sneak into the kitchens. Bring tea, honey, and whisky. Try not to be seen."

Dougal glanced at the front doors then back to Eleanor. He nodded and took off back up the stairs. Eleanor hurried to the doors and flung them open just as Knox staggered into the doorway.

"Are you out of your mind?" she demanded as she caught him around the waist and steered him, dripping, across the marble floor to the staircase.

"I went for a walk," he mumbled.

"In a fucking thunderstorm?" She half stumbled with him up the stairs to as the first floor and started up to the second floor. The closer they got to his room the more he leaned on her.

"Wasn't raining when I started," he said in a low voice.

"You *are* out of your mind."

"Someone finally noticed. I need to sit down." He started to drag her toward one of the antique chairs along the end of the hallway to his room.

"Don't you dare. I'll never get your ass back up. Just a few more feet."

She managed to move them staggering into the huge bedroom and closed the doors behind them. His two dogs leapt down from the bed and crossed the room tails wagging, giving low, short, happy woofs.

"Hello, you two," Knox murmured as he clumsily patted each wooly head. "Been waiting for me, have you?"

"They're not the only ones." Eleanor shoved him into a chair in front of the fireplace. She grabbed the poker and stirred the low burning embers. "Where the hell have you been all day? McGinty's been looking for you. I've been looking for you."

"Aye, and Mrs. Wallace has been looking for him as well," Dougal said as he emerged from a side door across the room, his arms loaded with towels. He handed several to Eleanor and dropped a few more on the table next to the chair where Knox sat slumped. "I turned the heat up." The footman indicated the electric thermostat on the wall. "His Grace prefers his rooms on the cooler side, but he looks to need warming up."

"I'm right here," Knox mumbled, and raised his head to glower at Dougal.

"So you are, Your Grace. I won't tell Miss Witherspoon we're using the electric heat if you don't." He gave Eleanor a wink. "Robbie's putting together a tray. I'll run and fetch it." He disappeared back the way he came.

"I hate it when they do that," Eleanor said as she grabbed one of the towels and started to dry Knox's hair.

He batted at her half-heartedly. "When they do what? I can do this." He tried to take the towel from her, but had trouble lifting his arms higher than the middle of his chest.

"Stop struggling, idiot. I hate it when they disappear

through a door and somehow end up downstairs in the kitchens. What is back there?"

"My bathroom, but this house is r-r-riddled with hidden doors, staircases, and p-p-passes." He began to shiver.

She stopped drying his hair. "Do you have a robe somewhere? A warm one?"

"Hook." He pointed weakly at the bathroom door. "In there."

His face had gone pale and his lip had a blue tinge. Eleanor ran into the bathroom and snatched the thick wool robe off the hook by the door.

"Come on," she said once she got back to Knox. "Out of these clothes. Now." She dragged his shirt over his head and reached for the belt that held his sporan. He grabbed her hips and tried to drag her onto his lap. "I don't think so, Your Grace." She pushed his hands away. "Get up." She dragged him to his feet and whipped his kilt off to find his cock pointing straight at her. "Is that damned thing always on alert?"

"Only when you're around." He swayed on his feet.

She dragged a fresh towel from the stack on the table and began to rub Knox's entire body as hard as she could. She did so to warm him up and stop his shivering. That didn't stop her checking out every inch as she worked the plush towel over his arms and chest, down his legs and finally down his back and over his very fine ass. Doing the back kept her eyes from dropping to the erection bobbing against his hard abs.

Just as Dougal backed into the room carrying a huge tea tray Eleanor managed to shove Knox into the robe. The footman dragged a tea table closer to the fireplace and placed the tray on it. He plugged in the electric kettle and set it to simmer. He took one look at the duke, who was still swaying on his feet, and poured a snifter full of brandy from the decanter on the tray.

"I think brandy first, miss. He still looks a bit blue around the gills."

"I'm still here." Knox waved an arm at Dougal and promptly collapsed back into the chair behind him.

"Have you been drinking as well as wandering around in the middle of a thunderstorm?" Eleanor took the brandy from Dougal and walked over to sit on the arm of the chair.

Knox looked up at her and smiled.

The footman picked up Knox's shirt and sniffed a stain down the front. "Stopped by the distillery, unless my nose has taken up lying." He grabbed the wet kilt and came over to remove the duke's shoes and socks. "Give him the brandy. Can't hurt now. A hot shower might help as well." He dropped the sporran and belt onto the bedside table across the room.

She wrapped Knox's hands around the snifter and pushed it toward his mouth. "Drink.That's not a bad idea, Dougal. Turn the shower on when you go back through and I'll get him in there. Leave the tray, and we'll try some tea and food after the shower."

"Yes, miss. Ring, if you need me." He went back to the bathroom door, Knox's wet clothes draped over his arm. He turned back at the last minute. "Miss?"

"Yes, Dougal?"

"Thanks for looking after him." He inclined his head and disappeared into Knox's private bathroom. She heard him turn the shower on and listened for the closing of the door that led into the hidden passageways.

When she turned her attention back to Knox he had drunk very little of the brandy, but he was shivering again and seemed ready to nod off. She took the glass and put it on the floor next to the chair. "Come on, Your Grace." She stood, grabbed both of his hands, and pulled him to his feet.

"Where we going, lass?" Apparently when he was frozen

to the bone and a little tipsy, the Duke of Turra's brogue came out to play.

She dragged him toward the bathroom. "To shower, you big goof. Hopefully, it'll warm you up and wake you up enough to tell me where you've been all day."

The bathroom was toasty warm and steamy. The glass enclosed shower was huge with shower heads at each end and a bench that ran down the back wall. It really was good to be the duke. Eleanor peeled the robe off of him, opened the door, and shoved him under the closest shower head. The sound of canine toenails on the tiled floor drew her attention to the door into the bedroom.

"Hello, Beira," she murmured as she went to scratch the big deerhound behind the ears. "What is it?"

Eleanor caught the muffled sound of voices far down the corridor. She kicked off her silk slippers and padded across the antique carpets to listen at the double doors of the duke's huge bedchamber. Everyone was coming upstairs to go to bed. She couldn't hear what they were saying. She and Beira stood there for a moment until the noise died down and doors began to open and close.

"Go back to bed," she told the dog. Tannus, sprawled at the foot of the giant bed raised his head and woofed softly. "You heard your man, girl. Go back to bed."

The deerhound butted Eleanor's thigh and ambled back to jump on the bed next to Tannus as she continued back toward the bathroom.

She'd managed to get Knox into the house and upstairs without anyone finding out, except Robbie and Dougal. She knew they'd keep their mouths shut. Eleanor had no idea why, but she suspected something bad had happened to Knox and the last thing he would want was for everyone to know he'd been walking in a thunderstorm all afternoon and evening. But she damned sure wanted to know and then some.

She entered the bathroom. "Okay, Knox, what exactly have you been— Oh shit."

he was slumped against the glass side of the shower, head tilted back and water pouring onto his face. She shimmied out of her dress and climbed into the shower in her chemise and stockings. Thank God she hadn't bothered with stays or petticoats this evening. She grabbed Knox's biceps and shook him.

"Hey," he said, as he dropped his head and immediately zeroed his gaze in on her nearly naked boobs beneath the wet, sheer chemise. "Whatever are you doing, Miss Witherspoon?"

She pulled him out of the shower head's spray and used a washcloth to dry his face. "Keeping you from drowning, Your Grace. Can you imagine what everyone would say if I let the Duke of Turra drown in his shower?"

"Hmm. Which would your Regency pupils object to most? My death, or my use of a modern shower?"

"You don't want me to answer that." She pushed him back under the hot shower and squeezed some of the very expensive men's body wash into her hands. He watched her with a strange smile as she lathered his shoulders and chest.

"Thank goodness this Regency experience didn't include you forbidding me from living in the modern world."

"If they saw this amusement park of a shower, they'd kill both of us. And forbid? Fat bunch of good it would do me to forbid you anything. Turn around." She spun him around and washed his back. Damn, his body wash smelled insanely good.

He laughed. "Would you like a list of everything you have forbidden or overruled me on since your arrival? Whoa. Do that again." She'd squeezed his ass and he'd flexed his gluts against her.

"Have you kept a list?"

Eleanor turned him around and used one of the hand-held shower heads to rinse him off. The shower had done more than revive him. The heat and her hands had brought his muscled and toned body to life beneath her fingertips. Eleanor should be able to resist that warm, sculpted flesh. Who the hell was she kidding? In a kilt, the man was sex in motion. Out of the kilt? She licked her lips and stepped closer until her breasts pressed against him and he stared down into her, eyes suddenly wide awake.

"Oh, I absolutely have a list of all of the things you have forbidden me." His voice came out in a low growled brogue that sent a shiver down her spine and a jolt between her legs.

The lightning outside had nothing on the Duke of Turra. She slid her palm down his chest, across his abs and down to his cock which she wrapped her fingers around and gave a long, tight stroke.

"Was this on that list?" she asked as she pressed up on her toes and sealed her mouth to his as she stroked again.

"No," he gasped when she finally let him up for air. "Thank God."

"Good."

She kissed him again, sucking his tongue into her mouth and sliding her hand around to caress his balls. He leaned forward to grab her ass with both hands and squeezed. Unfortunately, he was still a little unsteady on his feet. When he stumbled forward, she stopped the kiss and clutched his elbows. She steered him to the bench along the back wall and pushed him down to sit. Knox pulled her to stand between his legs and cupped her breasts. He gave her a wicked grin before he sucked one nipple into his mouth while his thumb circled the other.

Eleanor threw back her head and moaned. He bit down gently and tugged her tender flesh between his teeth. She clutched his head and held him to her. He dropped his free hand down to palm her pussy, and she rocked against his rough palm. Eleanor hissed at the delicious pain he tortured from her breast only to have him drag his mouth over to the other and suckle that nipple hard, alternating with flicks of his tongue. He pressed his thumb to her clit and rubbed in slow circles.

The faster she rocked against his hand, the harder he sucked and teased her breast. She clutched his shoulders so hard she knew her nails had to be digging in, especially when he growled and leaned into her.

"Knox, please," she gasped.

She wanted to stop. She wanted his cock, but more than anything, she wanted to come. She was too damned close not to and he knew it, damn him. He slid a finger into her pussy and released her breast to press his head against the wall and gaze up at her, his expression almost feral.

"Come for me, Eleanor. I want to watch. That's it. Take it. Take it."

Her orgasm crashed into her like a storm. Her entire body spasmed over and over as incoherent cries echoed in the shower, sounds over which she had no control. Her legs went wobbly and Knox caught her by the hips. He licked and nipped her breasts which caused an orgasmic aftershock to shoot through her body.

"Eleanor, I—"

She kissed him hard and shoved him back against the wall. "You're not getting off that easy, Your Grace." She straddled him, kneeling on the bench, her knees on each side of his thighs. With one hand braced on his shoulder she rose up and grabbed his cock. He reached between them to help her.

She took him inside, just the tip at first, sliding up and down, but never completely off.

"Damn," Knox gasped. "What are you doing to me, woman? Oh. God. Don't stop. Fuck." He drew the last word out on a low groan.

"I intend to." She braced her hands on the wall over his head and slid completely down onto his cock. For a moment she simply rocked. She loved the feel of him inside her. She loved the way her pussy pulsed around him, full and stretched. She loved the way his eyes nearly rolled back in his head and he panted, his forehead pressed to the cleft between her breasts.

"You're killing me, lass. Killing me."

"Not yet." She rose onto her knees again and began to ride his cock up and down from tip to root. Once she fell into the most sensuous rhythm, he palmed her hips and pushed up into her with powerful thrusts. They moved as one while the water poured over them from all directions. The shower echoed with the sounds of the water and their gasps and moans of pleasure while the storm raged on in the distance.

Eleanor's entire focus centered on the place where their bodies joined. Another orgasm, slower building, but no less powerful, started and her body flushed in anticipation. Knox quickened his thrusts. His muscles flexed and locked. He angled his body so her clit was flush against his groin as he pumped faster and faster, his gasps for air keeping time with his body.

"Yes," he growled. "Fuck me. Fuck. Me. Damn!"

"Knox!"

Her vision went white. Heat seared through her in waves. She could hardly breath as she collapsed onto his lap and dropped her head onto his shoulder.

"Good God," Knox finally said hoarsely. "I think you have killed me." He slumped against the tiled wall. He kissed the side of her breast and wrapped his arms around her. "Can we stay here all night? Just like this?"

Eleanor sighed. "No, we can't. Eventually we'll run out of hot water. And I need to get you into bed."

"Sounds like a wonderful idea. If you take me to bed will you have your way with me again?"

His little sound of protest as she separated their bodies and pushed to her feet made her smile. She took his hands and pulled him to his feet. They took turns with the hand held shower head and washed each other. Eleanor turned off the water and led Knox out of the shower. She handed him a towel from the towel warmer and he used it to dry her off. With another toasty warm towel, she did the same for him.

"You do realize, if the others find out I not only enjoyed your modern shower, but I used the towels from the electric warmer, that I'll be drummed out of Regency boot camp."

"I'm more worried about them finding out you just shagged me nearly unconscious." He knelt to peel down her wet stockings and dry her legs and feet.

"Are you ashamed about us?" Eleanor had to admit her heart sped up a bit.

"Of course not." He stood and wrapped his robe around her. "Its just…I'm your employer, even if you are in charge and well…I don't want to talk about this now."

"What do you want to do?" She traced her fingers over the dark circles under his eyes. "You look tired. Weary."

"What do I want to do? I want to crawl into that bed in there with you and sleep, wake up, make love again, and sleep some more."

She had questions. Hundreds of them. But in that moment she wanted what Knox wanted. And looking at him, really looking, she suspected he needed sleep more than anything right now. He'd been through some emotional event, an event that sent him wandering his estate most of the day. But now was not the time.

"Come on then." She took his hand and led him into the bedroom. While she turned the lamps out he crawled into the bed and flipped the covers back so she could join him. The dogs raised their heads, then settled back down across the foot of the bed.

Eleanor turned out the last of the lights and turned the antique key in the lock that spanned the two doors. The room was toasty warm and Eleanor had to admit she'd be glad when the Regency experience and the filming of *A Matter of Honor* came to a close. Fireplaces and candlelight and baths filled with buckets of hot water could be charming. But so could electric heat and that magnificent shower. Dougal had built up the fire in the hearth and the flames lit the room enough for her to get back to the bed without running into anything.

"Knox?" She took two tries to haul herself into the high ancestral bed of the Dukes of Turra. Her foot connected with the top of the bedside table and knocked his sporan into the floor with a metallic clank.

"Hmm?" He threw his arm around her waist and dragged her across the bed until her naked body was flush against his.

"My hair is wet," she said as he drew the covers over them both. "I'll soak the pillow."

"There are at least half a dozen pillows across the head of this bed." He blinked his eyes open, gazed at her and smiled. "Do your worst." He brushed several tight wet spiral curls away from her face. "Thank you, Eleanor. For looking out for me. For…being here."

"Where else would I be?" She traced the lines of his face and was drawn to the dark circles under his eyes again." Where were you today? Why were you walking in the rain?"

His body stilled. His eyes widened just a bit and then closed for a few seconds.

"I went for a walk."

"A walk? All day? No one has seen you all day, Knox. Not even McGinty. He was—"

"Very well. A long walk. I went to the mausoleum and then I just…walked." He rolled onto his back away from her. "I had some things I needed to sort out."

"The mausoleum? What kind of things?" She threw her leg over his and pulled herself on top of him.

"You keep that up, Miss Witherspoon, and the talking part of the evening will be over." He nudged his hips up.

"Nice try."She pushed his hair back and pinched his ear. "Talk to me, Knox. What's going on in that handsome head of yours?"

He sighed heavily and tilted his head back so he wasn't looking directly into her face. "As much as it pains me to tell you, and it does pain me, you were right about one thing."

"Just one thing?"

He narrowed his eyes.

"Fine. Tell me the one thing."

"I was angry at Lachlan. I am angry. Sometimes. When he came back so broken and strange, I knew he'd never be able to take over once our father died. Then when the old bastard did die, and I had to give up everything and come home, I was even angrier. I wanted to shake him or smack him or something." Knox looked at her. "I feel guilty as hell about that. I have no right to be angry at him."

"Of course you do. Jesus, Knox, you're only human. Though you've convinced most of the people around you that you aren't. I'm sure Lachlan knows you're mad, and I'm even more sure he knows you feel guilty about it. Talk to him about it. Tell him."

"Tell him? Oh, by the way, Lachlan, I was really pissed

that you came back from the Middle East completely fucked because that meant I had to take over once Father died and I have been resentful ever since." He worked his hand under the covers and stroked her back. "I don't think so."

There was more to his long walk than some old guilt and resentment. Hadrian had gone to speak to Knox that morning. Something the New Yorker told him set him off. Something he was avoiding talking about.

"You might want to work on that speech, especially if you're going to deliver it in front of Lily."

"You may be right."

"What else were you trying to sort out wandering around in a thunderstorm?"

"Nothing." He cleared his throat and tried to look away.

"Bullshit, Your Grace." She used her fingertips to tilt his head so that he was looking right at her once more. "What did Hadrian say to you this morning?"

"Hadrian? What has he got to do with anything?"

"A lot, I suspect. Did he ask you about Elsbeth? Did he ask you about whatever it was that chased me down in the tunnels?"

"Not this nonsense again."

His voice tightened. He dropped his hands onto the bed away from her. She shivered at the loss of his hand on her back, but she refused to back down.

"It isn't nonsense, Knox. Something is going on at Rosemount Manor. Something that has to do with your ancestors, and your childhood, and whatever is happening now. How can you not believe when the evidence is so overwhelming.? You know it is, no matter how much you deny your connection with Elsbeth."

He grabbed her elbows and maneuvered her onto the mattress. "I have no connection to Elsbeth." He thrust his legs over the side of the bed and sat up, running his hands through his hair. "I can't."

Eleanor pushed up onto her knees and came up behind him. She wrapped her arms around his shoulders and rested her cheek on his back. "Why can't you? Please tell me. I want to understand."

"I can't believe because if I believe in any of it, I have to believe in all of it. And all of it is too sad and horrible to contemplate. That's why I spent the whole day walking, trying to sort it all out. There are things…things you don't know. I'm fighting so many battles and…." He shook his head. "I'm tired, Eleanor. I'm just so bloody tired."

"Come back to bed."

She kissed a spot between his shoulder blades and pulled him gently back onto the mattress. He rested his head on her shoulder and buried his face in the crook of her neck with a sigh. Eleanor resettled the covers over them and stroked his hair. In minutes, he was breathing the soft, rhythmic breaths of a man in the sleep a weariness of the mind as well as the body.

Knox slept. But Eleanor couldn't sleep. The rain had stopped, as had the wind. But the lightning continued to flash outside the windows like an invader trying to peek into a room.

Chapter Twenty

KNOX SHUFFLED THROUGH THE STACK OF PAPERS ON HIS DESK and tried his best not to reveal he hadn't been listening to McGinty for the last five minutes. He probably hadn't succeeded as the heat of an actual blush crept up his neck and didn't stop until his hairline. How the hell was he supposed to focus on the repaving of the roads from the distillery to the railway when Eleanor's scent still clung to his skin?

The last three days and nights had been an idyll for him. Hadrian Cross hadn't said anything to Eleanor. The filming had gone on out of his sight and out of his mind for the most part. He spent his days managing Rosemount's affairs, his evenings living in the nineteenth century with the Regency boot campers, and his nights in Eleanor's arms. Rousseau and Salazar were back from their honeymoon and, as much as he hated to admit it, Knox trusted them to keep the explosions and stunts safe and to a minimum.

"Maybe we should save this discussion fer later, Yer Grace." McGinty's brogue always got thicker when he was chastising Knox, the way he had when Knox was a boy.

"No, I'm sorry McGinty. I have a few things on my mind that I need to settle today. But I do want this situation with the road paving settled as well."

"Well ta settle it ye may have to meet his price. He doesn't strike me as the sort ta back down."

"Really? Well neither am I. You tell him if he cannot do the job for his original estimate we'll find someone who can."

"Aye, and where will we find that someone?" McGinty asked with a grin.

"We'll burn that bridge when we come to it. Maybe he'll call my bluff, but I have to actually bluff before he can call it. Anything else?"

A brief rap at the door interrupted them. "Come."

Eleanor, dressed in a gold and bronze striped Regency dress, strode into the room. The woman never made an unobtrusive entrance. Knox fought a smile.

"Nothing that won't wait, Yer Grace." McGinty gathered up his papers, tucked them into the battered leather case he carried, and offered Eleanor a bow. "Good morning, Miss Witherspoon. Yer as lovely as a sunny day this morning."

"And you, sir, are a terrible flirt. I think Erik is asking for you." She made a point of not looking at Knox at all.

"Wonderful." McGinty rolled his eyes. "I'm off ta see what the Hollywood Yank wants." He inclined his head. "Yer Grace." The old Scot lumbered out of the room, but not before he turned and gave Knox a curiously suspicious look.

Knox waited until the heavy footsteps led away from the door before he left his chair and sauntered around his desk.

"Flirting with my steward, Miss Witherspoon?" He he cupped her elbows and drew her against him. "How many men do you need worshipping at your feet?"

"Only one, Knox." She kissed his chin and reached around and under his kilt to squeeze his butt.

"Good answer. Did I kiss you this morning?"

"Define morning."

He pressed his mouth to hers, once, twice, and then succumbed to the lure of those plump lips. He sank into the kiss, his tongue caressing hers and his hands stroking her back. The heat of her body and the scent of gardenias surrounded him. When he kissed Eleanor, he entered a world he never wanted to leave—no responsibilites, no worries, no family curses, just peace. Well, a peace that was morphing into arousal pretty damned quickly.

Eleanor slowly ended the kiss and propped her hands on his biceps. "Don't start something that we don't have time to finish."

"We don't?"

"No," she sighed. She handed him the papers in her hand. Papers he had not noticed until this moment. "Now that Bas and Teddy are back, Erik has revised the shooting schedule. Here's the new one."

Knox lean his butt against his desk and studied the printed schedules. "Does Lachlan know about this?"

"What?" Eleanor had begun to wander around his study. When he spoke she jumped as if she'd forgotten he was in the room.

"Lachlan. He needs to stay away from where some of this is going to happen."

"Oh." She smiled. "Of course. Lily has already filled him in. I just wanted you to know so you can stay clear of all of the noise and smoke. I know you hate it."

"Yes. I do." He noticed her hands clasped behind her back. "Have you talked to Hadrian today?"

"Hadrian?" She frowned. "Not since we all had breakfast together. "Why?"

"I need to speak to him about something." For some reason the hair on the back of his neck began to creep up.

"I think he's going to be in his and Anna's room writing

all day. He's trying to organize his…research. I think. What do you have planned for the day?"

He reached out and caught her hand, which she had suddenly begun to swing back and forth at her side. "I have a stack of paperwork to get through so I'll probably be stuck here all day," he said as he massaged her fingers. "You'll be with Wentworth herding your charges, I assume?"

She laughed, but the sound was hollow, not at all the rich, dark, sexy laugh he had grown to crave. "Something like that. I just wanted you to know so you could avoid the noise and concentrate on your…" she waved her free hand at his desk, "paperwork."

"Eleanor, what is it?" He wanted to cringe at the needy concern in his tone. Knox didn't know when she'd become so important to him that her every emotion evoked a physical response in him.

"Nothing." She stepped between his legs, cupped his face in her hands, and gave him a slow, deep, lingering kiss. "Will you be gracing us with your presence at supper tonight?"

"Another candlelight supper with your Regency boot campers? I wouldn't miss it. Which of those lovely evening gowns will you be wearing?"

"You only want to know so you can figure out how long it will take you to get me out of it, playboy."

"Untrue. I love to anticipate how gorgeous you'll look in the gown. And then how hot and tempting you'll look out of it. Both are equally important."

She patted his chest. "You'll just have to wait and see. I'm off."

She turned and crossed his study as if she was late for a train at St. Pancras station. Had Hadrian talked to her? Why would she keep it from him if he had?

"Eleanor?"

"Yes?" She stood in the open doorway, her hand on the doorknob.

"I…." He had so many things he wanted to say to her. Too bad the words were backed up in his throat like a log jam in the narrows of the loch. "I'll miss you."

"Knox. I'm not going anywhere." She shook her head and her eyes glittered like jewels. "Don't work too hard. I want you to be happy. You know that don't you?"

"I am happy."

"I hope so." She swallowed, gazed at him in silence, and after a few moments disappeared down the corridor.

He glanced back at his desk and then at the open door. In three strides he stood just outside his study and contemplated going after her. "For pity's sake," he muttered. "You've got it bad." He walked back to his study and dropped into his desk chair. Hadrian said three days. Today was the third day. Would he really tell Eleanor everything he had discovered in the first duke's diaries?

Probably.

Which meant Knox had better do something about talking to her. He dropped his hand to the bottom drawer of his desk. The diary that had gone missing was in that locked drawer. A brave man would sit Eleanor down and tell her the whole story himself. A coward would drop the diary on her bed and run. Face the consequences later. There had to be a middle ground.

Maybe this was all nonsense, and she wouldn't believe any of it. None of what he'd read and allowed to invade his already overloaded subconscious would matter to her. She was an intelligent, twenty-first century woman, in spite of her obsession with nineteenth-century England. Which was exactly why she and her merry band of actors, writers, and creative types, including his brother, had actually entertained the idea of digging up Knox's dead ancestor to reunite him with his equally dead love.

A not so gentle breeze blew across his desk from somewhere. Papers went flying.

"Fuck."

Knox pushed out of his chair and started gathering the various documents, pages, bills, and God only knew what else was in those stacks of paperwork. He had to crawl under a side table to collect some of them. And, of course, he banged his head on the way back out.

"Dammit, Elsbeth. If you've got something to say, say it. This is bullshit." He sat down in the floor and shuffled the papers into some sort of order. "My parents were right. I am out of my mind, none of this is real, and what I really need is a long stay in a hospital somewhere."

"I'm not talking about a holiday. Just leave. Go back to London and let me take over."

Had Lachlan really meant those words. That was the answer. He'd plead insanity and go away somewhere and let Lachlan take over. He lurched to his feet and picked up the last few straggling pieces of paper. He returned all of them to his desk except for the ones in Eleanor's handwriting. The warm June sunlight spilled into his study from the floor to ceiling window at the end of his study closest to his desk. He went to the window and gazed out at the expansive green lawns and the gentle hills beyond them.

Rosemount was beautiful in the sunlight. Then again, he'd discovered his home was beautiful even in the darkest, most savage weather. He'd stood on the banks of the loch in the rain and contemplated what Eleanor said as they'd left the mausoleum.

"How can you not be as one with the land that has been yours since before you were born?"

Walking the hills and fields and gazing over the loch as the rain pounded down and the thunder rumbled, he'd wondered the same thing. That day was probably the longest he'd actually spent exploring the land since he'd returned after his father's death. There had been no time at first. His father had left everything in such a damned bloody mess. Then later, he had no desire to spend time *bonding* with the one place he despised for all he'd had to give up. Why was he not one with Rosemount?

"My bloody bastard of a father, that's why."

Father was dead. Knox was here. All the dead people in his life had apparently ganged up on him to make him resentful, angry…and unhappy. Until now. Until Eleanor. He glanced down at the pages in his hand. The new shooting schedule appeared packed with explosions, cannon fire, cavalry charges. Had Lily really warned Lachlan off? How close was the fake battlefield to the mews, where his brother would be working with his birds? Lily wasn't in the battle scenes. Where was she now?

"Damn." He tossed the schedules onto his desk as he passed by on his way out of his study. He still needed to talk to Eleanor about the duke's diary, but some odd sensation told him he needed to make certain Lachlan was okay first. *Odd sensation?*

"Shut up, Elsbeth," he said as he took the stairs two at the time all the way down into the foyer.

Two hours later, Knox was over odd sensations, movie schedules, and sunny June weather. Lachlan wasn't answering his phone. He wasn't at the mews. He wasn't in his cottage. Neither was Lily. In fact, Knox hadn't seen very many people at all. The house and grounds were usually teeming with movie people, servants, and people from the village.

"This is beyond ridiculous."

He started up the stairs to return to his office when he

heard noise from the direction of the ballroom. Lachlan might not be in there, but Lily could be, learning the waltz or the Regency tango or something. As he got to the doors, he heard Erik Wentworth shouting at someone. He pressed his ear to the door to make certain Mrs. Wallace wasn't the one on the other end of that shout. The last place Knox wanted to be was between his housekeeper and the American who had dared to scratch her floor. He opened one of the double doors a crack. He didn't recognize any of the men in the ballroom, nor the equipment they were crawling all over. In fact, Wentworth was the only person he knew.

"Hey, Your Grace. Can I help you or did Mrs. Wallace send you to throw me in the dungeons?" The idiot directed grinned while his men cracked up.

Knox opened the door. "Mrs. Wallace is more likely to ask me to throw you in the loch with an anvil around your neck."

"Nice. What can I do for you?"

"Nothing really. I'm looking for Lady Lachlan. Have you seen her this morning?"

"Lady…Oh, Lily. No, I haven't seen her. We're not shooting today so I didn't expect to see her." One of his crew handed him a clipboard. He glanced at it and handed it back.

"Not shooting?"

"No. We're checking lighting in here and then we'll be setting up some shots in the west wing for tomorrow. Why?"

"I was given a revised schedule that indicated you would be shooting some battle scenes today."

"Not today. We'll be doing that the day after tomorrow. Bas needed more time to set some things up." Wentworth studied him carefully.

Time to get out of the ballroom and figure out what the hell was going on. Knox nodded briefly and left the ballroom. Wentworth called after him, but frankly he didn't have time for polite conversation. He shrugged at the twitch between his shoulder blades, the twitch that indicated he needed to be suspicious. But of what or whom, that was the question.

He stood in the foyer for a moment. Yes, something was going on and for some reason Eleanor had given him a bogus schedule. Maybe his suspicions were valid or maybe his guilty conscience was getting to him. All the hours he spent in her bed or with her in his, and not once had he even brought up the subject of superstitions, ghosts, or missing diaries since that stormy night.

"Good morning, Your Grace." Mrs. Wallace met him on the staircase, a pristine starched table cloth over her arm. She looked in the direction of the ballroom. "Has that Wentworth man done anything to my floor?"

"Not that I noticed. Have you seen Lady Lachlan, or my brother, or anyone of Miss Witherspoon's merry band for that matter?"

"Not in quite a while. The last I saw of them, they were on their way to the stables. Urquhart might know where they are. One of the lads said Lord Lachlan had asked them to have a team of the Suffolks hitched to one of the hay wagons for him early this morning."

"Thank you, Mrs. Wallace." He nodded absently to acknowledge her curtsy and headed slowly back to his study.

That little tingle of suspicion had turned into a bigger, more confused tingle. Pieces of information began to rico- chet around his head. The shooting schedule was wrong. No one was actively involved in filming or lessons today. Lachlan needed a wagon and a strong team? And through it all Hadrian's threat about the duke's diary kept popping up like a shark fin off an Australian beach. He closed his study door behind him and leaned back against the thick cool wood. No matter how hard he tried, he couldn't fix on what about the entire morning was bothering him.

Liar!

"Fine!"

He stomped to his desk, retrieved the bottom drawer key from the hidden slot under the lip of his desk, and opened the bottom desk drawer. He settled into his chair for a moment and stared at the frail leather-bound volume. As if he was afraid the book might bite him, he slid his hand underneath the dry, rough cover and lifted the last diary of the first Duke of Innes onto his desk. With a deep breath, Knox made his decision. He'd found his middle ground. He'd give the diary to Eleanor, but he'd be present when she read the contents. She'd either be furious with him for with-holding information—again—or she'd help him sort out how he felt about what the duke had written.

He glanced at the drawer once more. The empty drawer. He reached inside and swept his hand all the way to the back. *What the hell?* He grabbed the handle and pulled the drawer completely out to the point it left the desk and fell to the floor. Nothing. He dropped onto one knee and searched the hole where the drawer fitted. *Think!* When was the last time he'd seen the ancient metal key ring, the one with the keys to the family mausoleum?

The day he'd taken his little rainstorm hike across the estate. The day he'd ended up soaked to the skin until Eleanor took him upstairs and took care of him in every way a woman could take care of a man. The keys had been in his sporran. But he'd worn his sporran since then, though he wasn't wearing it today. He assumed he'd put the keys back in the drawer. He went through every drawer in the desk, but somehow, he knew he wouldn't find the keys. That sinking feeling in his stomach wasn't the return of his breakfast.

As if his limbs were suddenly filled with lead, Knox picked up the diary and staggered to his feet. He left the study and somehow made his way to the foyer. He turned back for a moment. Perhaps he should look for his sporran. No point. The keys weren't in his sporran. Like pieces of a child's wooden puzzle, everything began to fall into place.

He strode out of the house to find McGinty's Range Rover parked on the far side of the fountain. His steward had a habit of leaving the keys in the vehicle, a fortunate habit for Knox. He climbed in, tossed the diary onto the passenger seat, started the Rover, and steered it onto the narrow lane that led from the front drive up to the mausoleum. As he drove he forced himself to ignore the path across the fields he and Eleanor had taken. *Taken.*

He ran the events of that stormy night through his mind. She'd stripped him out of his clothes. But Dougal had picked them all up. He remembered the footman leaving with the clothes over his arm, and the shoes in his hand, and…the sporran was on the floor next to the bed. Had she planned this all along? He hit the brakes just in time to avoid running the vehicle into the steps leading to the mausoleum.

Not that it mattered. The iron gates stood wide open. He climbed the stairs like a man approaching the gallows. Of all the things careening through his thoughts, one agonizing fact burned like a comet. Eleanor had betrayed him. She'd taken the keys to the mausoleum, lied to him about the film schedule, and made certain he was going to be too busy to notice that she and the people he'd begun to count as friends had.…

"*Mhac na galla.*"

He stepped into the cold dark chamber and stared at the opened tomb in disbelief. They'd slid the first duke's *tumba* across the floor, pried up the slab beneath it, and took the contents out of the block vault beneath. He closed his eyes, counted to ten, and opened them again. Nothing had changed.

Lachlan was in on this. He'd ordered the wagon. Hell, he'd

likely driven the wagon, unless that Amazon of a wife of his had decided that was her job. His heart raced. Heat flooded his body. He shook his head to try and clear the roar in his ears. Didn't work. Suddenly, he wanted all of them gone—the boot campers, the film people, the director. Eleanor. Fate had dragged him back to the ruins of his childhood, to the place where he'd questioned his own sanity, and now they'd all run mad and intended to take him with them.

"Fuck that," he muttered as he staggered to the mausoleum doorway and braced one hand against the open ancient iron and oak doors.

His chest hurt with every breath. He'd been lied to, worked around, and deceived by them all. Yet, Eleanor's face was the one that invaded his brain and refused to leave. Why? Why had she done this?

A hot wind blew in from the fields below the mausoleum. The sun shone brightly onto the deep green expanse, but Knox shrugged against a cold, damp sensation between his shoulder blades.

A loud crash *sounded behind him.*

"Shite!"

He shoved open the door and jumped out onto the covered portico, then spun to face the tomb of his ancestors. His body went from hot with rage to cold as death in a split second. The eerie creak of glass cracking drew his eye to the stained-glass window at the back of the mausoleum. The one that bore the Innes family crest. The four-foot-tall black marble urn that sat before the window had fallen against the window sill and a crack ran up the middle of the crest.

He stepped into the room, his intention to figure out how the urn, which weighed as much as four grown men, had fallen. An eerie sensation crept over him. He stared into the empty vault in the floor. The darkness drew him in. He stepped closer. The walls seemed to pulse around him. Rage washed over him. Confusion. He had to get out of there. He had to figure out a way to stop the superstitious insanity that had taken over his life.

Once he stepped out of the mausoleum and closed the doors and gates behind him, Knox's equilibrium returned somewhat. He was choking on the hurt, anger, and disbelief swimming in his veins like some exotic soup. For a moment, he nearly missed the view across the estate from the top of the hill where he stood. The narrow hedge-lined lanes used by generations of his family and the families of those who worked on the estate rose out of the fields and led to the estate's church. And outside the front doors of that five-hundred-year-old church stood a wagon to which four of his finest rare Suffolk punch draft horses were hitched.

Knox reached the Range Rover in moments. He sped down the country lanes so fast the back of the vehicle swayed from side to side and occasionally tilted to one side or the other. He skidded into the final turn and slowed so as not to startle the horses. By the time he slammed the car into park and turned it off, Bas Salazar and Viscount Staines, rather Teddy Rousseau, emerged from the church to meet him.

"The vicar is on his way," Teddy announced.

"That's not what I bloody want to know." Knox stepped around the sword master and shrugged off the grasp of the stuntman Teddy had recently married. "Is the first duke's corpse in there?"

He stormed through the nave and into the cavernous stone church. On a bier before the altar sat an intricately carved stone coffin. They'd done it. They'd dug up his ancestor and carted his body, or what was left of it, to the church.

"Why is he here?" Not what he really wanted to know, but this was the first question that came to mind.

His question met with silence which gave him the opportunity to carefully peruse the group of people gathered at the front of the church. Danny Arneaux and his wife, Samantha, stood to one side of the bier. They both dropped their heads the moment Knox turned his attention to them. On the other side of the bier, Lachlan, arms crossed over his chest, and Lily, one hand propped on her hip, gave him their best defiant glares. Anna Chase leapt from her seat in the front pew and turned to face Knox. He sensed Bas Salazar and Teddy Rousseau behind him, waiting for him to do something, anything. Hadrian stood on the far side of the bier, standing on one of the altar steps.

He glanced around the interior of the church once more. "Where is she?"

"Here, Your Grace. I'm right here." Eleanor rose from the Innes family pew, a bouquet of dark red roses in her hand.

She walked to the stone coffin, placed the roses on top, then faced him, chin up and face composed. Her eyes, however, those incredible brown eyes that shone like the deepest of topaz, revealed her uncertainty and yes, dammit, her sympathy. She'd robbed his ancestor's grave and she had sympathy for *him*. He couldn't look at her.

He turned to Lachlan instead. "Why? Why did you allow them to do this?"

"Now just a minute you tight-assed, arrogrant son-of-a—"

"Lily, that's enough." Suddenly Lachlan was no longer the broken young man who dragged himself back to Rosemount to hide.

Knox should be happy. He wasn't. He was pissed.

"Son-of-a-bitch, sister?" Knox smiled. A chill suffused him. "I'm the son of a long line of bitches and some right bastards as well. So is your husband, but I think he got the best they had to offer and I got the worst. How long have you been planning this? What in God's name possessed you to—"

"God had nothing to do with it." Arneaux stepped forward to stand next to Eleanor, which forced Knox to look at her too. "Some weird shit has been going on around here, in case you haven't noticed. Maybe taking this thing out to that island won't help, but it sure as hell can't hurt."

"This isn't Louisiana, Arneaux. There's no voodoo here. Just old superstitions and my bad childhood dreams." Knox closed his hands into fists so tight his nails dug into his palms.

"Shit, Knox. Where the hell do you think those damned ideas in Louisiana came from? Not all of them came from voodoo. There are Scots in Louisiana too."

"You're right," Hadrian said. "We're not in Louisiana. Maybe this has nothing to do with ghosts and curses and superstition. Maybe its just the right thing to do. How about that?"

"Knox?" Eleanor's voice cut through the fog in his brain.

He couldn't remember her ever calling him by his name in front of anyone. He couldn't remember her voice so soft and gentle except when they were alone together. If he wanted to say anything to her, if there was anything to say he couldn't open his mouth to save his life. All he could do was stand there, lost in her voice and her expression that said things he'd never imagined he'd ever see.

"How long have you been planning this? Was that was the night of the storm was about, stealing my keys?"

"I didn't steal them. They fell out of your sporran. Of course I didn't plan to—"

"Betray my trust after everything I said to you, everything I told you? You have a funny damned way of showing it."

"I meant what I said, Knox. I want you to be happy. Something has hold of you and won't let you go. I don't know if it is your father or Elsbeth or the weight of the family legends, but something is keeping you from being who you were meant to be. Who I think you want to be. Maybe." She stepped closer and placed her hand on his arm. "Maybe us doing this will help."

He stared at her hand as if he meant to memorize each finger or perhaps memorize the moment. Slowly, he studied their faces one by one. He gazed at the stone coffin carved with symbols of his clan and the long line of men and women who pressed down on him with a weight he never wanted. This whole thing started as a result of betrayal after betrayal and it occured to him that perhaps that was all he was meant to have. *Fuck!*

"Do whatever you want. I don't care anymore. Try not to let the story get to the village or it'll be in the damned papers." He gave a brief dark laugh. "Or did none of you think of that? Then again, maybe headlines about grave robbing would be better than the headlines about our father fucking the help, right, Lachlan? Right, Eleanor?"

She gasped as he turned to go. From the corner of his eye, he glimpsed the fist coming at him, but too late, hard knuckles crashed into his jaw. His head snapped back. He tasted blood and saw stars. Swayed a little on his feet. When his vision cleared, he saw Teddy Rousseau shaking his hand out.

"You're a fucking asshole," Bas said. "Better be glad Teddy told me it wasn't okay for a viscount to cold-cock a duke or I'd lay your ass out next to your long dead grandfather."

"Of course its not okay. I outrank your husband. But we'll just keep this between us." Knox turned back to the others and swiped his hand across his bleeding lip. "After all, we're all friends here, aren't we?"

Samantha had her arm around Eleanor who raised her head and met his eyes, unafraid.

Knox ignored the throb in his jaw and shoved past Teddy and Bas only to run into the vicar. "What's he here for?"

"To bless the duke before we take him out to the island." Hadrian said. "Twelve years of Catholic school told me it might be a good idea."

"You and I both know why that won't help, but I'm not in charge of any of this, am I?" He shook his head and walked out of the church. "Do whatever the fuck you want. I don't care anymore. About any of it."

He managed to make it to the Range Rover before his legs gave out. He started the engine and peeled back onto the lane, but not in the direction of Rosemount. He needed to drive, to get as far away from the hurt in her eyes, the sharp pulsing pain under his ribs and the stinging sensation behind his eyes. He kept his gaze on the rising hills and low mountains on the horizon. Dark clouds had formed and appeared to rush toward him like an invading army.

Good!

He hoped they all got soaked trying to haul that stone box of bones down to the loch and across to the island. He wanted them cold, wet, and filled with regret. The same regret he felt for ever having met Eleanor Witherspoon. The same regret he felt for being so damned cruel to her that he wished Teddy had let Bas beat the shite out of him.

Chapter Twenty-One

ELEANOR HAD FORGOTTEN HOW TO BREATHE. SHE MUST HAVE. She'd only managed short little sips of air since Knox stormed out of the church and sped down the lane in a hail of dirt and gravel. Holding her shoulders back and her head up, she refused to cry. Knox had been a complete asshole. He'd shown her who he truly was, and she no longer had time or energy to muster anymore sympathy for him. Sitting on the wagon bench between Lily and Lachlan she congratulated herself on her sensible, feminist, twenty-first-century logic.

The fact her chest hurt like someone had cracked it open with a hammer and chisel? Yes, she was full of shit. She knew the minute she saw those keys lying on his bedroom floor after he'd left to go to breakfast ahead of her so as not to arouse suspicion that she intended to take them. The entire time she hid them wrapped in one of his fancy bathcloths in her dress pocket and hunted down Hadrian she knew she was betraying Knox. She'd done it anyway. And now?

As her Jamaican grandmother always said, "Eventually, everybody's bill comes due."

"Are you okay, Eleanor?" Lachlan asked as he steered the team of four back to the stables. "My brother—"

"Is a fucking jerk."

"Yes, Lily. You've said that three times since we left the church." Lachlan glanced at Eleanor who gave him a weak smile.

"She's just getting warmed up," Danny said from his spot in the back of now empty wagon where everyone else had climbed for the ride back to the manor. "Trust me."

"Regardless," Lachlan said in that rich quiet tone of his, "I want to apologize for his behavior. I expected him to object to all of this. For a lot of reasons. But I never expected him to take it out on you."

"It isn't your job to apologize for him." Eleanor looked over her shoulder at the church. "I'm the one who took the keys. I should have told him. I just didn't think he'd ever allow us to do this."

"Why?" Teddy asked. "If he doesn't believe in all of this what difference does it make? And if he does, I'd think he want us to lay the Innes Witch to rest."

"The witch is already at rest," Hadrian observed. He shifted on the hard floor of the empty wagon so that Anna was seated more comfortably on his lap. "We're laying the duke to rest."

"You haven't seen her," Danny said. "Trust me. That woman is *not* at rest. I'm just hoping once he's in that fancy-assed tomb with her she'll stay put."

"So we're pimping for a dead woman." Lily's expression was dead serious, though everyone else appeared to be ready to burst into laughter.

Eleanor's aching heart lifted a little. They were trying.

"If that's what it takes? Hell yes. Just call me Huggy Bear," Danny said, and laughter did erupt then, though Lachlan and Samantha appeared confused. "We'll introduce you to Huggy

Bear once Eleanor and Wentworth lift the ban on electronics." Danny winked at Eleanor who actually managed to give him a playful swat.

"So, when are we carting that big stone box of bones across the lake?" Bas asked. "And more important, *how* are we going to do it?"

"You have such a way with words." Teddy rolled his eyes, but the statement was made with such fond affection Eleanor had to smile. Teddy owning he was gay and marrying Bas had actually turned him into the decent guy he probably always was.

"We'll ferry him across on a barge the shepherds use to rescue sheep when the meadows are flooded. Sheep tend to crowd around high ground, trap themselves and refuse to budge across fast water." Lachlan guided the wagon into the stableyard and the lads who worked there scrambled to unhitch the horses.

The rest of the *grave-robbing* party scrambled down and began to walk toward the manor.

"Sounds good," Hadrian said. "What time? McGinty said we might have some bad weather movng in tomorrow or the next day."

The men strolled slowly and continued to discuss the weather and the logistics of moving the first duke's body from the chapel to the elaborate sepulchre on the island. Eleanor worked to put one foot in front of the other. Her entire body had grown heavy. She was tired, so tired. And frightened, though she wasn't certain of the source of that fear.

"Are you all right, Eleanor?" Samantha looped her arm through Eleanor's as they went into the manor and climbed the stairs. "You must realize the duke was upset and likely didn't mean all of the—"

"He meant every word, Samantha." Eleanor smiled

bitterly and shook her head. "Knox Innes doesn't say anything he doesn't mean."

"Bollocks," Samantha replied as they stopped in front of Eleanor's room. "Duke or not, he *is* a mere mortal. He feels betrayed and confused about all of this hocus pocus. Give him some time. Or better yet, beard the lion in his den and give him the ass-whoopin' he deserves."

"Ass-whoopin'?"

"Not Regency, I know. But my husband says an ass-whoopin' can be quite therapeutic when someone is being a complete wanker." She squeezed Eleanor's hand and walked down the hall to the room she shared with Danny Arneaux. "See you at dinner?"

"Of course. Thanks, Samantha."

Eleanor went into her room, closed the door behind her, and slid down that closed door to sit on the floor. She wanted to cry, but discovered she couldn't. Everything in her body—blood, tears, heat, even her heart—had frozen in the chapel and now refused to move at all. Well, except her mind which raced back and forth between guilt and burning anger. She shouldn't have taken the keys. She shouldn't have gone against his wishes. He'd be angry, she conceded that much. But why *so* angry? Angry enough to be cruel. Knox was never deliberately cruel. He'd had many opportunities since she'd started working for him. What was the difference when things converged around the Innes Witch and the first duke?

A cold breeze swept through the room. Eleanor struggled to her feet and straightened the skirts of her Regency dress, then walked to the tall windows on either side of her bed. Neither had been left open. She checked the door to her dressing room then the door to the bathroom she hadn't used since the Regency experience had started. Both were secure. The temperature continued to drop. Thunder rolled in the distance outside her windows.

"Okay, this is some crazy woo-woo shit," she muttered.

Very un-Regency but, frankly, at this point, she didn't give a fuck. Knox was being an ass. She and the rest of her friends had dug up a seven hundred year old grave, and she was probably about to lose the best job she'd ever had.

"What?" She stood in the middle of the room and spun slowly in a circle. "What the hell do you want? Is that you, Elsbeth? Grandma?"

Thunk!

Eleanor jumped in spite of herself. Persephone had climbed halfway up her enclosure and banged her nose against the glass again. Hard.

"Shhh, sweetie." Eleano reached the huge glass case in a few steps and pressed her hand against the place where the python had struck. "What is it? What do you see?"

As she assessed her pet's attitude, she followed the line of sight from the snake's slightly undulating head across the room to the dark corner by the dressing room door. Thunder rumbled once more, still far away, but close enough to vibrate the windows.

She paced slowly toward the dressing room door, but stopped when she passed the window. For a moment she swore she saw a woman in white standing there gazing out across the estate. Once she'd closed her eyes and opened them again, the woman was gone. Was this what is was like for Knox? Had this been his life as a child, seeing and hearing things that weren't really there? Or were they?

"Okay, Elsbeth, what were you looking for?"

She marched to the window and swiped the curtains farther apart. Nothing. The sky appeared blue and clear all the way across the front lawn and up to…the mausoleum, or at least the hill where the mausoleum stood. You couldn't really see the monstrous family vault from that distance but you could see the hill and the outline of the building. Except now there was a bank of dark clouds over that outline. The entire sky from that point across the horizon was black.

Eleanor leaned her forehead against the glass and laughed. "Wonderful. Knox hates me, Elsbeth is ignoring me, and apparently someone in the mausoleum is pissed we dug up the first duke." Her eyes burned and glazed over. She blinked furiously. "Tough shit!" she all but shouted. "Tough damned shit."

Then she burst into a full-blown ugly cry all over Mrs. Wallace's nice clean windows.

His Grace the Duke of Turra didn't deign to bless them with his presence for dinner. Eleanor vacillated between gratitude and being highly pissed at the bastard. Erik Wentworth had come to dinner and had even allowed Bella Stepford to dress him in the evening clothes of a Regency gentleman. He'd taken everyone else's smart-assed remarks with a few remarks of his own, and dinner was a pleasant and chatty experience. Very different from when Knox bothered to show up. McGinty had offered the stubborn man's apology and said *Himself* was busy with estate business. Even Lachlan had snorted at that, but Erik didn't seem to notice. McGinty glared at the younger Scot before taking his own seat next to the empty seat at the head of the table.

Eleanor had taken great care getting dressed for the meal, not that it mattered. She wore a beautiful emerald green silk gown, whipped up by Bella from a pattern she'd created for one of Lily's costumes for the film. Everyone had complimented Eleanor, and she had taken an elaborate bow at their praise. Bridie had done her hair in a very elegant style, after she'd walked into Eleanor's bedroom, taken one look at her red eyes, and sent down to the kitchens for some cucumbers and ice. In true Scot's stoic style, the maid hadn't said a word until she'd pronounced Eleanor ready and pushed her out the door.

"Us below stairs think yer doing right by the Witch," she'd said, then disappeared through one of those doors hidden in the hallway wall to keep servants out of sight and out of mind.

At least somebody thought she was doing the right thing. *Doing right by the Witch.*

She hadn't been thinking about Elsbeth Dunhomme when she'd taken his keys. She'd been thinking about Knox. He needed the legend to be put to rest, to be able to move on with his life and accept who he was. The resentment he held for Rosemount, for the responsiblities, and for what his relationship with a seven-hundred-year-old ghost had done to him as a child made it impossible for him to commit to anything or anyone because he didn't want even one more person to depend on him for a damned thing. She couldn't decide if that made him selfish or if he was just trying to survive. With what she knew of Knox, the latter was the most likely.

The table erupted into laughter. Eleanor hadn't been paying attention. Wentworth, however, sounded as if he were enjoying himself, and that was good for her. Because if Knox fired her…. She wasn't going to think of that now.

"What's so funny?" she asked. "I was thinking about tomorrow's…outing."

Everyone but Wentworth and McGinty mumbled some sort of agreement. The director looked curious. McGinty? Yeah, he was just as pissed as Knox, if that was possible.

"Arneaux here has just explained what I'm eating," Wentworth said, his complexion a suspicious green tint.

"Aye," McGinty said. "And our Cajun friend lied just ta see

that look on your face, Sassenach." The big Scot was grinning now and everyone else at the table laughed. "Yer nay eating haggis, mon, not ta worry."

"Thank God," Wentworth said with a sigh of relief. "Because until he said that, I was really enjoying whatever this is." He forked some more of the food on his plate and took a big bite.

"Aye," McGinty said with a wicked glint in his eye. "It's eel pie you be eating. Eel fresh caught from the loch this morning."

Erik Wentworth's eyes bulged as he fought to swallow what he'd just eaten. He grabbed his wine glass and chugged it like a frat boy. The minute he fumbled it back onto the table Robbie stepped forward to fill the glass again. Once he'd drained that glass, he glared at the rest of them as they tried to rein in their laughter.

"Were people really this cruel during the Regency?" he finally asked when he'd caught his breath. "Or just you people?"

"We've been eating like this for weeks, Wentworth," Teddy said. "You'll get used to it."

"Like hell," Erik said. "I'll take my meals at the pub in the village. And you people better not show up to tell me what I'm eating because I happen to like the food they serve."

"Lightweight," Bas said.

"Be nice, gentlemen," Anna said. "He hasn't had the benefit of Eleanor's Regency boot camp regime to toughen him up."

"Regime?" Erik waved his hand around. "Living in this beautiful mansion and waited on hand and foot. What's so tough about that?"

"No electronics," was Lily's immediate response.

"No electricity," Hadrian added.

"No modern toilets or showers," Samantha put in.

"No heat but a fireplace in March," Danny grumbled. "Almost froze my *couilles* off."

Erik raised his hands in surrender. "I stand corrected. Now what is this outing tomorrow? I know we don't have any filming scheduled, but are you going to be doing anything that might look good in the film?'

"*NO!*" They all answered so quickly and with such vehemence the crystal rattled on the table.

"Excuse me, Miss Witherspoon?" Abercrombie, Rosemount's very proper butler, stepped into the dining room, silver salver in hand. He gave Eleanor a brief but correct bow and offered her the salver where a sealed note rested.

"Thank you, Abercrombie." Eleanor recognized the handwriting and the seal at once. She opened the note, read it, and placed it back on the salver as if it might bite her. "Tell His Grace I will be up in a few minutes."

"Very good, Miss Witherspoon." He glided out of the room as quietly as he had entered.

Eleanor stood and the men at the table were immediately on their feet. Erik was a little slow, but apparently even he knew something was up.

"Samantha, if you will lead the ladies to the drawing room for me. Gentlemen, we will leave you to your port. Try to be nice to Mr. Wentworth." She inclined her head and when she looked toward the far end of the table McGinty met her gaze with one of sympathy, but encouragement too. He tilted his head as if to say *Chin up.*

Damned right. She refused to cower to Knox Innes now.

By the time she'd climbed the stairs and marched down the corridor to Knox's study, she had a full head of steam and more than a few things to say to His Fucking Grace. She didn't bother to knock but flung the door open and slammed it behind her once she was inside his lair.

Seated at his desk in that thronelike chair, he neither flinched nor raised his head.

"Please have a seat, Eleanor. I'll be right with you."

He turned to snatch a few pages as his printer spat them out. After a quick scan of the pages, he grabbed his pen to sign one of them and folded them all to place them in an envelope. She didn't get the chance to read the contents but they were printed on his official embossed stationary. He didn't seal the envelope, but did press his ring into a blob of wax on the back of the envelope. When he began to organize the rest of the papers on his desk, Eleanor was done.

"You've made it abundantly clear you don't want to *be* the duke so I'll be damned if I am going to treat you like the duke, Knox Innes. What do you want? I have things to do."

"Planning on digging up some more of my relatives?" He raised his head and fixed her with flat blue eyes.

"No, but there *is* a vacancy in your family mausoleum. You might want to take that into consideration before you keep wasting my time and pissing me off." She folded her arms across her chest and leaned back in her chair.

His mouth curled in a slight smile. "Duly noted." He sighed and flattened his hands on his desk. "What are we going to do, Eleanor? What do you want me to do?"

"About what?" The instant the words left her mouth, she wished she hadn't uttered them. There were some things she didn't want to know—like how badly she'd screwed up this thing with Knox, whatever it was. Whatever she hoped it might be.

"For God's sake, woman. Us! You and me. You took my keys. You went against my express wishes. You didn't even talk to me about it. You just assembled your troops and raided my ancestor's tomb and—"

"I did talk to you about it, Knox. You didn't listen or you simply chose to act like I hadn't said anything."

"I said no. More than once. You just decided to go ahead and do what you thought was best...for a couple of dead people." The vehemence of that last part struck her. There was more to this than he was letting on, but he refused to tell her, to open up to her when that was all she wanted in the world.

"Dead people don't ruin a child's life, Knox. Dead people don't show up periodically to try and speak to the rest of us. Dead people don't control our every move unless we let them."

"What are you talking about?"

"You tell me. Everyone in this house knows you've seen the Innes Witch, that you have spoken to the Innes Witch, that the Innes Witch cost you your childhood and your relationship with your brother. You hate Rosemount. You hate being the duke. All because of a dead person who, apparently, is a lot less dead than you want her to be. I took your keys. And tomorrow the rest of us and I are going to do what we hope will put the Innes Witch to rest forever.

"We're hoping to set you free, Knox. Because, whether you want to admit it or not, whatever is going on here has prevented you from taking your place here, from loving your brother, from loving your home and from allowing anyone close enough to you to...love you." She fought the sting of tears and gulped a breath. "Your parents are gone, Knox. But Lachlan is here. Your people are here. This group of movie invaders is here. I'm here."

"I know you're here, Eleanor. I've never been more aware of someone's presence in my life. And I...." He erupted from his chair and started to pace back and forth behind his desk. "You were the one person I wanted to trust, Eleanor."

"But you don't trust me, Knox." Her voice broke but she pushed on. "You trust me with your doubts and fears. You trust me with your b-body. But you don't trust me with yourself. With whatever has this hold on you that keeps you from"—she threw her hands up in frustration— "letting go of this person you seem to think you have to be." She jumped up in front of him and grabbed his hands. "I've seen glimpses of that man. Haven't you?"

He laughed. The sound frightened her. "That's so easy for you to say, Eleanor. Typical American *just-be-yourself* attitude. My life is so much more complicated than that."

"Bullshit. You make your life complicated." She dropped his hands and walked away and then back to stand toe to toe with him. "You want to know why I took your keys? Why I am trying to lay Elsbeth, my ancestor, to rest? To give you peace. To make you realize you aren't cursed, and you *can* be happy, and the duke, and loved."

"If that does happen, it will have to happen without you, Eleanor."

He stared into her face and his expression twisted into one of such pain she wanted to reach for him. She didn't get the chance. He strode to the desk and picked up the envelope and some other papers from his desk. With one last look at them, he thrust them toward her.

"I have terminated our contract. When the film is over so is your position here. I've written you a letter of recommendation, and I will tell anyone who inquires what an amazing asset you have been to the estate. I'll tell them you are worth more than I can pay you." He finally looked into her eyes again. "It's the truth."

"I see." She took the papers and folded them into a bundle. Her entire body shook, but she tried to tell herself he didn't see. She waited for her throat to open, which took a minute or two. "More than you can afford to pay me to be your event planner? Or more than you can afford to pay me to be your lover?"

"You know that's not true. I've never seen what's between us as something ugly or fake."

"That's not what you said when you busted up into the chapel and lost your mind."

"I didn't mean it. I was angry." He swept his fingers through his hair. "I don't remember what I said, but—"

"I do." She pressed the bundle of papers against her chest. "I'll never forget a single word. I didn't deserve that, Knox."

"You don't deserve any of this, Eleanor. That's why I am letting you go. Get away from here. I wish I could, but I can't, any more than I can get away from the legacy of the men in this family." He slid a drawer open and withdrew a very old, thick, leatherbound book. "This is what Hadrian Cross found in the archives in the west wing. The first of many. Every Duke of Turra since the first one has kept a personal journal." He placed it on the corner of the desk closest to her. "Everyone except me."

"What does this have to do with—"

"She didn't curse the Dukes of Innes. He did." Knox's eyes remained locked on her face with that keen, piercing way of his.

Eleanor put her hand on the journal and sat down in the chair in front of his desk. An icy fog settled into her brain. She'd heard the words but couldn't make out what he'd actually said.

"What?"

"Elsbeth Dunhomme didn't curse the men of this family. The first duke did. After her death, he spent every waking moment in the library in the west wing. He consulted every witch, wizard, druid, and conjurer in Scotland. He sent for books. While his mother had Elsbeth's village burned and most of her family murdered, he sat in that west wing dungeon studying black magic. He didn't save the two children Elsbeth had with her first husband, McGinty's ancestor did. He put them on a ship to Jamaica while the duke searched for a way to avenge Elsbeth's death."

"Oh my God." Eleanor didn't know what to think or what to feel. Her very sensible twenty-first century self had just been picked up and dumped in the middle of a seven-hundred-year-old soap opera, a bad one.

"God left this family on its own a long time ago. All the while my ancestor was stirring up this curse, he was married to the woman his mother picked for him. Once he got her pregnant, he didn't touch her again, didn't talk to her again. She died in childbirth, like I said. He never bothered to have anything to do with his son. By that time, he'd found the curse he wanted and that curse required a sacrifice, a human sacrifice."

"So, he killed himself." Eleanor touched her fingers to her mouth. She wanted to know, she'd kept saying she wanted to know. This was insane. He'd fired her. And he was telling her all of this. Why?

"The Dukes of Turra were Catholic. Big no-no. But he didn't care. He wanted revenge on his mother, and he didn't care about anyone else or anything else. Poor sod."

"Knox, surely you don't believe in…."

"In curses?" He shook his head. "No," he said as he turned back to her. "Read the journal. The man was a raving lunatic right to the end. And so was his son. And his grandson. Hadrian will get through all of the journals eventually, right up to my son-of-a-bitch of a father who was bipolar, by the way. *That* is the curse of the Dukes of Turra. Murderers, wife beaters, schizophrenics, suicides. My father didn't send me away because he thought I was crazy. He *knew* I was crazy."

"Knox, no. You're not crazy. If you are, then we all are. The things we've seen? The things that have happened here?" She dropped the papers on top of the journal and went to him. He'd folded his powerful arms tightly across his chest.

She clutched his forearm with both hands and shook him. "There is nothing wrong with you. Other than being an arrogant, tightly wound, stubborn, pain in the ass Scot. We can make this right, Knox."

He unfolded his arms and cupped her cheek in his hand. "I told you before, love. I cannot believe in any of this. It's been hanging over my entire life, and I am going to rid myself of it once and for all. It ends with me, whether it is a curse or hereditary mental illness. It ends with me."

She started to open her mouth to say that things couldn't end with him, if he never married Lachlan's son would be the next duke, but he rubbed his thumb across her bottom lip and Eleanor wanted to cry. He was truly walking away, from her and from what might have been between them.

"Knox, please."

He kissed her forehead and walked around her to pick up the journal and the paperwork. "I want to thank you, Eleanor. For a little while at least I got a taste of what being happy was like. I almost believed, and you gave me that. I'm just…." He shrugged, his eyes suspiciously bright.

A wave of heat washed over her. She snatched the journal and papers from him. "A coward. You're a coward, Knox Innes. The ghost? The family history? It's all a bullshit excuse for a man who refuses to risk the work it takes to build a relationship. Fucking is easy. A relationship is hard. All these dead people from the first duke up to your fucking father have made you so afraid to live you hide behind your brother's PTSD and your shitty childhood so Rosemount won't touch you. And you hide behind this fear that Elsbeth isn't real because you don't want to risk getting your h-heart broken."

"No worries on that account, Eleanor. You did a bang-up job of that when you took my keys." He dropped back into his desk chair and dragged a stack of paperwork in front of him. "Good night, Eleanor."

She swept his desk clean with one arm and folded the other arm against her chest to keep her pounding heart from falling out on the floor. "Fuck you, Knox. Goodbye."

She made it out the door and halfway down the corridor before her body seized in a noisy bone-shaking sob. She plopped down on one of the sturdy velvet-tufted benches and buried her face in her hands where she alternated between crying and screaming into her palms. The journal and the papers and his letter of recommendation lay at her feet.

Against her every instinct she had fallen in love with a man determined to hold himself responsible for every flaw, real or imagined, except for his own. He was claiming a legacy of cruelty, hate, and revenge to avoid dealing with his own fears. Life was so much easier when all she had to worry about in men was whether they had a job and if they had a side chick who was going to show up and key her car.

A large clean handkerchief appeared in her lap.

"Don't gie up on him, lass," McGinty said. "He's a good mon, and the way he is isn't his fault."

She wiped her face and offered the handkerchief back. He closed his hand around hers. "I know it isn't his fault, McGinty, at least not all of it. But he is who he is, and that man just fired me and expects me to be gone once the film is done."

"He didn't mean it. If you don't stay…if you don't try, he'll stay broken."

She gathered up the things she'd dropped and pushed to her feet. "Then he'll have to stay broken. A woman who takes on a man thinking she can fix him will spend the rest of her life doing just that. I don't want to fix him. I want to love him, and he just won't let me."

Eleanor patted the old Scot's shoulder and walked calmly down to the drawing room. When she entered everyone else was gathered around a table covered in some sort of hand-drawn plans. Hadrian spotted the journal in her hand, but when he raised his eyebrow she shook her head. Pieces of her heart peeled off and dropped into her gut, but the entire time she smiled and put a bounce in her step.

"So," she said as she sat down next to Samantha, "what's the plan?"

Chapter Twenty-Two

KNOX FINALLY UNDERSTOOD WHAT THE WARNING "BE CAREFUL what you wish for" truly meant. After the last twenty-four or so hours, all he'd wanted when he finally flung himself from his bed that morning was peace and quiet. Flung himself from his bed because he had slept very little and had experienced peace even less. As he left his study and carried the tray bearing the remains of his lunch down to the kitchens, he discovered the only thing more hollow than an empty London apartment or an empty London office building in the middle of the night was an empty Rosemount Manor. At least, he assumed the house was empty.

He'd neither seen nor heard a soul all day save for Robbie, who had delivered his breakfast tray then retrieved it and had, less than an hour ago, brought up his luncheon. The lad had said very little. A sure sign the servants heard about Knox firing Eleanor. He wasn't an idiot. His entire staff had been suspicious of Eleanor, then resentful, and now they adored her. Perfectly understandable. That was exactly how Knox's relationship with the red-haired beauty had gone.

Now they adored her.

So did he, dammit. But he couldn't trust her. Maybe if he told himself that every day for the rest of his life he'd eventually believe it. What he did believe was rather than risk saddling her with a man who was or would become mentally ill, he'd decided to let her go. Aye. He didn't believe that either.

"Your Grace," several voices exclaimed, accompanied by scraping chairs and clattering dishes. The servants stared at him as if he were a unicorn at a tea party or something like that.

"Please continue your lunch." He handed the tray to Mrs. Gordon, who scowled and muttered something unintelligible as she handed the tray off to one of the maids.

"I told that lad to fetch your tray before he went running off to do God knows what," she grumbled.

"It's fine, Mrs. G." Knox kissed her cheek and reached around her to filch one of the little fried pies cooling on the work table. "Where was our Robbie off to this afternoon?"

Mrs. Gordon swatted at him just as she had when he was a boy. The servants settled back down at the table, several even flashed grins at him as they did. One or two refused to look at him. Just as he suspected, something was up. He ate his pie and waited as they all went back to eating their lunch. Mrs. Gordon bustled about and tried very hard to look busy.

"No one knows where Robbie went?" he finally asked. Suddenly they all had mouths full of food. Knox sighed. "Maybe McGinty will know." He turned to leave.

"Lord Lachlan sent for him, Your Grace," a footman named Seamus said. "Not twenty minutes ago."

"Thanks, Seamus."

Trouble was, once Knox had that information and walked back upstairs from the kitchens, he had no clue what to do next. Something *was* going on this afternoon. They were going to take the first duke out to the island. He wanted nothing to do with that. If he never heard another word about this misadventure it would be too soon. He rubbed the back of his neck in the hope of eliminating the electric pulse that had his hair on end. That was usually the first sign Elsbeth was nearby. He'd had the sensation all morning, but she'd never appeared. More evidence he was losing his mind.

He stopped in front of the library doors. His chances of being able to concentrate enough to read a book were slim. Nevertheless, he needed a break from estate business and a distraction from…everything else. Seemed like a perfectly good idea until he walked into the library and saw McGinty at the front of the spacious room staring out the tall windows that looked over the front lawns.

"Anything interesting?" he asked as he crossed the library to join the burly Scot.

"Don't like the look of those clouds," McGinty said without turning around. He nodded toward the horizon.

Knox came to stand next to him. The skies were blue and clear over the fountain and front drive and even over the perfect green carpet of the expansive lawn that stretched from the drive toward the hills in the distance. At the top of the hill, however, spread across the horizon like a cloak, an inky darkness blotted out the shadow of the mausoleum and the skies beyond that hilltop. He couldn't remember ever seeing a storm move in like that. He shuddered at the sensation like the trail of fingertips across the back of his neck.

"You did say to expect storms this afternoon, didn't you?"

"Aye, Yer Grace. I did at that." McGinty turned to look at him, his expression as grim as Knox had ever seen. "But that isnae a normal storm. When it breaks it willna be pretty, I'll tell yer that much. Not a fit time ta be out on ta loch."

"Are they? Out on the loch?" Knox evened his tone and made the question as casual as he could.

"They are or soon will be. They spent the morning organizing the sheep barge and lines across the loch. They sent Robbie and some of the lads with the wagon ta the chapel to fetch…." McGinty rubbed the bridge of his nose with his forefinger.

"The body," Knox all but growled. "Or rather the box of bones. Not much of a body left, I expect."

"Word has it, ye made a damned loud bloody fuss about that box of bones." McGinty lumbered across the library to peer out the French doors that led onto the terrace.

"It wasn't the box of bones that made me angry. It was the way they went about it, and the fact they dug up the box of bones when I asked them not to." Knox stayed where he was, his body at war with the desire to see what McGinty might see of whatever was happening on the loch.

"The way they went about it or the way *she* went about it?"

"It doesn't matter."

"Apparently it does. Ye dismissed the lass over it."

"She's not a lass she's a grown woman."

"Ye noticed, did ye? Did ye ask this grown woman why she took yer keys and did what ye told her not to do?"

"She said she did it for me." He shrugged at the feel of some sort of silky fabric brushing against his bare forearm. One of the library doors creaked open behind him. He refused to look back but strode to the place where McGinty stood.

"Did she now?" the older man murmured. "I suspected as much. And ye still let her go."

"I'm not interested in talking about this anymore. Can you see the loch from here?"

"Only a bit. Cannae see what they're doing."

One of the French doors slammed open and a damp, heather-laden wind rushed into the room. He and McGinty looked at each other, but didn't move.

"Ye first, Yer Grace. She's yer ghost." The big bastard was dead serious.

"She's not *my* anything. *She* doesn't exist."

"As ye say, Yer Grace." McGinty rocked on his heels and nodded toward the open door. "She's right though. If we want ta see what that lot's about with yer dead grandfather, we won't see it standing around in here."

"Oh, for fuck's sake," Knox muttered. He turned and stomped to the doors, then out onto the terrace with McGinty close on his heels. "This is ridiculous. I have—"

Crack!

"Bloody hell." McGinty threw up his hand to shield his eyes from the fierce spear of lighting that split the nearly black sky and sizzled down toward the loch. The wind picked up and began to howl in an ungodly shriek. They were surrounded by the sort of darkness one expected just as the sun set, yet it couldn't be later than two in the afternoon.

"We can see the loch from the tower." Knox grabbed McGinty's arm and half-dragged him through the gardens and across the ha-ha bridge toward the castle ruins.

Once they reached the bottom of the tower, he fumbled with his keys to unlock the ancient wooden door into the room he'd turned into his private retreat. He didn't tarry once he got the door open but raced across the room to the door that led to the stairs up the tower.

With every narrow, slick, treacherous step his heartbeat increased. He swallowed against the sense of dread that poured over him like a bucket of loch water. Something was wrong. Very wrong. By the time he reached the door to the roof of the tower, he was gasping for breath. Somewhere behind him, he heard McGinty struggling to keep up.

Once on the battlement, Knox saw and felt the magnitude of the storm that spewed from the area of the mausoleum and crept across Rosemount like an oil spill on the ocean.

The wind came from all directions and howled like the *bean nighe* Mrs. Wallace had frightened him and Lachlan with when they were children. But this *bean nighe* sounded too damned real and big enough to scare a fair share of adults. Lightning shot from the blackness to the ground along the shore of the loch.

"Where are they?" Knox shouted as he prowled along the parapet that faced the loch. "I can't see them." McGinty moved along the wall, studying the loch with every step.

"They should be right along here." McGinty pointed toward a spot in the middle of the loch. "The island is somewhere along—"

"There!" Knox nearly knocked the older man over as he pointed.

There, as if floating on the water, stood Elsbeth Dunhomme, dressed in white and staring at Knox. She and Eleanor did look very alike, but he could tell the difference. His childhood companion raised her arm and pointed to a spot halfway across the loch. There, amidst a whirl of powerful waves, the sheep barge rose and fell higher and higher against a storm one might see off the coast of Cornwall, not in an inland lake in the middle of Scotland.

Knox was past the point of denying what he saw now. Real or not, he needed Elsbeth to show him what to do. Dread clung to him like a second skin. Dread for all of the fools out on the water on the romantic mission they all insisted on undertaking. Sheer near paralyzing terror that he might never have the chance to tell Eleanor how sorry he was and how very much he needed her.

"What the hell is all this?" McGinty swiped the rain from his face. The storm reached the tower and dropped a near wall of water on them.

"What the fuck?" Knox leaned over the parapet to get a better view. "Why are there women on that damned barge?

What the *hell* was my brother thinking? Jesus Christ. We've got to get down there." He started down the stairs and had to grab at the stone walls to keep from sliding all the way to the bottom. "Hurry up, McGinty, dammit."

"If I hurry too much faster, I'm going to knock us both ass over teakettle."

"Eleanor's with them, isn't she? And that she-devil my brother married."

"I think all of the ladies went. They wanted to be there to—"

"I could give two shites *why* they're there. They have no business out there in this storm."

"I don't think this storm was brewing when they left the shore. This storm's like nothing I've ever seen. You'd think the witch doesn't want her mon laid to rest beside her."

"What they hell are you saying? That Elsbeth is responsible for this?" Knox waved his hand at the driving rain pelting them like a hail of pebbles. "This isn't Elsbeth. Come on."

Knox sprinted down the narrow lane around the loch. Surprisingly, McGinty kept up with him pretty well. They reached a landing that jutted out into the loch and Knox gave thanks that some row boats and a couple of jet skis were tied there. They bobbed precariously in the wind and waves, but he seized the handle of the nearest jet ski and dragged it closer.

"How do you know?" McGinty shouted above the wind as he untied the jet ski.

"What?" Knox straddled the jet ski and turned the key. The engine roared to life

"How do you know it isnae Elsbeth?" Their gazes met.

"I just know." Something in him shifted. He drew in a deep breath. "Go fetch the lads. Have them bring the big speed boat from the boathouse. Hurry, McGinty. Something is wrong." He glanced back toward the mausoleum, then across the loch where Elsbeth still shimmered in the darkness. "Very wrong. Go."

"Be careful." McGinty slapped him on the back and jogged up the lane toward the stables.

"Too fucking late for that," Knox muttered, and he gunned the accelerator with his right hand. The jet ski shot across the rolling waves.

He'd chosen today of all days to wear a kilt and hiking boots and a polo shirt, which meant he'd been soaked to the skin before reaching the loch, and his balls were turning into damned waterlogged ballcicles. Not to mention, said ballcicles being banged about against the seat of the jet ski as he bounced across the water.

"Fuck!' He swiped his hand across his eyes to clear his vision.

Where were they? How couldn't he see the barge that was right there just a minute ago. It had to be…. *Shite!*

A little over halfway across the loch the barge rose and fell higher and harder with each wave as Lachlan, Arneaux, Bas, Rousseau, and Hadrian Cross fought to pull the barge closer to the island by way of the rope and pulley system they'd devised to drag the barge and its contents to shore. The system was sound, though labor intensive, had the loch been calm and the skies clear. Now? They'd be lucky if they, the long-dead duke, and the women huddled against the casket hanging on for dear life didn't end up at the bottom of the loch.

"Bloody film people." He gunned the jet ski toward the barge.

Eleanor spotted him first. She stood, fool woman, one hand tight around the ropes holding the casket in place and one outstretched toward him. Dear God, he felt that hand reaching for him. With every fiber of his being he wanted her hand clasped in his because if he had her hand, he'd never let her go. Never.

"Knox!" Her voice carried across the water and wrapped around his heart.

He neared them, slowed, and struggled to bring the jet ski alongside the barge, an impossible task. "Bas," Knox shouted. "Come grab the jet ski when I move it close enough!" he screamed at the top of his lungs to be heard over the roar of the wind, waves, rain, and thunder. The storm had actually increased in force the closer he'd raced to the barge.

"Are you fucked in the head?" Bas shouted back.

"I'm not the one on a sheep barge in a bloody thunderstorm all for a damned dead man." Knox angled the jet ski so it bumped nearly sideways against the barge. Bas grabbed the handlebars and steadied himself on the deck of the barge. Knox leapt off the jet ski and strode straight to Eleanor whom he enveloped in his arms. "Are you okay?" he demanded.

She nodded.

"Good. Now get on the bloody jet ski with Bas and take your ass back to shore. You are barking mad to be out here like this. All of you ladies," he called over the storm. "Bas is going to take you off this damned barge and back to shore one at a time."

"I am?" Bas fought to hang onto the jet ski. Knox glared at him. "Apparently I am." The stunt master shrugged.

"Knox, we have to get the duke onto the island." Eleanor wrapped her hands around his bicep. "We can't leave him out here."

"The hell we can't. He wouldn't *be* out here if you lot hadn't dug him up." He tried to drag her toward the jet ski.

She grabbed the ropes holding the casket in place and held on tight. The rain began to lash sideways. The other men fought to hold the ropes steady enough to keep the barge at least still in the middle of the loch.

"Whatever the hell we're going to do we need to do it quick," Arneaux said. "I didn't sign on to be in a remake of *Titanic*." Samantha stood between his outstretched arms as he grasped the ropes in his leather-gloved hands. The poor woman looked terrified though she did manage a weak smile at the Cajun's remark.

"McGinty's gone for the speed boat, but I don't know if we can wait that long. That's why we need to get the women off this barge as quickly as possible."

Anna stood and grabbed the rope next to Eleanor. "Can't we all work the ropes and get the barge to the island?"

Knox rolled his eyes and looked to Hadrian for help. The big American nodded toward the casket. Now Knox's sister-in-law had joined the ladies. Great! No way he was going to take on Lachlan's wife.

Bas manhandled the jet ski onto the deck of the barge. "Come on, Your Grace. I'll fight the storm and the damned jet ski, but I'm not about to fight—holy shit!"

The barge lurched into the air. The jet ski slid across the deck and crashed into the stone casket. Knox stumbled against the casket. Teddy and Lachlan struggled with the ropes on the far side of the barge. Arneaux and Cross began to pull at the ropes on the other side in order to move the barge toward the island, but with little luck.

Knox pushed himself upright. As he did, his vision became fixed on the island. *Elsbeth.* The woman in white was no longer watching him. Her gaze was fixed on a spot in the distance, on the skies over the mausoleum where some sort of maelstrom boiled in the black clouds shot through with lightning. Three ear-splitting blasts of a horn echoed across the lake.

"What the fuck?" Lily shouted as she lurched with

another wave and clung more closely to the rope. She wore sweatpants and Wellingtons. They all did. No Regency costumes today, thank God, because they might have to swim for it. "Knox, what is that?"

She'd called him Knox. Lachlan's wife never called him Knox. But he'd heard her as if from a long distance away. The sound of the ancient horn reverberated in his ears. He gazed at Eleanor.

"Knox?"

That one word. From her, his name was a plea to save them all. But he heard his name from another place too. From the island, where the Innes Witch stood staring into an impossible vision in the distance. From Elsbeth, his name was something more. The sound of bagpipes rose all around the loch, as if drawn from the last tones of the ancient battle horn.

"If this is all special effects and Wentworth is filming it," Teddy gasped, "I am going to cut his balls off with a blunt dagger."

"If this is special effects"—Lachlan stopped pulling the ropes—"what the hell is that?" He pointed at the black swirling mass over the mausoleum. "Knox?"

"I've seen that before." Eleanor locked eyes with Knox. "In the west wing. I saw that…thing. Knox!"

The barge tilted. Eleanor slid across the deck and went over the side. Knox dove into the loch. He gasped at the iciness of the water.

"Steady!" Lachlan shouted. "Hold the damned lines steady. Stay where you are, dammit!"

Knox spun in the water and spotted Eleanor hanging onto the side of the barge, waves banging her into the lip of the sheep transport. He swam to her, fighting the choppy water, until he trapped her between the barge and his body. He wrapped an arm around her waist and shoved her up the side of the barge. With a firm hand on her arse, he pushed her onto the deck. She crawled around and grabbed his hand

"You'll fall back in, you madwoman," he shouted into the screaming wind.

"She should let you, asshole." Lily grabbed his other arm as he tried to climb back onto the barge.

Before he knew it, Anna and Samantha were there, kneeling on the deck and dragging him by his shirt until he landed on top of Eleanor.

"I told you lasses to say where you were." Lachlan leaned around the casket. "You alive, Knox?"

"Barely." He crouched over Eleanor and studied her face. "Don't ever do that again." He kissed her hard and fast. "To be continued."

He lurched to his feet and helped her up. The combination of the pipes and the storm grew nearly deafening. He led her to the casket and raised the ropes to push her under them so she was tied in, flattened against the monstrous stone box.

"The rest of you ladies, strap in. Now." To his amazement they did as he said, even Lily. When he looked up Arneaux grinned at him.

The horn no longer sounded, but the call of the pipes echoed from every hill on all sides of the loch. He couldn't see the pipers, but they no longer worried him. Whatever was happening here and now was beyond the practical considerations of an English educated, London employed architect.

This was the Highlands.

"Who the flying fuck is that?" One hand on the ropes and the other pointing into the maelstrom, Bas pointed.

Knox turned to face into the storm.

"The witch?" Lily shouted.

"No," Eleanor called back. "That's not Elsbeth."

Knox glanced to the island. Elsbeth met his gaze, her face

resigned but proud. "No, Elsbeth is on the island. Waiting for us." He stepped to the edge of the barge, his feet planted wide to brace against the roiling deck and his head thrown back to stare into the face taking shape in the swirling mass of stygian clouds. "I know who that is."

Lachlan turned toward him, both hands still gripping the ropes. "Knox? Knox, what are you doing?"

Knox crossed his arms over his chest and met the horrific red eyes glaring out of the darkness.

"Is mise Knox Alexander Wallace Innes, Diùc Turra! Tha mi ag àithneadh dhut air ais gu ifrinn gun a bhith a 'tilleadh le àithne mo riaghladh air mo fhearann. Rach! A-nis!" he shouted.

The pipes went silent. An ungodly howl took their place. The wind shrieked and the lightning flashed continually. The loch roiled like a boiling cauldron.

Knox flung his arm out and pointed to the mausoleum hill on the mainland. *"Air ais gu ifrinn a sheana ghalla! Tha an Tighearna Turra ag àithneadh dhut!"*

As quickly as it had arisen, the storm began to abate. The inky maelstrom shrank back toward the mausoleum as if sucked in by some unseen force. The winds died down and the loch settled slowly into gentle waves. The rain slowed but didn't stop. It was steady and damned cold. In fact, Knox was chilled to the bone and suddenly had to shake off a sense of light-headedness. He stumbled back and made his way to Eleanor, bedraggled with a scrape on her face, and yanked her into his arms, the ropes holding her between them.

"Don't go," he murmured against her soaking wet curls. He kissed her forehead and then her lips. "Don't go. Never go." His mind swam through a series of images—the storm, Elsbeth, the face glaring out of the darkness, Eleanor going into the loch. Eleanor, always Eleanor. She wiped his face with her hands.

"Knox, please. Are you all right? You're shaking. What happened? What did you say?"

"He told her to go back to hell," Lachlan said, his arm around Lily. "He told her he was the fucking Duke of Turra and he ordered her back to hell."

His brother's voice struck him hard in the chest, but Knox kept gazing into Eleanor's eyes, his forehead pressed to hers. She rubbed her hands up and down his arms. They were both soaked to the skin, but she was trying to keep him warm.

"Who?" Anna asked. "Who did he tell? What was that?"

"Here comes the cavalry." Arneaux pointed toward the speed boat racing across the loch. "What the hell is Wentworth doing here?"

"I don't know," Teddy said. "But I'm definitely over this laying the first duke to rest thing. I vote we take him back and try another day."

"No," Knox said. "We do this today." He kissed Eleanor again and squeezed her hand. "Elsbeth is waiting for us." He looked toward the island.

"Holy…is that…" Arneaux shook his head. "That's her. That's the Innes Witch."

They all looked to the shore of the island where a faint image of a lady in white stood waiting. From the gasps of the other people on the barge, they all saw her as well. She looked to Knox and exectued a decorous curtsy. He inclined his head, and the figure in white disappeared into the trees on the island.

"Did everyone see that?" Lily asked.

No one said a word.

Robbie maneuvered the speed boat alongside the barge. "Everyone safe?" he asked. "What are you looking at?" He peered at the island.

"Nothing," Hadrian said. "Nothing at all. About time you got here."

"We had a devil of a time what with the storm and all."

"What storm?" Arneaux asked with a grin.

"Ladies, into the boat, please." Knox led Eleanor toward the speed boat.

"Now wait a minute," Samantha started. "We started this and—"

"And you'll finish it," Knox said. "Robbie, once the ladies are on board take them to the island."

"*Seadh, a Ghràisg.*" Robbie bowed and extended a hand to Eleanor.

Wentworth jumped onto the barge and helped the other ladies safely into the boat.

"Holy shit," Bas said. "I feel like I'm in an episode of *Highlander* without subtitles."

The other guys laughed as Robbie steered the boat slowly toward the island.

Knox managed a weak smile. "Lets get this done." He went to man the ropes on the side of the barge with his brother. "I don't know about you, but my balls are about to fall off from this bloody rain."

"I've felt that way since I arrived in Scotland," Wentworth said as he went to the other side of the barge with Hadrian and Teddy. Danny joined Lachlan and Knox. Bas worked to steer them toward the island. "Its June for fuck's sake. When does it warm up here?"

"If it ever happens we'll be sure to let you know," Lachlan said with a grin.

Knox watched his brother carefully. So much had changed in Lachlan, and he hadn't noticed. Or maybe he hadn't wanted to notice, that's what Eleanor always told him. He'd spent the entire time since his father died seeing everyone and everything in Scotland the way he wanted to see it because that fueled his anger at all he'd lost. He'd never bothered to think about what he might have gained.

"What *are* you doing out here on the loch, Wentworth?" Teddy asked.

"That big bear in a kilt threw me on the boat after I tried to get him to get my phone back from Eleanor's snake."

"Now there's a sentence I bet you never thought you'd say," Arneaux said.

"No shit. She took my phone last night before dinner and I forgot to get it back. When I got the house, all hell had broken loose. Someone named Seamus told me where to find my phone. The snake was losing its shit banging on the glass, and I had no intention of fucking with that. I asked where everyone was, and when I got to the lake, I got dragged onto the boat and told to *Haud yer wheesht!* So, I sat down, shut up, and held on. I don't suppose anyone wants to tell me what the fuck this was all about?"

"Why?" Knox asked. "So, you can film it?"

"Do I *look* like I have a camera on me?"

"Shame you didn't get your phone from Persephone," Lachlan said. "Get ready. We're about to hit the shallows."

"Snake? Big snake, going crazy? Remember? Should have asked Lily for that phone she keeps shoved in her corset or whatever the hell it's called." Wentworth tried to wring the water out of his shirt.

"My wife does *not* keep a phone shoved in her corset." Lachlan jumped off the barge onto the shore and tied the mooring line around a giant rock along the narrow beach.

"Bullshit!" Danny coughed the word.

"I haven't been married long, but I think I know the shape of my wife's tits by this point. If she'd had a phone, we could have called for help once the storm hit."

"I'm dead," Knox muttered. "I'm dead, and hell is a discussion of the shape of my sister-in-law's tits."

"We got the only help we needed." Hadrian wiped the rain from his face. He leveled Knox with a dead serious expression. "Nice job, Your Grace." Hadrian executed a brief bow.

Knox inclined his head, and Teddy rolled his eyes.

"When we get through here," the sword master viscount said, "we're going to get royally drunk and the duke here is going to tell us who that was and exactly what he said to her. Because that was definitely a woman's face in those black clouds."

"Wait! What?" Erik looked from one to the other of them as they fitted the sides of the casket with the poles through the carrying frame that they'd obviously attached to the sides of the stone casket.

"Mr. Rousseau," McGinty called from up a narrow path that led away from the shore.

The women were standing with him. Knox gazed at Eleanor, and she smiled. Suddenly he wasn't cold. His chest no longer hurt and his shoulders felt lighter than they had in longer than he could remember.

"Go ahead and lead them to the tomb," Bas told his husband. "We've got this."

"You sure?" Teddy grasped his fingers.

"Yeah. We'll be right behind you." Bas squeezed his hand.

Teddy strode up the path to where Eleanor, Anna, Samantha, and Lily waited. Robbie, ever the efficient servant, had apparently thought to bring warm rain slickers for them. Knox really needed to give that lad a raise in pay.

"Come along, ladies," Teddy said, and ushered them up the path. "I'll show you the sort of tomb I expect Bas to have made for me."

"Give me a break," Arneaux muttered.

They all chuckled, but only for a moment. By some unspoken agreement, Knox and Lachlan took up positions on either side of the front of the casket. Arneaux and Bas spaced themselves out behind Knox on one side. Hadrian and McGinty moved to the spots behind Lachlan.

"Wentworth, get back on the speed boat. Robbie, watch him," Knox ordered.

"Watch me? What the hell?"

"This is between us and the first duke," Eleanor said. "Please, Erik."

The American threw up his hands and went back to the boat.

"Ready?" Lachlan looked at Knox as they hefted the casket up and started off the barge onto the shore.

"More than ready," Knox replied. "Let's take him home."

Home.

Could that be it? The sense of peace that had settled over Knox? Was that home? As they finally reached the brilliant white tomb and saw the rest of the party standing at the entrance, he shook off a nervous tremor. Not quite. He had one more thing to do once this was over. One more thing before the Duke of Turra was finally home. And the thought of that one thing scared him more than any evil bitch ancestor or any dangerous storm.

Chapter Twenty-Three

Knox stood at the head of the two stone tombs, side by side now, with one hand on each, and Eleanor thought he'd never looked more handsome nor more changed. He caught her gaze and smiled. The others had gone on to the boat. It was just the two of them inside the monument the first duke had built to his love.

"Happy now?" he asked.

"I only hope they are." She brushed a hand across Elsbeth's beautiful sarcophagus. "I hope they're at peace."

"Hmm," was his only reply.

"He wasn't a monster, Knox. I read the diary. All of it. He was simply heartbroken and so angry. So very angry." She moved along the side of the sarcophagus and put her arm around him. "Rage like that can make a person do desperate things. And I think…he came by that rage honestly." She reached up to cup his cheek and tilted his head down so she could look into his eyes. "It was her, wasn't it? The storm. His mother. We dug him up and brought him here, and she tried to stop us. *Mad awd bitch*, as McGinty calls her."

"Yes. It was her. Remind me to reseal her tomb as soon as

possible. I'd really rather not deal with her again." He wrapped his arms around her and held her close. "She was after you, and I couldn't let her hurt you. I'll never let anyone hurt you, Eleanor. Especially not me. I'm so sorry. I never should have—"

"Hush." She touched two fingers to his lips. "How did you know? How did you know what to say? How did you—"

"Elsbeth. She told me what to do."

He said the words so simply, as if they made perfect sense. They *did* make perfect sense to him now. She saw that in his face, in the way he stood, in the way he'd ordered what he might have said was an illusion before today to go to hell.

"You've had a big day, Knox Innes." She kissed his chin.

"To quote our Cajun friend, *no shit.*"

Eleanor threw her head back and laughed. "I don't know about you, but I'd like a hot bath, a meal, and a long nap." She took a deep breath and an even deeper risk. "Care to join me?"

"There is nothing I'd rather do more, but there is one more thing I need to do. I'm going to do it now while we're alone because I don't want you to feel pressured. Well, and I don't want my ego to be any more bruised than it is."

Eleanor frowned. His expression was such a mix of emotions she couldn't read him at all. Which was a little scary. He stepped back a bit and clasped her hands tightly in his.

"You were right. I suspect you always will be." He grinned for a moment, but then went solemn again. "I haven't been the Duke of Turra, not really, not since my father died. But I want to be. I truly want to be, even with all that means."

"I think after today no one will doubt that, Knox. I think—"

This time it was his turn to touch her lips and silence her.

"This job is a pain in the arse. And I am bollocks at it, but

I think I could give it a decent go." He squeezed her hands. "If I had the proper duchess to keep me in check and keep me from being too great an idiot at it."

Eleanor swore she'd been sucked into some kind of vortex where all she heard was the thumping of her heart and the sound of his words as if from far away.

"I know I don't deserve another chance with you. I've treated you like crap. I've taken you for granted. I've fought you every step of the way. I've…. Feel free to stop me at any time."

"On no. You're doing fine, Your Grace."

He laughed. "That's just it, Eleanor. I'm not doing fine. But I will be…if you'll marry me."

"What?" She'd suspected, but until he said the words she'd told herself she was nuts. Maybe she *was* nuts. Some seven-hundred-year-old bitch had tried to kill her. She was entitled to be a little crazy at this point.

"I love you, Eleanor. More with every passing day that you put up with me. I lied when I said I didn't believe in the family curse. I always have. I never expected to find happiness or love. And I still may end up being bonkers as a loon, but somehow, I think, with you here with me even that won't be so bad. Because I know you'll lock my arse up in the tower if I get too hard to handle."

Eleanor gasped to catch her breath. Her eyes stung like hell even though she kept blinking like some nineteen-twenties movie star. She couldn't think. Or maybe she didn't want to think. All her life she'd analyzed and organized everything in order to keep herself from being hurt. She'd led such an ordered life on the inside and such a free life on the outside just to prove to her parents she could. Once she'd decided against medical school they'd been determined to see her as a failure, not out of meanness, but out of some twisted idea they could bring her back into the fold.

"Eleanor, please say something." Knox stared at her, his face so earnest and a little battered.

"What?" She cringed.

"Something besides *what* perhaps? Anything? Knox, you're mad if you think I'll marry you. Knox, that was the worst proposal I've ever heard. Knox, I don't even like you, let alone love you?"

She pulled one hand free and punched him in the arm. "Don't be ridiculous."

"Ouch!"

"Of course, I love you. How could I not love you? You're a complete mess. Someone has to love you."

"Uhm…Thank you?" He rubbed his arm. "Does that mean you'll marry me?"

"Do I get a coronet?" She'd just stepped into a *Lifetime* movie, and she was going to ride that fucker all the way home.

"Yes."

"And a tiara?"

He pulled her into his arms so hard she was afraid he'd cracked a rib. "An entire walk-in closet of them actually, along with assorted other jewelry. All the way back to the first duchess, but not the first duke's mother. She was buried with all of hers. Although since we are now in the business of digging up my relatives I guess we could—"

"No!"

"No to digging up the *awd bitch* or no to…marrying me?"

"Of course I'll marry you." She threw her arms around his neck and kissed him hard. "I can't leave you running around Rosemount unsupervised. God knows what would happen to you."

"I'd be lost." He kissed her then, softly and sweetly, and as if he never wanted to stop. He was shaking. They both were. Of course, they were. They stood there in sopping wet clothes in a tomb, no less, and… "Promise me you'll never leave me, Eleanor. Never."

"I promise. You're stuck with me, Your Grace. Forever."

"That *might* be long enough."

A loud horn honked from the vicinity of the lake. Knox rested his forehead against hers and Eleanor wished they could stay like that forever. No such luck and not very practical. If she was going to be a duchess, she'd have to be practical at least part of the time.

"Lets go. I'm sure everyone else is ready for a hot bath and dry clothes too." She took his hand and led him toward the door of the beautiful mausoleum.

Knox lingered long enough to rest his hand on the foot of Elsbeth's sarcophagus. "Thank you," he said softly as he wrapped his free arm around Eleanor. "I'll take good care of your granddaughter, Elsbeth."

They walked to the boat in silence, although they kept looking at each other as if they couldn't quite believe what had happened. Eleanor imagined that would happen a lot in the days to come. Once on the boat, they all sat huddled on the seats in the back wrapped in blankets the ever-useful Robbie had brought along. McGinty passed a flask of whisky around and not a single one of them turned down their turn. There was little conversation. They all kept glancing back at the island and then toward the ancestral mausoleum on the hill.

"Where are all of those other pipers?" Danny finally asked as the tower came into sight.

A lone piper stood there in silence and watched as the boat crossed the loch. Eleanor couldn't tell, but she was certain he had to be Lachlan's friend from the last time, the last time the horn had sounded and all hell had broken loose. She shuddered. Knox pulled her closer and wrapped the blanket more tightly around her,

"All right?" he murmured.

"Never better."

"What other pipers?" Lachlan asked.

The rest of the group stared at him in disbelief.

"Are you fucking kidding me? The rest of you didn't hear that damned army of pipers blaring away in the middle of that shitstorm? Right about the time His Grace here pulled his *get-the-hell-off-my-lawn* routine with the first duke's mama? That was her in that big black cloud trying to drown us all, right?" Danny pointed toward the mausoleum.

Get-the-hell-off-my-lawn? Teddy mouthed.

"It was her." Knox said with such solemnity that no one replied.

Robbie steered the boat alongside the dock where the men from the stables and Urquhart stood ready to help everyone ashore. Knox gave Eleanor's arm a squeeze, then took two quick steps to Robbie and said something to him in a low voice. The young man's brows show up, then he gave a quick nod.

Robbie jumped onto the dock, followed by the other men who helped the woman from the boat. Knox was the last to leave the boat. The moment he stepped from the dock onto the shore, the lone piper on the tower began to play. McGinty turned and grinned at Eleanor.

"*Highland Laddie,*" she said.

McGinty's grin turned into a broad smile, then he strode up the lane toward the manor ahead of them, with Robbie already far in the lead. Knox stopped long enough to squint into the setting sun and offer the piper a salute. Their little band huddled together and hurried toward the manor. The rain had turned to a faint drizzle.

"You still didn't tell me where those other pipers were," Danny grumbled. "I know you all heard them. Sounded like they were everywhere all at once." He stopped to adjust Samantha's blanket.

"You know where they came from," Lily said over her shoulder as she walked arm in arm with her husband. "Same place the Innes Witch came from."

"Wait." Erik ran to catch up with them. He'd been staring at the piper. Probably planning to ask the poor man to be in the film. "Where who came from?"

Everyone else kept walking. Danny stood in the middle of the lane and looked back at the tower and then at the lake. Samantha grabbed his hand and dragged him along with the rest of them.

"The fuck you say," he muttered.

Knox laughed quietly, and he held Eleanor so closely to his side the laughter vibrated against her. "Wentworth, you are welcome to stay the night, but if you try to film anything, I'll put you in the empty spot in the family mausoleum. I'm cold, wet, hungry, and not in the mood to put up with even one more minute of shite."

Eleanor glanced behind them to see Wentworth standing stark still in front of the fountain. "Shame on you, Knox. You scared him. And we need him to finish the film for the money."

The doors burst open and footmen and maids hurried out with dry blankets to bundle everyone indoors.

"Come along, Wentworth," Knox called back to the director. "Only joking." He leaned down to whisper in Eleanor's ear. "A little bit at least."

She and Knox stepped into the foyer and were immediately surrounded by servants and friends from the film and an entire room full of people. Knox stepped away for a moment to speak to Mrs. Wallace. Bella and Sylvan crowded around Eleanor to ask what had happened on the loch. Everyone talked at once.

The entire scene was surreal and wonderful and completely ridiculous. Poor Erik stood like a ragdoll and allowed two of the footmen to dry him off, then strip off his coat and shirt.

"Excuse me." Knox now stood at the top of the stairs.

Robbie, Eleanor noticed, stood in the hallway behind him.

Knox extended a hand toward her, then motioned for her to come to him. She frowned and pointed at herself. He smiled and nodded. The crowd of people separated, and her faced warmed as she climbed the stairs to the landing. McGinty and Mrs. Wallace started shushing everyone. The hair on the back of Eleanor's neck stood up.

"What are you up to?" she whispered as Knox took her hand.

"You haven't changed your mind, have you?" he asked as he went down on one knee.

She'd read about a collective gasp and even seen some in movies. Nothing compared to the real thing as the noise echoed off the domed ceiling of the foyer of Rosemount Manor. The Regency boot campers had pushed to the front of the crowd to join McGinty and Mrs. Wallace.

"Of course I haven't." She leaned close so their audience wouldn't hear. "Why are you doing this?" His gaze was so intense and serious she straightened to keep her balance against the power of his regard.

"I love you, Eleanor." He said the words so loudly and clearly, she swore she heard them echo over the surprised murmurs at the bottom of the stairs. "I've fought it tooth and nail, and I am man enough to surrender. I love you, and I cannot imagine my life without you. Wentworth, if you use the phone my sister-in-law just pulled out of her bust to record this, I will throw you back into the loch." He never took his eyes off Eleanor, but she glared at the director just in time to see Mrs. Wallace snatch the phone from him and tuck it into *her* bust.

Knox opened his hand to reveal a very old heavy gold ring topped with a brilliant emerald. "Miss Eleanor Witherspoon, I would consider it my greatest honor and the very best thing to ever happen to me if you would agree to take me as your husband. I know it will be a monumental task, but I am certain the servants and all of our…friends will help you any way they can. Lily alone would be happy to kick my arse anytime you think I need it."

"Count on it," Lily called out from the foyer.

"Will you marry me, Eleanor?"

His voice had broken ever so slightly on the word *friends* and her heart turned over at the realization she'd brought more than love into his lonely life.

"I believe I will marry you, Your Grace," she said as she fought to smile through tears. "Someone has to try and keep you on the straight and narrow."

"Good luck with that," Bas called out.

Knox surged to his feet and wrapped her in his arms so quickly and with such force he nearly dropped the ring. "Here," he said, his voice shaking. "This was your grandmother's ring. The one my grandfather gave her when they married."

"How did you…." Eleanor's hand trembled as he slipped the ancient ring on her finger. "This ring is seven hundred years old." She ran her finger over the rough gold and the angular stone. "Where on earth did you find it?"

"Elsbeth showed me where it was hidden in the west wing a very long time ago. I didn't know why, but I do now. It has been sitting in a drawer in my bedside table all these years." He kissed her finger. "She wanted you to have it."

"But how—when—" Then she remembered him whispering to Robbie on the boat. She looked past Knox at the young man, who grinned so wide, Eleanor thought his face might break.

Knox abruptly swept her into his arms and kissed her long and hard. The hoots and whistles and applause of those watching from the bottom of the stairs nearly deafened her.

Eleanor marveled at the surge of wonder and excitement that swept through her. He loved her. He wanted to marry her. They'd argue. They'd fight. But they'd make it. She knew that beyond a shadow of a doubt. Knox grasped her hand and turned to face their audience. He raised her hand to kiss her knuckles and his face broke into a wide, for him at least, grin.

"Ladies and gentlemen, I present to you the next Duchess of Turra. God help her because she's going to need it."

"That's the damned truth," Erik Wentworth stated loudly.

"My first act as an almost duchess is to declare tonight as a free night from boot camp. For one night only, you can use the showers and hot water in your rooms because I think we're all freezing our asses off!"

The boot campers didn't have to be told twice. They thundered up the stairs pausing only long enough to hug her and shake Knox's hand. Even Wentworth came up as he'd been assigned a room for the nights he chose to stay at the manor.

"Can I assume you will *not* allow me to film the wedding?" he asked as he shook Knox's hand.

"You're learning," Knox replied.

"Congratulations, Eleanor." Erik kissed her cheek. "He is a very lucky man."

"Yes, he is." Eleanor flashed Knox a grin.

"Yes, he is," Knox murmured, and pressed his forehead to hers.

Mrs. Wallace had come up the stairs to stand just one step below them. "What would Her Grace like to be done about supper?"

Eleanor glanced at Knox expectantly.

"*Her Grace.*" He nodded at Eleanor and smiled.

"Oh!" Eleanor shook her head. Now *that* was going to take some getting used to for sure. "With the afternoon everyone has had, I suspect we will all be ready for bed after we shower and get into some warm clothes. Would it be too much trouble for trays to be brought up to everyone's rooms with some of Mrs. Gordon's beef stew, some fresh bread and butter, and whatever dessert she had planned for tonight?"

"No trouble at all. Perhaps some tea and a bottle of wine from the cellars for each room as well?" the housekeeper suggested.

"Perfect, Mrs. Wallace. Thank you." She squeezed the housekeeper's hand.

The older woman wrapped both her hands around Eleanor's, then dipped into a curtsy. "Welcome home, Your Grace," she said softly, then rose and retreated down the stairs to scatter the servants with orders barked like an army drill sergeant.

Eleanor blinked furiously, but the tears that burned her eyes spilled over her cheeks.

"What's this?" Knox wiped her tears with his thumbs and cradled her face in his hands. "Don't cry. Whatever has you in tears, I'll fix it, I promise. Always."

She punched his shoulder. "There's nothing to fix, you big Scots goober. Everything is perfect. Come on. I'm freezing."

"You've been spending entirely too much time with our Cajun friend."

He put his arm around her and they climbed the stairs and made their way to his bedroom. The dogs launched their giant wooly selves from the bed and came to lean against Eleanor, pleading for attention.

She hugged Beira and Tannus in turn. They licked her face and nearly knocked her over in their enthusiasm to love her. She looked up to find Knox leaning against the bedpost. His expression took her breath away.

"Knox?" She straightened, a hand resting on each deerhound's head.

"What did I do without you, Eleanor? How did I survive? And how did I ever think I could send you away?"

She snorted. "You sent me away because I went against you express orders, Your Grace. And if you think marrying me is going to stop me going against your orders when they're wrong then you're sadly mistaken. I am not going to—"

Laughing a rich deep laugh she'd never dreamed of, he had her in his arms and was kissing her while the dogs wove around their legs. "You're not going to give me a moment's peace are you Eleanor soon-to-be-Innis? You're going to be trouble and mischief and stubborn and insanity and...."

"Passion and common sense and so much love you'll never doubt for a single second that you and I deserve to be happy for the rest of our lives."

"You're going to make me happy for the rest of my life?"

"We're going to be happy *with each other* for the rest of our lives, no matter what life throws at us." She pushed his still damp hair off his face. "I promise."

She filled those words with everything she felt for this complicated, passionate, impossible man who had ordered a seven-hundred-year-*awd bitch* back to hell for her, had proposed to her with a centuries old ring, and had allowed her to turn his entire world upside down, with only a little complaint.

"Even better, *mo ghràdh*," he breathed.

And it was. For the rest of their lives, it was.

Epilogue

Late July, 2024

"Do we want to know what they're doing up there?" Eleanor asked as she stepped just outside the terrace doors and peered up at the top of the ancient tower.

"Probably not," Lily said from her chair by the fireplace. "It's the night before your wedding, and my brother-in-law and his band of merry boot campers have been up there in the dark for at least an hour."

"How much whisky have you taken up there, Robbie?" Samantha checked her appearance in the full-length mirror they'd had brought into the drawing room for the last-minute alterations Bella Stepford was making to their gowns for the wedding.

"I am sworn to secrecy, Dr. Arneaux," Robbie said solemnly. "Shall I send up more tea before I make my next run to the tower?"

"Yes, please," Anna said. "And perhaps some more of those macarons that are supposed to be for the reception?"

Robbie gave her a thumbs up as he left the room.

The film's costume mistress had insisted on creating Eleanor's wedding gown and the gowns that Lily, Samantha, and Anna would wear tomorrow. They had commandeered the drawing room for their final fittings tonight, and for the hair and makeup, and for getting dressed tomorrow.

The other women would wear heather colored silk gowns in the style of fairy queens, all elegant falls of fabric from an empire waist, simple and elegant. They would also wear flower wreaths in their hair made by Rosemount's gardener. Their leather slippers had been died lavender a share darker than their gowns to match the single long ribbon tied just beneath their busts.

The men would wear Innes family plaids as traditional kilts with the swath thrown over their shoulders pinned with thistle pins, gifted to them by Knox that very evening at dinner. Bella had tailor-made their period ivory linen shirts herself, in spite of the fact Teddy complained the entire time about having to wear a *pirate shirt.* He had discovered fellow sufferers in Eleanor's father and brother who had arrived a week ago.

Eleanor was thrilled her family had come, but after hearing the family history between their long dead relatives, minus the ghost stories and the encounter on the loch, her parents were still a bit uncertain about it all. Her brother had been so stoked by the movie making activities and hanging out with Danny Arneaux that he and Eleanor had patched up their entire strained relationship in the first twenty-four hours.

"Come here, Your Grace," Bella called from the sewing area she'd set up in the middle of the drawing room. "One more check of that gown and we must hang it up on the rack and let Mrs. Wallace set a guard before the poor woman has a seizure."

"Will you stop *Your Gracing* me, Bella?" Eleanor crossed

the room and stopped in front of the mirror for one last look. Her gown was like the others, a fairy queen elegance of ivory silk with a sash of Innes plaid across her shoulder and tied at the waist with an antique diamond and gold kilt pin securing it in place. "You have outdone yourself. I can't believe this is my wedding gown."

She went to stand before Bella who checked every seam and every covered button. When she finished, the other women helped Eleanor out of the gown so it could be hung on the roller rack with the rest of their clothes. The men had suffered through final fittings earlier before they'd adjourned to the tower to drink.

"What I cannot believe is this tiara you'll be wearing." Anna lifted said tiara from its ornate inlaid box. "This thing is gorgeous."

"I still can't believe out of an entire *closet* of jewels and crowns you chose this beautiful but simple piece to wear tomorrow." Lily took the tiara from Anna and placed it on her own head, then checked herself out in the mirror.

The tiara was several hundred years old. It was made of hand-hammered gold, a plain circlet with gold vines and leaves woven around to make the entire piece appear as if it was made from nature or perhaps conjured by a forest elf. The tiara sparkled with small jewels placed to look like flowers throughout the woven vines.

"Once I am officially the duchess, Lily, you can borrow anything from the Innes family vault you care to borrow." Eleanor slipped into the quilted banyan she'd lifted from Knox's closet and claimed as her own.

"Did I tell you you're my favorite sister-in-law?" Lily returned the tiara to its box.

"I'm your only sister-in-law but thank you." Eleanor followed the others as they went out onto the terrace and left Bella to her sewing.

Someone had lit torches all around the top of the tower which enabled them to see Knox, Lachlan, Teddy, Bas, Hadrian, Danny, and Eleanor's brother, Anton gathered around the parapet while it appeared McGinty and Dougal devoted themselves to refilling everyone's glasses.

Her heart filled as she watched Knox with the others behaving like any other man the night before his wedding, happy and carefree. The last few weeks had been hectic and sometimes stressful between planning the wedding and Wentworth trying to keep to his filming schedule. They'd gone back to living Regency style, well, except for Knox, who declared one part of finally acting the duke meant dressing the way he wanted, using electricity, and availing himself of that monstrous luxury shower as often as possible, usually with Eleanor joining him.

Yes, they'd gone after each other like a couple of teenagers every night, but more than that they'd talked about anything and everything for hours. He'd involved her in decisions about Rosemount and taken her around to meet all the people who lived and worked on the estate and in the village and in the various businesses tied to Rosemount. And these were the people who would come to the wedding—family, friends, their people. This would not be a big Hollywood wedding nor would it be a British aristocracy wedding. Knox had nothing to do with those people. In fact, Teddy Rousseau was the only other titled person there. Eleanor had asked, and Knox had agreed so quickly she realized she knew him far better than she ever imagined she would.

"Listen." Samantha hurried down the steps from the terrace into the garden and continued to the bridge over the ha-ha.

The others quickly followed with Eleanor bringing up the rear.

"They're singing," Anna looked up at the tower as they reached Samantha. "They're actually singing."

"And not too badly," Lily put her arm around Eleanor's waist.

"*The Parting Glass*," Eleanor murmured, and smiled. "A very old Scots folk song. Most people think it is a funeral song, but it isn't. Men sing it at bachelor parties in Scotland as a sort of farewell song to a man's bachelor days."

"That they do, Yer Grace." Robbie offered them all a glass of champagne from the silver tray perched on his hand.

"This isn't tea, Robbie." Eleanor took a glass.

"Nae, it isn't, but we thought tea wouldn't do for a night like this."

"We?" She looked up at the terrace where a crowd of servants stood looking up at the tower, pointing and talking and laughing.

"What the fuck?" Lily called out. "What is he doing?" She pointed at the tower and took a long swig of her champagne.

Eleanor shielded her eyes as she gazed up at the tower. The light of the torches and the glow of the full moon created a brief glare until her vision cleared. Standing atop the parapet, Knox had something cradled in his arms. The others continued to sing as McGinty and Lachlan stood on each side of Knox and held him in place though he swayed slightly. Then she heard the sound and realized Knox had bagpipes against his chest, bagpipes, and he was playing them.

The crowd on the terrace went silent as the sound of the pipes and the men's voices raised in song echoed across the valley. Eleanor's friends gathered round her. Robbie stood transfixed as Knox played to accompany the singing. The men sang loudly and only a little offkey, but the bagpipes melody was perfect, note for note. She'd heard the song at the pub in the village many times. She couldn't speak. Her throat had closed and a few tears slipped from the corners of her eyes.

She turned to look at the faces of the people on the terrace. Mrs. Wallace and Mrs. Gordon. Bridie and Emma and Tilda and the other maids. Urquhart and the men from the stables. Shepherds and farm workers and distillery workers. Seamus and the other footmen. All Knox's people, her people now. They stared up at Knox in wonder with such smiles on their faces, such happy and truly joyous smiles. She'd stepped back in time or perhaps not. There had been so much sadness at Rosemount and now….

"He's perfectly safe," Anna said. "Mr. McGinty and Lord Lachlan won't let him fall. Did you know he could play the bagpipes?"

Eleanor shook her head.

"Mrs. Wallace knew," Robbie said, speaking of his grandmother, Rosemount's housekeeper. "And now I owe her a hundred quid thanks to you, Yer Grace."

Eleanor laughed. "It's my fault he knows how to play the bagpipes?"

Robbie grinned. "He learned when he was a boy. My gran said he'd play again now he'd found his duchess. I never thought he would. Should have listened to Gran."

"I think we'd all do well to listen to your Gran, Robbie," Samantha said.

"You've the right of it there," he agreed.

The singing and the bagpipes drew to a close. The terrace erupted into applause. Lily added a series of long, loud whistles to the noise. The men saw they'd attracted a crowd and came to the edge of the parapet to lean over and take a bow. Knox stood on top of the parapet, bagpipes in hand and gazed over the gardens and terrace below. Slightly drunk he appeared to be enjoying it all. Would he be sober in the morning?

She'd never let him forget this moment, not if they lived and loved to be a hundred. No one present tonight would. The latest Duke of Turra was creating new legends, and tomorrow she would be a part of that legend.

◈

KNOX FOUGHT THE URGE TO SWIPE HIS HAND ACROSS THE BACK of his neck for the third time in the last five minutes. The ancient chapel was relatively cool. Scotland in July was warm, but never hot. Until today, dammit. The one day he was outfitted in full Scots regalia and the chapel was crowded with people, the sun shone entirely too bright, and it wasn't even noon yet. He tried not to think about the time.

"She isn't late, Knox." Lachlan, standing at the front of the church with him, exchanged a look with the vicar from the village.

The old man smiled kindly and shook his head.

"It is not yet eleven, Your Grace."

"It isn't? Thank you, Vicar." Knox tried and failed to return the officiant's smile.

"Has Eleanor ever been late to anything since you've known her? She'll be here. Her mother's here and so is her brother." Lachlan nodded at the two people seated in the front pew.

Eleanor's father stood at the back waiting to walk his daughter down the aisle, once she showed up—and if he didn't try to talk her out of marrying Knox. For some reason, Dr. Witherspoon hadn't warmed up to Knox at all.

The small pipe organ at the back of the altar began to play. Knox let out the breath he'd been holding. Arneaux and Samantha strolled down the aisle. Samantha went to one side and Arneaux continued to the dais to stand with Knox and Lachlan. Hadrian and Anna came next. Rousseau and Bas walked down the aisle and took up posts at the head of the first pews on either side of the altar. Lily came down the aisle alone and took up position across from Knox. When McGinty stepped into the arched entrance to the chapel and began to play his bagpipes, Knox finally relaxed.

Playing *Flower of Scotland,* Rosemount's steward announced the entrance of the bride. He paced up the aisle and the music reverberated in the stone chapel to fill the sanctuary with sound. McGinty was halfway down the aisle when Eleanor appeared on the arm of her father and the entire congregation rose to their feet.

She was glorious. There was no other word to describe her. She was like something out of a dream and appeared to float down the aisle. The ivory fabric of the dress made her golden-brown skin glow. Her riot of tightly coiled curls fell to her shoulders and down her back and the tiara she'd chosen sparkled in those curls. She carried a bouquet of heather and other Highland wild flowers run through with ribbons in the Innes plaid.

A quick glance at her father, dressed in a very expensive tuxedo gave Knox pause.

"He looks like he wants to cut off my cods," Knox muttered.

"He'd do a good job," Arneaux observed. "The man's a surgeon." He and Lachlan snickered until the vicar cleared his throat and gave them a dirty look.

Once Eleanor reached his side, however, Knox grew calm as a cucumber. Nothing mattered now except saying the I do's.

Dr. Witherspoon put her hand into Knox's and gave him a hard glare. "Take good care of my daughter," he said.

"I will as much as she'll let me," Knox replied.

He regretted his words at once. The man didn't crack a smile. At first.

Then he snorted and grinned. "Good luck with that," he murmured, and Eleanor kissed his cheek.

"No fair ganging up on me," she whispered as her father joined her mother and brother, and she and Knox stepped up to the altar.

"So long as he doesn't cut off my body parts, we're fine," Knox said solemnly

Eleanor looked horrified. Arneaux snorted, and Lachlan elbowed him.

Eleanor took it all in, then smiled at Knox with such joy it took his breath away. *This* was his life now. With her. He tried to sear every moment of the ceremony into his brain. He'd never imagined he'd be marrying, let alone getting married to such an amazing, impossible woman. Before he knew it, they had exchanged rings and vows, and the vicar was telling him he could kiss the bride. He didn't have to be told twice. He took her in his arms and seared his mouth to hers. Eleanor grabbed his arms to hang on as he leaned her back.

"Let the woman breathe," Arneaux said in a not so quiet whisper. "She's yours now. She won't run away."

The chapel broke into applause and some laughter. McGinty made his way to the front and played the first strains of *Highland Laddie*. Knox ended the kiss and steadied Eleanor before she took his arm and they turned to follow McGinty. As they started down the aisle the people packed into the chapel stood then, as if choreographed, bowed and curtsied. Knox checked out his new in-laws shocked expressions and exchanged a look with Eleanor as they walked slowly down the aisle and acknowledged everyone.

Once outside, Knox hurried her to the decorated open carriage waiting to take them to the reception. He lifted her inside and joined her on the seat as the congregation and wedding party spilled out of the chapel cheering and applauding. He pulled Eleanor into his lap and kissed her again.

"You are so beautiful, Your Grace. We'll have to have your portrait painted in this dress for the portrait gallery."

"We'll have our portrait painted together, Your Grace," she said. "I insist. *And* we'll have Elsbeth and the first duke's portraits moved to the main drawing room too."

"Already done." Robbie had told Knox what Eleanor wanted, and he'd had the portraits moved right after the wedding party left for the chapel. "They'll be watching over the reception. Your parents will be stunned, I'm certain."

"You did?" She planted a loud kiss on his mouth. "Thank you so much. What a perfect time to show them off."

"Speaking of the reception," he said, and held her close as Urquhart turned the carriage toward the manor, "how long do we have to stay? We only have a week for this honeymoon at the hunting lodge, and I don't want to waste a minute."

"Knox, really. Mrs. Wallace has gone to so much trouble. Don't you want to enjoy our reception?"

"What I really want to enjoy is a nice long honeymoon somewhere on a tropical beach with my wife. It's bad enough we have to wait until the film is done and then clean up the estate before we can go on a proper honeymoon. I really— Eleanor?" He recognized that look. He was in serious trouble. Serious Eleanor trouble. "What have you got up your sleeve?"

"About the film ending," she started. "I mentioned to one of the people working on the film that there are a lot of bachelors working here on the estate. Lonely bachelors."

"Eleanor." The hair on the back of his neck stood on end.

She had that look in her eye, that *hopeless romantic combined with determined planner* look.

"They want to film a reality show here, where they bring women in who are looking for husbands. This show runner says they would pay us a fortune to do the reality show here. And she's certain it would be a hit because, after all, I found my Highland Scot here."

"Eleanor, you promised."

"I know, but the show will only be for about six weeks. Two months tops. And—"

"That's what you said about the boot camp." He knew now how his ancestors felt when the English overran them.

"It'll be perfect. I will run the entire thing. You won't even have to show up except maybe the first night or so. If we start right after the film wraps, the reality show will be finished right before the baby gets here and we'll be—"

"Baby?" He shouted.

Knox's heart stuttered. Terror gripped his knees as they pulled to a stop in front of Rosemount Manor. Urquhart came around and opened the carriage door. Knox forced himself to step out and immediately collapsed to sit on the cobblestone drive.

"Knox!" Eleanor jumped down beside him.

Urquhart was laughing. He went to the fountain and soaked his handkerchief under the stream of water arching out of the horses' mouths. He handed the handkerchief to Eleanor, still laughing.

"Knox, darling, say something." Eleanor bathed his face and stroked his hair.

Suddenly he began to laugh. Hard. His belly started to hurt, he was laughing so hard.

"Ye've got yer hands full with this one, Yer Grace, and no mistaking it. Not a dull moment 'til they carry ye up to yon hill." Urquhart reached down and helped Eleanor pull him to his feet. He gave them both a salute and went into the house.

Knox took Eleanor into his arms. "Is every day married to you going to be like this?"

"Like what?" She touched her forefinger to his chin.

"Glorious chaos."

"I'm afraid so," she replied.

"Well thank God for that."

He bent to take her mouth in a long, sensuous kiss. A lavender scented breeze wafted around them. He glanced up at the tall windows at the front of the house and swore he saw a figure in white smiling down at them.

He returned his attention to Eleanor. "And thank the Innes Witch for bringing you to me, mo ghràdh."

"I love you, Your Grace," she whispered as they wrapped their arms around each other and walked into Rosemount Manor. "And about the Innes Witch…."

Rosemount Manor
LOVE REGENCY STYLE

Cajun in a Kilt
Sassenach in Stilettos
Critic with a Claymore
The Stuntman and the Swordmaster
The Duke the Witch and the Party Planner

Stay tuned for the next Rosemount Manor series THE PRICE OF LOVE

www.scarsdalepublishing.com

www.ingramcontent.com/pod-product-compliance
Lightning Source LLC
Chambersburg PA
CBHW030933120726
47906CB00002B/566